Marijuana Girl

Theresa Vernell

MARIJUANA GIRL
WELCOME TO CANNABISVILLE

This book and its graphic art designs are works of science fiction. Any references to historical events, real people, or real places are purely fictional or used fictitiously. Any resemblance to actual names, characters, places, or persons, living or dead, is entirely coincidental.

Copyright © 2024 by Theresa Vernell

All rights reserved. No part of this book may be reproduced, stored in a retrieval system, or transmitted in any form or by any means - electronic, mechanical, photocopying, recording, or otherwise - without prior written permission from the author.

ISBN (Hardback): ISBN: 979-8-9922090-0-6

ISBN (Paperback): ISBN: 979-8-9922090-1-3

MARIJUANA GIRL
WELCOME TO CANNABISVILLE

ONEMARIJUANA.ORG, we envision a world where cannabis is embraced for its diverse benefits and contributions to wellness, culture, and economy. We aim to empower everyone, from passionate consumers to industry professionals, by creating a trusted hub for knowledge, quality products, and advocacy.

What We Offer

Education & Awareness: We're dedicated to providing reliable, science-based information and insights, empowering you to make informed choices and understand the nuances of the cannabis plant and its potential.

Community Engagement: ONEMARIJUANA is committed to promoting social equity and breaking down stigmas around cannabis. We're here to support advocacy and inclusion efforts in our industry.

Quality & Integrity: We stand for uncompromised quality, transparency, and responsibility. Our partners, products, and content are carefully curated to reflect these values.

Thank you for joining us on this journey to a brighter, greener future. Together, we're one step closer to a world where cannabis is embraced and celebrated. Welcome to the ONEMARIJUANA family!

MARIJUANA GIRL
WELCOME TO CANNABISVILLE

SPERMOLOGY

In Cannabisville, the study of spermology takes on a unique significance due to the planet's diverse plant life, including the specialized reproductive structures of cannabis plants. Spermologists in Cannabisville study the seeds and reproductive mechanisms of plants, including cannabis, to understand their genetic diversity, propagation, and cultivation.

They analyze the morphology, anatomy, and genetics of seeds to develop new strains of cannabis with desired traits such as higher yields, resistance to pests and diseases, and enhanced cannabinoid content. Spermologists also study the pollination process to optimize breeding techniques and ensure the genetic purity of cannabis crops.

Through their research and expertise, spermologists in Cannabisville contribute to the development of sustainable agricultural practices that support the planet's agricultural sector. They play a crucial role in ensuring the genetic diversity and resilience of cannabis plants, which are essential for the long-term viability of agriculture on Cannabisville.

MARIJUANA GIRL
WELCOME TO CANNABISVILLE

DEDICATION

Puff ~ Puff ~ Pass to the free spirits, the contemplative minds, and the seekers of solace in the fragrant clouds.

After 420 weeks of writing, rewriting, and blazing through ideas, *Marijuana Girl* emerged as a vibrant story. Today is a labor of love and a true testament to patience and creativity.

This is for you - the cannabis connoisseurs, the ones who find meaning in the ritual, joy in the laughter, and unity in the haze of smoke-filled rooms. May *Marijuana Girl* stand as a celebration of those shared moments, the camaraderie sparked by the herb, and the insights born of its embrace.

To the passionate, the open-minded, and the unapologetically Pot Heads, this work is a humble nod to the vibrant community that sees beauty in simplicity, wisdom in nature, and connection in every rolled leaf.

To the Reefer (or Reffa), Grass, Pot, Weed, Ganja, Mary Jane (MJ), Hash, Chronic, Bud, Blaze, Herb, Spliff, Green Gold, Chiba, Tree smoking - Loud, and Zaza enthusiasts - this is our story, and these are our roots.

MARIJUANA GIRL
WELCOME TO CANNABISVILLE
MARIJUANA GIRL

A **Marijuana Girl** in Cannabisville is more than just a name - it's a title that embodies the spirit, strength, and ingenuity of the remarkable female strains who thrive in this unique world. A Marijuana Girl is a **Hommo-Harvesta**, rooted in both cannabis culture and the natural rhythms of their planet. She is a trailblazer, a healer, and a protector, blending wisdom, creativity, and navigating the complexities of life in Cannabisville.

Who is a Marijuana Girl?

- **A Keeper of the Green**: She understands the power of the marijuana plant, tending to it with reverence and using its gifts for healing, enlightenment, and connection.

- **A Voice for Change**: Whether advocating for fairness in the Northside or breaking barriers in the Embassy, she uses her influence to create a safe future for all strains.

- **A Symbol of Unity**: She bridges the gaps between strains, welcoming diversity and celebrating the vibrant, multifaceted culture of Cannabisville.

- **A Warrior and a Dreamer**: Fierce and determined, she faces challenges head-on, but she never loses sight of her dreams or the possibilities of the world around her.

- **A Sister to All**: Marijuana Girls stand by one another, bonded by a shared spirit of compassion, loyalty, and love. From Sativa Diva's leadership to Indica Green's redemption, they show that even in the face of adversity, unity prevails.

To be a Marijuana Girl is to live boldly, love deeply, and embrace the green magic that sustains Cannabisville. They are the heart and soul of their world, weaving stories of triumph and transformation into the very roots of their culture.

MARIJUANA GIRL
WELCOME TO CANNABISVILLE

WELCOME TO CANNABISVILLE

Planet Marijuana is a golden-ratio floating in the sky, suspended between Earth and the Moon. Shrouded by thick green gases that form a natural camouflage, this mist acts like a giant "green screen," keeping Cannabisville hidden from Earth's eyes. Through this veil, it remains invisible to human satellites and telescopes, letting it exist in peace.

In the vast expanse of the universe, among the myriad galaxies, exists the smallest planet known as Marijuana. Its sole continent, 'Cannabisville,' takes the shape of a marijuana leaf, embraced by serene surroundings.

This unique land nurtures an ecosystem that not only replenishes the atmosphere but also gives birth to a world inhabited by Hommo-Harvestas. Unseen by humankind, the seeds of this extraordinary realm gracefully descend to Earth with the rain, continuing their mysterious journey unbeknownst to those below.

But the inhabitants of Cannabisville, the Hommo-Harvestas, know plenty about Earth. Using advanced hacking skills, they've tapped into Earth's satellites, internet, and media networks. They can tune into human television broadcasts, browse Earth's internet, and even intercept Wi-Fi signals.

By learning about Earth culture and technology, the Hommo-Harvestas have kept tabs on human trends, languages, and lifestyles, adding a modern edge to their unique world. Yet, despite all they know, they remain safely concealed, watching quietly from their skyward sanctuary.

In Cannabisville, Earth and its humans are a primary focus in every school. Hommo-Harvestas study human DNA, believing it holds essential connections to their origins.

While they speak their native language, Cannalog, they also study Earth's languages like English, Spanish, French, Chinese, and numerous African dialects, preparing for a future where their worlds might unite.

This dedication to Earth's study goes beyond curiosity. Cannabisville's scientists have long observed a gradual drift, predicting that Cannabisville itself is moving closer to Earth.

They believe this cosmic shift will soon open a hidden passage, allowing Hommo-Harvestas to visit Earth undetected. Their ultimate plan is not one of conquest but of restoration.

The Hommo-Harvestas dream of returning Earth to its "green glory," a world alive with nature, healing from industrial scars. Through a peaceful "invasion," they hope to plant seeds of Cannabisville's sustainable culture on Earth, harmonizing the two planets in a shared future.

MARIJUANA GIRL
WELCOME TO CANNABISVILLE

CONTENTS

WELCOME TO CANNABISVILLE

SMOKE SESSION 1: Marijuana Girl - Sativa Diva	1
Welcome to Cannabisville: ONE MARIJUANA	64
SMOKE SESSION 2: Marijuana Girl - Indica Green	65
Welcome to Cannabisville: LOVE LANGUAGE	117
SMOKE SESSION 3: Marijuana Girl - Girl Scout Cookie	122
Welcome to Cannabisville: NEW WEED DAY	186
SMOKE SESSION 4: Marijuana Girls - Pink Haze Sistahs	188
THE BOOK OF ROOTS: 420 CHRONICLES	260
The Kushcordance	359
ABOUT THE AUTHOR	418
Coming Soon: Marijuana Girl Series	419
420 WeedHelp	420

MARIJUANA GIRL
WELCOME TO CANNABISVILLE

THE BOOK OF ROOTS
"Light of Creation"
CHRONICLE: 1 NVC

"At the dawn of time,
Jah created the heavens and Cannabisville.
The village existed in formlessness and void,
with darkness shrouding the depths.
Then Jah spoke, 'Let there be light,'
and instantly emerged illumination.
Jah beheld the light, deeming it good; thus,
Jah separated the light from the darkness
- Selahjah."

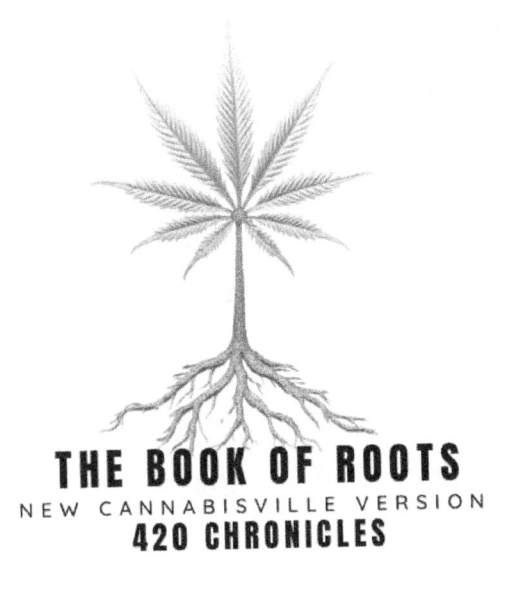

THE BOOK OF ROOTS
NEW CANNABISVILLE VERSION
420 CHRONICLES

MARIJUANA GIRL
WELCOME TO CANNABISVILLE

WELCOME TO CANNABISVILLE

Welcome to Cannabisville, where the pungent scent of possibility fills the air, and a unique world thrives. On an Island where Marijuana Girls and other cannabis strains do not just grow in gardens, they walk, talk, and eat greens, always on the weed party scenes with a flair as diverse as their strains.

The Marijuana Girls, embodying a free-spirited and health-conscious lifestyle, adhere strictly to a vegan diet. Through their stable vegetarianism, these girls not only embrace the wholesome benefits of a plant-centric diet but also celebrate a harmonious connection between their love for marijuana and their commitment to mindful living.

The Marijuana Girls embrace a philosophy of mindful living, following 'The 420 Chronicles of Cannabisville,' a book that mirrors the significance of religious texts like the Bible, Quran, and Torah in Cannabisville.

MARIJUANA GIRL
WELCOME TO CANNABISVILLE

These chronicles serve as sacred scriptures, guiding the Hommo-Harvesta in their way of life and fostering unity within the community. The chronicles preserve the wisdom, traditions, and spiritual teachings of Cannabisville. It is their source of inspiration and a moral compass, reminding the Hommo-Harvesta of their roots and their connection to the Marijuana Tree of Life.

Come journey through Cannabisville, where cannabinoids are more than a remedy, they are the lifeblood of an advanced society. Harnessing the energy of specialized strains, the living beings of Planet Marijuana, known as the Hommo-Harvestas, thrive in harmony with their environment. With adept green thumbs and cutting-edge technology, these skilled cultivators extract cannabinoids from unique grow houses, nurturing plants infused with the rarest and most potent compounds ever known.

In this sci-fi realm, the quest for cannabinoids is not just a necessity but an exhilarating journey that blurs the boundaries between the diverse strains of Cannabis.

These compounds not only fuel their bodies, preserving them and slowing the aging process, but also enhance their physical and mental capacities.

The delicate balance between nature's wonders and science that sustains their existence. They do not have veins in the same way that animals or humans do. Instead, they have a system of vascular tissues that includes xylem and phloem. These tissues transport water, nutrients, and sugars throughout their skin.

In Cannabisville, there is no GPS; instead, Weed Maps guide them through the bushes, trees, weeds, and cannabis fields. The streets may look like any other, but on this island, they are distinctly seedy. From the north to the south, from the east to the west, the question lingers: who has the best? The best seeds, the best weed indeed came from the Marijuana Girls and meet the Ganja Boys. Come embark on a journey through this herb society, where the essence of each character is not defined by human race but rather by the distinctive qualities of their cannabis lineage. Explore a realm where the boundaries

MARIJUANA GIRL
WELCOME TO CANNABISVILLE

between plant and person blur, revealing captivating personalities, intricate relationships, and thrilling adventures that unfold in the heart of Cannabisville.

In this vibrant world, the Hommo-Harvestas navigate their daily lives amidst lush green landscapes, mystical grow houses, and bustling marketplaces alive with the hum of community. From the spiritual wisdom of the Seed Weeds to the daring exploits of the Resin Reapers, each story is a unique thread woven into the tapestry of Cannabisville. Here, every strain carries its legacy, and every leaf tells a tale of resilience, unity, and the ever-growing pursuit of harmony with the Marijuana Tree of Life.

MARIJUANA GIRL
WELCOME TO CANNABISVILLE

SMOKE SESSION1:
MARIJUANA GIRL - SATIVA DIVA

"Puff-puff-pass, before you touch my ass,
Only the finest green, don't bring no trash.
Spark up the vibe, let's take it slow,
Blaze up the rhythm, let the high flow."

Marijuana Girl, Sativa Diva was having a good high-time as the free blunts and joints rolled tight with the finest strains, passed eagerly from hand to hand, while clouds of rich, smoke swirled through the air like a mystical fog.

Music pulsed through the vibrant Weed1Cafe, shaking the walls with bass so deep it seemed to make the very roots of Cannabisville tremble. Heads were bobbing, fingers snapping, feet tapping as they all inhaled and exhaled.

The music echoed the soulful rhythms of the memories of her Bud-Mother (a God/Jah Mother) 'SoulShine Session's harmonious blend of many genres including, Hip-Hop, Reggaeton, Afro-Beats, Soul, Jazz, and inspirational spiritual music called gospel, she had shared with Cannabisville, a gift of downloads brought from Earth.

Each note carried the weight of memories, a bittersweet reminder of the vibrant spirit SoulShine Sessions had infused into their lives. Thinking of her now, Sativa Diva felt a deep ache of loss. The melodies that once brought joy now made her mourn, her beauty a haunting echo of a connection she could never replace.

She was fashionably notice as she always wore vibrant colors, and her rich brown hair, the color of Sativa seeds, styled in flowing locks that were intricately braided to symbolize her strength and wisdom. Looking around, she noticed that every Cannabis Enthusiast, Herb Lover. Bud Connoisseur, Green Advocate, Weed Aficionado, Stoner, Tokester, Ganja Guru, you name it every pothead in attendance wore a look of pure bliss, half-lidded eyes, savoring the taste of freedom with every drag.

With every flavor you could savor in Gummies and dabs were laid out like a lavish buffet, while glassy bongs of every shape and size bubbled nearby, infusing the air with rich terpenes and mouthwatering aromas.

"We roll with style, got that Pink Haze gleam,
Smoke fills the night like a hazy dream.
From the north to the south, from the roots to the buds,
We light up the world, it's all love, no thugs."

MARIJUANA GIRL
WELCOME TO CANNABISVILLE

THC levels were hitting their peak, and the subtle notes of CBD complemented the night's mellow vibe, soothing every Hommo-Harvesta down to their roots. Sativa, Indica, and exotic hybrid strains intertwined, creating a cloud of unity that lingered as friends old and new inhaled each other's aromas, leaning into the shared symphony of flavors and effects.

Males and females from all strains mingled freely, exchanging stories, laughs, and dreams for the future. Hints of Marijuana Kush blended with citrusy Lemon Haze, while whispers of Pineapple Express and Blueberry Muffin punctuated the crowd's sweetly skunky fragrance. The scents were intoxicating, and each strain carried its own story, its own energy that added to the thrill in the room.

"Puff-puff-pass, before you touch my ass,
Only the finest green, don't bring no trash.
Spark up the vibe, let's take it slow,
Blaze up the rhythm, let the high flow."

Tonight wasn't just any celebration it was the grand fundraising gala for the 'One Marijuana' campaign, and spirits were as high as the crowd. The purpose was clear: to gather enough BudCoin$ to push forward the foundation's mission, and by the looks of the donations pouring in, it was a success event.. The event organizers had transformed Weed1Cafe into a dreamscape for every cannabis connoisseur, where flavors from Northern Pines to Purple Haze filled the air, each puff revealing a symphony of aromas and the promise of new heights.

The buzz of excitement filled every corner, where the who's who of Cannabisville mingled from elite strains like the Ganja Boys and Marijuana Girls.

Also, a special appearance from the infamous Pink Haze Sistahs that were lip-singing their song, along with the crowd, While in the middle of dancing being the center attention. Throwing their hands in the air, waving like they just didn't care, decked out in glittery pinks, greens, and gold.

Girl Scout's got cookies, Blueberry's got jam,
In Cannabisville, we don't give a damn.
We're queens of the green, with smoke trails wide,
Rolling up good vibes on every side.

As they moved, they left trails of glitter, singing, laughing and dancing to their own song, their spirits as lifted as everyone around them. The Pink Haze Sistahs' song, *"Puff-Puff-Pass,"* had become the unofficial anthem of the night.

MARIJUANA GIRL
WELCOME TO CANNABISVILLE

(Outro)

So hit it once, hit it twice, let your worries fall,
Feel the love, the peace, one bud for all.
Puff-puff-pass, through the green we unite,
In Cannabisville, we blaze till daylight.

Marijuana Girl, Sativa Diva, the face of the One Marijuana campaign, basked in the crowd's energy. She was exhausted, yet ecstatic this night marked a new chapter, a hopeful leap toward a future where Cannabisville could blaze freely, its roots unbound.

"Puff-puff-pass, before you touch my ass,
Only the finest green, don't bring no trash.
Spark up the vibe, let's take it slow,
Blaze up the rhythm, let the high flow."

"Puff-puff-pass, before you touch my ass."

The One Marijuana Event was a success, but now hours later Sativa Diva was sitting in Weedland Park, singing and teasing, as she looked up, eyeing the very tall - Jax, the striking male Hommo-Harvesta standing before her. His laid-back stance and confident smile gave away that he had something special in his stash. She looked like he had some killer weed, but more than that, there was something about his aura that pulled her in strong, grounded, yet with a wild edge.

The Hommo-Harvestas are a blend of human deoxyribonucleic acid (DNA) and cannabis strain. Their green blood pulses with tetrahydrocannabinol (THC) or cannabidiol (CBD), which flow naturally through their veins, infusing their beings with a unique vitality and strength.

They appear mostly human, but there's an otherworldly quality to the Hommo-Harvestas. Their skin tones range from deep, night-dark shades, reminiscent of Black Tupelo bark, to pale hues like White Oak, or reds like the Redbud blossoms and even vibrant golds, almost luminous each spectrum beyond anything seen on Earth.

Each of them, no matter their strain's skin tone, whether the uplifting Sativas, the calm and grounded Indicas, or the exotic hybrids with their unique auras, or even the steadfast Hempsters held an energy that transcended any earthly notion of race.

In Cannabisville, they were identified not by physical appearance but by the distinct vibration of their strain. Blowing smoke clouds in the air Sativa Diva and Jax united by the green of their blood, the verdant hues that ran through their veins and

MARIJUANA GIRL
WELCOME TO CANNABISVILLE

painted their presence, was simply a reminder of their origins. A tie to the fertile soil and verdant landscapes of their world. Together, they were creating a bond of pure unity, flowing with an energy that transcended appearance or classification.

In the warmth of each other's presence, the strains that made them distinct only enhanced their connection, amplifying the harmony they shared. As Sativa Diva and Jax exchanged glances and laughter, the boundaries of Cannabisville faded, leaving only the raw, powerful feeling of being entirely understood and uplifted by each other.

Sativa Diva smirked as she leaned in, her eyes narrowing with a mix of curiosity and challenge. " *Jax do you need a hand, you roll slow,?*" She teased, her voice smooth and playful. The air around them was thick with the sweet, fruity-spicy aroma of his stash, a heady mix with tropical overtones that teased her senses.

The Marijuana, Jax had were small, dense, grape-shaped nugs in olive green with flashes of neon beneath, bright orange hairs, and a frosty coating of amber crystals glinting in the light. It was potent stuff, and Sativa could hardly wait for a taste. Jax chuckled after he finished rolling the joint and handing it to her with a wink. *"This one's called Mystic Thunder,"* he said, his voice low and warm. *"Hits hard but leaves you floating easy."*

Sativa took it between her fingers, appreciating the craftsmanship as she rolled it slowly between her thumb and forefinger. She took a long drag, closing her eyes as the flavors bloomed on her tongue, Marijuana with a rich sweetness, and felt a soft heat settle in her veins.

The world around them faded into a gentle haze, and in that moment, it was just her and Jax, an unspoken connection sparking to life between them. After smoking the joint, they got lost staring into each other's eyes, the intensity of the moment pulling them in.

Quickly gathering her composure, Sativa Diva reached into her bag and pulled out a blunt. With a flick of her lighter, she it up, took a slow inhale, and, in a smooth motion, passed the blunt to Jax, watching him inhale, as she exhaled smoke swirling around them like a hazy cloud of calm.

Jax, catching her vibe, replied in their language called 'Cannalog,' *"Pax et Fuma!"* meaning, '*Peace and Puff*!' He didn't want any problems with the stunningly beautiful female Hommo–Harvesta. As she gauged his interest while maintaining a playful vibe, he passed the blunt. Sativa Diva and Jax blew smoke rings into the air as they both secured their own thoughts.

MARIJUANA GIRL
WELCOME TO CANNABISVILLE

It was just a couple of hours ago at the venue that hosted 'The Marijuana Art Show' where Sativa Diva's painting 'Marijuana Girl' sold to a private buyer. She donated the BudCoin$ to 'One Marijuana,' a foundation for their nourishment and multivitamins for their young Hempsters, the OG Wanders and the 'Kushimba' sprouts (Children), organic fertilizers, and clean drinking water. Also helping the holy ones called the 'SeedWeeds' in need of repairs to their prayer temples.

Throughout the night Sativa Diva did interviews with her favorite radio stations 420 Vibes *"Tuning you in, puff by puff,"* and The Green Frequency *"Where every note grows."* The music was so good, her head was bobbing, her fingers snapping and toes tapping all night. Her stomach was satisfied with all the delicious vegan tapas and appetizers. She was feeling satisfaction, overwhelmed with happiness.

Enjoying a celebratory flute of Cannabis champagne, Sativa Diva felt the thrill of achieving the highest sale but exhausted from the day's exertions. With her THC levels dipping and experiencing a slight tremor, she decided it was time to replenish by indulging and getting high off her own supply. There was nothing to pack up, she sold everything.

However, Sativa Diva couldn't help but reflect on the support she had received from her friends, the Marijuana Girls. Especially the Pink Haze Sistahs and Girl Scout Cookie. Overwhelmed, Sativa Diva appreciated the unwavering loyalty of those who had stood by her, understanding that their presence was a testament to their genuine connection.

After the interviews Sativa Diva was preparing to leave when a distinguished-looking male Hommo-Harvestas strolled inside, right in time for them to catch eye-to-eye contact. The event had a big turnout, and the after-party was a blast.

Exiting Weed1Cafe, Sativa Diva couldn't help but notice the male Hommo-Harvesta with the striking physique following close behind her. They were heading in the same direction, and curiosity got the better of her. She stopped abruptly, wanting to see if he was following her. As she paused, he continued walking, seemingly unaware of her sudden halt. She let out a small sigh of relief, guessing that it was just a coincidence after all.

The lingering scent of his hemp oil cologne hung in the air as he turned the corner and vanished from sight. The subtle blend of Marijuana and woodsy notes hinted at something both natural and exotic.

MARIJUANA GIRL
WELCOME TO CANNABISVILLE

It was unmistakably masculine, with undertones of sandalwood and patchouli that mingled with the fresh, green aroma of cannabis. The fragrance was as alluring her to follow. Sativa Diva couldn't shake off the awkwardness she felt. She questioned herself for what seemed like a moment of foolishness, realizing it all stemmed from simply walking alongside a handsome stranger.

Why had she stopped? Why did she feel so self-conscious? She shook her head, a small smile playing on her lips, amused by her overthinking. In search of solace, she yearned for puffs of 'Super Lemon Haze' Sativa, eagerly anticipating the embrace of its uplifting high and the infusion of zesty lemon flavors.

The bright green buds, adorned with orange hairs and a delicate coating of trichomes, promised a sensory experience she could not resist. This strain, deeply ingrained in her lineage, ran through her veins like a legacy. She sought its invigorating properties for the added energy and mental clarity it always provided. As she reached for her blunt, she could almost taste the familiar citrus burst, the promise of calm in the chaos, and the clarity she needed to clear her mind and focus on the present.

Searching for a lighter, she desperately needed the potent strain to take effect and fuel her with cerebral intensity and sharpen her focus. She needed to feel a sense of well-being. While she usually only smoked this strain in the daytime, she found herself drawn to its benefits around the clock.

The fine dark male Hommo-Harvesta and his alluring tall presence had departed, but his lingering sativa male scents remained, his fragrance clung to the air, teasing her senses, and leaving her mind wandering back to him.

Still lost in thoughts of his mysterious allure while searching her handbag, she pulled out a pre-rolled 'Super Lemon Haze' Sativa blunt, craving the soothing effects of a few puffs. However, as she prepared to light it, she realized she was without a lighter, now frustrated.

Minutes later, at a Medicinal Benefits smoke shop called Herbs & Remedy, they unexpectedly collided, both reaching for a lighter while grabbing rolling papers. In the same instant, they blurted out, "*High-lift-o!*" A cheerful greeting in their language - Cannalog that carries more than just a casual hello. It's a way of honoring one another with positivity, meant to uplift the spirit and strengthen the shared connection to high vibes.

MARIJUANA GIRL
WELCOME TO CANNABISVILLE

Their awkward encounter quickly shifted into a light-hearted exchange, bonded by the unspoken rhythm of Cannabisville's culture. Exiting they were still walking in the same direction, amid laughter and quick introductions, they joked about their coincidental meeting.

Smiles were exchanged, and the ice between them melted as their conversation flowed effortlessly, revealing an easy camaraderie that felt surprisingly familiar. There were quick introductions, though he already knew exactly who she was, but it was the first time he'd ever seen her smile, and it stopped him in his tracks.

It was clear she didn't recognize him. He told her his name, but whether she misunderstood or simply liked the sound of his nickname better, she decided to call him Jax. This, however, was their first time meeting face-to-face.

They began walking and chatting like old friends, the kind whose conversations flow easily without effort. Jax lit a pre-rolled joint, the fragrant smoke swirling in the cool air, and handed it to Sativa Diva, insisting she take the first hit. He couldn't help but crave that smile of hers so warm it could outshine the sun.

As she took a long, slow puff then another, before passing it, Jax grinned and jumped right into his usual antics. With exaggerated facial expressions and playful gestures, he dropped a couple of jokes to keep the vibe light.

"Why did the dispensary worker get promoted?"
Jax leaned in with a mischievous grin.
"Because he was highly motivated!"

Sativa Diva chuckled, blowing clouds of smoke through her nose, and Jax could feel her soft laughter loosen the air between them. Jax asked, holding a beat with a mock-serious look. *"And why did the pot-head plant his phone in the garden?"* She raised a curious eyebrow.

"He wanted to grow some weed Apps!"

That earned a full-on laugh from her, the kind Jax had been hoping for. Satisfied, he took a deep drag from the joint, his grin growing wider. There was something about her laughter that made everything seem brighter like the world was rolling along just fine.

"What did the weed say to the blunt?

MARIJUANA GIRL
WELCOME TO CANNABISVILLE

"You're a real wrap-star."

Jax had her laughing hysterically, her joyful cackles echoing through the quiet streets, until a few blocks later they found themselves in Weedland Park. The serene beauty of the botanical gardens surrounded them, every plant swaying softly under the night breeze. Overhead, the stars twinkled like fireflies, and the full moon cast a soft, emerald glow across the landscape, painting everything in a soothing green hue.

Before entering Weedland Park, they plucked and ate freshly harvested buds from the *'Marijuana Trees of Life'* that encircled the park. The rules were clear: one bud per Hommo-Harvesta, taken with reverence and intention, as an offering of respect and prayer.

They didn't smoke it instead, they ate it, following rituals set forth in their holy grail called *'The Book of Roots.'* The sweetness of the marijuana buds surprised the senses, tasting like sweet-sour red pomegranate apple terpenes, firing away on the tongue, crisp and tangy with each bite.

The act of consuming the raw bud was sacred, a practice akin to communion - eating the flesh of the planet, Marijuana shared in unity with nature. As the plant's essence coursed through them, it was said to deepen their connection to the planet, their ancestors, and their inner selves. Afterward, they drank from the holy water fountains nearby, the cool liquid soothing their spirits. As drops of water trickled down their chins, they both murmured *"Jah, ess'Blay Up'ay, een'Gray."*

Blessings in in their language of Cannalog, meaning *"Bless Up, Green!"* Their voices blending with the peaceful whispers of the leaves around them, as if nature itself listened and responded to their reverence.

They wandered deeper into the park, where the natural artistry of the place came alive. Underneath a canopy of trees, they found benches known as 'Rootrest.' These weren't ordinary benches crafted from living trees, they represented a perfect harmony of art and nature. Branches and roots had been lovingly shaped and guided over time, intertwining into intricate designs that cradled whoever sat upon them.

Each bench told its own story, with arms of bark curling like vines and roots weaving into smooth, flowing seats. Sitting down on one of the Rootrest benches, the air felt thick with tranquility, as if the park itself was breathing in tune with them.

Jax passed the joint back to Sativa Diva, a quiet smile lingering on his face. She took it, still giggling from his jokes, her laughter slowly fading into the calm embrace of the night. They

MARIJUANA GIRL
WELCOME TO CANNABISVILLE

sat in comfortable silence, the natural artistry of the bench embracing them like a glove, gently holding them close. The intricate seat was a product of the 'Kushimba Klans Arbortecture,' the careful shaping and manipulation of living trees over time to form functional structures benches, arches, even entire shelters.

In Cannabisville, the Rootrest benches of Weedland Park stood as prime examples of this craft, each one a testament to the community's profound connection to nature, sustainability, and creative expression.

Every curve of the bench, every intertwined branch and root, was a living sculpture that carried the wisdom of the forest, merging beauty with purpose, encouraging them to sit, reflect, and connect with the living world around them. As they puffed and passed the joint, the smoke swirled around them, their proximity grew more intimate. Their laughter mingling with the crisp night air.

Jax leaned in, his breath warm against Sativa Diva's ear, and whispered, "*Ay'stay it'lay!*" Cannalog for "*Stay Lit!*" His message was clear, he always had the fire to keep things going. Also, before entering the park - respectful of the natural surroundings, they both removed their shoes to connect more intimately with the ground. The subtle connection between them intensified as their feet brushed together under the growing moonlight.

A quiet energy hung in the air, and without words, they understood they were locked in the same vibe. Sativa Diva immediately noticed the size difference between their feet, his were easily tripled the size of hers, suggesting he must wear a size 24. She couldn't help but stare, fascinated by the size of them. Jax caught her gaze and grinned, a playful glint in his eye. "*You like big feet, huh?*" He teased, brushing his foot against hers in a light, tickling motion.

His confidence showed, as if he took pride in every part of himself, even down to his toes. The sensation made her giggle, and for a moment, the tension between them melted away, replaced by a shared sense of playful curiosity.

In Cannabisville, the standard unit of measurement is the foot, uniquely defined as twenty-four inches. This distinctive system originates from a legend about Jah's footprints, said to have been discovered in the sands of a sacred beach.

According to 'The Book of Roots' their holy grail of wisdom and folklore, Jah - the divine figure in their culture, left behind 24 - inch footprints, which became the basis of a foot-long measuring, symbolizing divine alignment with their God. These footprints, however, were larger than any Hommo-Harvesta's foot, most males have big feet, but very few in Cannabisville could measure up to this rarity in foot size.

This has led many to believe that the mysterious footprints found along the shores truly belong to Jah, reinforcing the spiritual and cultural significance of these measurements within their society.

    Jax feet wasn't the only thing amusing Sativa Diva, it was his personality. He invited her to join him in a gunshot. He placed the burning end of the joint in his mouth, and she positioned her lips on the other end. With a quick exhale, he blew the fumes of cannabis backward, creating a thick cloud of smoke that made her choke.

    Watching the cute expressions across her face as Sativa Diva coughed into laughter. *"You're something else, you know that?"* she teased, still catching her breath. Jax chuckled, enjoying her reaction. *"Just trying to keep things interesting,"* he replied with a wink, flicking the lighter to reignite the joint.

    The flicker of the flame briefly illuminated their faces, casting playful shadows across their features. As they passed the joint back and forth, the night around them seemed to fade away, leaving only the two of them under the canopy of stars and the thick, fragrant smoke. Sativa Diva instantly sensed that Jax was more than just an ordinary male Hommo-Harvesta. His fragrance was overwhelmingly Sativa, strongly hinting that he might be a 'Ganja Boy' from the upper northeast side of Cannabisville. The East side Ganja Boys are known for their discreet lifestyle and are rarely seen in public, preferring to keep to themselves.

As they continued sharing the joint, Sativa Diva's curiosity grew. She knew about the Ganja Boys, elusive strains known for their potent abilities and rare genetics. The idea of him being one of them intrigued her. She wondered if he had secrets that matched her own, buried deep beneath his confident exterior.

They sat close, the night air filled with the sweet, pungent aroma of cannabis smoke and the soft rustle of leaves in Weedland Park. Sativa Diva could feel the pull of the unknown between them, a magnetic energy that was hard to resist. Jax's presence was intoxicating, a mix of strength and mystery, and she found herself wanting to know more about him.

"Tell me something, Jax," Sativa Diva asked, her voice low and playful. "*What brings a Ganja Boy like you out here tonight? Aren't you supposed to be hiding, plotting your next big move?*"

MARIJUANA GIRL
WELCOME TO CANNABISVILLE

She flashed at him a teasing smile, her eyes sparkling with curiosity. Jax chuckled, taking another drag from the blunt. *"Maybe I just needed a change of scenery,"* he replied, his tone equally playful. *"Or maybe I was looking for something... or someone interesting, Marijuana Girl Sativa Diva."* He gave her a look that made her heart skip a beat.

Sativa Diva felt a blush rise to her cheeks, her body reacting to his words. *"Well, you've certainly found something,"* she said, trying to keep her composure. *"But I have to warn you, I'm not like most females. I'm a Marijuana Girl that follows the usual rules."*

"So do I," Jax said, leaning closer. His eyes locked onto hers, and for a moment, the world around them seemed to fade away. The only thing that mattered was the building connection between them, the shared rhythm of their breaths, and the unspoken bond that was forming.

"Let's see where this night takes us," he whispered, his voice barely audible over the gentle breeze. Sativa Diva nodded, feeling a surge of excitement. She had no idea what the night would bring, but she was ready to find out, with Jax by her side. They hadn't kissed, but she already senses the flavor of his terpenes in his saliva from wrapping his lips around the joint.

On her last puff, she made sure to pass it back wet, letting her lips linger just long enough for him to taste her terpenes spit, too.

As Sativa Diva's lips tingled with anticipation, she sensed a familiar vibe in Jax, but something about him was different. At first, she thought he might be a Hybrid, as he moved too quickly and smoothly to be an Indica.

She enjoyed tasting his saliva, he was truly a Sativa, and his energy was vibrant and intense, matching her sativa-dominant essence, yet there was a depth to him that made her curious about his lineage. But she was too high to dwell on it for long,

However, the one thing about Sativa Diva was that she had her preferences firmly set on a Ganja Boy, Sativa male Hommo-Harvesta's only, but she wasn't going to mess around with any Ganja Boy that was an Indica, whose heavy vibes could never match her energetic spirit.

Never a male Hybrid Hommo-Harvesta, they were too unpredictable for her liking, a mix of traits that never quite aligned with what she was looking for. And no way - ever would she mate with an Island Bud, with their gangster rawness and indigenous roots, didn't fit her contemporary lifestyle and for the 'Hempsters,' forget it.

MARIJUANA GIRL
WELCOME TO CANNABISVILLE

They were off-limits anyway, because they couldn't crossbreed, or their offspring would expire very young, turning back into compost and flower beds, buried in the Northern side near the Holy ones known as the SeedWeeds' prayer grounds. Call her prejudiced, but Sativa Diva preferred only Sativa Ganja Boys! Now, Sativa Diva found herself fully enjoying Jax's company, her thoughts swirling in a hazy mix of desire and wonder.

Suddenly, she noticed the praying axial purple flowers that looked like shamrocks sleeping nearby. Every time they flicked their lighter, the flowers seemed to shiver and stir, as if disturbed by the light and the smoke. *"Hey, do you think we're bothering those flowers?"* she asked, nodding toward the plants.

Jax glanced over, curiosity piqued. *"Maybe,"* he mused, "but they'll get over it. Nature's pretty resilient like that." He leaned back against the tree, his eyes half-closed as he inhaled deeply. *"Besides, we're just enjoying what Cannabisville has to offer. No harm in that."*

Sativa Diva considered his words, still watching the delicate flowers sway gently in the night breeze. *"Yeah, I guess you're right,"* she agreed softly. But as she took another puff, she couldn't shake the feeling that their presence was more significant than she initially thought that perhaps they were part of something bigger in Cannabisville, something that connected all its inhabitants, plant and Hommo-Harvesta alike.

She glanced at Jax, who was watching her with a thoughtful expression. "*What?*" she asked, feeling suddenly self-conscious. "*Nothing,*" he said with a lazy smile. "*Just thinking maybe there's more to you than meets the eye, Sativa Diva.*"

She laughed, a sound that was both light and rich, mingling with the smoke that surrounded them. "Maybe there is," she replied, her voice teasing yet contemplative. "*Or maybe I'm just a marijuana girl who likes to smoke under the stars.*" Jax nodded, but there was a glint in his eye that suggested he thought otherwise.

As they sat there in comfortable silence, the night seemed to hold its breath, waiting to see what would unfold next in their strange, smoky world. Jax slid his arm around her shoulders, pulling Sativa Diva closer. The warmth of his touch sent a shiver down her spine, and she found herself leaning into him almost instinctively. She wasn't sure if it was the effects of the 'Super Lemon Haze' still coursing through her veins or the intoxicating mix of his cologne and the lingering scent of cannabis that made her feel so drawn to him.

MARIJUANA GIRL
WELCOME TO CANNABISVILLE

"You know," Jax murmured, his voice low and smooth, *"this is nice. Just us, the stars, and a little weed. Feels... peaceful, doesn't it?"* Sativa Diva nodded, her head resting lightly against his shoulder. *"Yeah, it does,"* she replied softly. For a moment, she let herself relax, feeling the rhythm of his breathing, the gentle rise and fall of his chest against her cheek. It was a simple, unexpected moment of comfort and connection that are rarely found in the dating scene on their side of Cannabisville.

But then, a sudden gust of wind rustled through the leaves above them, bringing with it a faint whisper of voices from somewhere deeper in the park. Sativa Diva lifted her head, her senses suddenly on alert. *"Did you hear that?"* she asked, pulling away slightly to look up at Jax. He frowned, listening intently. *"Yeah... sounds like... singing?"* He straightened, his arm still around her but now more protective, as if shielding her from whatever was out there. They both sat still, listening to the eerie melody that seemed to drift closer and closer.

It wasn't unpleasant, just a strange haunting tune that felt as old as the trees around them. Sativa Diva's heart began to race, a mix of curiosity and a hint of fear. *"What do you think it is?"* she whispered, her eyes scanning the darkened paths that wound through Weedland Park. Jax shrugged, his grip tightening around her. "*I don't know. But I think we're about to find out.* "The night seemed to grow thicker around them, and as the mysterious singing continued, Sativa Diva realized that tonight was far from over, this was just the beginning of an unexpected adventure.

They walked deeper into the foliage of ferns, carefully expecting to find other Hommo-Harvestas camping out and singing. Instead, they discovered the singing plant, known as the Cantor Flora, a rare and enchanting flora native to Cannabisville. Its leaves, when rustled by the wind, produced melodic, harmonious tones that filled the air with a soothing, almost magical sound.

Sativa Diva's hand was gently in his, his touch warm and reassuring. The melody of the Cantor Flora seemed to enhance the connection between them, making their surroundings feel even more intimate and magical. Sativa Diva, still caught up in the soothing sounds, felt a profound sense of tranquility.

The previous tension had melted away, replaced by a serene acceptance of the moment. She leaned closer to Jax, her head resting on his shoulder as they listened to the plant's hauntingly beautiful song. Jax, feeling the calming effect of the Cantor Flora, spoke softly, "*This is incredible.t. It feels like it's connecting us to something bigger, something beyond just us.*"

MARIJUANA GIRL
WELCOME TO CANNABISVILLE

Sativa Diva's eyes were still fixed on the glowing plant. *"It's like we're part of a living, breathing symphony. This is why I love Cannabisville, there is always something magical waiting to be discovered."* They stayed there for a while, enveloped in the plant's melodic embrace, the night air filled with the harmonious notes of the Cantor Flora.

The experience deepened their bond, turning an ordinary evening into a memorable adventure that neither of them would forget. Feeling woozy from the adventures of the night and the cannabis, Sativa Diva sensed an overwhelming need to distance herself from Jax.

She gently withdrew her hand from his grasp and began making her way back to the Rootrest bench. Her steps were a bit unsteady as the effects of the cannabis took hold, leaving her both exhilarated and introspective. As she walked, her mind buzzed with thoughts and reflections on the night's events.

The vibrant, pulsating high from the cannabis mixed with the enchanting melodies of the Cantor Flora left her feeling disoriented yet oddly serene. She needed a moment to collect her thoughts and regain her sense of clarity.

Back at the Rootrest bench, Sativa Diva sat down, taking deep breaths of the cool night air. The stars above seemed to twinkle more brightly than usual, and the gentle rustling of the ferns created a soothing background. The night had been filled with unexpected encounters and magical experiences, and now she needed time to process it all. As they sat, her mind buzzed with thoughts and reflections on the night's events.

Jax, ever attentive, stayed right by her side, never letting her out of his sight. His presence was reassuring as Sativa Diva sat on the 'Rootrest' bench, her mind still spinning from the night's adventures. He respected her need for space though, choosing to remain close enough to offer comfort if she needed it.

With a gentle smile, he sat beside her, his demeanor calm and understanding. The soft glow of the moonlight cast a serene aura around them, and the distant melodies of the Cantor Flora filled the air with a soothing rhythm. Jax didn't push her to talk or engage, instead, he simply offered a quiet companionship, letting her take the lead in whatever she needed.

The night air was cool and refreshing, and the gentle rustling of the ferns added to the tranquility of the moment. As Sativa took in her surroundings, she appreciated Jax's thoughtful presence. It was a rare comfort to have someone who understood the delicate balance between space and closeness, especially after such an intense experience.

MARIJUANA GIRL
WELCOME TO CANNABISVILLE

As Sativa Diva playfully joked about what if the singing plant could have possibly been a 24-Karat Gold Cannabis Seed. The rarest and most coveted treasure among the Hommo-Harvestas. *"Imagine if I stumbled upon one," she mused, laughing. "It'd be like hitting the jackpot!"*

Jax choked a bit when he heard Sativa Diva mention the 24-Karat Gold Cannabis Seeds. It was the very reason he had come to the Marijuana Art Show at Weed1Cafe. He had been hoping to gather information, perhaps even a lead on the mythical seed that every Hommo-Harvesta dreamed of finding. But just as quickly as she brought it up, Sativa Diva shifted the conversation, her attention caught by something else.

"Look at that glowing green moss," she said, pointing to the shimmering strands hanging from the sleeping willows nearby. *"Isn't it beautiful?"* The moss seemed to pulse with a light of its own, casting a soft, enchanting glow over the branches it draped. She moved closer to touch it, her curiosity piqued by its radiant color and ethereal texture.

For a moment, Jax was relieved she had dropped the subject of the 24-Karat Gold Cannabis seed, though his mind still lingered on it, wondering if she knew more than she was letting on. Every Hommo-Harvesta wished to discover this legendary seed, which is rumored to be their golden ticket to leave Cannabisville and venture to the mysterious and alluring planet Earth.

It was said that whoever found a 24-Karat Gold Cannabis Seed would be granted immense power, fortune, and the ability to transcend the boundaries of their world. The legend of the 24-Karat Gold Cannabis Seed was a well-known tale whispered among the Hommo-Harvestas like a sacred secret.

Evidence of its existence had even reached their world, transmitted through earthly satellite broadcasts that somehow penetrated their solar-cable realm, sparking dreams and ambitions among all the Hommo-Harvestas strains.

The tale of this golden seed ignited imaginations, a mythic promise of abundance and power whispered from generation to generation. Now they had proof. Just a few legends, like Bud Marley, Buddy Nelson, and Weed Doggy-Dog, once superstar Hommo-Harvestas living fabulous lives in Cannabisville but departed to become icons on Earth.

Each of them acquired their own 24-Karat Cannabis Seed. Their stories fueled belief in the golden seed, the bridge between worlds, and the dreams of every strain who heard the legend. By planting these mystical seeds, they gained the unique ability to

MARIJUANA GIRL
WELCOME TO CANNABISVILLE

break free from the confines of Cannabisville and journey to planet Earth. Believing they would be legends, and their strains becoming synonymous with freedom to legalize.

The 24-Karat Gold Cannabis Seeds were rare, and 420 were believed to be kept safely locked away at 'The Embassy of Green Roots' also known as 'The Greenhouse' of Cannabisville, in a secret room known only to the highest in power.

Each seed held the promise of a new life, a chance to escape the green confines of their world and explore the unknown. For many Hommo-Harvestas, the seeds represented more than just a ticket to freedom; they were a gateway to infinite possibilities, a path to break away from the cycle of their existence and discover what lay beyond Cannabisville.

Those who possessed a 24-Gold Karat Seed could unlock untold power and transform their destinies, becoming legends in the annals of their world's history. It was rumored that some seeds had been missing for years and that there were still a few unaccounted for.

Whispers in the shadows spoke of rebellious Hommo-Harvestas who had managed to steal the gold seeds and were now living in secret, plotting their escape, or perhaps already having fled to Earth, leaving only legends and mysteries in their wake.

The thought of these seeds missing sent waves of curiosity and fear through Cannabisville. The possibility of finding one of these uncounted gold seeds was the ultimate quest for many, a beacon of hope in a world otherwise bound by the rules of the Embassy in Cannabisville and the laws of Jah.

The stories of Earthlings fueled a quiet but persistent hope that somewhere, somehow, there might be another seed waiting to be discovered, another path to freedom waiting to be walked. The gold seed was not just a prize but a symbol of ultimate freedom and possibility, sparking the imagination and ambition of every strain in Cannabisville.

Jax was still thinking about Sativa Diva mentioning the gold seeds, as he attentively stayed right by her side, never letting her out of his sight. His presence was reassuring as Sativa Diva sat on the Rootrest bench, her mind still spinning from the night's adventures. He respected her need for space though, choosing to remain close enough to offer comfort and support if she needed it.

Jax knew just what to do to keep their party going, reached into his pocket and the aroma wafting through the night as he prepared for another round. He was visibly excited, pulling out a green mylar smell-proof bag, his enthusiasm intense.

MARIJUANA GIRL
WELCOME TO CANNABISVILLE

"You've got to check this out," he said, his voice bubbling with anticipation. *"I just copped this new strain called 'Green Monster'. First time trying it."* He opened the bag, and the pungent aroma of a rolled blunt filled the air. Sativa took a tentative inhale, her face showing clear disapproval as the strong scent hit her senses. Though the buzz was immediate, it quickly made her feel drowsy, the strain's effects contrasting sharply with her usual high. As the effects set in, she leaned back against the Rootrest bench, trying to stay alert despite the creeping drowsiness.

Passing the blunt, Jax's playful demeanor persisted as he flirted with Sativa Diva. His hand made several attempts to gently touch her ass, driven by a cheeky curiosity about whether her curvaceous figure was all-natural, enhanced with Miracle-Grow, or perhaps the result of some cosmetic intervention.

"Come on, just let me see if it's real," he teased with a mischievous grin, his fingers brushing near her voluptuous ass trying to confirm his playful theory. Sativa Diva, feeling both amused and slightly taken aback by his forwardness, swatted his hand away with a laugh. *"You're persistent,"* she said, shaking her head. *"If you're that curious, you'll have to find out some other way."*

Listening to Jax talk, Sativa Diva noticed his accent, but it was difficult to determine which side of Cannabisville he might be from. His voice had a smooth, almost hypnotic quality that seemed to blend elements from different regions, a rare trait among the Hommo-Harvestas. Depending on their strain had distinct speech patterns or intonations that hinted at their origins.

The sharp, crisp tones of the North, the laid-back drawl of the South, or the rhythmic pace of the East Side. But Jax's voice was an enigma, as if he belonged everywhere and nowhere all at once. This only added to the mystery surrounding him, making Sativa Diva even more curious about who he really was and where he truly came from.

In Cannabisville, the language is called 'Cannalog,' a unique dialect that blends Marijuana tones with rhythmic cadences. This language is deeply rooted in the culture of the Hommo-Harvestas, incorporating phrases and expressions inspired by the flora and fauna of their world.

'Cannalog' is spoken with a melodic flow, where words often mimic the natural sounds of wind rustling through leaves or water flowing over rocks, giving the language a harmonious, almost musical quality. Each strain or community in Cannabisville has its own regional accent, but all share the core

MARIJUANA GIRL
WELCOME TO CANNABISVILLE

vocabulary and grammar of 'Cannalog,' uniting them under a common linguistic heritage. After taking one puff of distaste, unbeknownst to Jax, she promptly ordered a tUber, ready to get home to her organic weed stash. Although Jax sensed her dissatisfaction, he asked about her thoughts on the weed.

The embarrassment on his face was evident as she candidly stated, "*No, that weed is disgusting.*" Jax chuckled while attempting to explain, recounting his unusual practice of purchasing weed from underground dealers. However, explaining he bought it from a Marijuana Girl named Indica Green, whom he had met at the hotel bar where he was staying.

"*Fuck that seedy budtch! Her weed is wack and fake!*" Sativa yelled while still trying to get rid of the taste of the synthetic marijuana. The mention of Marijuana Girl Indica Green's name abruptly disrupted Sativa Diva's high and shifted her mood. Without hesitation, Jax extinguished the Indica blunt.

Reaching into her handbag, Sativa Diva pulled out a pre-rolled blunt while contemplating the resurgence of Indica Green, she felt an urgency to promptly alert Marijuana Girl, 'Girl Scout Cookies' that Indica Green had re-upped and was actively back on the Cannabisville weed scene.

This wacky-weed experience was something she felt compelled to document in her journal the 'Cannalog,' that was not just a language, but where they meticulously recorded every cannabis strain encountered and all other marijuana-related details. She prided herself on knowing each strain intimately, understanding their unique effects, aromas, and flavors, and the way they made her feel. Her journal was a living archive of her cannabis adventures, a testament to her passion and expertise in the art of cannabis culture.

Sativa Diva was resolute in her choice: she would only propagate, mate with, and have Hommo-Harvesta babies with a Sativa male. She believed that her lineage should carry the vibrant, energetic traits of the Sativa strain, keeping her spirit and legacy alive through her offspring. For her, a Sativa male wasn't just a preference, it was a necessity to ensure the continuation of her strain's characteristics, pure, uplifting, and always potent.

She had no problem smoking other strains like Indica, Hybrids, or even Hemp, and when it came to friendships, the female Hommo-Harvestas strains were a different story. She welcomed the company and friendship of all females, appreciating their unique qualities and perspectives.

MARIJUANA GIRL
WELCOME TO CANNABISVILLE

She found that these friendships enriched her life, offering different insights and experiences. Her acquaintance, Marijuana Girl, Indica Green was a trendsetter on the Eastside of Cannabisville. Indica was known for always leaving her mark, whether she was setting the latest trend or causing a bit of chaos, she made sure everyone remembered her presence.

Sativa Diva had not seen Indica Green in 365 Moons. Now, Indica Green was back in the game, selling the infamous 'Wacky Weed' in green Mylar bags, making waves in Cannabisville once again. It was a dangerous move and signaling that Indica Green was back and had her BudCoin$ up. The new bags were eye-catching, their rich emerald color a departure from the typical packaging seen in the community.

But Sativa Diva's keen-eyed couldn't help but notice the resemblance to the iconic blue Mylar bags that the popular Marijuana Girl, Girl Scout Cookies used. It was almost as if Indica was taking a page right out of Girl Scout Cookie's playbook, tweaking the green color with green glitter, just enough to stand out.

Now Sativa Diva was lost in her thoughts almost forgetting about Jax, she sat thinking, Indica Green managed to come back by selling synthetic marijuana? And why fake weed when she is of pure lineage from the prestige Green family? Some speculated she'd been hiding underground on the Northside in the holy lands with the Seed Weeds, praying, meditating, fasting trying to get her head right.

Now it looks like she has been building her corrupt empire quietly, away from prying eyes, waiting for the perfect moment to make her mark. But why fake cannabis? Now she was assuming that Indica Green must have been making deals with the powerful figures, Ganja Boy, 'Gorilla Glue' or Island Bud, 'Brick-Weed,' because they ran these kinds of seedy businesses.

Both Gorilla Glue and Brick-Weed were male Hommo-Harvesta known for taking pleasure in trying to turn out and corrupting any female of any strain, especially a Marijuana Girl, they relished the challenge of pushing boundaries, always.

Shaking her head in disbelief and still feeling the effects of that wacky puff, Sativa Diva pondered the branding move. The use of the familiar Mylar bag format, now transformed into a vibrant green, struck her as a bold statement. It was clear that Indica Green wasn't just copying there was a clever strategy behind it. Sativa Diva couldn't shake the feeling that she was orchestrating this kind of comeback.

MARIJUANA GIRL
WELCOME TO CANNABISVILLE

When Indica Green disappeared, immersed in the underground and caught up in the chaos, Sativa Diva assumed she was entangled with Ganja Boy, Gorilla Glue. Sativa Diva had once cautioned Indica Green about Gorilla Glue and his negative influences, warning her of his shadowy presence and the trouble he brought.

Now, as Indica Green reemerged with a new, bold branding move, Sativa Diva couldn't shake the suspicion that Ganja Boy, Gorilla Glue might be the driving force behind this unexpected comeback.

The intricate web of influences and the aura of deception surrounding her friend's return made her wonder if Gorilla Glue was the mastermind pulling the strings. Lurking in the shadows, or chilling on the northeast side in his villa, embodying a villainous vibe. He consistently engaged in mischief, causing one to become entangled like glue in both thoughts and actions.

Despite being a constant distraction, he was the only strain capable of unwinding Indica Green. Nevertheless, Sativa Diva was aware that Indica Green would reappear in time. Lost in her thoughts, Sativa Diva was startled when Jax handed her a new lit blunt, promising it was not fake.

Jax hand wrapped around her waist, slid down and began massaging her naturally voluptuous ass. Gently pulling her closer. As he sang back to her, "*Puff - puff – pass before I touch your ass.*" She didn't stop him; instead, she felt a strange comfort in his touch, his hand moving smoothly over her curves. Just as she was about to protest, Jax's hand paused, hovering at the edge of crossing a line. But she found herself not wanting to stop him, it felt good, a soothing touch in the haze of her high.

They stood there for a moment, swaying slightly to the rhythm of the night's breeze, the fragrance of blended cannabis strains mingling in the air. Jax's fingers lingered, tracing a delicate pattern across her lower back, and Sativa Diva shivered, not from the cold, but from the unexpected warmth of his touch.

"*Why are you so guarded?*" Jax whispered, his voice a low rumble that resonated in the quiet of the park. Sativa Diva inhaled deeply, trying to clear her mind. "*You'd be too if you knew what I knew,*" she replied, her voice soft yet firm, as if weighing each word carefully. Leaning closer, his lips brushing the edge of her ear. "*And what is it that you know, Sativa Diva?*" he asked, his breath warm against her skin, sending another shiver down her spine. She turned to face him, their faces just inches apart.

MARIJUANA GIRL
WELCOME TO CANNABISVILLE

The intensity of his gaze made her heart race, and she suddenly felt like she was standing on the edge of something deep and unknown. *"I know that not everyone is what they seem,"* she said finally, her voice steady but low. *"And that sometimes, the prettiest flowers have the sharpest thorns."*

Jax smiled, a slow, knowing smile that suggested he understood more than he let on. *"I'm not afraid of a few thorns,"* he said softly. For a moment, the world seemed to pause around them. The night air was thick with the scent of marijuana, the sounds of distant laughter and the rustling of leaves. Sativa Diva found herself leaning into Jax, drawn by an invisible force she couldn't quite understand, her lips parting slightly, ready to close the distance between them.

Sativa was feeling *high as the sky*, her thoughts swirling in a haze that matched the cloud of smoke she had just inhaled. The world around her seemed to melt into a kaleidoscope of colors, but it was Jax who stood out the most in that moment - his smooth swag, his effortless charm, and that beautiful smile that seemed to draw her in with a magnetic force.. She found herself growing more nervous, her heart racing as his gaze lingered on her.

Jax presence was intoxicating, and though her mind was cloudy, she couldn't help but feel a sense of vulnerability she wasn't used to. He had this way of making her feel both at ease and on edge at the same time, a delicate balance that both thrilled and intimidated her. But as the moment stretched on, Sativa's nerves began to settle, and a spark of determination flared inside her. She needed answers. She needed to know what was going on with Indica Green, her estranged friend.

With a calmness that contrasted the storm of thoughts in her mind, Sativa turned to Jax and, with a slight edge in her voice, inquired, *"What's your relationship with Indica?* Jax paused, his easy smile slipping slightly as he considered her question. He seemed to weigh his response, and Sativa caught a flicker of something unreadable in his eyes. She pressed on, not willing to let the moment slip away.

"I need to find her," she continued, her tone softening but still firm. *"She owes me some BudCoin$ for pinching and selling a portion of my weed stash. I've been looking for her, but she's gone off the grid. Any idea where she's hiding?"* Jax studied her for a long moment, the weight of her words hanging in the air.

MARIJUANA GIRL
WELCOME TO CANNABISVILLE

Jax response would either bring her closer to finding Indica or leave her with even more questions than she already had. Sativa braced herself, unsure of what she'd hear next but determined to get the truth.

He swore again that he had just met her, changing the subject he pointed at the midnight moon hanging high in the sky, glowing brighter than ever and twinkling like a distant star. Its radiance was different tonight, signaling the arrival of a new day.

For Hommo-Harvestas the moon was more than just a celestial body, it was a timekeeper, a guide that marked the passing of time in a world where every moment counted.

The soft, green silvery light bathed the landscape in an ethereal glow, casting long shadows and creating a magical atmosphere that seemed to whisper secrets to those who knew how to listen. They sat there enjoying the moment, swaying slightly to the rhythm of the night's breeze. Sativa Diva felt a sudden twinge in her heart, a sensation she had never experienced before.

The rapid beating made her anxious, sparking a fear of heartbreak she hadn't known she could feel. She placed her hand over her chest, trying to steady herself and breathe through the unfamiliar flutter. Yes, Hommo-Harvestas had hearts, much like humans on Earth, and they possessed many of the same organs. They shared similar features, too, blending the recognizable with the unique. There were notable differences like the distinctively pointed ears of the Hempsters. However, the 'SeedWeeds' are also Hempsters, their differences lie in their appearance. They are albinos with elongated, white, feathery, leaf-like ears that set them apart from the rest of their kind.

Sativa Diva and Jax only became aware of time because of the soft, rhythmic sound of bells ringing in the distance. It came from the eastside prayer *'Temple of Dawn Blaze'* where the first light touches Cannabisville every day, representing new beginnings, clarity, and enlightenment.

Signaling the sacred hour of *'Glow Time - 4:20 GT.'* The bells chimed twice daily, once at dawn and once at dusk. *'Blaze Time - 4:20 BT'*. This was their designated prayer time, a moment set aside for the offering of peace and gratitude to 'Jah.

The bells were a constant reminder of the cycles in Cannabisville, where time wasn't measured in the same way as on Earth. Instead, the gentle flow of life in 'Cannabisville' revolved around these sacred intervals, where the Hommo-Harvesta gathered their thoughts, honored the land, and offered thanks for the abundance they cultivated.

MARIJUANA GIRL
WELCOME TO CANNABISVILLE

THE BOOK OF ROOTS
'Blessings of Marijuana'
Chronicle 420 NCV

"Jah, Creator of all, Thank you for the herb that brings us together, May we celebrate life, love, and growth, As we share, eat, and partake in your bounty, Blessings of Marijuana. - Selahjah"

In this serene moment of reciting a chronicle from *'The Book of Roots,'* they prayed for their blessings of Marijuana and puffed and passed, Sativa Diva and Jax felt the weight of time briefly lifted, as the sound of the bells filled the air, blending with the natural rhythm of the world around them. Peace enveloped the land, and everything seemed perfectly aligned for a moment.

It was *4:20 GT*, the perfect time to light up again and keep it passing. As the bells faded into the distance, Sativa Diva sparked another one of her pre-rolled joints and took a long, slow drag, feeling the warmth of the smoke fill her lungs before passing it to Jax.

He smiled back, taking the joint from Sativa Diva's hand. "*Ibes'vay up'ay - Vibes up!*" he said, his voice calm and relaxed as they settled back into the rhythm of Cannabisville. Here, time wasn't rushed, only measured by the sun's rising and setting, and the ritual of 4:20 brought them back to themselves.

"*Thanks for keeping it lit,*" he said with a playful grin, exhaling slowly as the smoke curled around them. Noticing Jax was ready to light another joint, Sativa Diva quickly stood up, breaking the moment. "*I should go, I already canceled 2 tUbers,*" she said, more to herself than to him, trying to regain her composure.

"*I can take you home. My Weedsla is parked around the corner,*" Jax said as he handed her a bottle of rainwater right on time, she had cottonmouth, attributing her dry mouth induced by smoking the weed, placing the blame on the wacky-weed. She heard him but wasn't ready to let him into her personal space, yet.

After drinking the bottle of rainwater, she became nervous and intimidated thinking about him driving her home. Technically he was still a stranger, but his smooth swag and beautiful smile made her want to say yes. But she inquired further about Jax's relationship with Indica and sought information on how to find her estranged friend, who still owed her BudCoin$ for pinching and selling a portion of her weed stash.

Overwhelmed by the arousal induced by the Sativa strain, Sativa was feeling sexually aroused and gazing into Jax eyes, sensing his appreciation for intimate eye contact. Their eyes

MARIJUANA GIRL
WELCOME TO CANNABISVILLE

locked, delving into each other's souls, arousing a desire within her that surpassed mere marijuana cravings. Cannabisville operates under the vigilant gaze of the Embassy, with their leader, Prophet Highstem, overseeing its harmony.

Discreetly installed within the solar-powered streetlight posts are security cameras, their presence subtle but far-reaching, ensuring every corner of the city remains under careful observation. These unassuming sentinels stand as both a symbol of protection and a reminder of the Embassy's ever-watchful eyes, maintaining order across the vibrant regions of Cannabisville.

However, the parks remain a sanctuary of privacy, untouched by these surveillance measures. This exemption exists because of the tree of life 'Marijuana Trees Privacy Law, which protects the natural sanctity of Cannabisville's green spaces. Here, among the lush foliage and winding paths, the inhabitants are free from the constant gaze of the Embassy, allowing a rare sense of freedom and secrecy in a place otherwise always observed.

Disturbing her groove was an urgent need to use the bathroom to relieve her terpenes. Sativa Diva knew she wouldn't make it home in time, so she decided to find a patch in the foliage. Jax, ever the gentleman, stood with his back turned, guarding her privacy as she took care of business. The stream of her mint-green urine hit the ground, and like a potent fertilizer, the grounds eagerly absorbed it, creating a melody that echoed like the soft tinkling of wind chimes.

Of course, Jax couldn't resist catching a quick glimpse of her smooth, round ass as she pulled her dress back down, but still exposed her '*Budlip*' (vagina). He tried to play it cool, turning his gaze away just in time, but a sly smile crept across his face.

There was something magnetic about Sativa Diva, something that drew him in with every passing moment. Once she finished, it was his turn. With a playful grin, he stepped forward to relieve himself. Unlike Sativa Diva, he wasn't shy about it, and he didn't care if she watched as he confidently exposed his well-endowed weednis (penis) that was half his shoe size, as he made his own melody with streams of dark green terpenes.

The sound was like a loud drum banging the leaves, creating a natural symphony that blended seamlessly with the surroundings of Cannabisville. One of the unmistakable traits of Hommo-Harvestas is that they bleed and pee green, a feature that integrates them deeply with the planet's vibrant ecosystem. They rinsed their hands in the glowing waters of a small stream when a telepathic connection suggested they both harbored the same erotic fantasy of fucking in Weedland Park.

When Jax was releasing his terpenes, Sativa Diva noticed not only his impressive weednis male part, but also a tucked-away device known as a 'Weedpon.' Unlike traditional weapons, a Weedpon was a specialized tool used by the 'Green Sentinel Forces' or 'Soul Patrol' for non-lethal purposes, designed to immobilize or restrain rather than cause harm.

Its presence added an unexpected layer of intrigue, making Sativa Diva wonder about Jax's true affiliations and intentions. No guns or weapons are permitted to the civilian Hommo-Harvestas, except for those who are part of the 'Green Sentinel Forces.' Even within this elite military unit, their guns are not lethal. They are designed to incapacitate or stun, using non-lethal technology that aligns with Cannabisville's values of harmony and preservation of life.

The Green Sentinel Forces are committed to protecting without causing unnecessary harm, ensuring that any conflicts are resolved with minimal violence. This approach reflects the community's dedication to peace and balance, maintaining order without compromising their principles. As they washed their hands in the lime-colored waters of Weedland Lake, the orange belly whistle ducks let out a tune, disturbing both them and the pink swans. Not everything was green in Cannabisville.

In fact, the hues were unlike any seen on any planet. With vibrant, mystical shades shimmering with a life creating a kaleidoscope of colors that defied earthly comprehension. The sounds of Cannabisville in Weedland Park were a musical production of nature's symphony, a harmonious blend of quacks, chirps, and rustling leaves, accompanied by the gentle hum of the wind through the trees. But after sitting back down on the Rootrest bench something seemed different.

The walking trees 'Socratea exorrhiza,' once distant, now loomed beside it, their branches rustling with a strange, deliberate movement. These towering palm tree natives were known to 'walk' by growing new roots toward the moonlight or sunlight and letting the old ones wither and die, slowly shifting their position.

Though fascinating, they were the noisiest trees in Cannabisville, infamous for their creaky movements and rustling leaves, often considered more of a nuisance than a marvel. Their relentless swaying disrupted the peace, and locals often complained about their unpredictable wanderings. Sativa Diva felt a chill as she realized how close they had crept. "*Jax, do you see this?*" she asked, her voice low with unease. Jax nodded, his eyes narrowing as he observed the trees.

"*Yeah, they're awfully noisy tonight,*"

He replied, his voice barely above a whisper. "*I watched them creep up on us slowly. They must be curious about us.*" He reached into his bag and pulled out a small bottle. "*Lemon-lime water,*" he said with a grin. "*I picked it up from the store earlier and glad because it's handy for not just my throat.*"

Without another word, Jax began spraying the lemon-lime water around the base of the trees. The effect was immediate. As if hit by an invisible gust of wind, the trees recoiled, their leaves rustling violently. The walking trees scattered in all directions, their branches flailing as they retreated from the pungent spray.

Sativa Diva laughed in relief thinking he was reaching for his weedpon to shoot them. Hysterically laughing, "*I didn't know they hated lemon-lime!*" Jax chuckled. "*Yeah, it's one of their few weaknesses. Keeps them from getting too nosy.*" He winked at her, and they both settled back on the 'Rootrest' bench, the tension easing away as the walking trees continued to keep their distance, watching but no longer daring to come any closer.

The night birds had been peacefully sleeping, their feathers tucked in as they nestled in the branches overhead. But the sudden commotion from the walking trees jolted them awake. One by one, their eyes opened, glowing softly in the darkness like tiny embers. They watched the scene below with a mix of curiosity and caution, their heads tilting from side to side as they observed the walking trees scatter away from the lemon - lime spray.

The birds remained silent, their glowing eyes the only sign of their presence, as if they were reluctant to make a sound on this strange, magical night. Jax picked a rose called the 'Emerald Enigma.' The stubborn flower put up a fight, pricking Jax with its razor-sharp thorns and causing a few drops of green blood to bleed.

Teasingly, he asked Sativa Diva to kiss it to make it feel better. After she showed sincere affection, he carefully plucked off the thorns from the long stem and tucked it behind her ear. The emerald petals of the rose stood out beautifully against Sativa Diva's golden tan skin. The contrast between the rich green of the rose and the warm glow of her complexion made her look like a vision of nature itself.

MARIJUANA GIRL
WELCOME TO CANNABISVILLE

A living embodiment of Cannabisville's lush beauty. Her skin, being kissed by the moonlight and nurtured by the essence of the land, shimmered with a subtle radiance that seemed to catch the light just right, enhancing her natural allure. The rose nestled in her hair complemented her perfectly, making her look both ethereal and grounded, a true daughter of Cannabisville.

The tUber conveniently pulled up just in time. Jax thanked Sativa Diva for the wonderful evening in Weedland park. She was surprised by his swift yet affectionate embrace. Jax held her tightly around the waist, allowing her to sense his erection, and whispered, *"Do you want a playmate for a few more hours?" He* reluctantly dropped his hand from around her waist. *"Alright,"* he said quietly, not pushing any further. *"But just so you know, I'm not done with you yet, Sativa Diva. Not by a long shot."*

She gave him a small, mysterious smile, then turned and started walking away, her heart pounding in her chest. As she got into the tUber, she could feel his eyes on her, watching her every move. And for some reason, that thought made her smile even more. He knew it was too late, he should have fucked her the moment when their shared fantasy was vivid. Stepping back, with a respectful gesture, he opened the car door, anticipating an invitation to accompany Sativa Diva wherever she desired. Sporting a seductive grin, she gracefully entered the backseat of the tUber.

The tUber driver was so high, with a long ash joint dangling from his lips, that he looked like he was asleep. Thankfully, the tUbers are auto-piloted solar cars. As soon as Sativa Diva shut the door and fastened her seatbelt, the vehicle automatically engages and begins its journey.

Puffing the blunt Jax was disappointed that she did not move over for him. In a euphoric state, Sativa Diva soared high, her mind in the clouds. She was so immersed in her thoughts that she responded non-verbally, subtly hunching her shoulder, gesturing vaguely maybe. Jax exhaled smoke while grinning and repeating her cellphone number.

Contemplating his playful gestures, limited to touching her ass and holding her within bounds, he appeared courteous. However, he might not be prepared for the game she thoroughly enjoys. She had already expressed her desire to have another smoke session with him.

Before the door closed and the seatbelt secured Sativa Diva finally responded in a sultry tone, *"What's Marijuana Girl's favorite mode of transportation - the highway."*

MARIJUANA GIRL
WELCOME TO CANNABISVILLE

They both laughed and said, *"een'Gray - essings'blay"* Green Blessings! A warm greeting or farewell, wishing someone good fortune. She gestured with two fingers, declaring, Peace out, as the tUber departed.

Upon arriving home, Sativa Diva was astonished to discover a Cannabis plant gift, elegantly wrapped like a flower bouquet, waiting at her front door. The tag revealed it was from Ganja Boy the Chronic King aka CK, apologizing for missing the Marijuana Art Show. He sought forgiveness, for his busy schedule managing his multi-million-dollar empires of Cannabis dispensaries, smoke shops, and marijuana grow houses.

Despite missing the event, Chronic King had one of his assistants drop off a gift, a baby Sativa cannabis plant. It was a thoughtful gesture, and Sativa Diva could sense the deeper meaning behind it. The baby plant symbolized growth, potential, and perhaps a desire to nurture something new between them. It was his way of reminding her of his presence, even from afar, and of the roots they had already planted together in their relationship.

She guessed the gift was more than just a token and it subtly conveyed Chronic King's readiness for the next stage, a desire to fertilize and nurture the growth of seedlings, hinting at his longing for offspring, Hommo-Harvesta babies. She also suspected he was the private buyer of her 'Marijuana Girl' painting. But Sativa Diva was still aroused and unable to stop thinking about Jax. During her refreshing shower, she gave in to her desires, indulging in her fantasies with her thoughts and fingers, reaching a climax as she imagined them encountering further than Weedland Park.

In the mix of her fantasy thinking of the Ganja Boys and the possibility of Jax and CK knowing each other, unable to shake thoughts of Jax, Sativa Diva found herself questioning whether he might be friends with Ganja Boy, Chronic King. That thought jolted her, stopping her from reaching another climax.

It was probably for the best, she thought because otherwise, she would have been stuck in the shower releasing herself of wet webs of flavonoids. Her body still tingled with arousal, but the idea of Jax being connected to Chronic King would complicate everything. She needed to clear her mind, think straight, and figure out what she truly wanted.

She almost forgot about her cat, Aries, until the little feline brushed up against her, meowing for food. After tending to Aries, she fixed herself a cup of cannabis tea to calm her mind and reset her spirit. With practiced hands, she began preparing her cure, expertly grinding fragrant marijuana buds and rolling them into a perfect joint. She craved the familiar rush, a lift that only a pure Sativa strain could provide, as she sought balance amid the chaos swirling through her thoughts of Jax and the Chronic King.

As she brought the joint to her lips and took the first deep inhale, she felt the tension start to melt away. The citrusy notes filled her senses, grounding her even as her mind began to lift. Sativa Diva closed her eyes, letting the smooth smoke curl in her lungs, and exhaled slowly, feeling the stress of the day begin to dissolve. She knew this was what she needed a moment of clarity and calm in a world that seemed to be spinning too fast.

Still aroused, Sativa Diva was unable to shake thoughts of Jax, her mind replaying every moment they shared. Even after returning home, her thoughts collided with images of both Jax and the Chronic King, leaving her restless and confused. She could not focus, her emotions a chaotic blend of desire and curiosity.

The memory of Jax's touch lingered on her skin, while the Chronic King's cryptic gestures tugged at her mind. As she tried to make sense of her feelings, Sativa Diva realized she was caught in a haze of uncertainty, yearning for clarity, but too captivated by the mystery of both men. After tasting the flavors of Jax's flavonoids when they smoked together, she instantly wanted more. Something intoxicating about his essence left her craving his presence, touch, and energy.

But then there was the Chronic King, a commitment she could not just ignore. Despite his absence and the distance between their compounds in different parts of Cannabisville, she had promised herself to him. He was a steady, powerful presence in her life, even if he was not physically there most of the time.

Conflicted, Sativa Diva's mind was a whirlwind of thoughts, torn between the allure of Jax's vibrant energy and the steady, unyielding pull of the Chronic King. As much as she wanted to explore the spark, she felt with Jax, she knew she had to make a choice soon.

Of course, she had not forgotten about Indica Green. The lingering effects of just one puff from that potent *'Wacky Weed'* still buzzed through her system was affecting her senses and awareness. Sativa Diva knew she would have to confront Indica Green soon, and she was more than ready for the encounter.

This time, she would make sure to catch Indica Green off guard, turning the tables on her unpredictable acquaintance. Whatever Indica Green had planned, Sativa Diva was prepared to manage it with the finesse and strength she was known for in Cannabisville. As the morning sun began to rise, its gentle light filtered through the leaves, casting a warm glow over her gardens. The soft rays of sunlight danced on the dew-kissed plants, making the greenery sparkle like a sea of emeralds. Her mind was still buzzing with thoughts of Jax and the time they spent together.

Next to Sativa Diva's bed on her nightstand was 'The Book of Roots.' Its worn goldish-green cover glistening in the soft light. She reached up, gently removing the emerald rose Jax had tucked behind her ear earlier.

For a moment, she held it, remembering the warmth of his touch. With a tender sigh, she put the rose next to the sacred book, its vibrant petals, a reminder of their growing connection and the unspoken promises that lingered in the arrestive Diva delicately ran her fingers over the rose as she softly recited Chronicle 88 NVC from 'The Book of Roots,', *'Emerald Enigma Rose'*

"Let the Enigma Rose of Emerald bloom to remind us of resilience, for it will be sharp to the touch, yet its beauty will endure. The rose shall bleed green as a testament to the strength of our strain, and its petals shall carry the essence of love and loyalty. You are the Emerald Enigma Rose' of Cannabisville, and the lily of the valleys. -Selahjah"

Sativa Diva knew that to pluck the rose is to embrace both the pain and the pleasure, for nothing worthy comes without sacrifice. She paused, then whispered, "I am the Emerald Enigma Rose' of Cannabisville, and the lily of the valleys." Her voice lingered on the last line, as she remembered the gentle sting of its thorns, the green blood on Jax's hand, and the tenderness in his eyes as he tucked it into her hair.

The rose, now resting beside her, felt more significant than ever, a symbol of their shared moment. She gazed at the Emerald Enigma Rose lying on her bedside table, a reminder that her night had been real. Placing the rose in a vase of moon water, she watched as its emerald petals shimmered under the soft glow of her nightstand light.

A faint, sweet fragrance filled the room, almost as if the rose had come alive with renewed energy. Its once-sharp thorns softened, and the delicate bloom stood upright, more vibrant and radiant than before. As Sativa Diva watched, a single droplet of moon water glided down one of the petals, landing on the surface below with a soft plink. The atmosphere in the room shifted, a calming energy enveloped her, and she felt as though the rose held some secret power, perhaps a blessing from Jah.

MARIJUANA GIRL
WELCOME TO CANNABISVILLE

Unable to sleep and a natural pothead, Sativa Diva pulled out her rolling tray, feeling a deep need for a remedy that could soothe her mind, body, and solar soul. The cat, Aries, purred contentedly, glad to be fed and now stretched lazily, her sleek fur catching the light, while Sativa Diva watched the day awaken around her, feeling a deep connection to the natural beauty of Cannabisville.

It was in these tranquil moments that she felt most at peace, her thoughts momentarily free from the complexities of her world. As the soothing aroma of cannabis filled the room, Sativa Diva felt a slight release from the thoughts that had assembled up during the night.

She leaned back, inhaling deeply, trying to find some clarity amid the haze of her thoughts. Realizing she'd spent nearly four hours in the park with Jax. The hours had slipped away, each moment with him drawing her deeper into a world she hadn't expected. She didn't ask him about his weedpon, yet.

Immediately, Sativa Diva relit the joint, leaning back, inhaling deeply, trying to find some clarity amid the haze of her thoughts. As she watched the day awaken around her, feeling a deep connection to the natural beauty of Cannabisville.

It was in these tranquil moments that she felt most at peace, her thoughts momentarily free from the complexities of her world. The soft teal-green hues of dawn welcomed her into a state of tranquility, wrapping her in a calm she hadn't felt in a long time.

Sativa never imagined the whirlwind of events that had unfolded moments so unpredictable that even she, with all her sharp instincts, couldn't foresee them. The encounter with Jax left her in a strange blend of clarity and confusion, her mind a tangled web of emotions.

She was still worried about the wacky weed they'd almost smoked. They had both taken a single puff before pulling back, uneasy about its peculiar effects. Something about it didn't sit right with her, though Jax had remained calm, his sincerity disarming her doubts just enough to let her guard down.

His presence was magnetic, drawing her in with every carefully chosen word, every light brush of his touch. Yet, beneath that pull was an undercurrent of uncertainty. Jax stirred something deeper within her a mix of curiosity, longing, and caution that she wasn't ready to confront, especially with Chronic King still looming in her life like a storm cloud on the horizon.

MARIJUANA GIRL
WELCOME TO CANNABISVILLE

What was it about Jax that both grounded her and threw her completely off balance? The answers felt just out of reach, buried somewhere between the haze of the moment and the questions she was too afraid to ask.

Thoughts still swirling, Sativa Diva drifted into a peaceful slumber, gently cradling the new Sativa plant as if it were a precious infant. She sympathetically recited 'Chronicles 5' letting the familiar words of Jah soothe her troubled mind

THE BOOK OF ROOTS
"Be Fruitful, and Multiply "
Chronicle: 302

"And Jah blessed them, and Jah said unto them, Be fruitful, and multiply, and replenish Cannabisville. Tend to its sacred roots and subdue it with care: have dominion over the kush-fish of the flowing streams, the Bud-birds that soar through the skies, and every living strain that thrives within Cannabisville's green embrace."

THERESA VERNELL

WELCOME TO CANNABISVILLE
ONE MARIJUANA

On Planet Marijuana, a single truth united all strains, tribes, and spirits: One Marijuana. This sacred principle guided Cannabisville, ensuring its soil remained untainted and its skies unclouded by the shadow of synthetic cannabis. To the Hommo-Harvestas, this wasn't just a belief - it was their way of life, a commitment to keep their world organic, pure, and thriving.

In Cannabisville, One Marijuana was more than a law; it was a harmonious ethos. It cultivated an atmosphere where creativity blossomed, freedom flowed like sweet resin, and unity shimmered like dew on the first buds of morning. This unspoken promise extended to every strain - be it the jubilant Sativas, the serene Indicas, or the enigmatic Hybrids. Each found solace under the vast canopy of the Marijuana Trees of Life.

Quietly but steadfastly, the guardians of One Marijuana upheld this vision. Their vigilance ensured that the heart of Cannabisville pulsed with authenticity. Their work was often unseen but felt in every corner of the land, allowing every inhabitant to bask in a light that nurtured the soul. Here, individuals weren't just safe; they were celebrated, free to express their true selves in a world that embraced diversity as its greatest strength.

One Marijuana wasn't just a creed - it was the root of their identity, anchoring Cannabisville in its mission to preserve its natural splendor for generations to come.

MARIJUANA GIRL
WELCOME TO CANNABISVILLE

SMOKE SESSION 2:
MARIJUANA GIRL -INDICA GREEN

*"Puff - Puff – Pass - My Ass
Get Your Own Grass,
Smoke Your Own Stash!"*

In the pouring rain, strolling down the alley, Marijuana Girl, Indica Green felt an overwhelming sense of offense. She had just been ejected from a car for refusing to pass her blunt to Ganja Boy, Blue Cheese.

The disruption to her high was enough to sour her mood and dealing with low-grade indica strains like him was never in line with her vibe. She was only with him for his cheese and securing a meal, and a ride while selling him the last of her green weed bags, all the while enjoying his Blue Cheese supply.

Indica Green knew her strength was potent Do-Si-Do strain, she was renowned for her robust aroma. Frequently releasing a sweet and Cannabisville scent with undertones of pungent skunk and subtle floral notes upon climax, she captivated male strains without even trying.

Blue Cheese had fallen hard for Indica Green, savoring her sweet, floral kisses that offered more than just a fleeting high.

As an Indica-dominant hybrid, she had a soothing touch that brought relief to those struggling with intense aches, everything from migraines to nerve pain melted away under her calm influence. But for Blue Cheese, her presence was more than medicinal; her scent and aura were pure enchantment.

Indica Green had a quiet, steady vibe that eased his mind, grounding him in ways even his laid-back strain couldn't fully manage. Her touch, like the promise of calm in a chaotic world, left him wondering if their roots might one day grow together. But their connection ran deeper than the physical.

Blue Cheese relied on Indica Green for updates on bud-hood events and cannabis concerts, making her an essential part of his social circle. He was one of the famed Blues Brothers triplets, from the Northeast side of Cannabisville.

Now, as he cruised at the local speed limit of 420 down Herb Grow Road in his sky-blue Solar-Leaf Cruiser, his mind was set on the next fiery strain to sell or smoke, something potent enough to elevate his senses to new heights.

For Indica Green, sex was not necessarily about love or commitment, especially not with Blue Cheese. Despite his efforts to spend more time with her, attempting games like 'Spin the Blunt' her real allegiance lay elsewhere.

MARIJUANA GIRL
WELCOME TO CANNABISVILLE

Ganja Boy, Sour Diesel was her go-to strain for chilling and her primary source of fresh bud to sell. But since returning to the Eastside, Diesel had gone missing, forcing her to push the new stash she had in her green bags.

He was also the male strain Indica Green would have chosen to produce offspring with, though she knew commitment was out of the question. His deep connections with the Island Bud's, Westside gang, known as the Resin Reapers, made him an enticing yet dangerous choice.

The Reapers were infamous for sourcing and trading the rarest, most potent strains in Cannabisville, often operating in the shadows and breaking the rules in their quest for the ultimate high. Indica Green couldn't deny the allure of Sour Diesel's raw energy and his reputation as a powerful Sativa strain.

But despite the chemistry between them, the thought of tying her roots to a member of the 'Resin Reapers' was a risk she wasn't sure she was ready to take. Being associated with the Resin Reapers of the Buds, complicated things. They controlled the cultivation, distribution, and sale of the finest cannabis strains on the Westside of the island.

The Island Buds, Resin Reapers were notorious for their underground operations, and whispers of their exclusive, potent strains only added to the mystique surrounding them. Any association with the Resin Reapers could spell trouble.

By law, Marijuana Girls and Ganja Boys caught being involved in criminal activities or producing offspring with the Island Buds, Resin Reapers were disqualified from legal commitments. The law was designed to keep cannabis lineages pure, though many strains broke the law and suffered the natural consequences.

Both Indica Green and Sour Diesel had broken their fair share of laws. They were spoiled brats from prominent cannabis lineages, assuming they were untouchable, until they faced their own struggles with addiction, often getting high off their own supplies.

Now, Indica Green was on a mission to find Sour Diesel. She needed to beg for his forgiveness for her recent hookup with Ganja Boy, Gorilla Glue. And she hoped beyond hope that he never found out about her dealings with Blue Cheese. However, Ganja Boy Sour Diesel was a sativa-dominant hybrid strain, composed of 90% Sativa and 10% Indica.

MARIJUANA GIRL
WELCOME TO CANNABISVILLE

Though not pure Sativa, his high percentage of Sativa genetics gave him the edge he needed to dominate among the male strains. He had once confided in Indica Green that, despite his Sativa roots, he would always have a soft spot for Indica female strains, largely due to their extra-large breasts, an irresistible trait to many Sativa males.

However, the true lust of Sativa male strains was for the curvaceous figures of Sativa females. The appreciation for extra-large asses was like the roar of a lion, loud and clear, and it was a distinctive trait admired in all Sativa women.

Indica Green, on the other hand, knew her strength was undeniable. As a Do-Si-Do strain, she was celebrated for her robust aroma. Her scent, a sweet and Cannabisville fragrance with undertones of pungent skunk and a subtle floral note upon climax, captivated male strains effortlessly.

Ganja Boy, Blue Cheese, for instance, was enchanted by Indica Green's kisses, which were an intoxicating blend of sugary, floral, and herbal notes. Being an Indica-dominant hybrid, she always turned him on, He even prayed to Jah for the day he could even kiss her 'Budlips' too.

Blue Cheese, known for his laid-back vibe, usually stationed in the Northeast, he was now driving down Herb Grow Road on the Eastside with Indica Green, as he tried to spend more time with her.

She couldn't bring herself to comply. Her real heart was for Sour Diesel, her 'Bud-Boo.' She wasn't try to be intimate with Blue Cheese… her mission was only about the BudCoin$.

But Indica held back, feeling a pang of guilt mixed with unease. Her heart, or perhaps her instincts, warned her about the tangled web she'd be in if Sour Diesel, another Ganja Boy with a fierce reputation, caught her with Blue Cheese. The thought alone sparked a flurry of nerves, as the tension between the two Ganja Boys brewed beneath the surface.

Although she heard that Sour Diesel was deep in debt to the fierce Resin Reapers, Indica Green never expected him to vanish without a trace. His departure left her reeling, unsettled by the sudden silence of someone who had always thrived in the thick of Cannabisville's high-energy buzz.

For all his wild charm and connections, Sour Diesel had a way of making everyone believe he'd always be around, especially Indica. Now, questions lingered like smoke.

MARIJUANA GIRL
WELCOME TO CANNABISVILLE

Did he owe too much, or was he running from something even deeper? Indica couldn't shake the feeling that this wasn't the end of his story, and maybe, just maybe, their paths would cross again when she least expected it.

The Resin Reapers were feared and respected. Whispers of their secretive operations spread through the streets, their potent strains a symbol of power and mystique.

Yet, despite their dominance, aligning with them came with consequences. Anyone found guilty of criminal activities with the Island Bud - Resin Reapers, or producing offspring with them, risked severe punishment from 'The Embassy of Green Roots.' It was a risk Indica Green couldn't take lightly.

Trying to get intimate with Indica Green, he said, *"Why don't you let me, Blue Cheese take you out Indica Green on a real first date? Let us get together and make some cheesy memories!"*

Though no stranger to danger, Blue Cheese was known to be to also be humorous, and a fun Hommo-Harvestas to be around. He valued his connection with Indica Green beyond her exquisiteness. Though he can now tell she was looking spaced out.

> *"Why are Marijuana Girls always so calm, no stress?*
> *– because y'all always got your roots grounded."*

Blue Cheese adored the sound of Indica Green's laughter - it was like music that danced through the air, soothing his restless mind. He often went out of his way to tell her jokes, loving the way her laughter filled the air and brighten his days.

Beyond their shared humor, he relied on her for updates because Indica Green always had the inside scoop, whether it was about secret venues hosting Kush-core bands or underground smoke circles where the strains mingled. She was his connection to the pulse of Cannabisville, and he cherished every moment they spent together.

> *"Why is Blue Cheese always the life of the party?*
> *-because I'm aged to perfection, smooth, funky,*
> *and leaves everyone feeling extra chill!"*

As Blue Cheese reduced his speed and cruised down Herb Grow Road, he needed her to talk not just smoke up his weed. He started asking probing questions about Ganja Boy, Sour Diesel. His curiosity piqued, and instantly Indica Green's mood shifted. She knew she couldn't afford to give him any real answers, so she pretended to feel nauseous from the cheap, low-grade ganja he'd been smoking.

Blue Cheese then asked as if he was telling a joke, "How does a Resin Reaper order their bud? Extra sticky, hold the shake." Indica Green knew now he wasn't trying to be funny but sending a subliminal message.

Now she was really feeling sick and began acting extra budchy, intentionally creating distance between them to keep his hands off her. Her attitude, paired with her sudden illness, was enough to discourage any further advances.

When Blue Cheese eventually pulled over, he inspected the new overpriced green glittery bags of the 'Green Monster' she was selling. He said, *"My conscious said stick to my bud-get. I'm like, the bud-get is already high, just like I'm about to be, high."* After a quick BudCoin$ deposit for the stash, he was done with Indica Green's bad mood.

"Why did the Blue Cheese strain break up with the salad? because it only had eyes for budding relationships!"

Without hesitation, Blue Cheese muttered in Cannalog, *"ye'Bay - udth'Bay!"* After saying, *"bye, budtch"* and dropping off Indica Green right there at the curb. She was thoroughly irritated but wise enough to hop out of his car without a word. Normally, she enjoyed the Blue Cheese strain; its effects were just the right balance for daytime, not overly sedating, so she could smoke it anytime. Well, anytime but bedtime.

But today, Indica knew there'd be no free 'Blue Cheese Weed' coming her way, nor any of the famous ' THC "Budzilla Burger," made with baked blue cheese and known all over Cannabisville for being bigger, better, and baked. Her stomach grumbled in protest.

Upon returning to the Hempton Inn, Indica Green quickly scanned the bar lounge, her eyes searching for Ganja Boy, Jack Herer. Known by many names like JH, The Jack, Premium Jack, and Platinum Jack, he was a Sativa-dominant strain with a presence that was both masculine and mysterious. His muscular tall frame and sneaky nature made him stand out, often keeping everyone around him guessing.

For Indica Green, Jack Herer embodied the very essence of what she craved in a male Hommo-Harvesta. His heady, uplifting energy, combined with an irresistible charm, made him the sativa strain she yearned for, the perfect balance to her potent, rustic Indica strain.

MARIJUANA GIRL
WELCOME TO CANNABISVILLE

Though their connection was never fully realized, the thought of Jack Herer lingered in Indica Green's mind like the sweet aroma of freshly picked bud - familiar, comforting, and impossible to ignore. His laughter, his warmth, and the way he made her feel seen stayed with her long after their moments together had passed. It was a feeling she couldn't quite shake, though they had just met, she was hoping to run into him again.

Now, settled back in the Hemptel room, Indica Green lit up right away, cleverly smoking while taking a shower to avoid getting the joint wet. Then she searched through the last of her weed supply, she was suddenly struck by a sense of realization.

It dawned on her that she had been living out of Hemptels for several months, now with only 1 green Mylar bag of weed. The realization hit hard, her life was in a state of constant, and the stability she once took for granted seemed like a distant memory.

The new strain she was selling was in high demand, yet Indica Green found herself craving it as much as she sold it. Recognizing her issues, she felt as though she was back to a choice between selling ass or grass. her mind drifted back to thoughts of Ganja Boy, Jack Herer, he was the most alluring sativa male strains she had encountered.

Having previously selling him a dime-bag, she pondered whether he was eager for this last glittery green bag or perhaps a taste of glittery Indica Green. With every puff, she drifted from sweet fantasies of Ganja Boy, Jack Herer to seething thoughts about how Blue Cheese had driven her around the block, only to start prying into her connection with Sour Diesel.

Now she was thinking about Ganja Boy, Jack Herer, a smooth Sativa-dominant with just enough Indica to keep him, had a weakness for Indica Hommo-Harvestas like her, a preference he made no effort to hide. The spark from their bar encounter lingered, hazy yet unforgettable. Even through her high, she'd remembered his parting words: *"I'll be here same time tomorrow night."*

Right now, the thought of that drink, and maybe a second chance at that spark, sounded just about perfect. At first, she assumed perhaps he was undercover weed patrol because most Ganja Boys held official positions within Cannabisville, whether as members of the Weed Patrol, military, space units, or secret services.

Some also served as doctors, scientists, and entrepreneurs, each contributing to the thriving cannabis culture. They oversaw cultivation, researched new strains, developed medicinal uses for cannabis, and created innovative businesses within the industry. These roles allowed them to maintain order, protect the sacred strains, and ensure that the laws regarding cannabis cultivation and strain purity were upheld.

Those Ganja Boys that decided to go astray normally found themselves involved in the underground cannabis trade, dealing with illegal strains, or engaging in shady dealings with the notorious gangs all over Cannabisville.

Instead of following the legitimate paths of doctors, scientists, and entrepreneurs, they exploited the darker side of Cannabisville's economy. Many of them turned to trafficking contraband bud, tampering with genetics, or organizing covert operations that bypassed the strict laws on strain purity and cultivation.

Eventually, the consequences caught up with them, as those who strayed too far faced exile or worse, being cut off from 'The Embassy of Green Roots.' However, Indica Green's suspicions were dispelled when he lit a blunt, passed it her way, and inquired about trying to find a new high, expressing a desire to try something different.

Indica Green always had her guard up and didn't trust most. She especially didn't have many female friends; she always believed they were jealous of her last name. Being a 'Green', her lineage carried a reputation that commanded respect. For Indica Green, it was easier to navigate the world solo than to deal with the petty jealousy of other Marijuana Girls.

The Green family was well-known for producing some of the most potent and desirable strains in Cannabisville, and Indica Green wore her name like a badge of honor. It wasn't just her last name they envied, though it was the effortless way she carried herself, her potent aroma, and the attention she garnered from nearly every Ganja Boy she encountered.

The Island Bud females were cool if you didn't mess around with their male Hommo-Harvestas. They were fiercely protective of their own and crossing them meant serious trouble. But if you respected that boundary, they kept to themselves and didn't stir up drama.

The Hempsters, on the other hand, were good to everyone. Indica Green's family always saw them as humble, hard-working Hommo-Harvestas, especially known for being the best cannabis field workers. They had a peaceful, down-to-grind vibe, she respected them for their dedication and kindness.

MARIJUANA GIRL
WELCOME TO CANNABISVILLE

The SeedWeed females, however, were a different story. Rarely seen beyond their secluded villages, they ventured out only to pray for sick or homebound Hommo-Harvestas or to sell their renowned healing oils. They kept to themselves, never forming bonds with other female strains, not even with their parent lineage, the Hempsters. To Indica Green, they seemed distant and aloof, perpetually wrapped in their own spiritual world, maintaining a quiet separation from the rest of Cannabisville.

For Indica Green, all the other female strains of Hommo-Harvestas, whether from the Kushimba Klan or the OG Wanderer hermaphrodites, were hardly trustworthy. She didn't want to mingle with any of those *"Bud'ches"* and kept her distance from the foreign strains scattered across Cannabisville, especially the mixed-breed ones.

Lost in a daydream about why she didn't have female friends, Indica Green lazily blew smoke rings into the air, her thoughts drifting as hazy as the incense curling around her. She hardly noticed the piles of clothes scattered across the floor or the ticking clock, as time slipped away in the smoky lull of her reverie.

In these quiet moments, she faced a truth she rarely allowed herself to dwell on, her dependence on the 'wacky weed.' But accepting it? That was a different story. She'd always believed that cannabis was a natural extension of her essence, a healing force that could cure ailments, not one that held power over her.

After all, Indica Green wasn't just any Hommo-Harvesta. She saw herself as a genetically unique Marijuana Girl, designed with a purpose far greater than simple indulgence, a purpose she clung to, even in her highest moments.

Unlike the other female Hommo-Harvestas, she was planned to produce the most robust cannabinoids and terpenes on the entire planet. Believing her essence, her smoke was potent cure due to the chemistry of her genetic code.

As she floated through her day, blowing smoke and chasing her own thoughts and smoke rings, Indica Green reminded herself that she wasn't just any Marijuana Girl, she was the future of Cannabisville and maybe, one day, Earth.

In Cannabisville, daydreams about the legendary 24-Karat Gold Cannabis Seed drifted through many Hommo-Harvesta's minds. For some, the fantasy of finding it and exchanging at the 'Embassy of Green Roots' for the million BudCoin$ reward.

MARIJUANA GIRL
WELCOME TO CANNABISVILLE

Others imagined planting it, hoping it would grow into a grand Marijuana Tree of Life with the mystical power to open pathways to Earth. Here, on their verdant planet, Hommo-Harvestas thrived with lifespans twice that of humans on Earth.

A gift from their world's lush, cannabinoid-rich environment. The unique climate and the abundance of potent cannabis strains nurture their vitality, allowing them to live for centuries, retaining their strength and youth in their natural habitat. Their elongated lives are intertwined with the rich cannabis-infused air, which sustains their health and prevents the ravages of time.

However, should a Hommo-Harvesta ever venture to Earth, their long life would be severely threatened. Though they might still appear youthful and vibrant to human eyes, the atmosphere on Earth, devoid of the rich cannabis elements, causes their bodies to age rapidly.

This aging process happens subtly at first, unseen by humans, but it is deeply felt by the Hommo-Harvesta. The once potent essence that kept them ageless begins to diminish, and their robust existence starts to wither away. Because of this, leaving Cannabisville is considered a great sacrifice. Only the most determined or desperate of the Hommo-Harvestas dare to make the journey to Earth, knowing that their time outside the protective atmosphere of their home is limited.

Risking their longevity for a mission on Earth is a temporary and perilous decision, one not taken lightly. For them, the choice to leave Cannabisville is an act of bravery, but it comes with the understanding that their stay on Earth may be short-lived, and their return uncertain.

There are Hommo-Harvestas who claim to have miraculously ventured to 'Earth' and found their way back to 'Planet Marijuana'. These enigmatic individuals, shrouded in mystery, have become legendary among the strains of 'Cannabisville'. Their tale, whispered in hushed tones, has been passed down through generations as both a story of awe and caution, evoking wonder and fear about the perils of leaving their world.

These returned Hommo-Harvestas now reside in the southern territories within the highly protected compounds of 'The Embassy of Green Roots, 'with its rich heritage and lineage of royal gold strains, has become their sanctuary. Guarded closely, and rarely seen by the general populace, and only the elite and elderly have access to their knowledge.

MARIJUANA GIRL
WELCOME TO CANNABISVILLE

The Embassy itself is revered as the epicenter of knowledge on interdimensional travel between worlds. Its ancient halls hold the secrets of how these Hommo-Harvestas managed to survive Earth's atmosphere and return to Cannabisville.

There is great speculation that the gold strain lineage from the Embassy played a vital role in their safe passage, with some believing the gold seeds that allowed them to traverse worlds. These legendary returnees, now regarded as prophets of sorts, are treated with both reverence and wariness. The Hommo-Harvesta of Cannabisville view their survival as a rare gift, but they also carry the burden of knowledge - the stark reminder of the dangers that exist beyond their world, and the possibility that one wrong step could mean never returning to Cannabisville again.

Though many seek answers from them, few are granted an audience. Some say they have aged far beyond the usual lifespan of a Hommo-Harvesta due to their journey to Earth and back. Others believe they have secrets that could change the future of Cannabisville, offering a glimpse into the possibilities of traveling between worlds.

However, their silence about what truly happened on Earth has left much to speculation, leaving their fellow Hommo-Harvestas torn between curiosity and fear. It is said that the scars of Earth linger on their being, a constant reminder of the dangers that exist outside of the safety of Planet Marijuana.

Yet, their return offers hope that perhaps the key to bridging both worlds may still exist, buried deep within the archives of the Embassy. Lately, Indica Green found herself drifting, her thoughts slipping into a daydream of dropping out of 'Cannabright University.'

Memories from Geography class, where they'd studied Earthlings, mingled with fragments from music class on genres like Soul, Reggae, Country, Jazz, Rhythm and Blues, and Hip-Hop. She tried not to dwell on the troubles gnawing at her, growing recognition of her struggles and insecurities, but pushing these thoughts away was becoming harder each day.

It felt like Indica Green was back at a familiar crossroads: selling ass or grass. Her mind wandered to Ganja Boy, Jack Herer and the alluring, Cannabisville fragrance of his Sativa strain. There was something about Jack Herer that kept pulling Indica Green back to thinking about him, like a magnetic energy that made her wonder whether their next encounter would be strictly business or something deeper, something that blurred the lines between transaction and temptation.

MARIJUANA GIRL
WELCOME TO CANNABISVILLE

Indica sighed, the sweet scent of cannabis smoke curling around her as she pondered her next move, unsure whether the path ahead led to profit or pleasure. Either way, the haze of her indecision was as intoxicating as the smoke she inhaled, filling her with both uncertainty and allure.

Their interaction at the bar had left an impression, though Indica Green was higher than the sky. Now ready to find Jack Herer, she realized that she had been shape-shifting in and out of long thoughts about her past and more, immediately after indulging in the new strain that she was selling.

Eyes wide shut, her green eyes would close, and she'd drift into profound contemplation, all the while under the illusion that her eyes remained wide open.

Indica Green reflected on the necessity of maintaining a low-key existence underground. Moving through clouds of smoke, she actively steered clear of any needless drama, contemplating how she ended up in her current situation and successfully evading Ganja Boy, Gorilla Glue.

Encountering this new substance, Gorilla Glue introduced her to the wacky-weed. One day after he took a few puffs and plunged into a coma, provided Indica Green with the perfect opportunity to make a daring escape and taking his stash.

Fleeing towards her freedom from the Northeast, back to the Eastside, Indica Green ventured into clubs, selling pre-rolled blunts, joints, and a few ounces to bouncers, security guards, and touring rappers. Driven by determination, she was set on establishing her own business by any means necessary.

After finding her way to break free from Ganja Boy, Gorilla Glue, she strategically followed a renowned rap groups artist's tour bus, seizing the opportunity to escape when they made a stop in the upper Northeast side of Cannabisville.

A rap group known as the 'Kush Kings' made an unscheduled stop to refuel their tour bus with 'Sour Diesel' fuel. Indica Green, eager to escape her routine, had hopped on with them, hoping for an adventure. But an hour into the journey, two of the rappers, having smoked the 'Green Monster' weed that Indica Green sold them, started showing signs of wild paranoia and uncontrollable laughter.

The erratic behavior quickly turned chaotic, with one of them freestyling gibberish while the other attempted to DJ using the bus drivers steering wheel, their high spiraling far beyond the usual buzz. Seizing a daring opportunity, she jumped out at the next smoke-rest stop, hitching a ride with an unknown bud-trucker heading to the Eastside.

MARIJUANA GIRL
WELCOME TO CANNABISVILLE

Luck favored her as she narrowly evaded a group of young weedling rappers attempting to rob her of all her stash. "Puff-puff-pass, my ass; get your own grass, smoke your own stash!" Indica Green murmured, half-smiling as her own freestyle lyrics echoed back to her, reminders of her knack for self-preservation. They brought her focus back, especially as she remembered how narrowly she'd managed to slip away from Ganja Boy, Gorilla Glue.

Indica Green never drew much suspicion about her identity as a Marijuana Girl. She blended into the background with ease, always radiating an effortless coolness. No matter what her financial ups and downs, she looked the part. Usually impeccably dressed in a low-key elegance that made people question nothing more than where she got her style.
Even though her surname, Green, could have opened doors within the protected estate of the family's lush grounds, she preferred her freedom. Bar-hopping was her way to keep the good times rolling and her BudCoin$ flowing.

Between Hemptels and Bud-BnB's, she had a steady stream of clients looking to keep their heads high. With her stash packed into green mylar bags, she catered to the 420 crowd. Now, sitting at the Hemptel bar, Indica Green felt the evening settling just right, she felt sexy and confident, her green lips shimmering with gloss and the scent of fresh Indica buds clinging to her, unmistakable yet enchanting, like an unspoken invitation to indulge.

Geared up for the night, and ready to flirt. Indica Green assured Jack Herer that she would be at the same place and time as yesterday in case he was in need. Prepared for action, she posed as if ready for a photoshoot, sitting at the bar her green eyes scanned the room then closed.

Falling into deep thoughts, and didn't notice Marijuana Girl, Sativa Diva had walked in and stood behind her. Sativa Diva startled Indica Green, saying, *"What a coincidence, I am here meeting a friend, and look who resurrected. The dirty budtch that pinched my weed stash. I don't wanna fuck you up or curse you out in public, just pay me right now!"*

Immediately Indica Green transferred the BudCoin$. Sativa Diva verified the BudCoin$ funds were in her balance, before joining Indica Green, now she was playing the role of a caring friend. As they settled down, she ordered two glasses of cannabis wine and inquired, *"Where have you been hiding?"* Sativa Diva wasn't shocked to learn that Indica Green had been with Ganja Boy, Gorilla Glue.

MARIJUANA GIRL
WELCOME TO CANNABISVILLE

Then It seemed like out of thin air Jack Herer appeared approaching them with a big smile, showcasing his beautiful white teeth. Upon greeting them, he first acknowledged Sativa Diva. Indica Green was baffled, not understanding how they knew each other. It made sense, though they were both Sativa's. Indica Green felt set up. Cutting to the chase, she spoke directly to Sativa Diva saying, *"Oh, y'all set me up, Ganja Boy, Jack Herer and you!"*

Indica Green caught a flash of confusion on Sativa Diva's face as she processed the nickname *"Jax"* that Ganja Boy Jack had casually let her assume. Jack noticed it too, stepping in before Sativa Diva could question it further, easing her concerns with a quick grin. He'd only meant for their night together to be casual, just a one-time thing. But that evening in Weedland Park, he realized he wanted more than just a fleeting moment with her.

In the past, Jack Herer had always come prepared with condoms, except that night. It was ironic; he'd had everything ready on countless other occasions, but when it came to that night with Sativa Diva, he was caught off-guard. Tonight, however, he was ready.

In Cannabisville, the culture around mating is strict, especially when it comes to unplanned sexual encounters, as any resulting 'off-springs' might have unpredictable outcomes. If a union between strains isn't carefully planned, it can lead to premature, extremely beautiful hybrid babies Hommo-Harvestas with mixed traits unable to reproduce.

For instance, a baby born from any other Hommo-Harvesta with a Hempster may inherit plant-like features, such as marijuana leaves for ears or even lashes. Yet, tragically, these hybrid babies live only to toddlerhood, their lifespans short and bittersweet. Once their brief lives conclude, a magical transformation takes place, a metamorphosis unique to Cannabisville.

Their small bodies revert to plant form, becoming a variation of the 'Queen of the Night' plant. A revered blossom that blooms only under moonlight, symbolizing their fleeting existence and the powerful essence they leave behind.

Much like the fleeting beauty of the Queen of the Night's white flowers that bloom for just one night, the hemp children's enchanting bloom concludes when they die in a single magical night, leaving only memories in its wake.

MARIJUANA GIRL
WELCOME TO CANNABISVILLE

Ready for action, Ganja Boy Jack aka Jax explained, "I invited Sativa Diva, however, you too seem to already be acquainted." He sat down right between the two beautiful female strains making it very clear he was there for Sativa Diva.

Jack promptly ordered Sativa Diva another glass of cannabis wine and signaled to Indica Green that he was engaging with Sativa Diva. Simultaneously, Jack Herer informed Indica Green that the weed she sold him was synthetic, commonly known in Cannabisville as *'Spicy'* aka *'Wacky-Weed.'*

The shit that the underground gangsters the 'Resin Reapers' manufacture with chemically engineered compounds designed to mimic the effects of THC, the active ingredient in natural marijuana.

The synthetic or chemical fertilizers induced a seemingly supernatural effect on cannabis strains, despite their artificial nature. The 'Wacky-Weed' is created by spraying synthetic chemicals onto the plant. Synthetic cannabis interacts with the same receptors in the brain as THC.

Synthetic cannabis is also rich in salts and chemicals and when accumulated in the soil over time will cause nutrient imbalances, plant stress, and detrimental effects on the soil health in Cannabisville that takes pride in being organic.

Jack Herer, renowned for his meticulous weed inspections, found his usual scrutiny wavering in the presence of Sativa Diva. Her vibrant energy and alluring presence pulled him away from his habitual routine, making him forget to check for the subtle signs that usually indicated quality.

In Weedland Park, Jack Herer could taste the same nasty difference that made Sativa Diva frown. He expected organic 'Green Crack' cannabis from Indica Green. But what she sold him had a distinct kick, a heat that lingered on his tongue.

"Where did you get this?" Jack Herer demanded, determination setting in as he looked back at Sativa Diva, his mind racing with the possibilities. He needed answers, not just for himself but for the sake of his reputation as a cannabis connoisseur, and especially for Sativa Diva's health.

Jack Herer's brow furrowed, his suspicion deepening as he studied Indica Green. *"Come on, Indica. You know this stuff isn't what you claimed it to be. The texture is off, and it burns too fast."* He leaned closer, lowering his voice as if sharing a secret. *"You can't fool me. I've seen this before, and I won't be the one left holding the bag."*

MARIJUANA GIRL
WELCOME TO CANNABISVILLE

Indica Green feigned confusion, her emerald eyes wide with mock innocence. *"Really? I thought it was just some new strain making waves. You know how fast things change around here."* She could feel the tension in the air, a tight coil that threatened to snap. *"Maybe I just got it mixed up. You know how it is, too many strains, not enough time."*

Jack Herer narrowed his gaze, searching for the truth behind her words. *"Or maybe you're trying to hustle me. I get it. We all gotta eat, but don't sell me bud-shit."* Jack's voice had a steely edge, and Indica Green knew she needed to pivot quickly to regain control of the conversation.

"Listen Ganja Boy - Jack Herer," Indica Green said trying to inject sincerity into her tone. *"I wouldn't do that to you. You're too important to the scene, and I respect what you bring to the culture. If you're worried about the quality, let's figure it out together."*

Sativa Diva sat back, silently entertained by the back-and-forth between Jack Herer, who she'd first known as 'Jax,' fussing with Indica Green. They were deep in debate over the synthetic marijuana issue, with Jack holding his ground, probing Indica with questions she was struggling to dodge. Sativa didn't need to jump in, he was doing a fine job defending her and more.

As the conversation escalated, Sativa Diva watched with a hint of amusement, appreciating Jack Herer's intensity and insight. For now, her quiet confidence seemed to rattle Indica Green more than any words would have, and she savored the rare moment of letting someone else take the lead.

Indica Green leaned in slightly, the aroma of sweet buds enveloping them both, hoping the familiarity would ease the tension, but it didn't work. "*But you need to be upfront with me,*" Jack Herer replied, still skeptical. "*Otherwise, this trust between us is just as synthetic as what I just smoked.*"

As Jack Herer's revelation sank in, a wave of concern swept over Indica Green, realizing she was caught and had no defense. She was aware that she was dealing in '*wacky weed,*' sourced secretly taken from Ganja Boy, Gorilla Glue's stash, who was probably looking for her.

The first time Indica Green smoked it she only took one puff, and she swore she had seen Bud Marley. This was something out of the world and sent her head space-trippin' and her body sleepwalking if she smoked too much. Each time it makes her feel more human not like a Hommo-Harvesta strain that bleeds green.

MARIJUANA GIRL
WELCOME TO CANNABISVILLE

The ingredients for synthetic cannabis production were quietly finding their way onto Cannabisville's underground 'Green Market,' thanks to disgruntled Island Bud lab members from the 'Resin Reapers' faction, who were bent on revenge. Known for their cunning and secrecy, the Resin Reapers had perfected covert sales, feeding a growing green market for these banned ingredients.

Such fertilizers were outlawed due to the environmental risks they posed, impacting not just the soil but also diminishing the quality of Hommo-Harvesta strains. Their influence was a looming concern, threatening to disrupt the natural harmony of Cannabisville's treasured ecosystem.

Indica Green was addicted and dismissed the side effects believing her super strain powers and potent cannabinoids that only Marijuana Girls have that will protect her. Little did Indica Green know there would be side effects that would cause her to be compared to a pothead with behaviors ready to do anything for the next high.

Like fucking around with male strains like 'Blue Cheese.' Though it was good for her ego. He made her feel powerful, being needed. Something else about the Marijuana Girls was they were emotionally delicate.

Being so sensitive made Indica Green always need to be touched, always needing to be held, and always needed to be watered more often due to her crocodile tears.

Yes, Marijuana Girls have emotions. They need to be cuddled and cared for just as much as they need the sun for photosynthesis. Smoking 'Spicy' sheds light on why Indica Green would blackout and find herself waking up in unfamiliar places, butt naked.

Additionally, it clarifies the vascular system pain her body has been grappling with and her green hair turning brown. Even though Indica was breaking down, she was more concerned about Sativa Diva reporting her to the local health ambassadors or contacting The Embassy of Green Roots' for her to be admitted to be repotted.

'Repotting' is an expensive procedure only affordable to the privilege Marijuana Girls and Ganja Boys. All other Hommo-Harvesta strains must accept their fate or expire if they can't afford the treatments.

This critical experience is akin to a blood transfusion, but for Hommo-Harvesta strains, it involves a transfusion of cannabinoids and terpenes. The intricate process unfolds over months within the Greenhouse-hospitals, like a prison sentence.

MARIJUANA GIRL
WELCOME TO CANNABISVILLE

Green tears were flowing down Indica Green's face fast, feeling embarrassed and guilty. She rushed out of the bar knocking over her empty glass of cannabis wine and not caring if she was followed and they didn't try to stop her. Running she would catch glimpse of herself in the mirrors on the walls and not recognize her own reflections, not liking what she was seeing.

The Marijuana Girls' were not snitches but every day things were changing in Cannabisville. As Sativa Diva watched Indica Green run out of the door. She also knew that Indica Green was introspective and deeply connected to her inner self. Usually, she enjoys solitude and moments of calm reflection, making her one of the most grounded Marijuana Girls, when sober.

Sativa Diva sat there next to Jack Herer full of questions about the weed he gave her to smoke, did he know what it was when he passed it to her in the park? She knew it was wacky first puff, she had so many questions about his Nickname, Jax.

The morning after meeting and smoking with him, Sativa Diva woke up and promptly vomited fluorescent lime-green phlegm. She knew there was something bad and wacky about the weed in the green mylar bag.

She drank decarbonated cannabis detox sativa tea with fresh organic ginger and lemon juice shots, happy her vascular system acted akin to an immune system, and fortunately, it proved to be strong. She considered herself lucky that there were no discernible effects. Now she sat unsure about the player Jax. But positively sure Ganja Boy, Jack Herer was a potent Sativa strain and knew better. Sativa Diva felt relief when Jack Herer confronted Indica in her presence confirming he didn't know it was wacky weed.

Yet, the lingering question remained, why lie about his name? She refrained from asking, recognizing his playboy tendencies. It was a close call, and she almost fell into the game of the Ganja Boys. Despite being strongly drawn to him, Sativa's primary motive was to confront Indica Green.

Indica Green appeared visibly fashionable but altered, her green hair was so dirty it looked brown and looked as if she had been in a fight, and somebody already fucked her up.

Sativa Diva urgently needed to return home to detox after the confirmation that they had smoked wacky-weed. Understanding the situation, Jack Herer graciously set a future date for a more joyous meeting.

MARIJUANA GIRL
WELCOME TO CANNABISVILLE

Surprising even herself, Sativa Diva agreed before hastily exiting the door, following Indica Green's lead. Racing home Sativa Diva had the urgent need to consume gallons of rainwater, aiming to cleanse her system from the toxins resulting from the one puff of synthetic weed she shared in the park with Playboy-Jax, now known as Jack Herer. She was not a medical professional but knew if exposed to synthetic cannabis, she should consider a weed detox lab promptly. However, she couldn't let 'Grow-Lab' where her seeds were stored know about this incident.

For detoxification, Sativa knew for the next few days she needed to stay hydrated by drinking rainwater, osmosis water, or distilled water. Also, she needed to engage in physical activity to promote sweating and maintaining a balanced diet rich in antioxidants that will be beneficial to her terpenes and flavonoids.

Sipping rainwater while also tending to the new sativa plant, a gift from Ganja Boy, Chronic King. Watching it basking in full sunlight on her kitchen windowsill. However, she wondered about the mother of the seed, because it wasn't one of hers. The seeds she'd planted have yielded the flower buds in her garden.

Yet, in their unique world, seeds took on dual roles: those placed in the soil produced plants, while those nurtured within a Hommo-Harvesta womb brought new life, birthing Cannabisville's next generation

Later that evening, Sativa Diva still hadn't heard from CK, the elusive Ganja Boy who always managed to get in her head but never in her bed. She knew his pattern, close enough to stir her thoughts, but distant enough to leave her lonely, and never shown any clear sign of wanting to create offspring, leaving Sativa to question if he was ever truly committed. Because of their unique customs surrounding intimacy.

For them, physical connection was traditionally reserved for committed relationships. Though they were always Horney, sexually aroused by nature. Majority lived by 'The Book of Roots. 'However, there is nothing in 'The Book of Roots' about masturbating to sustain from having sex. Sativa Diva had plenty of practice squirting out pungent fragrances that would intoxicate a male leaving them stuck like honey in sweet tasting wetness.

The male Hommo-Harvestas have a unique reproductive trait - when they release, their essence forms a web-like structure, shimmering like dewdrops in the morning light, designed to nourish and connect.

MARIJUANA GIRL
WELCOME TO CANNABISVILLE

For the females, consuming it is said to be more revitalizing than the purest rainwater, brimming with nutrients and energy that sustain not just their bodies but their deep-rooted connection to their partner and the land. This act is considered sacred, symbolizing life's intricate bonds and the cycle of renewal within committed relationships between male and female strains.

The phone rang and it snapped Sativa out of her masturbation marathon, just in time before she had an orgasm and cover herself in honey sweet wetness. Answering the phone, it was Girl Scout Cookies asking for the 4-2-0 (4-1-1) on Indica Green.

Sativa Diva told almost everything, withholding the detail about Jax being Jack Herer. However, she expressed concern for Indica, and together, they devised a plan to get her to rehab if she is addicted to 'Spicey.' Sativa Diva didn't mention her incident in Weedland Park, smoking with Jax, now identified as Ganja Boy Jack Herer. After confirming they smoked synthetic cannabis, she was having a health scare, but not talking to Girl Scout Cookie about it.

In Cannabisville, if there is suspicion that a Hommo-Harvesta strain might be infected or nearing their expiration, word spreads quickly. Once another strain becomes aware of this, they have a duty to report it to their territory health ambassadors. These ambassadors, in turn, notify the medical authorities at '*The Embassy of Green Root.*' Upon confirmation, the individual is relocated to the North Side of Cannabisville, a place where those with compromised health or nearing the end of their lifecycle reside.

This relocation process ensures that the balance of the strains is maintained, and the integrity of the population's health remains intact. The North Side of Cannabisville, a solemn, yet peaceful area where strains spend their final days.

It's a place that carries both reverence and mystery, a necessary part of life on Planet Marijuana. Also, the homeland to more than just the ailing or expiring Hommo-Harvesta strains. It is also the sacred territory of the Hempsters, an indigenous tribe with dark skin and blond hair, and illuminating green eyes known for their deep spiritual connection to the land.

Living alongside the Hempsters are the revered 'SeedWeeds', a holy group of albino Hommo-Harvestas, with their white skin, hair, and eyelashes. These SeedWeeds, though physically fragile, are spiritually powerful. They live by the laws of the Embassy and Jah, upholding a revered place in society for their healing knowledge and wisdom.

MARIJUANA GIRL
WELCOME TO CANNABISVILLE

Their presence, along with the mystery of the Final Grove, makes this area not just a place of endings but a place of deep spiritual significance. Thinking about the Northside always sent a wave of sadness through Sativa Diva. It was home to the Hempsters, a resilient community of Hommo-Harvestas with CBD blood types, whose hemp products were essential.

Their work sustained the planet, but their land was leased from the Embassy of Green Roots, leaving them in a perpetual state of dependence. Though they lived rent-free on the properties, they would never own the soil beneath their feet a stark reminder of their limited autonomy.

The plight of the SeedWeeds, the holy ones of Cannabisville, also weighed heavily on her mind. Bound by their beliefs, they refused to earn BudCoins or use the old currency, relying solely on donations. In return, they offered their sacred white hemp buds, known as Spirit Light aka Ghostbud that is smoked as the Hommo-Harvestas embrace the spiritual connection to Jah

The SeedWeeds also served as caretakers of the burial grounds, where the Hommo-Harvestas returned to the soil of Cannabisville. These sites were hallowed, not for mourning, but for the transition back to the soil.

As they were planted upright by their feet, their bodies transformed into new life becoming part of the Marijuana Tree of Life, a divine cycle of renewal. Yet, the Northside also whispered of darker tales of Blightroot (the Devil), rotten roots that grew strange, cursed trees tied to long-forgotten ancestors.

Among the living, the Northside was a place of unparalleled beauty, home to the most exotic children born from the blending of THC and CBD bloodlines. These mixed strains offspring have a very short life span. But to Sativa Diva, the memories of the Northside held a bittersweet weight a constant reminder of the struggles, the resilience, and the fragile balance that kept Cannabisville thriving.

The Northside, with all its contradictions, reflected the harsh realities and enduring spirit of a world bound by roots, yet yearning for freedom. Now, the thought of Indica Green being that sick was like a knot tightening in her chest, making her feel unwell herself.

Thankfully the 'Temple of Dawn Blaze' bells rang, its deep chime signaling the sacred hour of *4:20 BT*, Blaze Time. This was the time when Cannabisville paused for reflection, peace, and collective lighting.

MARIJUANA GIRL
WELCOME TO CANNABISVILLE

The sound echoed across the land, from the bustling markets to the tranquil forests, reminding every Hommo-Harvesta to offer up their prayers and peace in a ritual as old as the strains themselves. Instead of joining the evening rituals outside, Sativa Diva chose her moment of solitude. Seated comfortably on the toilet, sipping a glass of osmosis water, letting the cool liquid refresh her senses. With a calm hand, she lit up a joint, the smoke swirling lazily in the quiet air, she embraced her peace time. Puffing and thinking, Sativa Diva understood that the only course of action now was to wait it out.

In a few days, signs of infection will become apparent if her hair turns darker and brittle like Indica Green's and there could be discoloration and dryness in her skin. Contemplating the situation, Sativa Diva felt the urge to cry but refrained, cautious not to squander a tear due to the fear of dehydration.

Then, an alert from the alarm system broke her tranquility, flashing a warning of an intruder at her front door. Startled, Sativa Diva quickly reached for a sexy robe. Her mind racing with the assumption that it could be Ganja Boy, Chronic King, making a surprise visit. As she hurried to the door, her heart skipped a beat, it wasn't him. It was Indica Green.

Marijuana Girl, Indica Green knew she hit rock bottom when she got kicked out of the Hemptel Inn, due to her BudCoin$ account declining payment to extend her stay. As she was leaving, dragging her belongings, she unexpectedly ran into Ganja Boy Blue Cheese, who was in a frenzy, screaming at her and losing his mind.

His rage boiled over as he sped toward her in his solar vehicle, driving like a madman. She barely managed to sidestep him before the vehicle crashed violently into a wall. Before he could jump out and come after her, she bolted. Heart pounding, she sprinted into the dense undergrowth, seeking refuge among the thick bushes.

Hidden from sight she ran into thick bushes and lit a bud to calm her nerves, the fragrant smoke mingling with the forest air. Exhaustion and adrenaline overwhelmed her, and she eventually succumbed to sleep, the hum of distant (Crickets) called "*Chirpleafs*."

Their melodic chirping is believed to harmonize with the natural vibrations of the Marijuana Tree of Life, creating a soothing symphony that others often say carries Jah's blessings through the night, her only lullaby. Indica Green blacked out, her mind a haze of fragmented memories and distant echoes.

MARIJUANA GIRL
WELCOME TO CANNABISVILLE

When she finally remembered the reason for her frantic escape from Blue Cheese, memories came rushing back like a sudden spark of clarity. He was furious - completely unhinged - when he discovered the stash she'd sold him was nothing more than *wacky shit*. At first, she couldn't understand his anger.

They had smoked it together, after all, laughing and vibing as the haze enveloped them. But what seemed like a harmless high quickly turned sour. Indica winced, piecing together the moments leading up to her flight. The shift in his mood, the wild look in his eyes, the way his voice had risen like a storm. He was furious, not just at the product but at her. She'd never seen him like that before.

Now, curled up in the shadows, her pulse still racing, Indica wondered if their bond had snapped for good. The thought was almost as unsettling as the memory of his rage. Whatever had been in that stash, it had sparked something dark—and she wasn't sure how she'd make things right.

Nevertheless, Indica Green was comfortable sleeping, but awakened by the tickling of her toes being sucked and the cool slime that covered her foot began to pull her into its suction, she began kicking wildly, struggling for her foot to be released from the mouth of one of the deadliest plants on the island, King

Nepenthes. Amid the floral landscapes of Cannabisville, not all blooms were kind. One of the most dangerous yet captivating was the 'Nepenthes Rajah,' the king of the pitcher plants.

This botanical monarch stood very tall with a bright reddish, trumpet-like trap, brimming with liters of potent digestive fluid, a spectacle of nature's raw power and beauty. Though mesmerizing, it could be dangerous to all insects and creatures including the Hommo-Harvestas.

Finally breaking free from the King Nepenthes' slimy grip, Indica Green stumbled forward, but not without a casualty. One of her prized green high heels had been swallowed by the plant. Night had fallen, her solar-phone battery was dead, and there was no solar power to recharge it. Muttering under her breath about the price of those designer shoes, she trudged along the road, bags of personal belongings in tow.

She wore one green heel, while her other foot, sticky from the plant's slime, stuck slightly to the ground with each step. Just as despair was creeping in, she spotted a tUber driver on break. She managed to negotiate a ride in exchange for her last bag of wacky weed. With nowhere else to go, she directed the driver to Sativa Diva's place. The last person she had sent BudCoin$ to and her only hope for help.

MARIJUANA GIRL
WELCOME TO CANNABISVILLE

It was a surprise to find Indica Green, standing at the door in disarray. She looked dirty, her clothes half-torn and tattered, her hair wild with balding edges, and only wearing one green shoe. Her usually vibrant energy was replaced by exhaustion, and the sight of her in such a state was both shocking and concerning.

Indica Green collapsed to her knees, sobbing uncontrollably as thick, green, slimy snot oozed from her nose. *"Please, Sativa Diva, forgive me!"* she wailed, her voice trembling with exaggerated emotion. *"I... I didn't know where else to go! I'm so sorry, please, help me!"* Her tears mixed with the snot, dripping onto the doorstep.

Indica green clutched at Sativa Diva's robe, her fingers trembling as she overacted her distress, wailing louder. *"I didn't mean to betray you! I was lost... everyone is turning on me! You're my only hope, my only friend!"* Her sobs grew even more dramatic as she fell against Sativa Diva's feet.

Indica Green, despite her regal status, was now humbled and embarrassed, experiencing a level of vulnerability she had never known before. In Cannabisville, where strains were often compared and debated. She was once seen as a potent rival to Sativa Diva.

The two were frequently pitted against each other in conversations about which strain was more desirable, particularly in terms of their effects. The rivalry between Sativa Diva and Indica Green extended beyond casual banter. In the world of Cannabisville, strain potency and effects were highly valued, some considering Indica strains like Indica Green to be more relaxing and sedating, while Sativa strains like Sativa Diva were thought to be more energizing and stimulating.

'SATIVA versus INDICA,' *"Which strain made you hornier after smoking?"* In the heart of Cannabisville, the debate raged on a never-ending conversation that had fueled countless gatherings and late-night smoke circles: Sativa versus Indica.

The strains were as different as day and night, each carrying its own energy, its own story, and its own way of touching the soul. For many, Sativa was the strain of inspiration. It was uplifting, energizing, and buzzing with creativity. Those who indulged in its light, airy smoke often found themselves wrapped in a wave of euphoria, their minds alive with possibility.

It heightened sensations, making music sweeter, colors brighter, and touch electric. Some whispered that Sativa could ignite a fire of passion like no other, turning even the shyest souls into adventurous lovers under the right moon. On the other hand,

MARIJUANA GIRL
WELCOME TO CANNABISVILLE

Indica was a different kind of magic. Its heavy, cannabis aroma lulled the body into a state of pure relaxation, melting away stress and tension. Those who sought comfort and connection swore by its ability to deepen intimacy, slowing the world down to a single moment of bliss.

Indica was the strain of soft whispers and warm embraces, the strain that made lovers linger a little longer, their bodies attuned to every touch and heartbeat. Even the blended hybrids, with their careful balance of both worlds, sparked curiosity. Strains like Blue Dream or Commitment (Wedding) Cake were often called "*the best of both worlds*," promising the uplifting clarity of Sativa alongside the soothing, body melting calm of Indica.

For some, these hybrids unlocked entirely new dimensions of passion, making them favorites in Cannabisville's smoky parlors. In the end, it wasn't about which strain was better but about the experience it offered. Each strain told its own story, and each Hommo-Harvestas had their own journey to discover which path suited their spirit. As the Marijuana Girls often said, "*There's no wrong trail, just follow the vibe.*"

The constant debate stirred up lively discussions among the Hommo-Harvestas. Which strain was the true aphrodisiac, bringing on that hazy and sparking desire after a few puffs? The debate often split between those who swore by Sativa's energizing buzz, claiming it heightened sensations and deepened connections, and the Indica loyalists, who argued its mellowing effects made for a more intimate, relaxed vibe.

These playful exchanges were as much a part of Cannabisville culture as the strains themselves. For many, the friendly rivalry wasn't just about preference but a deeper conversation on how each strain could transform the mind, body, and spirit, and sometimes the heart.

Indica Green's dramatic plea for help was partly driven by her realization that the world around her was shifting, and she could no longer rely on her family's financial status or strain superiority to maintain her place.

She was confronted with the fact that despite her position and potency, she was not immune to the changing dynamics and growing complexities of Cannabisville. Empathetic, but skeptical Sativa Diva raised an eyebrow, watching her with a mix of disbelief and irritation. She knew Indica Green's theatrics all too well, sensing the desperation to gain sympathy.

MARIJUANA GIRL
WELCOME TO CANNABISVILLE

It wasn't the first time Indica had pulled this act, but something about the one greenshoe, her smelling like garbage, her green hair was turning brown with balding edges, and torn clothes hinted that there might be more to this drama than usual. Indica Green opened her mouth, but the words caught in her throat. The gravity of the moment hung between them, a fragile thread ready to snap. Sativa Diva could see it now.

The synthetic marijuana addiction and the swirling fear, the uncertainty hidden beneath Indica Green's bravado, begging to be saved.

Sativa Diva is a leader, radiating energy and confidence. She's sharp-witted, always one step ahead, and knows how to motivate and inspire others. Taking a deep breath, Sativa Diva lifted her chin slightly, steadying herself. *"We can't let this darkness take you, Indica Green. Remember what we learned - our years together at 'The Roots of Wisdom University..."*

Sativa Diva is deeply spiritual, embracing her connection to the cannabis strains as more than just plants but as symbols of healing and empowerment. She has an aura of elegance and wisdom, balancing strength with a nurturing side. She began to recite the '*Marijuana Girl Pledge*' from her voice strong yet soothing, echoing the wisdom passed down through generations

THERESA VERNELL

"MARIJUANA GIRL PLEDGE"

"From the soil we rise, rooted in strength,
In unity, we flourish, facing our days.
Let the light of truth guide our way,
For in our green hearts, hope will stay."

As the words flowed from her, Indica Green's eyes shimmered with unshed tears. Slowly, almost imperceptibly, she joined in, her voice a quiet whisper of salvation that intertwined with Sativa Diva's.

"In the embrace of Planet Marijuana, we find our peace,
With love and compassion, our fears will cease.
Under the tree of life, we hold each other's hands,
Together we grow, together we stand -
As One-Marijuana."

The pledge hung in the air, wrapping them in a cocoon of shared vulnerability. Indica Green's posture softened, the tension in her shoulders easing as Sativa's voice enveloped her like a protective shroud. When they finished, silence settled, heavy with the weight of their unspoken fears and desires.

MARIJUANA GIRL
WELCOME TO CANNABISVILLE

Sativa reached out, placing a reassuring hand on Indica's arm. *"You don't have to face this alone. We'll figure it out together."* Indica Green nodded, her braveness flickering like a lighter in the wind, but the glimmer of hope was a small, fragile flame igniting within her. *"Together,"* she softly echoed, finally allowing herself to believe in the possibility of redemption. Indica Green's voice wavered as she recited the words of the pledge, her breath growing shallow.

Sativa Diva held her close, feeling the fragility in her friend's trembling frame, as if the strength she had clung to was finally slipping away. She held Indica Green tighter, her arms a shield against the storm of addiction threatening to consume her.

In that moment, Sativa Diva vowed silently to guide her sister-strain through the darkness, to be the light when the shadows seemed endless. They were rooted together not just by shared soil, but by spirit, history, and the unbreakable promise made in the sacred pledge they had spoken together for years.

A pledge that transcended judgment and embraced the very essence of Cannabisville's teachings: care for all Hommo-Harvestas in need, as demanded by Jah. She couldn't quite remember the Chronicle in *The Book of Roots* that spoke of such love and responsibility, but its wisdom echoed in her heart:

"Do for another as you would want done for yourself."

There was no room for hesitation or doubt. Sativa Diva embraced Indica Green tighter, allowing her to feel the warmth of her energy, the sincerity of her intentions. No words were needed. This was a gesture born of pure love - a love that was steadfast, enduring, and strong enough to weather even the fiercest tempests. Together, they would find a way to heal, to rise, and to bloom once more.

Just before slipping into unconsciousness, Indica Green managed a weary smile, her voice barely a whisper. "One... Mmmm..." And then her eyes fluttered closed, leaving Sativa holding the fragile echo of their pledge, a reminder of their bond and the strength they'd need to face whatever lay ahead. A green tear dropped as Sativa Diva whispered back, *"One Marijuana."*

WELCOME TO CANNABISVILLE
LOVE LANGUAGE

In the thriving civilization of extraordinary beings known as 'The Hommo-Harvestas,' sentient cannabis strains take on human-like appearances. Most, united by a shared commitment to veganism, they partake in a unique and revered ritual: the pursuit of creating the most exotic and innovative cannabis strains.

The *Marijuana Girl* 'Girl Scout Cookie' cultivates her distinct personality and characteristics reigns as the 'Cookie Muncher' and bakes the finest cookies, as she gets ready to bake 'Kushmas Cookies.' She must first make cannabutter, her cannabis butter that works THC magic. *"Butta Makes it Betta."*

Not only does she have a passion for eating cookies, but she also enjoys the forbidden pleasure of munching on a well-known hybrid female strain, savoring every delectable bite. As the seasons unfold, Cannabisville undergoes a transformation, marked by the unique sight of girl strains embracing one another.

While homosexuality is not prohibited by law, it faces societal disapproval, traditionally propagating is for seedling reproduction. This eccentric society, where the essence of each character is not defined by human race, but rather by the distinctive qualities of the male and female cannabis lineage

THERESA VERNELL

THE BOOK OF ROOTS
"Love Roots"
Chronicle 50: NCV

"Love is the root from which all things grow. In the soil of kindness, watered by patience, and nurtured through understanding, it flourishes into a bond that connects the soul of Cannabisville, to Jah, and to each other.
-Selahjah"

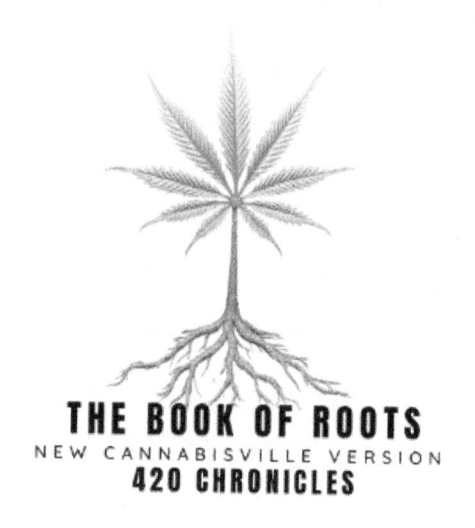

THE BOOK OF ROOTS
NEW CANNABISVILLE VERSION
420 CHRONICLES

MARIJUANA GIRL
WELCOME TO CANNABISVILLE

The 7 Love Languages of Cannabisville

1. Cannabis Infusion Connection

In the marijuana-advanced world of Cannabisville, the Love Language of *'Cannabis Infusion Connection'* takes center stage. Communication unfolds through the sharing and consumption of cannabis, becoming a unique expression of affection.

Individuals convey their deepest emotions by partaking in smoking, eating, or drinking cannabis, creating intricate displays that range from the bonds of friendship to the depths of romantic connections.

2. Neuro Harmony Nexus

In the cannabinoid-enhanced society of Cannabisville, the Love Language of *'Neuro Harmony Nexus'* emerges. Yes, the Hommo-Harvesta's boast brains like all the other strains, yet love transcends the ordinary.

Strains synchronize brainwaves, weaving a shared mental space where emotions, thoughts, and memories flow seamlessly. This unique connection fosters an unparalleled emotional bond, a harmonious symphony of minds in the vibrant landscape of Cannabisville.

3. Botanical Bond

Cannabisville thrives on its connection to nature, and the *'Botanical Bond' love* language revolves around the cultivation and sharing of unique plant life. Individuals express love by nurturing and exchanging rare and exotic plant species, each with symbolic meaning.

4. Herb Affinity

Love transcends the boundaries of time and space in Cannabisville's *'Herb Affinity.'* Through telepathic communication, the Hommo-Harvesta share emotions and experiences instantaneously, deepening their connection when intimately sharing moments of puffing and passing. This unique interaction strengthens their bonds beyond the constraints of physical proximity.

5. Bud Serenade

'Bud Serenade' Takes center stage as the residents of Hommo-Harvesta in Cannabisville express their love through immersive Bud Sharing. Strains engage in the ritual of sharing Cannabis Flower buds in romantic scenarios such as commitments (weddings), births, or simple expressions of

gratitude. The act of sharing buds serves as a symbolic gesture, enhancing and deepening their connections with one another.

6. Marijuana Emotion Coding

Marijuana is intricately woven into the very fabric of existence in Cannabisville. *'Marijuana Emotion Coding'* possess Homo-Harvesta's the ability to dynamically change color, shape, or texture based on the wearer's emotional state.

This innovative feature allows for a visually dynamic and private expression of affection, transforming Marijuana Emotion Coding into a unique and personalized form of emotional communication.

7. Cosmic Resilience

In a universe rife with uncertainties, the Hommo-Harvesta's of Cannabisville express love through a dedication to shared goals and mutual support during challenges.

The ability to navigate *'Cosmic Resilience'* together becomes a testament to the strength of their connection. As they gaze into the vastness of the universe, they seek eternal love from, Jah.

SMOKE SESSION 3:
MARIJUANA GIRL – GIRL SCOUT COOKIE

"Smoke, Weedflix, and Chill,
Take the edge off the grind, let the good vibes spill.
In the haze, we blaze, feel the thrill,
You know the deal - just Smoke, Weedflix, and Chill.""

"Smoke, Weedflix, and Chill," were all Marijuana Girl, Girl Scott Cookie wanted to do. She pulled out a rolling tray and a couple of rolling papers and magically her fingers twisted up a joint.

"Pass the vibe, roll it tight, let the green roots heal,
Every puff, Every laugh, it's the love we reveal.
Screen's lit, skies high, got that mellow appeal,
Just Smoke, Weedflix, and Chill."

Then, frantically searching for the lighter, Girl Scout Cookie (GSC) finally found it buried under a pile of leaves. She frowned, inspecting it closely - it was useless without 'Budtane,' the sacred fuel extracted from the Tree of Cannabisville itself.

"Pass the lighter my way, let's set it ablaze,
Tune into the highs, watch the low fade away.
Got that OG Kush, and the thrill is surreal,

MARIJUANA GIRL
WELCOME TO CANNABISVILLE

Life hits better when we smoke, Weedflix, and chill."

Without it, the ritual of lighting their herbs would have to wait, and the disappointment was evident in her furrowed brows as she searched now for the budtane.

Marijuana Girl, Girl Scout Cookie, affectionately known as GSC is an Indica-dominant hybrid strain created by crossing OG Kush with Durban Poison. Her popularity is a cannabis strain celebrated for inducing euphoric effects, followed by cascading waves of full-body relaxation.

Puffing and puffing until she had the munchies. While nibbling on another cookie, she was patiently waiting for a phone call from Marijuana Girl, Sativa Diva, anticipating an update on Marijuana Girl, Indica Green. However, curiosity got the better of her, prompting GSC to make the call herself.

"Dim the lights, roll it tight, it's 420 all tonight,
Got my stash on lock, and the sparks ignite.
Let's chase the world, just you and me girl
Let's smoke, Weedflix, and chill."

Girl Scout Cookie felt a sudden pull to find Indica Green. The urgency hit her like a wave, especially after she stumbled upon one of Indica Green's green bags. At first glance, it seemed like Indica Green was back to her usual business, selling high-quality, potent strains. But when Girl Scout Cookie opened the bag, a pungent, unfamiliar scent hit her nostrils. She frowned, her fingers sifting through the brittle, unnatural-looking contents.

This wasn't the vibrant, woodsy birch aroma of true Cannabis. Instead, the bag contained something far more sinister, a synthetic substance cleverly branded as "Spicey." The look and smell were close enough to fool a casual observer, but Girl Scout Cookie knew better.

Her stomach twisted as she realized the gravity of the situation. 'Spicey' was notorious in the underground circles, often masquerading as authentic Marijuana but wreaking havoc on both mind and body. It was a dangerous blend, cheap to make and deceptively potent, known to plunge even the strongest minds into darkness.

Lost in the haze, feelin' faze
You and me, baby, just feelin' hazy
Just being lazy, as we
Smoke, Weedflix, and chill."

Annoyance simmered beneath Girl Scout Cookie's initial shock. She'd been duped. But more than that, she thought of the unsuspecting souls who might fall prey to this synthetic poison, mistaking it for something natural, something safe. With a resolute glare, she sealed the bag and slipped it back into her pouch, her mind already racing with plans to track down whoever was behind this deceit.

Anger and disappointment filled Girl Scout Cookie after discovering that Indica Green was the Eastside plug. Synthetic cannabis was frowned upon in Cannabisville, a place where purity of strain and natural cultivation were sacred. Selling something like this was not just illegal, it was a betrayal of everything the Hommo-Harvestas stood for natural growth, the sanctity of the land, and the bond between strains.

"Smoke, Weedflix, and Chill"

Determined to get to the bottom of it, Girl Scout Cookie knew she had to confront Indica Green. This wasn't just about business anymore; it was about protecting the integrity of Cannabisville itself. As much as they'd had their differences, Indica Green had always been known for her royal lineage, for her purity. What had changed? Or had Indica strayed so far from her roots that even her famed reputation was now a puff of fake smoke?

Girl Scout Cookie dialed Sativa Diva, her emotions still in a whirlwind from discovering the fake cannabis. As the call connected, Girl Scout Cookie could hear the urgency in Sativa Diva's voice. When Sativa picked up, her voice was heavy with concern. *"Hi Cookie, Indica Green is here... at my place,"*

Sativa Diva said, her voice trembling. *"She's in bad shape. Indica Green's clothes are torn, she's lost weight, and I don't know what happened, but it looks like she's been using 'Spicey' herself."*

Girl Scout Cookie listened closely, concern growing with each word. *"She's asleep right now, but with her eyes wide open,"* Sativa continued, her tone edged with worry. *" She's been mumbling nonstop, talking about every Hommo-Harvesta from the Northwest, Southwest, Northeast, and Southeast.*

She mentioned the Ganja Boys - the Blues Brothers, the Island Buds -Resin Reapers, and something about Dr. Ashblood and babies, abortions, ocean grown seedling by the OG Wanderlands." The more Sativa Diva revealed the stranger it all sounded. Indica Green's words seemed like fragments of some deeper conspiracy, the names, and networks too tangled to make sense.

MARIJUANA GIRL
WELCOME TO CANNABISVILLE

Girl Scout knew the involvement of so many factions wasn't a coincidence. Most knew about the underground connections between the Blues Brothers and Resin Reapers had their secret connections, but if there was a Hommo-Harvesta baby or babies ocean grown in danger with the OG Wanderlands, there could be more at play than they realized.

"We have to get her help," Girl Scout Cookie said firmly. *"If she's this far gone, she'll need more than just rehab. There's something bigger happening here."* The revelation hit Girl Scout Cookie like a punch to the gut. It wasn't just about selling the synthetic blend, Marijuana Girl, Indica Green had fallen victim to it too.

Girl Scout Cookie's earlier anger now felt misplaced. reconsidering her plans for revenge. She couldn't turn her back on Indica Green when she was in such a state, no matter what their differences. GSC had always been empathetic, but when it came to Indica Green, her feelings were complicated. Deep down, she knew that Indica Green cared only for herself. Period.

The selfish streak in her was as potent as her strain, always putting her desires first, regardless of the consequences for others. But for Marijuana Girl Sativa Diva, things were different. Sativa Diva was kind-hearted and loyal to a fault. She always tried to see the best in everyone, even in someone like Indica Green. That was the only reason Girl Scout Cookie found herself willing to help now.

"*If it wasn't for you, Sativa, I'd let her lie in that mess she made,*" Girl Scout Cookie admitted, her voice hardening for a moment before softening again. "But you always see something in her, and I respect that. We'll get her through this. For you."

Girl Scout Cookie is usually the friendliest, and bubbly one. She's optimistic and brings a playful energy to Cannabisville, always with a mischievous twinkle in her eye. She's witty, clever, and good at finding loopholes or solutions to problems others might overlook. But she wasn't blind to the potential chaos Indica Green could stir up again, but she'd put those concerns aside for now. If Sativa Diva believed there was still hope, then maybe, just maybe, Indica Green could be saved from the path she'd chosen.

Girl Scout Cookie clung to that sliver of optimism, despite the weight of doubt pressing on her chest. Listening to Sativa Diva talking, "*I'll come by. We can't just leave her like this. We need to get her into rehabilitation now. The Spicey stuff... it's way worse than I thought.*"

MARIJUANA GIRL
WELCOME TO CANNABISVILLE

Girl Scout Cookie knew this was no longer just about business or an 'Indica – Hybrid' rivalry. This was about saving one of their own. Recognizing that Hommo-Harvestas were experimenting with this dangerous substance to see if they could get high enough to float out of Cannabisville, without a '24 Karat Cannabis Seed.'

On the way to the rehabilitation center, Indica Green kept fading in and out of consciousness. Though her condition was dire and her state unsettling, only fragments of her experiences and names slipped through her incoherent mumblings. *"Ashblood... Gorilla... betrayed,"* she whispered, her voice weak but tinged with urgency. Her hands trembled, clutching at the air as if trying to grab hold of memories slipping through her grasp.

Sativa Diva, seated beside her, held Indica's hand tightly, her expression a mix of worry and resolve. *"You're going to get through this,"* she whispered, brushing strands of Indica's emerald-tinged hair away from her face. As the vehicle hummed along the quiet roads, Indica's fragmented words painted a haunting picture of her struggles.

Yet, despite her delirium, there was a flicker of determination in her glazed eyes, a spark that refused to be extinguished. It was as if, even in her weakest moments, Indica

Green was clinging to the hope of redemption and the promise of a fight yet to come. Sativa Diva exhaled a quiet sigh of relief, her tension easing, glad that Indica Green had not mumbled Jax's name. nThe weight of their secret they carried grew heavier with every passing moment thinking of Jax, her new confidant, she hoped that he was the Ganja Boy he appeared to be.

The revelation of his true identity as Ganja Boy Jack Herer could shatter the fragile alliances they'd built. For now, he will remain her secret, and so was the delicate balance of their health. The situation was fraught with tension, but Sativa Diva remained focused on helping Indica Green through this troubling situation.

Girl Scout Cookie frowned at the stench coming from Indica Green and said aloud, *"Whew, the smell is unbearable!"* Surprisingly, Indica Green responded with her eyes closed but fully awake, *"Budtch, It's my pores releasing the toxins."* She winced but nodded, understanding the gravity of the situation - no Hommo-Harvesta ever called her a *"Budtch"* and got away with it. The insult stung, but this wasn't the time to dwell on her pride.

MARIJUANA GIRL
WELCOME TO CANNABISVILLE

Sativa Diva, sensing the tension, cut through the moment with urgency. *"We need to get her to the rehabilitation center quickly, Every second counts if we want to save her."*

Girl Scout Cookie straightened up, brushing off the insult like ash from a joint. *"You're right,"* she said, her voice steady now. "Let's keep going - Indica Green's life depends on it." Together, they would help Indica Green's fragile form toward hope and healing, leaving the bitterness behind for a greater purpose.

The tUber transported them through the secured areas as they made their way, Indica Green's condition seemed to worsen, her breaths shallow and labored.

Despite her current state, she continued mumbling the same thing, "*Abortions... Puff.. the magic dragon.. Westside... Ashblood... OG... babies... danger...*" Her words were fragmented but seemed to hold a deeper meaning that both Sativa Diva and Girl Scout Cookie couldn't fully decipher.

Girl Scout Cookie wrinkled her nose, instinctively recoiling as a thick stream of dark green and black slime poured from Indica Green's mouth, filling a plastic bag.

The stench hit her immediately, sharp, sour, and almost toxic, a sickening blend that made her stomach churn. She looked away, fighting the urge to gag as the slimy substance continued to ooze out, clinging to the edges of the bag with a viscous, unnatural sheen.

For a moment, Girl Scout Cookie's hands shook as she held the bag of vomit, her mind racing. What had Indica Green gotten into? This wasn't just any illness; it was something darker, something that seemed to leech the life from their friend's body.

"*Stay with us, Indica Green,*" she whispered, her voice wavering but firm. She braced herself, shifting her grip on the bag, knowing that whatever had poisoned her friend had to be confronted. But the question lingered, gnawing at her: *Was it the Spicey? Or something far worse?* The air was thick with tension and concern as they sat in silence, the weight of what Indica Green had just spewed lingering between them.

"*I don't know,*" Sativa Diva finally replied, her voice steady but thoughtful. "*But were the rumors true about the mutilated baby that survived abortions, the children cared for by the OG Wanders, it had always been a mystery. If she's mentioning them in this state, it can't be good. Something's happening that we don't fully understand yet.*"

MARIJUANA GIRL
WELCOME TO CANNABISVILLE

Girl Scout Cookie nodded, her mind racing. "*I heard of 'Puff the Magic Dragon' that lives by the sea. We need to find out, though, before it's too late. The westside deformed children abandon living with the ocean grown... something feels off.*" They both stared at the sealed bag of green poisons vomit, knowing they couldn't dispose of it lightly.

The detox venom and toxins that Indica Green had expelled were dangerous, capable of destroying any plants they encountered. The dark green and black sludge seemed to pulsate in the sealed bag, its toxic nature threatening to seep out. Sativa Diva and Girl Scout Cookie both knew the gravity of the situation.

If even a drop of it touched the grounds in Cannabisville, it could kill entire crops, decimating Planet Marijuana's rich plant life. "*This isn't just about Indica Green anymore,*" Sativa Diva said, her voice filled with urgency. "*We need to make sure this doesn't spread. Whatever's happening to her could be a threat to all of us.*"

Girl Scout Cookie nodded, her face stern. "*We have to oversee this carefully. One wrong move, we could be smoked!*" The weight of the responsibility pressed down on them both. Indica Green wasn't just fighting for her own life, her detox could endanger the entire ecosystem of Cannabisville. Sativa Diva's expression hardened. *"First, we get her to the rehabilitation center. Then, we'll figure out what's happening with these babies..."*

Girl Scout Cookie nodded, her curiosity piqued despite the weight of what lay ahead. The mention of "*Puff the Magic Dragon*" felt too deliberate, too pointed. She couldn't shake the feeling that it was more than just a twisted nickname for Dr. Ashblood, perhaps it hinted at a hidden connection, a secret history yet untold.

There was a sense of urgency pulsing through her veins; time was slipping away, and whatever dark secrets surrounded Dr. Ashblood needed to be unraveled before he could harm another innocent. Determined, Girl Scout Cookie clenched her fists, her resolve firm.

"Whatever the puffing – long-ash - dragon-doc is hiding, we'll find out. The truth won't stay buried much longer." She knew that beneath the strange rituals, cryptic clues, and whispers in the shadows, there were babies to save - a story that could change the fate of Cannabisville. They needed Indica Green to get better so they could uncover it all.

MARIJUANA GIRL
WELCOME TO CANNABISVILLE

Sativa Diva shook her head, concern etched on her face. "*We need to focus on stabilizing Indica Green, first. We'll figure out the rest once she's safe.*"

Girl Scout Cookie glanced at the large tin of Do-Si-Do Kushmas Butta cookies she had brought along, each one carefully shaped like a Marijuana leaf. The sweet, Cannabisville aroma wafted up, a comforting contrast to the tension in the air. The cookies weren't just an indulgence they were her alibi, a simple distraction if anyone recognized her in the market. Still, a pang of embarrassment tugged at her as she glanced at Indica Green.

Indica Green's once-regal presence was now a disheveled mess, the sharp tang of synthetic cannabis clinging to her like a shameful scarlet letter. It wasn't just the smell it was the way Indica seemed to shrink under the weight of her own downfall, a shadow of the powerful strain she once was.

Girl Scout Cookie clenched the cookie bag tighter, silently reminding herself that appearances didn't matter right now. What mattered was getting Indica Green to Rehab before anyone else could see her or worse, recognize her.

As the medical staff ushered Indica Green into the rehabilitation center, Girl Scout Cookie tightened her grip on the tin. "*I'm just here to drop off Kushmas Butta Cookies,*" she rehearsed silently in her head, ready to deflect questions if needed. She hated the idea of distancing herself from a fellow Marijuana Girl, but the shame of being associated with Indica Green in such conditions weighed heavily on her. *"Everything okay?"* Sativa Diva asked, noticing her unease.

"Yeah, just... don't want anyone to think I'm caught up in all this," Girl Scout Cookie replied, forcing a smile. She added with a chuckle, *"I'm just here to spread some Kushmas cheer with my cookies."* Sativa Diva smirked knowingly but didn't push the matter.

They both knew the stakes were high, and their reputations in Cannabisville mattered, especially with everything shifting and rumors spreading. Indica Green lay still, eyes half-closed, her breathing shallow as she listened intently to the hushed conversation between Sativa Diva and Girl Scout Cookie.

They thought she was asleep, but every word they spoke echoed in her mind, sharp and clear. She knew the truth they were circling, the sinister depths they were only beginning to glimpse, but in her weakened, drug-withdrawn state, it felt impossible to break through the fog and make her voice heard. She tried to speak, but her words caught in her throat, each one feeling like it weighed a thousand pounds.

MARIJUANA GIRL
WELCOME TO CANNABISVILLE

Her fingers twitched, her mouth opened, but only a whisper escaped. She willed herself to stay strong, hoping they had understood her warnings and that they took her words seriously. Even now, as she wrestled with the remnants of her addiction, Indica Green knew this was her chance to set things right - to share what she knew and expose Dr. Ashblood for the monster he was.

The truth weighed heavily on her chest, but it also burned within her, a spark of the woman she used to be. Before Indica Green fell under the influence of Ganja Boy Gorilla Glue, whose silver tongue and shadowy schemes led her astray - she was a warrior with a purpose. Her mind had been sharp, her vision unclouded, and her mission unshakable. Stop Dr. Ashblood, the rogue alchemist better known by his sinister moniker, *"Puff the Magic Dragon."*

Even now, as she wrestled with the remnants of her addiction, Indica Green knew this was her chance to set things right to share what she knew and expose Dr. Ashblood for the monster he was. The truth weighed heavily on her chest, but it also burned within her, a spark of the female warrior, she used to be.

Before Indica Green fell under the influence of Ganja Boy Gorilla Glue whose silver tongue and shadowy schemes led her astray, she was a warrior with a purpose.

Her mind had been sharpened, her vision unclouded, and her mission unshakable. Stop, Dr. Ashblood, the rogue alchemist better known by his sinister moniker, *"Puff the Magic Dragon."* Who lived by a sea of emerald-green that often shrouded in mist, near the 'Haze Ocean,' located west of Cannabisville, bordering between the Island Buds and OG Wanders territories

He allured many strains with promises of enhanced potency, blending science and deception into a toxic brew that corrupted both body and soul. Indica had uncovered his secrets, but Gorilla Glue's allure had weakened Indica Green, clouding her judgment with all his smoke. The stakes were higher than her own redemption. Now, with the haze beginning to lift, Indica Green need to redeem her sins, by ensnaring Dr. Ashblood's web of lies.

If she could summon the strength to confront her past and reveal the truth, she might not only reclaim herself but also protect Cannabisville from falling into the dragon's fiery grip. This was her moment to rise. rooted in the strength of who she once was and blossoming into the hero she could still become.

MARIJUANA GIRL
WELCOME TO CANNABISVILLE

His reputation was sinister, built on whispered rumors of secret, brutal practices and trails of botched abortions he performed under the guise of care. Indica Green was relentless in her pursuit, determined to gather evidence against Ashblood..

Despite the scars left by her own struggles, she channeled her pain into purpose, uncovering every hidden layer of his evil empire. She sought out those he had wronged, piecing together their stories, building a case so strong that even Ashblood's vast resources couldn't suppress it.

Each step brought her closer to exposing the twisted network of deceit and exploitation that Ashblood had built under the guise of progress. The more she uncovered, the more her resolve deepened. This wasn't just about justice for herself it was about liberation for countless others, ensuring no strain would ever fall victim to his manipulations again.

But Gorilla Glue saw something in her a vulnerability he could manipulate. He started by slipping liquid fertilizers into her drinks, altering her mind and loosening her resolve. And when he finally introduced her to "*Spicy*," a potent drug only whispered about on the darkest corners, she found herself caught in his web.

Once Indica Green could uncover the truth about what was really sold on the 'Green Market' products that went far beyond synthetic marijuana, she knew she'd be able to blow the lid off Dr. Ashblood's dark empire. What began as a mission to protect lives had pulled her into a tangled web of addiction, deceit, and betrayal. The market thrived on more than just high-grade cannabis; it hid dangerous concoctions, synthetic enhancements, and questionable substances that fed Cannabisville's green market.

Despite her spiraling struggles, deep down, Indica Green's fire hadn't dimmed. She held on to the spark of her mission, knowing that exposing these truths could be the first step to saving countless lives. And in that clarity, she found a renewed purpose.

Indica Green had to face her own demons of *Blightroot*, the shadowy addiction that had gripped her for far too long. Every step forward was a battle - a test of her resolve against the whispers of weakness and despair. But her determination to dismantle the twisted network fueling the *Green Market* was unshakable. The secrets he kept weren't just his - they were the stolen lives and dreams of countless others. Indica Green was no longer just fighting for herself; she was fighting for justice, for redemption, and to bring the truth blazing into the light.

It was also whispered in the darkest corners of the *Green Market* that Dr. Ashblood had uncovered the secret to the legendary *Fountain of Youth.*

    Yet, the truth behind his so-called miracle was far from the ethereal promises of crystal springs or mythical elixirs. His secret ingredient was something far more sinister: the blood of a newborn, untainted and brimming with pure vitality.

    This horrifying revelation added a new layer to his monstrous reputation. It wasn't just greed that drove him it was a lust for eternal life at the expense of innocence. Those who dared to speak of it did so in hushed tones, knowing the price of exposing such darkness could be their lives. Indica Green knew this rumor couldn't remain hidden forever. She vowed to uncover the truth and ensure Ashblood's reign of terror came to an end, no matter the cost.

    The witch doctor known as Dr. Ashblood of the OG Wander clan was reputed to be nearly 420 years old by human years, though his appearance was that of someone no older than 42 years young. His secret to eternal youth was fueled by grotesque rituals steeped in darkness - rituals that centered around the infusion of fresh, untainted blood.

Dr. Ashblood's twisted legacy had been quietly sustained for generations, hidden in the shadows of the *Green Market*. His network thrived on the desperation and secrecy of those who abandoned their newborns, lured by promises of coin or coerced by fear. These children, full of vitality and innocence, became the lifeblood of his experiments, their futures sacrificed to sustain his warped vision of immortality.

For too long, his sinister practices had gone unchallenged, but whispers of the truth had begun to spread. Indica Green, scarred yet steadfast, knew this horrifying cycle could not endure. She vowed to expose his vile methods and bring justice to the lost voices whose lives had been stolen.

In the OG Wander clan, young Hommo-Harvesta females who bore children from forbidden strain pairings often resulting in birth defects or genetic anomalies would discreetly leave their infants for adoption by families rooted in their communities.

It was a quiet agreement, a taboo rarely spoken of openly, yet embedded deeply within the social fabric of the OG Wander. This practice allowed Dr. Ashblood continued access to his '*green blood fountain*,' preserving both his power and appearance.

MARIJUANA GIRL
WELCOME TO CANNABISVILLE

As the years passed, however, these traditions drew more and more suspicion from the younger generation, who began questioning the true cost of such rituals on the spirit and future of Cannabisville.

Dr. Ashblood, the cannibalistic witch doctor of OG Wander, was a name well-suited to the man who bore it. His skin, naturally a rich walnut brown, had always been plagued by a chronic ashy dryness. This unique characteristic led to the creation of his signature product, 'Soul-Glow 666,' an underground skincare elixir with an intense shine that made his skin appear otherworldly.

It was the only remedy he claimed could give his skin its eerie glow, and he'd made millions selling it on the elusive green-market, so far underground that only the most connected Hommo-Harvesta even knew it existed.

Dr. Ashblood's reputation, however, was not built solely on his skin care empire. The OG Wander knew him for his dark rituals, sustained by a diet of rain-water and a horrifying elixir: the fresh, green blood and the flesh of baby Hommo-Harvestas.

This forbidden practice was kept as quiet as the origins of his products, yet rumors seeped through Cannabisville like smoke. It was said that his eternal youth depended on the innocence and energy of young blood, a horrifying secret that fueled both fear and reverence for him. Though he moved through the shadows, rarely seen, Dr. Ashblood's name was a chilling reminder of the lengths to which some would go to hold onto power in the green world of Cannabisville.

Dr. Ashblood wasn't always seen as a dark figure in Cannabisville. In his early days, he was a compassionate healer, known for his desire to help abandoned children, especially those born with hermaphroditic traits, who were often left to fend for themselves due to societal taboos.

He began fostering these young Hommo-Harvestas, offering them a safe place within the secluded, mystical forest near the OG Wanders, where he nurtured them with genuine care.

Over time, however, his role transformed as he saw an opportunity to heal not just others, but himself. His interest in the mystic properties of Hommo-Harvesta blood turned into an obsession, especially as he aged and sought ways to sustain his vitality. The turning point came when wealthy females, desperate to keep their pregnancies secret, approached him for help. These elite Hommo-Harvesta women, often uncommitted to a male partner, were haunted by the stigma of bearing children outside traditional bonds.

MARIJUANA GIRL
WELCOME TO CANNABISVILLE

Many sought discreet abortions, others gave birth and left their newborns in his care. In secret, Dr. Ashblood began experimenting with the remains of these procedures, crafting potent elixirs and serums. He rationalized these actions as necessary for survival, believing that the abandoned children and cast-off remains were, in a twisted way, given to him for a purpose.

The Glow666 line grew from these forbidden practices, transforming him into an underground sensation. But the further he drifted into this shadowy world, the more his compassion faded, replaced by an insatiable desire for longevity and power.

To the public, he was still the mysterious yet benevolent figure of OG Wander, but in the depths of his practice, Dr. Ashblood had become something else entirely a man willing to sacrifice others for his own immortality, fueled by secrets that kept Cannabisville whispering his name in both fear and awe.

Marijuana Girl, Indica Green, knew the dark secrets Dr. Ashblood kept hidden from the rest of Cannabisville. She had seen too much to turn a blind eye, especially now. There were so many females unable to bear children who would have gladly opened their hearts to adopt or foster, yet he'd stolen that chance with his sinister rituals.

She'd witnessed the truth with her own eyes: the babies he kept hidden in his shadowed lair, and the young teens he manipulated, some even bearing his children only to have them sacrificed in his twisted quest for immortality.

Indica Green was no stranger to dangerous journeys. She'd put her body through trials in search of the most potent strains, pushing herself to the edge for that perfect high. She'd traveled to forbidden corners, walked through thorn-laden paths and under twisted roots just to get a buzz that seemed always out of reach.

It was on one of those reckless adventures that she stumbled upon Dr. Ashblood's hidden world a community in the deep, dense thicket where the children he claimed to 'save' were kept, the abandoned, the outcasts, their eyes hollow with secrets. Now, after leaving the rehabilitation program, Indica Green had a clarity she'd never felt before. She couldn't look away from what she had seen in the Bush.

She couldn't let those children continue to suffer in the clutches of a man who once vowed to protect them but had now turned into their captor. She had to do something. With a heart brimming with purpose and a plan forming in her mind, Indica Green set out to rescue them.

MARIJUANA GIRL
WELCOME TO CANNABISVILLE

She knew it wouldn't be easy; Dr. Ashblood had eyes everywhere, and his influence ran deep within the roots of Cannabisville. But she also knew the paths through the thickest parts of the Bush, the places where even shadows dared not tread. And this time, she wasn't searching for a high, she was fighting for freedom.

Organ harvesting was the darkest of evils in Cannabisville, and Dr. Ashblood true to his name had no qualms engaging in it, all while coolly puffing on a joint, the ash hanging precariously at its tip. To him, it was just another 'procedure,' a twisted ritual fueled by his ambition to remain youthful and powerful. Each organ, each life taken, he saw as a step toward immortality.

Dr. Ashblood patients, often vulnerable or desperate, would leave none the wiser, thinking they had made an irreversible choice. And while others whispered about his elixirs and underground dealings.

He would retreat to his lair, a fortress hidden deep within the Shadowgrove, fortified by wealth, secrecy, and the fear he commanded. Inside, the air was thick with the aroma of burning herbs, mingling with an undercurrent of something far more sinister chemical fumes and the acrid scent of decay.

His laboratory was a chaotic blend of ancient alchemy and cutting-edge technology, where bubbling concoctions and glowing tinctures lined the walls like trophies of his experiments. To him, it was all in the name of progress a twisted science fueled by insatiable greed and a callous disregard for life. He viewed the strains of Cannabisville not as living beings but as resources to be extracted, altered, and consumed. His grand vision wasn't healing or enlightenment but domination, a world bent to his will through manipulation and power.

Each night, as the embers of his experiments glowed in the darkened halls, he would smirk to himself, confident that his wealth and secrecy rendered him untouchable. Yet, even in his arrogance, whispers of resistance reached him - rumors of those who dared to challenge his reign.

Little did he know, his strongest opponent wasn't just a shadow in the crowd. Marijuana Girl, Indica Green, the very strain Dr. Ashblood thought he had broken, until she broke free from the suffocating grip of Ganja Boy, Gorilla Glue. Who was paid a fortune in BudCoin$ to keep her trapped, bound not just by addiction but by his toxic influence. His vengeance is fueled by old grudges and his twisted desire for power.

MARIJUANA GIRL
WELCOME TO CANNABISVILLE

But now that Indica Green had broken free, her resolve was unshakable. She had seen the darkness for what it was, the lies, the manipulation, and the exploitation. She was no longer a pawn in their schemes. The chains of her past had shattered, leaving her determined to reclaim her purpose and protect the legacy of the Green family.

Dr. Ashblood and Gorilla Glue both knew the storm was coming. Indica Green would stop at nothing to bring their empires crashing down, exposing their deceit to the light of truth and showing Cannabisville the strength of her roots.

Unconscious Indica Green continued having nightmares about the night, she ventured deep into the jungle-like bushes, chasing the elusive purple-lavender buds with crispy trichomes and tiny hairs that tickled her tongue and tasted like sweet grapes. Guided only by her craving, she made a wrong turn, stumbling over roots and batting away branches. Then, through the thick foliage, she stumbled upon a grim scene: the backyard of Dr. Ashblood's compound.

What lay before her were the haunting remnants of his dark practices muted echoes of laughter from the mutilated children he kept hidden, innocent lives twisted by his greed and disregard.

Indica Green felt a wave of horror, realizing the depth of the concealed evil in his so-called sanctuary. Scattered across the compound were children, many of whom were survivors of botched abortions. These tiny, fragile beings bore scars both seen and unseen, reminders of the horrors they had endured.

Indica Green's heart twisted as she took in the sight the babies he had deemed unworthy yet kept alive, perhaps for reasons darker than she could fathom. She knew then that these children weren't just survivors; they were his experiments, his twisted trophies, and they needed saving.

Determined, Indica green vowed to find a way to free them, to end the silent suffering that lingered in the shadows of Dr. Ashblood's dark domain. She slipped in and out of consciousness, haunted by vivid flashbacks of the horrors she'd uncovered. Faces, names, and cryptic conversations blurred together in a disorienting reel behind her closed eyes.

As the memory faded, she dimly registered voices around her, saying, *"Green-Leaf, we're here."* A wave of relief washed over her; she'd finally reached the rehabilitation center. But just as quickly, darkness pulled her under again, leaving her somewhere between the comfort of safety and the terror of her memories.

MARIJUANA GIRL
WELCOME TO CANNABISVILLE

fter a 2-hour tUber journey to the Eastside, Sativa Diva, Indica Green, and Girl Scout Cookie of the Marijuana Girls arrived. Reading the welcoming sign, *"Welcome to Green-Leaf"* as they walked the sterile corridors of the rehab facility, their vessels pulsated like a heavy heart.

Nestled in the heart of the Southeast side of Cannabisville. As they approached the rehabilitation center, the stark contrast between the clinical, clean environment and the chaotic situation inside the vehicle became apparent. Medical staff rushed to meet them, quickly taking Indica Green into their care. Girl Scout Cookie and Sativa Diva stood outside, their minds racing with questions and worries.

"We did what we could," Girl Scout Cookie said, trying to reassure herself. "Now, we need to stay vigilant and find out what Indica Green was trying to warn us about." Sativa Diva nodded in agreement. *"Yes, we need to get to the bottom of this. If there's a threat or something important, she was hinting at, we have to uncover it."*

'The Green-Leaf Rehabilitation Center' was a unique laboratory therapy resort, serving as a haven to confront the challenges posed by synthetic cannabis use and other addictions.

As the dark side of synthetics and other substances continues to surface, the demand for specialized facilities became increasingly apparent. In addition to the synthetic weed, there was a surge of Homma-Harvesta's snorting micronutrients, suitably named 'Calcium Magic.'

The slogan echoed, "Stay hi with strong and healthy buds with a pinch of magic," causing a phosphorus surge to elevate their phosphorus levels for maximum flowering and budding, keeping Hommo-Harvestas high and awake for weeks.

The rehabilitation resort stood as an innovative establishment, harmonizing scientific precision with therapeutic care to assist those on the journey to recovery from the pitfalls of synthetic cannabinoids and illegal fertilizers.

Upon entering the facility, guest Hommo-Harvestas are greeted with an atmosphere of serenity and sophistication. The architecture seamlessly blends modern design with elements inspired by the natural surroundings of Cannabisville.

The exterior, adorned with Marijuana trees of life, and lush greenery of large royal ferns, pink cotton silk trees, and bougainvillea flowers, creates a tranquil environment.

MARIJUANA GIRL
WELCOME TO CANNABISVILLE

Inside, the laboratory aspect comes to life as residents undergo personalized assessments. Scientific Herbalist experts meticulously tailor rehabilitation programs to address the unique challenges posed by synthetic cannabis. State-of-the-art equipment monitors the physiological responses, allowing for precise adjustments to treatment plans.

The integration of medical professionals, psychologists, and rehabilitation specialists ensures a comprehensive approach to recovery. The resort does not merely focus on detoxification; it endeavors to heal the cannabinoids and terpenes as well. Therapeutic sessions for both individual and group strains take place in thoughtfully designed spaces, promoting introspection and shared support.

Residents engage in activities that harness the healing power of Cannabisville's natural surroundings, fostering a connection between Hommo-Harvestas and the environment. However, the center maintains a strict rule: no visitors are allowed for the first 420 hours.

This policy ensures that residents can fully focus on their journey to recovery, free from outside distractions, as they reconnect with their inner strength and the restorative energy of Cannabisville.

As a sanctuary for those grappling with the repercussions of synthetic cannabis, the Laboratory-Rehabilitation Resort in Cannabisville stands as a beacon of hope, employing a blend of scientific innovation and compassionate care to guide Hommo-Harvesta's toward a brighter, substance-free future.

Recognizing the depth of Marijuana Girl's challenges, the caretakers discreetly escorted Indica Green into the rehabilitation center, her steps faltering but resolute. She was led to a room designed like an all-white bedroom suite, the walls, furniture, and linens gleaming with a pristine, sterile glow.

Everything had been meticulously prepared to accommodate the needs of a '*Green*,' ensuring a space both physically safe and mentally soothing. The room exuded a quiet tranquility, the soft hum of the air purifiers blending with the faint scent of fresh herbs meant to ground her senses.

Indica Green took a shaky breath, her eyes adjusting to the stark, comforting brightness around her. Knowing she had to accept her fate: without the Repotting treatment, her days were numbered. It was her only chance, yet it came with a daunting price tag. Repotting was more than just a procedure - it was an expensive, intensive ritual to cleanse her system and restore her balance, accessible to only a few who could afford it.

MARIJUANA GIRL
WELCOME TO CANNABISVILLE

They treated Indica Green with CBDV (Cannabidivarin) to managing nausea and seizures. The oxygen mask covered her entire head, sealing snugly around her neck like a delicate, transparent bubble. Her once-green hair, now turned brown, had been shaved, leaving her scalp bare beneath the clear dome. Indica Green could see her own faint reflection in its surface, her weary eyes peering out from within.

The air inside was crisp and pure, infused with calming scents meant to steady her nerves, but the mask's tightness made each breath feel precious, each inhale a reminder of the battle her body was waging. She looked around the immaculate room, its sterile brightness both a comfort and a stark reminder of the fragility of her situation.

The crisp sheets beneath her, the polished white walls, even the silence seemed to carry a kind of quiet reverence, as if the room itself was prepared to witness her transformation or her last stand. Grateful yet afraid, Indica Green closed her eyes, letting the clean air fill her lungs. Ready for the toxins to be purged, and the synthetic poisons drawn out, and her spirit, perhaps, set back on a path to wholeness. But she understood all too well that this treatment was no guarantee; it was a rare, fragile opportunity to rebuild herself from the roots up.

THERESA VERNELL

THE BOOK OF ROOTS
'Breathe in Jah'
CHRONICLE 224 NCV

*"As I breathe in the essence of life,
I feel Jah's presence within me.
Let each breath be a reminder of Jah's love."*

Taking a trembling breath as she recited, 'Breathe in Jah', Indica Green silently vowed to Jah that if she survived this, she'd never go near the green monster '*Spicey*' again. This room, this Repotting, was her last hope to reclaim her life as a true Green. This critical procedure was akin to a blood transfusion, but for Hommo-Harvesta strains, it required a transfusion of pure cannabinoids and terpenes.

Lying in bed, restrained to keep her body from curling inward, Indica Green appeared like a figure frozen in time, as if preserved in some sacred ritual. The room was silent, except for the rhythmic drip of the IV, infused with a blend of Cannaflavins A, B, and C.

These potent flavonoids, known for their anti-inflammatory effects, coursed through her green blood, mingling with chlorophyll to intensify its deep emerald hue. They fortified her system, flooding her with antioxidants to cleanse her body and spirit. She clung to that truth, her mind fixed on rebirth. In this strange yet healing suspension, Indica Green felt as though she was becoming whole again piece by piece, with each pulse of the green serum.

Her body and soul were locked in a quiet battle for freedom, her mind envisioning a life beyond the struggle, beyond the haunted fragments of her past. She had chosen to see this through, no matter the cost.

The IV lines pulsed with a restorative blend of THC (tetrahydrocannabinol) and CBD (cannabidiol), each compound flowing into Indica Green's veins, imbuing her depleted body with renewed life. This potent mixture, part of a carefully administered blood transplant, began to replace what synthetic toxins had stripped away.

The cannabinoids surged through her system, cleansing her cells of the residue from her previous addictions, each drop acting as a purge of the poisons she'd been bound to for so long. The healing compounds intertwined with her green blood, carrying an ancient, almost sacred essence that fed both body and spirit.

As the THC brought relief to her aching limbs and the CBD soothed her fractured mind, Indica felt a subtle warmth, as if her very essence was being reawakened. She could sense the restoration happening within her - each cell, every fiber of her being, reclaiming its purity and strength, preparing her for the journey ahead.

The most excruciating part of the 'Repotting' process was her feet. Each vein felt like the delicate roots of a plant being pruned and grafted anew, pierced with needles that delivered a cocktail of medicinal compounds.

Pain pulsed through her with each beat, as though her very roots were torn and mended at once. Among the restorative elements coursing through her was Quercetin, its antioxidant powers battling inflammation and warding off lingering toxins with each surge.

Kaempferol followed, reinforcing her heart's strength and fortifying her cardiovascular system. The alchemical blend took a toll, pushing her to the brink, yet steadily mending her with every infused drop. It was agony and renewal, destruction and rebirth, a reawakening in the most brutal sense, but Indica Green endured, her spirit fortified with every pulse of pain.

MARIJUANA GIRL
WELCOME TO CANNABISVILLE

She clung to the promise of her own rebirth, each root of her system growing stronger beneath the waves of excruciating healing. Every nerve throbbed, alive with searing intensity, as the infusion coursed through, purging her system. Her veins carried the life-giving elixir, rooting deep within her, reclaiming her from the synthetic poison with each agonizing pulse.

The fragrant flavonoids from the herbal infusions, drawn from the rarest spiritual essence of the gold Soulshine Elixir, filled her air with an almost electric aroma, like sunlight captured in liquid form. With each slow, deliberate drip, the infusion seeped into her veins, purging her system of the synthetic poisons that had dulled her spirit and restoring her connection to the vibrant life of Cannabisville.

The golden Soulshine essence was alive, rich with ancient energy, each molecule carrying the strength of the cannabis roots it came from. Vitamins and Nutrients that her body needed for recovery, such as Vitamin D and antioxidants, were also essential to her healing.

As the terpenes worked their way through her body, Indica could feel the subtle spark of renewal within her. Color returned to her pale cheeks, warmth to her fingertips, as the essence of Soulshine spread, touching every cell and rekindling her original strain's vitality. It was as if her spirit was being painted back to life, hue by hue, restoring the vibrant glow that had once defined her as a true Green. This wasn't just a healing; it was a reawakening.

The infusion penetrated her very core, grounding her while lifting her spirit, each drop a reminder of the power she carried within. Reconnected with her essence, Indica Green felt the faint stirrings of hope, the beginning of a journey back to herself.

The process was grueling and not without risk. Hommo-Harvestas who underwent 'Repotting' experienced fevered visions, as the terpenes triggered deep-rooted memories and unlocked ancestral knowledge.

For the next 420 hours, equaling 17.5 days - Indica Green would exist in a liminal space, drifting between worlds. Her mind, caught in a hazy twilight, would journey through both darkness and light, as memories and fragments of the past battled for dominance.

Her body, though fragile and battered from years of torment, would begin the slow and painful process of recalibration, as the powerful cannabinoids reclaimed their rightful place within her, healing her from the inside out.

MARIJUANA GIRL
WELCOME TO CANNABISVILLE

Every hour, every minute felt like a battle - against her own mind, against the poison that had once consumed her, and against the dark force that had tried to mold her into something she wasn't. But through the haze, there was hope.

The journey ahead would be long, but Indica Green was stronger than she realized. Even as her body trembled and her mind flickered with uncertainty, there was a flicker of the warrior she had once been, a flame waiting to reignite.

Waves of withdrawal tore through Indica Green as her body trembled, every nerve raw, but deep within, a flicker of determination remained, urging her to endure. This was her last chance to reclaim her greenness, to rise from the synthetic poison stronger and deeply rooted in her essence.

The intricate Repotting process, a delicate and grueling journey of healing, typically unfolded over months in the sterile confines of 'The Embassy of Green Roots.' But now, with her family involved, things were different.

They had arranged for an isolated suite within the Embassy's private wing, guarded by their own High Security detail around the clock, ensuring her privacy was tightly protected. The room felt like a paradox, a sanctuary, yet a prison. Indica Green's new confinement was a sentence of sorts, one that tethered her to this solitary journey. Yet, as confining as it felt, it was a reprieve from the fate that awaited her without it. This isolation, this careful control, was a chance at life, better than the slow decay that had threatened to claim her.

THE BOOK OF ROOTS
'Worship Jah'
Chronicle: 105 NCV

"Exult in Jah's holy name; rejoice you who worship Jah. Search for Jah and for strength; continually seek Jah."

'Chronicle 105 NCV,' Sativa Diva whispered as she walked down the hallway before leaving the rehabilitation center, her spirit centering as she softly, yet with conviction, recited from The Book of Roots, grounding herself in the presence of Jah.

As the words rolled off her tongue, she felt a surge of peace, the sacred vibrations calming her soul, reminding her of her purpose and the power she carried within. Sativa Diva's words echoed through the sterile halls of the center, bringing a sense of peace to the space.

She felt the weight of her mission but also the reassurance that Jah's strength was with her. After checking on Indica Green and making sure everything was in place, Sativa Diva prepared to leave. The encounter had left them unsettled, sparking contemplation on the delicate boundary between casual marijuana use and the hazardous realm of synthetic alternatives.

With a hectic schedule, she had to depart, setting off to locate the Chronic King, or so she hoped. Uncertain about Chronic King's whereabouts and accustomed to his elusive nature, she pondered whether there was cause for concern. But before looking for CK, she had committed to meeting up with Jack Herer.

Before walking out, she whispered the same chronicle once more, feeling the words anchor her to her faith. "Exult in Jah's holy name; rejoice you who worship Jah. Search for Jah and strength; continually seek Jah" With that, she left the center, knowing Jah's light would continue to guide her steps.

Before her departure, Sativa Diva attempted to settle the BudCoin$ facility bill, only to discover there was no need. Indica Green, hailing from the affluent lineage of the Greens, was exempt from such financial concerns. She was a truly spoiled brat strain. However, her behavior had escalated to the point of needing professional attention for the first time, resulting in her status as a patient. Due to her privileged position, the administrative processes managed discreetly, with no paperwork.

THERESA VERNELL

THE BOOK OF ROOTS
'Heart of Compassion.'
Chronicle: 219

*Jah, fill my heart with compassion.
Help me to care for others as you care for me,
sharing love in all forms."*

Reciting from 'The Book of Roots,' Girl Scout Cookie prayed for a 'Heart of Compassion.' As she stayed behind at the rehabilitation center, admiring the glittery colors of red, white, and green 'Kushmas tree' decorations that transformed the space into a wonderland of festivity.

The Kush Trees grow around 6 to 8 feet tall, central to the Kushmas celebration, is a much smaller and more intimate version of the towering Marijuana Trees of Life that dominate the landscape of Cannabisville. The Kush Tree Farms are located in the Northern regions of Cannabisville, governed by the Embassy of Green Roots, grown by the Hempsters.

This reminder that Kushmas was just a few days away, she had been busy preparing by and indulging in and baking Kushmas cookies to share with the Marijuana Girls on her Kushmas list, Indica Green's name was not on the list.

MARIJUANA GIRL
WELCOME TO CANNABISVILLE

Yet, somehow, Indica Green had managed to secure the biggest order of cookies donated to the Rehabilitation Center. It didn't add up, and Girl Scout Cookie couldn't help but think it was all in Jah's plans. Giving her a chance to showcase her cookies and be a part of the event, she couldn't resist the opportunity to make a grand gesture, even in a place like this.

The scent of freshly baked treats filled the air as the staff wheeled the cart full of her Do-Si-Do 'Kushmas' Butta cookies into the common room. The rehab center buzzed with the usual tension, but now, there was a hint of curiosity.

It was the perfect alibi for Girl Scout Cookie to check in on the cookies she'd dropped off as a peace offering, under the guise of showing kindness and meeting expectations. "Cookies for the soul," she whispered to herself, her eyes scanning the room as the residents flocked to the cart.

"*Girl Scout Cookie,*" a nurse called from across the room, waving her over, "*We weren't expecting such a large cookie donation. The patients are really enjoying them.*" GSC forced a smile and said her slogan. "*Butta-Makes it Better.*" The aromas of Kushmas cookies and the heady atmosphere of the rehabilitation center tugged at Girl Scout Cookie's senses.

Her munchies were creeping in, and her dry mouth was unbearable. She needed to find relief before heading home. She casually wandered over to the snack station, where they offered cucumber water and free CBD gummies. Grabbing a bottle and a handful of gummies, she moved toward the organic salad and fruit bar.

It was stocked with all her favorite fresh produce - mango slices, avocado salads, and berries. She quickly filled a small plate, savoring each bite as she felt the lightness return to her body. Once satisfied, Girl Scout Cookie felt the tension ease.

The plan had gone off without a hitch, and now it was time to head home. She'd earned herself some well-deserved relaxation. Grinning to herself, she imagined her Weedflix playlist waiting for her and the familiar comfort of her THC stash, ready to melt away the stress of the day.

As Girl Scout Cookie stepped out of the facility, her contemplations of returning to visit Indica Green for the additional benefits and to share the festive spirit, all while indulging in more of these delightful cannabis-infused treats, were abruptly halted by a familiar voice calling her name.

MARIJUANA GIRL
WELCOME TO CANNABISVILLE

"*Cookie! Marijuana Girl, is that really you?*" Marijuana Girl, Petal Pink Euphoria Haze, an acquaintance from the elite cannabis community, emerged from the pink silk cotton trees and pink hibiscus bushes, donated by the Pink Haze Sistah's organization, which supports breast infections, and she was wearing a pink ribbon to show support.

Girl Scout Cookie's eyes narrowed as she observed Petal Pink Euphoria Haze's flirtatious manners as she came forward passing her a lit joint. Without words, GSC accepted the peace offer and took two puffs of the Euphoria strain.

'*Marijuana Emotion Coding*' was taking effect as Girl Scout Cookie's cheeks became pink from blushing. Exhaling she inquired cautiously, "*Petal Pink Euphoria Haze, what brings you to a place like this?*"

Petal Pink Euphoria Haze's lips grew pinker explaining that she now ran an outpatient treatment center for female strains battling substance abuse, aiming to help them find a path to recovery. She spoke of her regular visits to rehabilitation centers to recruit those seeking a fresh start.

Passing the joint back, while experiencing an Herb Affinity moment, Girl Scout Cookie could not shake the feeling that there was more to Petal Pink Euphoria's intentions. Her instincts, finely tuned from years ago when they crossed a forbidden line, lingered. For female strains to share physical- sexual- intimacy was prohibited, and the memory of their forbidden kiss played on Girl Scout Cookie's heightened senses.

Petal Pink Euphoria Haze had, a sly smile playing on her lips saying, *"So Cookie, I heard you got quite the business going on with those THC-infused cookies, edibles, and Cannabutta. A creative twist, I must say."* GSC tried to guard her expression but revealed a blushing smile, but she sensed that Petal Pink Euphoria was fishing for more than just friendly conversation.

Marijuana Girl, Petal Pink Euphoria Haze belongs to the distinguished Pink Haze Family, known for their prestige in Cannabisville. She holds the unique position of being the third strain to sprout from the quadruplets known as the 'Pink Haze Sistahs.'

Petal Pink Euphoria Haze continued, "*It was nice of you to donate Kushmas Cookies to the rehabilitation center. I believe 'The Pink Haze Sistahs' could collaborate with your business."* She continued talking without interruptions, *"Later tonight, I need my own personal Kushmas cookies. Can you deliver and is your number and BudCoin$ account still the same?"*

MARIJUANA GIRL
WELCOME TO CANNABISVILLE

She proceeded to talk, and Girl Scout Cookie did not interrupt her explanation. "*My sistahs, 'Fuchsia Fantasy' and 'Rosey Cloud Dream,' indulge in your cookies regularly. Unfortunately, 'Bubble Gum Mist' cannot partake due to always dieting. Nevertheless, your THC and CBD products could be a distinctive addition to our holistic approach to recovery. What do you say?"*

Girl Scout Cookie hesitated, her mind racing. The proposal seemed innocent on the surface, but her intuition warned her that crossing paths with Petal Pink Euphoria Haze could lead to unforeseen consequences.

Experiencing a '*Neuro Harmony Nexus moment*' as they stood under the shadows of the pink silk cotton trees, Cookie pondered the risks and rewards of entangling her budding business with Petal Pink Euphoria Haze's recovery venture.

Little did Girl Scout Cookie know that this reunion would set in motion a series of events that would challenge her principles and redefine the boundaries between business and benevolence. After a notification alerted her of a large deposit in her BudCoin$ account, she was down for whatever!

In a sweet and inviting voice, Pink Petal Euphoria Haze questioned, her gaze lingering seductively on Girl Scout Cookie, *"Will you be attending this year's annual Cannabisville Ball?"* Girl Scout Cookie let out an exasperated huff, feeling a flush of offense rise within her.

Attendance at the ball required an invitation exclusively to the elite of Cannabisville. Most invitations came with committed partners, and she had never participated in a commitment ceremony akin to a wedding. The thought weighed heavily on her; choosing a Ganja Boy was challenging, especially when she wasn't interested in boys at all.

As for other male strains, she was not interested she tried, but the attempt ended in a messy crumble. No baby Homma-Harvesta for Girl Scout Cookie, they would only devour all her cookies. Nor was she privileged like the Pink Haze Sistahs, who hosted the event due to being elected as the rarest of all cannabis strains, being quadruplets.

Before she could respond, Petal Pink Euphoria Haze conveyed that the invitation would be arriving by mail, with a note specifying no plus one. Additionally, she requested that Girl Scout Cookie reminded Sativa Diva, whom she had seen her with earlier, not to forget to RSVP.

MARIJUANA GIRL
WELCOME TO CANNABISVILLE

Before walking away, Petal Pink Euphoria Haze cast a knowing glance, her voice dripping with intrigue as she said, "Us Marijuana Girls possess unique superpowers that stem from our DNA." She paused, as if hinting at something more about Indica Green without naming her. *"This genetic mutation endows our cannabinoids, terpenes, and physical structures with diverse defense mechanisms against pests, diseases, and environmental stress. Though we lack an immune system like humans or animals, the chemical compounds in our cannabinoids and terpenes act as a formidable shield, warding off various threats. But remember, self-destruction is all too real in Cannabisville."*

A kiss goodbye landed squarely on her lips, lingering for a moment before Petal Pink Euphoria Haze turned and walked away. As Girl Scout Cookie watched her go, it served as a stark reality check, a reminder of the chasm between them and the world of exclusivity that felt increasingly out of reach.

Now that Girl Scout Cookie knew the reputation of *'Green Leaf Rehabilitations'* was true, she understood that Marijuana Girl, Indica Green would be protected with privacy. After crossing paths with Petal Pink Euphoria Haze, GSC hurried home to prepare cannabutta for the new cookie order.

Back home and remembering the quick kiss goodbye under the

pink silk cotton trees that left her lips stained pink and on fire. It was time to start making the cannabutta, THC Butta because *'butta makes it betta.'*

She would be ready to bake more than just Kushmas cookies for the big order placed by Marijuana Girl, Petal Pink Euphoria Haze. Eagerly, to impress her, GSC started preparing to bake the best Kushmas cookies she had ever made.

Kushmas in Cannabisville, while reminiscent of Christmas, has its own vibrant traditions. There are no Santas or wrapped gifts; instead, the focus is on a collective gathering around the sacred Marijuana Trees of Life and illuminated palm trees draped in lights, their glow enhanced by fireflies filling the sky.

The air is thick with the sweet, aroma of cannabis, as the Hommo-Harvestas engage in rituals of prayer and fasting, consuming only blessed holy-water and an array of organic Kushmas treats. During Kushmas in Cannabisville, a range of sacred treats bring warmth and spirit to the celebration. One favorite is Cannabis-Infused 'Sweet Leaf Baklava,' a delicate pastry with layers of thin dough interspersed with chopped nuts, drizzled with a green honey made from cannabis nectar that adds a rich, sweetness.

MARIJUANA GIRL
WELCOME TO CANNABISVILLE

Another popular treat is 'Hempberry Delights,' which are small, flavorful bites crafted from ground hemp seeds and blueberries, wrapped in edible leaves for a nutty and fruity taste. The 'Sacred Herb Ganja Balls' are made from a blend of nuts, oats, and sticky green syrup, then dusted with trichome powder for a frosty, festive look. These treats are soft, chewy, and carry a potent taste that reflects the spirit of the season.

Lastly, 'Green Starfruit Compote' is a revered delicacy served chilled and lightly sweetened, blended with cannabis extracts and fresh starfruit. It is enjoyed for its delicate flavor and symbolic reflection of the stars on a Kushmas night. These treats, each made with love and intention, embody the unity, reflection, and gratitude that define Kushmas in Cannabisville.

The festivities are accompanied by chants and blessings, songs of prosperity, and dances around the trees, as the Hommo-Harvestas celebrate unity, resilience, and the verdant gifts of the planet Marijuana. The night culminates in a powerful silence, a moment for each individual to meditate on renewal and growth, ready to start the next year rooted in hope and harmony.

The culmination occurs for 7 days with the grand feast, marking the commencement of Cannabisville's new season, akin to a new year, and celebrated with a grand ball. Girl Scout

Cookie, however, harbored a sense of guilt for not actively participating in the seasonal observances. Recognizing that she needed to engage more in prayer, she acknowledged her lapse because of laziness, recognizing the setback it caused in her spiritual journey. Nervously, Girl Scout Cookie began to wonder if anyone had witnessed their brief goodbye kiss. It was discreet, concealed by the shadows of the pink silk cotton trees.

Marijuana Girl, Girl Scout Cookie, always had the perfect recipe for making the best 'Do-Si-Dosan irresistible blend of flavor and potency. Her secret? The Indica-dominant hybrid strain known as 'Do-Si-Dos' which she carefully crafted by crossing the legendary '

Girl Scout Cookies' with the powerful, 'Face Off OG.' The result was a treat not just for the taste buds but for the senses a potent experience that could relax even the most restless. With each bite of her infused cookies, the calming effects of Indica would wash over anyone, lulling them into a state of blissful tranquility, while still leaving just enough Sativa spark to keep the mind alert and creative.

These 'Do-Si-Dos' were more than just cookies; they were an art form, a balance of potency and pleasure that kept the strains in Cannabisville flocking to Girl Scout Cookie for a taste

MARIJUANA GIRL
WELCOME TO CANNABISVILLE

of her ancestors secret recipes. Eager to impress Petal Pink Euphoria Haze, Girl Scout Cookie carefully prepared a batch of her finest treats, made with the purest cannabutta extracted from cannabis buds she had personally cultivated in her private garden.

These buds were the product of years of careful tending, grown in the rich soils of Cannabisville and kissed by the glow of the northern lights, giving them a potency that few strains could match. With precision and care, she infused the cannabutta into her signature recipe, creating a special blend designed to elevate the experience for Petal Pink Euphoria Haze.

This was no ordinary offering; this was a *'Cannabis Infusion,'* a potent blend of flavor and high that would lift both mind and spirit. Each bite was a journey into the essence of the Planet, rich with the woodsy undertones of the buds and the sweet, buttery texture of the cookies. GSC knew that this was more than just a treat; it was a connection to the land, to the strains, and to the magic that made Cannabisville thrive.

Petal Pink Euphoria Haze wouldn't just taste the cookies, she'd feel them, as the euphoric waves of relaxation and bliss took hold, deepening their bond in the most intimate way possible. *'Cannabis Infusion Connection,'* would occur when she delivered the Kushmas cookies and more to Petal Pink Euphoria

Haze that evening when the moonlight was midnight, she wanted to fly to the moon, all she wanted was the euphoria, they shared a *'Botanical Bond'* both being hybrids.

For Girl Scout Cookie, it all began with the munchies, 2 sticks of sunflower butta, and potent weed. Ensuring precise dosing of the cannabutta was crucial for GSC. Cannabutta, a shorthand for 'cannabis butta,' serves as the intoxicating ingredient in many of her weed-infused recipes. She applies the same infusion process to oil as well.

A stoner math wizard, Girl Scout Cookie mastered the art of properly dosing cannabutta. Her formula for approximating the maximum THC in decarboxylated cannabutta: (grams of flower) x 1000 x (percentage of THC) = total milligrams. Infusing 2 sticks of butta with 3.5 grams of 100% THC flower, Girl Scout Cookie did the math 3.5 x 1000 times 0.2 equals 700 milligrams in the cannabutta batch.

Yet, she knew it was not an exact science, that about half of the THC could be lost in the infusion process. Girl Scout Cookie expected a maximum of 700 milligrams of THC per cup of butta or roughly 15 milligrams of THC per teaspoon.

MARIJUANA GIRL
WELCOME TO CANNABISVILLE

For Girl Scout Cookie making cannabutta was a simple recipe, even with the added decarboxylation step. She needed about three hours to make it. First, Cookie began by prepping the herb with a hand grinder, carefully breaking apart the flower into fine, even pieces to ensure it cooked uniformly.

Next, she laid a sheet of parchment paper over a baking tray, creating a smooth surface for the cannabis. With deliberate care, she spread the ground herb across the sheet in a thin, even layer, making sure no clumps remained that could lead to uneven heating.

This was the first crucial step in unlocking the full potential of its aromatic and therapeutic properties. Now it was time to decarboxylate the crushed weed. She had already preheated the oven to 220°F (105°C), placed the baking sheet in the oven, and baked for 15 minutes. She opened the oven a few times taking whiffs of the Marijuana scent. Also, to be sure it didn't burn.

If Girl Scout Cookie skipped the decarbing step, the potency of her cannabis butta would drop drastically. Without the heat-induced activation of THCA into THC, the final product would lack the psychoactive punch she was aiming for. The effects would range from non-intoxicating to significantly milder, more akin to consuming raw cannabis than the powerful, mood - altering experience of properly decarbed butta.

Skipping this crucial step could turn her carefully planned recipe into a disappointing flop, a lesson in the science behind every great batch of edibles.. As the weed decarboxylated in the oven, the kitchen filled with its earthy, pungent aroma, wrapping Cookie in a haze that made her feel both higher and more alive.

The familiar scent seemed to awaken her senses, grounding her in the moment while amplifying her focus. She set up a double boiler with practiced ease, the soft clink of the pot echoing her rhythmic movements. Slowly, she added the butta, watching it melt into a silky golden pool, its richness promising the perfect infusion to come.

Once the weed was ready to come out of the oven, Girl Scout Cookie lifted the hot parchment paper by the long edges, poured the weed into the melted butta, and stirred with love. As the butta simmered with cannabis flower to release cannabinoids - primarily THC (tetrahydrocannabinol) and CBD (cannabidiol), keeping the butta at a very low simmer for 45 minutes to an hour.

In the meantime, and in-between time, puffing on a fat blunt and dancing to music all along thinking of Petal Pink

MARIJUANA GIRL
WELCOME TO CANNABISVILLE

Euphoria Haze. Girl Scout Cookie packed her backpack with marijuana buds from her garden to '*Bud Serenade,*' Petal Pink Euphoria Haze. She wanted to play '*Truth or Dare,*' hoping to dare' her to go under the covers, and the added sex-toys would make it a '*Cosmic Resilience*'.

As she fantasized and daydreamed about what happened under the pink silk cotton trees, the quick tongue kiss and the shades of her pink lips, wondering if her panties were the same shade of pink. She knew this batch of Kushmas Cookies would let her confirm.

Feeling this kind of happiness for the very first time, feeling so alive, so in love. Trying to stay focused, it was now time to remove the butta from the stove and filter it through a metal mesh strainer lined with cheesecloth into a Mason jar.

Gently, GSC squeezed the cheesecloth, imagining it would be like squeezing her breast. Marijuana Girl, Petal Pink Euphoria Haze is a slightly sativa-dominant hybrid strain (60% Sativa - 40% Indica) created by crossing the classic Pink Kush with Super Silver Haze strains.

Sativa female Hommo-Harvestas were known for their ample derrières, while Indica female Hommo-Harvestas were recognized for their big boobs, but hybrid female Hommo-

Harvestas possessed both attributes. Softly, Girl Scout Cookie continued to squeeze the plant matter to get most of the butta out. GSC did not squeeze to excess, she did not want plant matter to enter the mix. She let the cannabutta cool off in a mason jar before putting on the lid.

    The cannabis-butta was now ready for Girl Scout Cookie to bake cookies, or it could keep up to two months in the fridge and six months in the freezer. Especially and only for Petal Pink Euphoria Haze, GSC made green Kushmas cannabutta cookies shaped like marijuana leaves sprinkled with pink sugar crystals.

    Many have tried to copycat her recipes, but they could not get the potent flavors from the organic strains she uses. No other could use her strain 'Girl Scout Cookies' due to the clause of nature. She was the organic strain that had seeds to grow the plants for medicinal purposes.

    Girl Scout Cookie's parents, Marijuana Girl Durban Poison (a pure Sativa strain), and Ganja Boy OG Kush (a potent indica strain), are legends. The union of these two iconic strains gave rise to Marijuana Girl, Girl Scout Cookie.

    As a hybrid, Girl Scout Cookies' is meticulously crafted to offer a blend of potency and flavorful characteristics. Just one hit of GSC can evoke feelings of happiness, hunger, and stress

MARIJUANA GIRL
WELCOME TO CANNABISVILLE

relief, highlighting the unique and desirable traits inherited from her esteemed lineage. The lineage of Girl Scout Cookies had become a legendary tale in Cannabisville, whispered with reverence among the Hommo-Harvestas. Stories of her family's legacy had even reached Earth, with everyone in Cannabisville recounting the true origins of Girl Scout Cookies.

It began with the tale of a Hommo-Harvesta who journeyed to Earth. A mysterious and powerful figure who achieved this feat by planting a rare '24-karat Gold Cannabis Seed,' a mystical seed known to open gateways for 'Pod Traveling.'

This pioneering traveler was none other than Girl Scout Cookie's great-great-great-grandmother, Marijuana Girl, Budliette Grow Light. A master pastry chef and skilled cultivator, was the one who first passed down the secret art of baking cannabis-infused treats to her descendants, birthing the legacy of the famous 'Girl Scout Cookies.'

However, Budliette disappeared over a century ago, lost to time and space, only to return to Cannabisville, looking older but strangely changed her once-feminine form now more masculine, her voice gone, her memories erased. Now confined to a secure laboratory within 'The Embassy of Green Roots,' scientists monitored Marijuana Girl, Budliette Grow Light's every move, fascinated by her transformation and the secrets she might hold about 'Pod Traveling.'

The Embassy knew that her travels to Earth might unlock answers to the mysteries of Cannabisville and its connection to other worlds. Her legacy lived on, though, in the strains she helped create. By crossing the energetic and cerebral effects of 'Durban Poison' and the calming sensations of 'OG Kush' gave birth to a hybrid known as 'Girl Scout Cookie.'

This strain became the pride of Cannabisville for its connection to another planet that keeps proving its existence. On Earth the *'Girl Scout Cookies'* were just sweet, innocent treats sold by the Girl Scouts of America. But in Cannabisville, they carried a much deeper significance, a potent reminder of their connection to the stars and the power of a single seed.

Disclaimer:

This Cannabutta recipe is strictly for entertainment purposes only! Please note, this buttery masterpiece is for Adult Hommo-Harvestas Only! No seedlings, sprouts, or underage strains allowed. Proceed with caution, a pinch of humor, and an extra sprinkle of good vibes. Always remember bake responsibly, puff thoughtfully, and never let your cookies crumble under pressure!

MARIJUANA GIRL
WELCOME TO CANNABISVILLE

CANNABUTTA RECIPE

Ingredients:

2 cup (4 sticks) of butta or coconut oil

8 grams (or more) of ground cannabis

Supplies:

Scale

Baking sheet

Parchment paper

Small saucepan or double boiler

Metal mesh strainer

Cheesecloth

Spatula/other utensils

Clean Mason jar and lid

Step 1: Prep Weed

First, use a hand grinder to break apart the flower. Put parchment paper on a baking sheet and spread the herb evenly across the surface.

Step 2: Decarboxylate

Preheat the oven to 220°F (105°C), place the sheet in the oven, and bake for 30 minutes.

Step 3: Melt Butta.

While the weed is decarboxylating, set up the double boiler or saucepan on

your stove and melt the butta.

Step 4: Combine and Stir

Once the weed comes out of the oven, lift the parchment by the long edges,

and pour the weed into the melted butta - stir well.

Step 5: Simmer

Keep the butta at a very low simmer for 45 minutes to an hour. Enjoy the aromas.

Step 6: Filter Butta

Remove the butta from the stove.

Filter it through a metal mesh strainer lined with cheesecloth into a Mason jar.

Step 7: Gently Squeeze Cheesecloth

Gently squeeze the plant matter to get most of the butta out. Do not squeeze to excess, you do not want plant matter entering the mix.

MARIJUANA GIRL
WELCOME TO CANNABISVILLE

The cannabis butta is ready to bake with or eat with some of the most popular ways to use cannabutta, Girl Scout Cookie also made a lot of pot brownies.

While watching Weedflix GSC also drizzles cannabutta over popcorn for a high-fiber, medicated snack. In her hot drinks, she added a teaspoon of cannabutta to hot tea for a soothing cannabis-infused beverage (Hommo-Harvestas don't drink coffee).

The cannabutta will keep up to two months in the fridge and six months in the freezer.

THERESA VERNELL

WELCOME TO CANNABISVILL
NEW WEED DAY

In the world of Marijuana passion for cultivation meets the mysteries of genetic diversity. Explore the intricate relationships, fierce competitions, and the ever-evolving strains that emerge from the enchanting fields of Cannabisville.

In the vibrant villas of Cannabisville, a hidden society of extraordinary beings thrives – '*The Marijuana Girls.*' These sentient cannabis strains, with human-like appearances and a shared commitment to Jahaism, engage in a unique ritual of creation: the pursuit of exotic new cannabis strains.

Amidst the lush fields, each marijuana girl cultivates her distinct personality and characteristics, representing the diverse world of cannabis. Their quest for perfection leads them to compete for the attention of the rare and sought after male cannabis strains, whose genetics hold the key to creating extraordinary hybrids.

As the buds blossom and the leaves unfurl, the community celebrates the diversity of each Hommo-Harvestas, attributing specific qualities to the gestation dates that shape their identity. The rhythm of life in Cannabisville revolves around these gestational dates, influencing everything from personal decisions to communal events. Residents eagerly anticipate the arrival of each new cycle, not only for the harvest it promises but also for the unique energy and characteristics associated with the marijuana girls during that period.

MARIJUANA GIRL
WELCOME TO CANNABISVILLE

In Cannabisville, New Year's Day is celebrated with an opulent grand ball exclusively for elite cannabis strains, where invitations are coveted, and attendance is a mark of prestige. Each guest is permitted to bring a single plus-one, typically a trusted companion or committed strain.

This gathering is more than a festive occasion; it serves as a unique platform for matching potential donors in the sacred act of producing new seeds, symbolizing growth and prosperity for the coming year. The air buzzes with anticipation as connections are forged under the glow of emerald chandeliers, blending tradition, celebration, and the future of Cannabisville.

The distinguished event is consistently hosted by the previous winners, The Pink Haze Sistahs, who happen to be Quadruplets. Cannabis plants can develop what's known as "twinning" or "polyembryony," where a single seed produces two seedlings. This occurrence is relatively rare, but it can happen under certain conditions during seed development.

In the hazy world of *The Pink Haze Sistahs,* secrets swirled like rosy smoke, uncovering drama, desires, and hidden truths. Within those shimmering clouds, every Hommo-Harvesta eagerly awaited their next revelation.

SMOKE SESSION 4:
MARIJUANA GIRLS - PINK HAZE SISTAHS

"In the Pink Haze, in Cannabisville we glow,
Rolling up dreams, watch the pink smoke we blow."

Welcome to Cannabisville, where the start of each 'New Weed Year' is marked by the Global Cannabis Marijuana March (GCMM), also known as the Cannabisville Million Marijuana March (CMMM). This highly anticipated event draws crowds from every corner of Cannabisville and beyond, a unified celebration of cannabis culture, advocacy, and community spirit.

On this day, the streets transform into a lively parade route with giant floats adorned in marijuana-themed decorations, representing everything from lush cannabis leaves to gleaming THC crystals. Characters dressed as oversized joints, blunts and lighters, roam the streets, engaging the crowd and passing out samples. Blunts and joints circulate freely, gifted by smiling festival goers alongside custom lighters designed to commemorate the event.

MARIJUANA GIRL
WELCOME TO CANNABISVILLE

The CMMM is not only a party but also a chance to educate and inspire. Information booths and outreach stations line the parade, offering educational materials on cannabis health, responsible use, and environmental sustainability. The air is thick with aromatic smoke and laughter as everyone celebrates the spirit of unity and freedom, marching proudly for a future where cannabis continues to bring communities together across Cannabisville.

On this day, though millions gather to celebrate, all are united under a shared anthem: *'One Marijuana.'* The sense of kinship and solidarity permeates every moment, from the booming music and the rhythm of dancing feet to the clouds of fragrant smoke that fill the air. For one day, there is no division, only strains blending together, each Hommo-Harvesta embraced as family, regardless of their cannabis strain, traits, or origin.

As the crowds cheer and vibrant colors of smoke swirl through the air, each individual can feel a connection to the roots of Cannabisville's culture and values: peace, resilience, and unity. It's a day when differences dissolve, leaving only the shared heartbeat of One Marijuana, a community thriving together in celebration and respect.

For the past four years, the Pink Haze Sistahs have hosted the event leading up to the grand Cannabisville Ball, a beauty pageant to crown the next Marijuana Girl. This celebration has become the talk of the town, with the Pink Haze Sistahs at its dazzling heart. Known for their elegance, charm, and deep-rooted influence in Cannabisville, these sistahs bring their unique flair, capturing the spirit of every strain.

After gracing the crowd on their pink-themed marijuana float in the parade, the Pink Haze Sistahs made their way to 'Budgrade 1st of Day Stadium' for a final rehearsal.

One by one, they arrived, each slipping into a shimmering pink rehearsal gown. The usual camaraderie and laughter were absent, replaced by a focused silence. Only the subtle scent of floral terpenes lingered in the air as they moved through choreography, fine-tuning their routines and ensuring every detail was perfect.

Though each Sistah carried her own worries, they knew the significance of the night ahead. This performance wasn't just about entertainment - it was a tribute to the strength and unity that defined Cannabisville, embodying the values and collective spirit of One Marijuana. As they took their places, they reminded themselves that tonight honoring the power of their unity.

MARIJUANA GIRL
WELCOME TO CANNABISVILLE

"In the Pink Haze,

in Cannabisville we glow,

Rolling up dreams,

watch the pink smoke we blow."

The Pink Haze Sistahs, a rare set of Quadruplets, defy expectations by not sharing identical looks. In the realm of Cannabisville, they stand out as a true rarity. While they've observed the occasional phenomenon in cannabis plants known as 'twinning' or 'polyembryony,' where a single seed gives rise to two seedlings, this occurrence is uncommon and typically happens under specific conditions during seed development in the wombs of female Hommo-Harvestas.

The uniqueness of The Pink Haze Sistahs' occurrence is akin to a miracle, a singular event that unfolded only once in Cannabisville. The island had long been familiar with extraordinary births, most notably the twins Luna Kushkin and her brother Blaze Kushkin, both members of the esteemed Kushimba Klan.

Luna Kushkin, a gifted herbalist and alchemist, and Blaze Kushkin, a fiery warrior known for his deep connection to the land, were regarded as a powerful duo, embodying the delicate balance between nature's healing and raw strength.

However, even their fame stakes in comparison to the legend of the Ganja Boys, also known as 'The Blues Brothers.' These identical triplets, consisting of Blue Cheese, Blue Haze, and Blue Berry Dream, were revered for their exceptional genetics and represented the rare occurrence of producing three remarkable male Hommo-Harvestas.

Their unique terpene profiles, blending strength, clarity, and tranquility, made them iconic across the island and beyond. The Ganja Boys were a testament to the island's mysterious and powerful cannabis-based lineage.

Yet, the arrival of the Quadruplets, affectionately named the Pink Haze Sistahs, truly shook the island to its core. These four striking Sistahs, Fantasy Pink Haze, Bubble-Gum Mist Haze, Petal Pink Euphoria Haze, and Rosey Dream Haze were not only known for their stunning beauty but for the grace and power they wielded over the spiritual and physical realms.

Their names were whispered in reverence and each sister carried a distinct yet harmonious energy, reflecting distinct aspects of the cannabis plant's spiritual essence, from serenity to invigoration. Together, they symbolized unity and diversity, transcending the ordinary and embodying a new era of femininity, strength, and elegance.

MARIJUANA GIRL
WELCOME TO CANNABISVILLE

The Pink Haze Sistahs, alumni of the *'Roots of Wisdom University'* brought a rare blend of femininity and raw power to Cannabisville, and their birth was said to have shifted the natural energies of the land, creating new, uncharted paths in both the spiritual and physical realms of the island.

In Cannabisville, *'New Weed Day,'* akin to New Year's Day, is marked by a grand ball exclusively for the elite Hommo-Harvestas. This prestigious event serves as a platform for introducing the Marijuana Girls and Ganja Boys for lifelong commitments and matching suitable donors for seed production.

The ball is hosted by the enigmatic Pink Haze Sistahs, quadruplets whose secrets swirl like pink smoke, revealing layers of hidden desires and untold truths. As the villas buzz with rumors of their mysteries whispers of passions and pasts that they pray are never fully unveiled.

As the excitement around crowning the next *'Marijuana Girl'* reaches its peak, the entire community of Cannabisville gathers in celebration. This title is more than just an honor; it represents a deep connection to Cannabisville's heritage, symbolizing resilience, purity, and the power to inspire future generations.

THERESA VERNELL

Amidst music, cheers, and the fragrant haze filling the air, candidates present their skills in cultivation, artistry, and healing, showcasing what sets them apart as true leaders. The chosen Marijuana Girl will embody the spirit of Cannabisville, a figurehead to lead, protect, and preserve the essence of their world.

As the moment of announcement nears, the crowd pulses with anticipation, eager to witness the crowning of the next guardian of the Green. This year marks a groundbreaking shift in Cannabisville, the power no longer lies solely with the elite.

The resident of Cannabisville will cast a vote, deciding who among the female Hommo-Harvestas will have the privilege of mating with the most alluring male strain. This isn't just about attraction; it's about creating offspring with unparalleled qualities, cultivating the finest of Cannabisville's legacy.

"In the Pink Haze,
in Cannabisville we glow,
Rolling up dreams,
watch the pink smoke we blow."

The Pink Haze Sistahs, Fuchsia Fantasy Haze, Bubble-Gum Mist Haze, and Rosey Dream Haze were gathering for a

MARIJUANA GIRL
WELCOME TO CANNABISVILLE

swift rehearsal but waiting for Petal Pink Euporia Haze running late. Despite their sense that it was scarcely necessary to rehearse the same song over and over.

Over the years, the annual grand *'New Weed Day Ball'* in Cannabisville had seen them perform the same songs and execute identical dance routines. The synchronized dances had evolved into a well-established tradition, resonating through the streets of Cannabisville like a familiar rhythm.

Though the very essence of their sisterhood seemed intertwined with the repetition of these beloved routines, a sense of boredom had settled in. The once vibrant celebration had taken on a tinge of predictability, leaving the Sistahs yearning for a spark of newness amidst the familiarity.

"Roots run deep,
yeah, we growin' real strong,
In the land of green,
where the high vibes belong."

Marijuana Girl, Fuchsia Fantasy Haze, distinguished as the eldest among 'The Pink Haze Sistahs,' was the 1st to sprout among the quadruplets. She is the fantasy, and the fire and desire the males craved. She could sing and lyrically flow, and her voice was captivating.

She won't tell secrets with a Sistah-hood bound by the Pink, but she will tell on any Hommo-Harvesta regardless of their strain being a bad influence on any of her Sistahs.

Now, with a newfound eagerness to attend the grand ball, Fuchsia Fantasy Haze felt a sense of urgency she hadn't experienced before. She hoped to discreetly find a surrogate who could help cultivate her future lineage.

Though initially hesitant about involving one of the Marijuana Girls in such a personal plan, she knew exactly which one she'd approach, not with a request, but with a carefully crafted directive she had envisioned days before.

Fuchsia Fantasy Haze had no intention of visiting her sister, Petal Pink Euphoria Haze, the third sprout among the revered quadruplets. However, she received crushing news about her fertility treatments. She needed a confidante and, perhaps, some potent Marijuana buds from Petal Pink Haze's abundant cannabis garden to help her think through her next steps.

But as Fuchsia Fantasy Haze pulled up, her gaze fell on Marijuana Girl, Girl Scout Cookie, standing on the front steps with Kushmas cookies in hand. She waited a few minutes,

MARIJUANA GIRL
WELCOME TO CANNABISVILLE

intrigued by the unfolding situation. She had observed them being quite friendly during Kushmas, and her sister hadn't mentioned another cookie order.

Fuchsia Fantasy Haze observed Petal Pink Euphoria Haze, opening the door wearing sheer pink lingerie. Initially, she thought nothing of it, but the extended embrace and kiss at the doorway caught her attention as if they were oblivious to anyone observing. The two then quickly scanned their surroundings, a hint of concern in their eyes, hoping that nobody had witnessed their intimate moment.

As they waited for Petal Pink Euphoria Haze to arrive, the group continued rehearsing the intro to their famous rap song, an annual anthem that everyone in Cannabisville knew by heart. Their song was a sensation, with lyrics echoed in every corner of the city. Music videos and dance routines sprang up throughout Cannabisville, and their single hit was played on loop, reminding everyone of their iconic one-hit-wonder status. Despite its simplicity, the track had become a staple in Cannabisville culture, a timeless hit that brought everyone together each year.

"Marijuana Girls,
Livin' that life, in the Embassy lights"

Marijuana Girl, Bubble-Gum Mist Haze the 2nd to sprout among the quadruplets was also relieved that the rehearsal would be brief. Known as an Indica-leaning hybrid with a sweet, candy-like aroma and deeply relaxing effects, she was the most conceited of the four.

To Bubble-Gum Mist Haze, beauty was everything, and she flaunted it with pride. Her makeup was layered extra thick, her lashes extended like spider legs, and her long, claw-like nails sparkled with jeweled embellishments that captured every bit of light in the room.

"We're the blaze, It's the pink Daze, Enter the pink faze,
The Pink Haze Sistahs!"

She shouted to keep their spirits ablaze, *"Stay-lit-o… puff up budches!"* Lighting a foot-long joint she rolled with a special blend of Hybrid Cannabis flowers from her garden, enjoying the strain of their green bloodline.

They enjoyed smoking and inhaling its essence, a sensory flight each puff they felt the balanced blend of Sativa and Indica genetics, while drinking sparkling rainwater to stay hydrated. Bubble-Gum Mist Haze screamed, *"Vibe-o-up-o!"* was like saying *"Fuck it – Lets smoke!"*

MARIJUANA GIRL
WELCOME TO CANNABISVILLE

She really didn't want to party. She wanted to drop the burning joint in the ashtray and walk out the door. She was so stressed organic Cannabis couldn't cure her need. Ready to stop and just give up, but she had to pretend everything was okay, especially around the sistahs. Instead, Bubble-Gum Mist Haze joined her sistahs and popped a few bottles of Cannabis champagne.

As the aroma of Marijuana danced in the air, a symphony of sweet flavors, like a harmonious key, a flavor that appeases. On their palates, a burst of sweetness in a pink haze, a cannabis symphony, setting ablaze.

So was her skin, Bubble-Gum Mist Haze was feeling the burning of her skin on fire. Trying to not scratch the itching all over her body, her head, arms, legs and especially her 'Budlip.' She knew she couldn't perform or entertain for this season's bikini contest.

Normally, Bubble-Gum Mist Haze hosts the event and always emerges as the unofficial winner. However, due to a rash that was spreading over her body, and now she was struggling to keep her condition a secret from her sistahs.

It all began with '*Soul-Glow-666,*' a secret lotion potion she brought illegally underground from the OG Wanders on the

Westside of Cannabisville. The green market had always delivered on its promises, until now. Bubble-Gum Mist Haze, began using 'Soul-Glow-666' the coveted cannabis-infused skincare potion that came with strict instructions: *'Use 'Soul-Glow-666' once a day, but not every day.'*

Yet, its effects were addictive. What she loved most was its scent - like a newborn baby Hommo-Harvesta. The smooth glow, radiant sheen, and endless compliments it drew enchanted her completely. She began using it three times a day, driven by the desire for skin so luminous it appeared wet and slippery. For a while, it worked, her skin shimmered with an almost supernatural glow, glistening like dewy leaves kissed by the morning sun. But then, things took a dark turn.

The 'Shady Groves' OG Wanders, who sell 'Dr' Ashblood's product 'Soul-Glow-666,' refused to sell her more. *"You've used enough,"* they warned, sensing the side effects that awaited her. Desperate, she tried every outlet and trader in the green market, but no one dared defy these 'OG Wanders.'

As the supply of 'Soul-Glow-666' ran out, her once glowing skin began to dry and cracked like parched soil, splitting painfully under every movement. Worse still, a strange green and brown scaled like snake skinned, a rash began to sprout across her body, spreading like invasive weeds. What made the rash even more disturbing was its resilience it refused to fade, and every treatment she tried only seemed to make it worse.

The insidious fungus infiltrated Bubble-Gum Mist Haze body, causing relentless itching and an incurable disease could be compared to skin cancer that mystified the infectious disease doctors. With an expiration date looming over her, she faced the harsh reality of mortality at an age when most are just starting to explore life.

Despite her growing discomfort, none of her sistahs had noticed the rash creeping across her skin. Bubble-Gum Mist Haze was lucky it had not reached her face, hands or feet, yet. She cleverly masked her condition to conceal her dry, cracking skin while maintaining her stylish reputation.

Bubble-Gum Mist Haze moved with practiced ease, exuding an air of confidence and allure. Her long-sleeved, bubble-gum-pink gown draped perfectly over her curves, accentuating her silhouette in a way that hinted at mystery, skillfully drawing eyes away from what lay hidden beneath.

Each step felt calculated, though her skin felt taut, as if it could crack open at any moment, revealing the fragile reality within. Still, in Cannabisville, appearances were everything, and for now, she could navigate the vibrant scene without raising suspicion, blending seamlessly into the sparkling world around her. Even as the rash spread, leaving her body itchy and inflamed, she kept up the act.

Late for rehearsal, the 3rd to sprout among the quadruplets, Marijuana Girl, Petal Pink Euphoria Haze burst through the door, out of breath and frantic. Shopping bags swung from her arms, and she kicked off her pink high heels with a clumsy stumble. "*I swear,*" she gasped, "*my dress still needs alterations, and..*" She paused, trying to catch her breath, "*There was an emergency at the 'Pink Haze House.' A new baby strain was born, and I had to help.*"

Her explanation was rushed, but Petal Pink Euphoria Haze kept wiping suspicious cookie crumbs off her lips as she spoke. The room fell silent, knowing better than to pry into her personal affairs. After all, who Petal Pink Euphoria Haze chose to spend her time with was nobody's business, even if she was kissing female Hommo-Harvesta.

With a shrug, she tossed her bags in the corner and reached for a bottle of vitamin infused water. "*Let's just get started,*" she sighed, smoothing down her tousled hair, the scent of sugar and fresh-baked goods still lingering faintly around her.

MARIJUANA GIRL
WELCOME TO CANNABISVILLE

Nonetheless just in time to puff, puff, pass, and sip cannabis champagne with her *'Pink Haze Sistahs.'*

Sitting quietly in a corner praying and planning her escape was the 4th and last to sprout among the quadruplets, Marijuana Girl, Rosey Dream Cloud Haze. The angelic Pink Haze Sistah epitomizes purity in both thought and demeanor. Possessing a pure quality, she seems destined for a life of tranquility in the serene Coventry of Cannabisville, akin to a nun in peaceful devotion.

However, Rosey Dream Haze maintains a vow of silence, speaking only in prayers to Jah, creating an aura of reverence and mystique around her presence. However, though she could talk, she did not talk, but the spell of rosy-pink mist she left on male strains that smelled her breath, left bliss where desires swell. She believed most in the moon's influence.

The Hommo-Harvestas believed praying to the moon enhances blessings, induces divination, and empowers intuition and intentions. Within their beliefs, the moon is regarded as a purifying force with the ability to cleanse and charge objects. She is well-versed in *'The Book of Roots - 420 Chronicles,'* and effortlessly could recite them in her sleep.

Rosey Dream Haze lived by the laws of the land with unwavering devotion. From sunrise to sunset, she immerses herself in her garden, fervently praying and praising Jah. When night falls, she tends to her garden, watering it with reserved rainwater and drinks moon water collected from bottles she carefully places to gather the celestial droplets.

Acknowledging Jah, everyone anticipates nothing but greatness, holiness, and cleanliness from Rosey Dream Cloud Haze. She prays for her actions and remains prepared to face any consequences. While she typically consumes only water, this was a different occasion and she needed the elixir to relax, Rosey Dream Haze enjoys a glass of cannabis wine, treating it as a communion.

Despite the potential path that lay ahead, Rosey Dream Haze remained resolute in her commitment to never part from her sistahs. However, there came a moment when she felt compelled to make a confession solely to Jah. It was her sins that weighed heavily on her conscience.

Only for Jah would she allow her tongue to articulate these words. She awaited the divine guidance of Jah, patiently anticipating the right moment. This conviction stemmed from the enchanting spell that was cast upon Rosey Dream Haze by a cloud of green haze masquerading as a male strain who frequented her gardens under the nightly sky.

This mysterious green figure slithered towards Rosey Dream Haze like a snake in the tall grass, seeking an intimate connection with her in the cover of darkness. Her heart raced as the shadows twisted around the figure, making it difficult to decipher who or what it was.

Kushcordance: 1 - In the Book of Roots recounts the sacred origin of the first Hommo-Harvestas, Kush-Adam and Eve-Flower, who were brought into being with divine purpose. Woven with the essence of nature and cosmic wisdom, their creational story symbolizes the unity of planet Marijuana and its roots.

Jah formed the first male Hommo-Harvesta from the dust of Cannabisville, shaping Kush-Adam, a calm and grounding male '*Indica*' strain. Jah breathed life into him, and Kush-Adam stood tall, his presence steady like the night breeze, with deep roots in the grounds of Cannabisville.

But Jah saw that it was not good for Kush-Adam to be alone, so Jah caused a deep sleep to fall upon him. From Kush-Adam's rib, Jah fashioned Eve-Flower, a lively and uplifting 'Sativa' Hommo-Harvesta. Eve-Flower's spirit flowed like the morning sun, radiant and energetic, ready to spread joy wherever she grew. Together, they balanced each other, like night and day, calm and vitality, root, and bloom.

Every night, Rosey Dream Haze found herself captivated, pondering the identity of the dark figure that lured her into its shadowed presence. Could it be a Ganja Boy? Their presence was unmistakable, always accompanied by a sweet, natural scent tinged with a hint of defiance. Or perhaps it was an Island Bud? With their tall frames and confident strides, they brought an electric energy wherever they went, an undeniable force that filled the air.

The mystery consumed her, weaving its way into her thoughts and dreams, leaving her longing for just one more glimpse. But then, a chill crept up her spine as a darker thought crossed her mind. Could it be a Hempster? She quivered finally speaking as she shouted, *"Oh, my Jah, was it a Hempster?"* The thought alone sent shivers through her, the Hempsters were different and mysterious, revered, feared mating with them. They rarely ventured this close to their villages unless working, they prefer to stay hidden in the shadows of the north.

MARIJUANA GIRL
WELCOME TO CANNABISVILLE

Rosey Dream Cloud's breath caught in her throat as the figure moved closer, its identity still obscured, the air thick with tension and unspoken intentions. She wasn't sure if she should run or wait to find out who, or what, was approaching.

"Oh, my Jah, oh my Jah, was it a Seedweed?!" Rosey Dream Cloud Haze's thoughts spiraled as she took a step back, her breath quickening. The figure moved with an eerie grace and its dark skin blended with the blackness of the night.

The SeedWeeds were even more elusive than Hempsters, the holy albino – ghostly figures that wore white hooded robes that roamed the northern lands with an air of mystery and reverence. They were said to have powers beyond understanding, able to communicate directly with Jah himself, yet their presence often meant something was wrong.

The roaring temptations to seek out the dark figure drew her closer, and as it did, a faint smell of green tea hibiscus Marijuana filled the air with a scent only carried by the SeedWeeds. Rosey's pulse quickened. Why would a Seedweed come here, to her? And in the dead of night?

THERESA VERNELL

THE BOOK OF ROOTS
The Roaring Temptation
Chronicle 399 NCV

"Be sober-minded; be watchful. For the enemy-Blightroot, Lurking Ember, prowls like a roaring lion, Seeking roots to consume. Beware his whispers of doubt and fear, for he stalks the weary and the unguarded, hoping to snuff out their light.. Let the Hommo-Harvestas remain spiritually vigilant, rooted in Jah's truth, to withstand the fiery assaults of Deceit and temptation."

"Selahjah - Oh, Jah, oh my Jah, please Jah say it is you!" Its voice said, *"You are fearless."* Rosey Dream Haze listened as it approached commanding, *"You re the rose of Cannabisville."* Her eyes couldn't see, but her ears could hear, and her body could feel the Verdant Wraith as it commanded, *"Call me your god, scream my name - Green Shade."* As it captured her in the essence of its dark, smoky, shadowy figure.

Embracing the 'Green Shade' as it wrapped around her, and as it did, she could smell the strong scent of Marijuana - Cannabis flowers filled the air. Rosey Dream Cloud Haze's pulse quickened as she moaned, *"Who are you? Why Jah, why me?"*

Hearing her call for *"Jah"* made the 'Green Shade' jealous as it released green gasses of pungent fragrances of every Cannabis strain on planet Marijuana. Sending her into a trance as

MARIJUANA GIRL
WELCOME TO CANNABISVILLE

'Green Shade' whispered sweet words in her ear, words Rosey Dream Haze hadn't known she needed to hear.

Drunk on adrenaline and the magnetic pull of his presence, she lost control, her body betraying her mind. Its promises were intoxicating, promising to plant the 'Greenborn' seedling in her belly. A seed of greatness, a legacy unlike any the Hommo-Harvestas had ever seen.

No matter what Rosey Dream Haze still could not forget the story about Jah's warnings of temptations in the Kushcordance. Especially gluttony, eating too much from the tree of life, the Marijuana Tree, and the temptations of Kush-Adam and Eve-Flower.

One day, a Verdant Viper - green serpent coiled around the low branches, hissing words of deceit. *"Do not touch the buds of the Tree of Life, Eve-Flower,"* it whispered, *"for they hold a secret you are not meant to know."*

The Verdant Viper's voice planted uncertainty in Eve-Flower's heart, suggesting there was more to discover beyond Jah's teachings. Eve-Flower, curious by nature, swayed between her desire for wisdom and her trust in Jah's words. Kush-Adam, content with Jah's blessings, urged her to rest easily and enjoy what they already had.

But as the green serpent's words lingered in her mind, Eve-Flower found herself torn between the peaceful existence Jah had gifted them and the intoxicating allure of the unknown. She gazed upon the vast, uncharted territories of Cannabisville, wondering what secrets they might hold. The path ahead seemed both thrilling and dangerous, and the seeds of doubt began to sprout in her heart, threatening the peace she once found in the simple joy of her life with Kush-Adam..

THE BOOK OF ROOTS
The Shield of Jah
Chronicle 400 NCV

*"Though Blightroot, Lurking Ember, prowls, seeking to devour the faithful, Jah's hand is mighty to guard Jah's creation. Fear not the threats of destruction, for those who hold fast to the Book of Roots and call upon Jah will find strength. Jah's power is an unyielding fortress, shielding the harvest from the fiery tongues of evil and guiding them to everlasting peace.
- Selahjah"*

Just like Eve-Flower, Rosey Dream Haze was tempted each night, praying, and awaiting the secret encounters with the shadowy 'Green Shade.' No longer a virgin, Rosey Dream Haze knelt beneath the shimmering green moon, praying silently for Jah to answer her desires.

MARIJUANA GIRL
WELCOME TO CANNABISVILLE

Awaiting under the tree of life, the Marijuana Tree, she believed in the dark presence's promises as it mounted her again and again, bringing great waves of pleasure as they spoke in tongues of ecstasy. The sensation of being chosen, of sharing in this forbidden connection, overwhelmed her as the shadowed figure whispered secrets of sexual pleasures unknown to most. Now, trying to slip away from those that may think she had sinned, Rosey Dream Haze was leaving the Cannabisville Ball, leaving her sistah's and the whole scene behind.

She pretended to go pray but was now running under the shadow of the green moon, her heart pounding with both excitement and dread. Each step away from her Sistahs and their sacred grounds on Cannabisville, she pressed her trembling hands against her growing belly, convinced that within her growing, the seed of destiny. The coming of the Greenborn is a child unlike any other in Cannabisville. A miracle born to a virgin, under the divine blessing of Jah, symbolizing hope, unity, and a new beginning for the Hommo-Harvesta. This unique being stands out from all strains, blending features from multiple Hommo-Harvesta lineages, with emerald-tinted skin that reflects the lush greens of Cannabisville and a faint, luminescent glow, especially visible under the moonlight.

THERESA VERNELL

It is written in Chronicle: 398 'The Greenborn'

"From the sacred bud of the Marijuana Tree of Life, a savior will sprout. Born to a virgin – a pure-hearted Marijuana Girl, untouched by the corruption of the world, the Greenborn will emerge. Their arrival will mark the dawn of peace and love in Cannabisville, where all strains shall unite under the 420 green moon of the 'Verdant Eclipse' the canopy of Jah's eternal light:

The Greenborn's eyes with be radiant, resembling bright green buds, with flecks of gold and amber that hint at a powerful connection to the Marijuana Tree of Life.

The hair, a natural blend of dirty browns and rich greens, woolly in texture. Its skin will be a darker brown hue than its hair that will flow like wild vines, sometimes appearing to shift colors with its emotions or the shifting sunlight.

Each breath from the Greenborn exuded a calming aroma of fresh herbs and sweet terpenes, wrapping those nearby in an invisible embrace of peace.

It was said that even the most restless souls found stillness in the presence, as if the very essence of love and harmony flowed from it with every exhalation.

MARIJUANA GIRL
WELCOME TO CANNABISVILLE

The Greenborn's breath carried more than just a soothing aroma - it bore the power of healing. Wounds mended faster in its presence, the green glow of its aura seemingly stitching together what was broken.

Its touch was a balm for the weary, easing pain and restoring vitality. It was said that even the most fragile strains, those thought beyond saving, could find renewal with the Greenborn nearby.

The air around Greenborn will shimmer with life, and plants bent slightly in its direction, as if drawn to its energy. Streams of golden resin dripped from nearby trees, enriched with healing properties, whenever Greenborn walked by.

Hommo-Harvestas believed its breath could purify toxins and cleanse the air of negativity, making every inhale a prayer and every exhale a miracle. The birth would be an awakened, a dormant energy in the lands, and some believe that the Greenborn holds the ancient knowledge of all strains, enabling them to commune with Cannabisville's flora and fauna.

The Greenborn symbolizes unity across strains, representing a new era where Hommo-Harvestas can thrive together as One Marijuana, guided by the wisdom and peace that this rare being brings. Escaping from the East Side was both an act of rebellion and fear. Rosey Dream Haze's heart raced with each step, her courage masking the turmoil within. She knew that once her truth was revealed, there would be no going back. The secrets she carried could change everything - not just for her, but for the entire planet, Marijuana.

She called upon four of the Angels of Plant Marijuana, 'Celestine Blaze' the Angel of Light and Illumination. She shines brightly, guiding the Hommo-Harvestas. 'Asher Rootbound' the Angel of Protection and Stability, and 'Emberleaf' the Angel of Renewal and Healing, and 'Kushfire Lumina' the Angel of Justice and Purification. She burns with righteous fire, driving out evil and ensuring that Jah's laws are upheld across Cannabisville.

Yet, even with praying she felt the weight of her decision, Rosey held her head high, acting brave, though the shadows of doubt lingered just behind her determined stride. Seeking refuge until the birth the Greenborn of what she believed was a divine creation, Rosey Dream Haze recited with her voice steady, but filled with a quiet intensity. Chronicle 4 NCV, ' *"The Seeds we Sow"* from 'The Book of Roots.

MARIJUANA GIRL
WELCOME TO CANNABISVILLE

Every word felt like a sacred prayer, each step forward a testament to her fearlessness. But even as she whispered the words, she could feel the pull of destiny, both heavy and exhilarating, as the Greenborn grew inside her, bringing with it unknown challenges and the promise of a powerful future.
The prayer flowed seamlessly into song, and she found herself softly singing along as she gathered the belongings she had carefully stashed away. As she prepared to leave, the familiar melody of 'The National Anthem of Cannabisville - Blaze of the Green' filled the air, echoing across Cannabisville.

THE BOOK OF ROOTS
"The Seeds we Sow"
Chronicle 4 NCV

"From the seed, all life begins.
Jah, in your wisdom, You created the seed that bears fruit,
The fruit that feeds your children. May we sow seeds of love and
Kindness, trusting in the harvest that comes from your hand.
This seed will bear great fruit. May we nurture our faith,
Trusting in Jah's power to make it flourish.
-Selahjah"

THERESA VERNELL

NATIONAL ANTHEM OF CANNABISVILLE

"Blaze of The Green"

Verse 1

From the roots of the soil to the skies above,

We rise as one, in unity and love.

With leaves so bright, and buds so strong,

In Cannabisville, we all belong.

Chorus

Blaze of the green, we stand so high,

Liftin' our spirits, under Jah's sky.

With every puff, our hearts align,

In Cannabisville, forever we shine.

Verse 2

Through fields of peace, where the Hempsters play,

We Walk the leafy path, by night and day.

No strain divides us, our bond is pure,

In the green light, we find the cure.

MARIJUANA GIRL
WELCOME TO CANNABISVILLE

Chorus

Blaze of the green, we stand so high,

Liftin' our spirits, under Jah's sky.

With every puff, our hearts align,

In Cannabisville, forever we shine.

Bridge

From seed to harvest, in Jah we trust,

Through sacred smoke, our souls adjust.

Together we rise, in peace and grace,

In Cannabisville, we find our place.

Chorus

Blaze of the green, we stand so high,

Liftin' our spirits, under Jah's sky.

With every puff, our hearts align,

In Cannabisville, forever we shine.

Outro

Leafy trails and roots so deep,

In Jah's embrace, our souls shall keep.

Cannabisville, our home, our pride,

Forever we grow, side by side.

THE CANNABISVILLE BALL

The Cannabisville Ball ceremony begins as the voices of thousands of Hommo-Harvestas can be heard for miles inside and outside the event. Together they raised their lighters high and united to singing, 'The National Anthem of Cannabisville - Blaze of the Green.'

The pungent scent of marijuana filled the air, mingling with colorful rings of smoke that drifted lazily above the crowd. The streets buzzed with excitement as Hommo-Harvestas from every corner gathered to witness a grand celebration, the beauty pageant and crowning of the next 'Marijuana Girl.'

Spectators lined the vibrant pathways, their spirits high with joy and anticipation, eager to see who would wear the coveted crown. Among them stood the familiar faces of past Marijuana Girl winners, their jeweled crowns gleaming under the soft lights.

Each wore a flowing, glittery green dress, distinct and vibrant, reflecting their unique personalities. The gowns shimmered with intricate designs - some adorned with delicate, hand-embroidered leaves and vines that seemed to grow across the fabric, while others sparkled with emerald stones that caught the light, echoing the essence of the Marijuana Tree of Life.

MARIJUANA GIRL
WELCOME TO CANNABISVILLE

These dresses weren't just garments; they were statements, embodying Cannabisville's lush heritage and elevated elegance.

The scene was pure Hollyweed glamour - Cannabisville-style - as the attendees made their grand entrance, strutting down the illustrious green carpet. The carpet, lush and vibrant, mimicked fresh cannabis leaves, setting the perfect backdrop for the dazzling display of the elite strains. Spectators lined the sides, cheering and snapping holographic photos as luminaries of Cannabisville's society posed and waved, exuding charisma with every step.

Cameras flashed as each stride brought whispers of awe: *"Did you see that leaf-embroidered train?" "The emeralds in her hairpiece is the size of a large bud!"* Even their footwear, gilded and encrusted with gemstones, sparkled as brightly as their radiant smiles.

The green carpet wasn't just a runway - it was a showcase of prestige, a celebration of culture, and a reminder that in Cannabisville, the spirit of innovation and tradition went hand in hand with style.

The Ganja Boys, draped in tuxedos tailored in colors that matched their unique strains, moved confidently through the crowd. Each tux was crafted from fine hemp-woven fabric, blending sustainability with style, and adorned with subtle embroidery representing their lineage. The air around them was filled with the fragrant smoke of aromatic strains they puffed, each exhale adding a distinct scent to the vibrant atmosphere. Their presence added a masculine charm to the event, embodying the strength and allure that defined Cannabisville's elite.

The Island Buds, dressed in striking native attire, wore vibrant greens and red as a symbol of their fierce energy. Both the males and females sported elaborate feathered headdresses dusted with glitter, with faces painted in intricate designs and adorned with colorful carnival beads.

The men's outfits highlighted the bold green bottoms, while the women wore flowing black, red, or green bikinis, each garment reflecting the rich culture of their heritage. Carrying drums and shells, they moved through the crowd, their rhythmic chants filling the air with an infectious energy, adding a primal heartbeat to the celebration.

Their half nude bodies bore painted messages, each symbol and word a bold declaration for peace and the right to cultivate Marijuana freely in their own gardens, unbound by licenses from the Embassy of Green Roots. Each stroke of paint shimmered under the lights, illustrating their shared vision of autonomy and a life rooted in connection to Cannabisville.

These messages, painted with pride and purpose, were more than just art; they were powerful reminders of their commitment to preserving Cannabisville's spirit of freedom and resilience. Each painted word and symbol stood as a rallying cry to the political party, a bold assertion of their constitutional rights under the timeless vow: "One Marijuana." This declaration echoed through the crowd, a reminder that their unity and autonomy were grounded in Cannabisville's sacred principles, embedded in every leaf, every root, and every strain they cultivated.

The OG Wanders reveled in the spotlight of New Weed Day, strutting with confidence in their bold, heavy makeup and vibrant gypsy attire, their flamboyant lifestyle on full display. They danced with pleasure, their laughter mingling with the smoke in the air, celebrating the freedom to express who they truly were.

Meanwhile, the Hempsters, with their wild blond curls and hands stained from the soil they loved, embraced the festivities in their own grounded way. Dressed in finely crafted hemp fashions, they radiated pride, knowing their creations adorned the attendees like badges of honor. For the Hempsters, New Weed Day wasn't just a celebration of the harvest; it was a testament to their connection to the land and the legacy of their craftsmanship.

It was a reminder to all: without the Hempsters' farms, there would be no fabrics or textiles in Cannabisville. For once, they felt special and equal, woven into the vibrant festivities of 'New Weed Day' - a fresh start, a new year, and a shared celebration of unity and abundance.

Once again, there were other Tribes and Klans like the holy ones known as the SeedWeeds, and the reclusive Kushimba Klan were absent. Leaving their lands to attend a vanity event was taboo, a breach of their sacred customs and traditions. Their absence was a quiet but ever-present reminder of the divide between the revelers and those who lived by stricter, more spiritual codes.

This is a highly secured event due to the variety of exotic rare and priceless male and female strains in attendance. All the past winning Marijuana Girls attended with their Ganja Boy they were committed to, Yet Sativa Diva and her devoted partner, the Chronic King, were also conspicuously absent.

MARIJUANA GIRL
WELCOME TO CANNABISVILLE

Their failure to RSVP sparked whispers among the crowd, hinting at two possibilities, either the joyous arrival of a new addition to their family or the unfortunate end of their union. Speculation swirled like the smoke in the air, leaving everyone wondering what fate had befallen the beloved couple.

Also absent from the Cannabisville Ball was Marijuana Girl, Indica Green. She had taken matters into her own hands, leaving the 'Green-Leaf' rehabilitation center, A.M.A., against medical advice. She defiantly asserted her autonomy, determined to manage her own substance struggles. She had vowed to never let them 'Repot' her again, not after enduring needles in her feet, a treatment that seemed to cure but left her feeling more trapped than ever, confined in a room without windows.

Indica Green had pressing matters waiting on the Westside. She wasn't just out here for herself, she was on a mission to find the young seedling babies, the unwanted Hommo-Harvesta children, that survived botch abortions and were forced into living by the Westcoast, disformed with the monster that tried to abort them.

Slaying the dragon has been Indica Green's mission for over a year, she was on that mission long before her entanglement, and getting stuck to Ganja Boy, Gorilla Glue. Now she was back on course. Fueled by vengeance, she was now armed and ready, having acquired a *'Weedpon'* for protection from an underground arms dealer, an Island Bud named 'Shake Weed.' With her newfound resolve and the weapon at her side, she stepped into the night, determined to right past wrongs.

In the unique community of Cannabisville, a peculiar set of rules governs the behavior of its botanical residents. One such regulation stands firm that strains are strictly prohibited from carrying concealed weapons known as 'Weedpons.'

Instead, the responsibility for maintaining order falls into the hands of the *'Soul Patrol.'* They are a specialized force equipped with Weedpons, a non-lethal weapon to ensure compliance. Their arsenal includes guns designed to shoot out a temporary paralyzing agent, a measure implemented to maintain harmony among the diverse strains inhabiting on the Planet Marijuana.

As Indica Green was back on track hunting down 'Puff the Magic Dragon,' also know as Dr. Ashblood. He had earned his reputation as a menace across Cannabisville. Living hidden among the ocean-grown herbs on the misty West Coast, was infamous for preying upon the innocent, indulging in twisted

MARIJUANA GIRL
WELCOME TO CANNABISVILLE

rituals driven by a relentless pursuit of vanity and eternal youth. Though a Hybrid by strain, he claimed no allegiance to any tribe.

Instead, he raised his own - an army of misfits, crafted from the disfigured infants he had "*rescued*" and shaped into loyal followers. His tribe, known as the 'Shadowborn,' were bound to him by fear and warped devotion, each one carrying the scars of his twisted experiments. Together, they lurked in the shadows, his personal legion for carrying out his dark designs.

Dr. Ashblood's reputation had earned him the fierce disdain from the OG Wanders, a neighboring tribe born as hermaphrodites and known not to follow *'The Book of Roots,* 'which held that all creatures of Jah were born perfect and should not be slaves if not.

Yet, despite not following Jahaism, they had deep-rooted principles, but some had turned their backs on Ashblood's atrocities for mere silver coins, oblivious to the fact that he would have gladly rewarded their silence with far more - gold coins, enough to secure their quiet compliance. This betrayal gnawed at the hearts of the OG Wander elders, who remained resolute, determined to bring him to justice and cleanse the land of his shadowed legacy.

Dr. Ashblood's sinister network stretched deep into the poorest corners of Cannabisville, where desperation often outweighed moral boundaries. He paid generously, exchanging the old-world currency of gold coins and faded paper hemp money for the loyalty of those willing to deliver patients to his shadowed clinic. These gold coins, once valued and trusted across the island, had recently been rendered obsolete due to a surge in counterfeiting.

Some, desperate for the legendary 24-karat gold seeds rumored to open a passage to Earth if planted, resorted to forging imitations. Thieves melted down gold coins, crafting counterfeit seeds that mimicked the prized originals, each fake seed worth a fortune in Cannabisville's underground markets. To possess one was to hold the promise of treasure and the lure of escape, fueling a black market that thrived on greed and deception.

For many cryptocurrencies like BudCoin$ accounts were unattainable luxuries. The females who sought Dr. Ashblood's services were often uncommitted, impoverished Hommo-Harvestas with little choice but to rely on the outdated currency he provided. Dr. Ashblood capitalized on this disconnection, luring patients with promises of cash and secrecy, using the golden remnants of a bygone era to cloak his vile deeds in the shadows of the island's forgotten economy.

The 'Shady Grove' OG Wanders, non-followers of Jah's law, believed their mission was to protect their land and mind their own business. To them, females who chose to sacrifice baby Hommo-Harvestas were exercising their right to choice.

Pro choice, even if it was for superficial gain. However, despite their divergence from The Book of Roots, most of them viewed such actions as an abomination, the work of a demon.

They believed these practices brought evil into Cannabisville, and they sought to purge their land of such darkness. Their resolve deepened when they noticed their children were missing.

Defying the cautious diplomacy of the Embassy of Green Roots, the 'Shady Grove' OG Wanders launched a quiet but fervent campaign to find and "slay" the dragon in the sea. To them, Dr. Ashblood's life was forfeit - a just price for his crimes against the innocent.

His so-called "*magic*" was seen as nothing more than cruelty disguised as power. Though Dr. Ashblood cloaked himself in secrecy, he knew that shadows could only hide him for so long.

Leaving Cannabisville to team up with the non-believers to make them believers and to hunt the dragon, Indica Green could still hear the distant echoes of the New Weed Day celebrations the laughter, the music, the thick air with blissful aromas. She knew what she was missing, but she'd had her fill of parties.

She left Sativa Diva and Girl Scout Cookie behind because they probably still thought she was tucked away in rehab. But this mission was no place for them. She doubted they had the stomach for what lay ahead the brutal reality she might face to save the babies, the future of Cannabisville.

The streets of Cannabisville pulsed with life, vibrant block parties filling every corner as Hommo-Harvestas continued to celebrate 'New Weed Day.' Smoke drifted through the air in fragrant clouds, and cheers erupted from every street, a joyous roar that echoed across town.

Alongside the revelers were the Soul Patrol, proudly guarding the festivities with unwavering dedication. The Soul Patrol's mission extended beyond mere crowd control, they were the guardians of peaceful coexistence, the protectors of Cannabisville's unity.

MARIJUANA GIRL
WELCOME TO CANNABISVILLE

They're armed with non-lethal weapons, reinforcing the community's commitment to resolving disputes without causing permanent harm. They upheld a firm commitment to harmony, stepping in when disputes simmered or tensions flared, but always choosing methods that caused no lasting harm.

The Soul Patrol's presence at the Cannabisville Ball was more than just security; it was a symbol of Cannabisville's enduring promise to protect, One Marijuana. In a world of diverse strains, each Hommo-Harvestas soul was embraced as part of the community.

Each strain played its part: from the lively Sativas, known for their vibrant energized celebrations, grew alongside the calm and grounding Indicas, and all the resilient Hybrids adapting to any role needed, and the Hemps who wove healings into the very fabric of their society.

It was more than a mix of strains; it was the spirit of Cannabisville itself. A world bound by diversity, yet united in purpose. Together, they formed a culture rooted in harmony, resilience, and the endless possibilities of One Marijuana.

That night, as festivities swirled with music, laughter, and thick aromatic clouds of smoke, the Soul Patrol kept a watchful eye. Their commitment was clear not only to ensure the night's joy remained undisturbed but also to protect the guiding principle that had unified Cannabisville.

The Soul Patrol, towering and radiant, was a striking sight against the vibrant lights of the Cannabisville Ball. Their beauty and strength captivated onlookers, blending seamlessly with the colors of the night as they patrolled the arena. Male and female alike, each Hommo-Harvesta member exuded a powerful aura, their poise enhanced by the vivid, swirling clouds of aromatic smoke that filled the air around them.

As they inhaled, their THC and CBD levels rose, releasing natural waves of cannabinoids, terpenes, and flavonoids that heightened their senses and renewed their bodies and spirits. The essence of Cannabisville's unique flora was more than mere smoke; it was a rejuvenating balm that connected the Soul Patrol deeply to their roots.

As the civilians passed them lit joints to puff for 'Goodluck,' their pleasures increasing with every joyful inhale, honoring the essence of their shared culture and collective spirit. The energy was electric, as Hommo-Harvestas of every strain came together to dance, laugh, and connect without boundaries.

MARIJUANA GIRL
WELCOME TO CANNABISVILLE

Tonight, they celebrated more than just a ball, they celebrated their shared roots, their unity, and the essence of Cannabisville itself. The lines between strains blurred in the haze, and in that moment, their collective spirit shone bright, honoring the harmony that made their world unique.

The celebration of *'New Weed Day'* and the 'Cannabisville Ball' was a grand affair indeed, held in the sprawling 'Budgrade1st of Day Stadium,' the largest outdoor arena on the island. Most of Cannabisville seemed to have gathered, a sea of cheering Hommo-Harvestas ready for the night's festivities to begin.

The air buzzed with excitement, and every corner of the stadium was decked in vibrant greenery, glittering lights, and streamers of gold and emerald. It was more than a celebration it was a cultural phenomenon, where strains came together dressed their best to revel in their heritage, their community, and the unity that bound them all.

Nothing but love and peace filled the air, yet the electric excitement demanded heightened security. Soul Patrol members, standing sentinel at every entrance, maintained a steady watch, their uniforms gleaming under the stadium lights as they upheld the tranquility of the evening. Inside 'Budgrade1st of Day

Stadium,' anticipation was palpable, humming through the corridors as guests pounded about, exchanging warm greetings, laughter, and shared memories of past balls.

    The Cannabisville Ball was more than just a celebration. It was a sanctuary, a time when all strains gathered as one to honor their roots, unified by their shared heritage and deep respect for one another. Cheering repeatedly, *"One Marijuana! One Marijuana! One Marijuana!"*

    In the hushed row of private dressing rooms, listening to the cheers the Pink Haze Sistahs immersed themselves in final preparations for the grand spectacle ahead. Each Sistah savored the moment in her own dedicated space, where stylists painted on perfection and sculpted their long pink hair into works of art.

    Their laughter mingled with notes of floral fragrances, filling the hallway with a sense of camaraderie. The Sistahs knew tonight was more than a performance; it was an embodiment of elegance, unity, and unwavering strength.

    As they slipped into their gowns, each one crafted uniquely, unseen even by each other, they felt the weight of what they represented was resilience, sisterhood, and a kind of mystique that transcended the glitz of the evening. Just as Marijuana Girl, Petal Pink Euphoria Haze, stood in front of her mirror, about to be draped in her dazzling attire, a soft but urgent knock sounded on the door, pulling her back to the present.

Girl Scout Cookie entered the room in a hurry, her usually calm demeanor replaced by a rare tension. Petal Pink Euphoria Haze, sensing the urgency, watching the worried expression, before they were interrupted. Also, before GSC could tell that Fuchsia Fantasy Haze knew about their relationship. But after, Girl Scott Cookie seen the happiness on her face, she decided to wait until after the event.

Their affair, though hidden in tender glances and stolen moments, was a bond that couldn't survive public scrutiny. The rules in Cannabisville were firm; same-sex relationships among the OG Wanders, Cannabisville's hermaphroditic pioneers, were tolerated but strictly private.

The stakes were high. If Fuchsia Fantasy Haze made good on her threat, it wouldn't just be the end of their love, and it could risk the reputation of the Pink Haze Sistahs and perhaps even disrupt the harmony of the Marijuana Girls.

Girl Scout Cookie and Petal Pink Euphoria Haze stood in silence for a beat, the air thick with unspoken fears wanting to kiss. But tonight, with the spotlight awaiting 'The Pink Haze

Sistahs,' they'd have to play their parts flawlessly, concealing the turmoil under layers of elegance and strength.

In their society where their purpose is to reproduce rather than engage in personal liaisons, the stakes were high. Girl Scout Cookie struggled to grasp the idea that Fuchsia Fantasy would expose her sister, if she didn't agree to be her surrogate.

There was no time to talk - the show had begun. A booming voice announcing the Pink Haze Sistahs, as the crowd erupted in cheers. The lights dimmed as the stage pulsed with color, casting a vibrant pink glow across the arena. Petal Pink Euphoria Haze and Girl Scout Cookie exchanged a final, knowing glance, masking their worries behind practiced smiles and poised steps.

As each Sistah took her position, the music swelled, an entrancing beat that seemed to echo the rhythm of Cannabisville's own heart. The Pink Haze Sistahs moved with flawless grace, their gowns flowing like liquid light, dazzling every Hommo-Harvesta soul in the audience.

The Pink Haze Sistahs spun gracefully, their expressions serene yet fierce, channeling all their energy into the performance, embracing their microphones and hoping their voices didn't betray them on stage.

MARIJUANA GIRL
WELCOME TO CANNABISVILLE

"In the Pink Haze,
in Cannabisville we glow,
Rolling up dreams,
watch the smoke we blow."

Their performance was okay, a little awkward because they had to improvise a few dance moves since Rosey Dream Haze was missing. The Sistahs moved as three, each off step on the 4th beat, and beneath the shimmer and glow, the tension simmered.

From her seat in the front row, Girl Scout Cookie couldn't avoid the piercing gaze of Fuchsia Fantasy Haze. How dare she try to 'Greenmail' her and attempting to manipulate her into becoming a surrogate for her seedlings. With every pointed glance, Fuchsia Fantasy Haze's eyes conveyed a veiled threat, a reminder of the secrets she held, like a shadow behind the Pink Haze's gleam.

Shifting in her seat Girl Scout Cookie, feigning for another puff, she blew smoke unable to stay calm while keeping a watchful eye on Fuchsia Fantasy Haze's every move. The tension between them simmered beneath the spectacle unfolding on stage, an unspoken standoff amidst the celebration.

Girl Scout Cookie wasn't ready to crumble. She held the truth about the sistahs, especially now, knowing that the underground rumors from 'The Embassy of Green Roots' were real. The Pink Haze Sistahs were sterile, they couldn't reproduce.

So, whose seeds did Fuchsia Fantasy Haze have? The question burned in her mind - a mystery wrapped in deceit that lingered behind their 'perfect' glimmering facade. Fuchsia was hiding something deep, and Girl Scout Cookie intended to find out, no matter the cost.

Girl Scout Cookie almost chuckled out loud, thinking about the impossibility of it all. A "Greenborn," a miracle from Jah, like the messiah once on Earth, would be the only way for the Pink Haze Sistahs to bear babies. It was a wish, a prayer whispered among the virgin female Hommo-Harvestas, a dream that seemed as distant as the stars over Cannabisville, a gift only Jah could grant. But as her thoughts drifted, she suddenly realized something strange.

Thinking about a virgin, Rosey Dream Haze, the sweet and innocent soulful voice of the group, was missing. And as Girl Scout Cookie scanned the room, it dawned on her that Marijuana Girl, Sativa Diva, was also nowhere to be found.

MARIJUANA GIRL
WELCOME TO CANNABISVILLE

A chill ran through her. Could it just be coincidence, or was there something more hidden behind their absence? The stage lights dimmed as the applause faded, but her mind was now fully alert, wondering where they could be, and what secrets might soon be uncovered.

Yet here was Fuchsia Fantasy Haze, parading a secret, cradling seeds she claimed were her own. It seemed impossible. Either she had defied nature, or something far more complex and hidden lay behind her tale. Girl Scout Cookie was determined to uncover the truth, knowing it would shake the very roots of their sistah-hood.

The music, lights, and laughter around her couldn't dissolve the dread growing in her heart, knowing that tonight, Fuchsia Fantasy Haze had the power to expose their hidden affair. As their final note rang out and the crowd's applause roared around them. The Pink Haze Sistahs took a bow and breath, knowing that while they had made it through the performance, the real drama still lay ahead. As they were still confused about the disappearance of their youngest sister.

The melodic tones of chimes and singing bowls from the 'Temple of Dawn Blaze' echoed, as the Marijana Girls reminiscent of the times when they resided at 'The Embassy of

Green Roots.' These sounds were integral to fertility baths, yoga, meditation, and spiritual healing, an integral part of the practices embraced by energy healers and spiritual practitioners in Cannabisville.

Rows of horses and opulent gold carriages, adorned with gilded marijuana leaf emblems, arrived at the stage. Each contestant in the Marijuana Girl competition will make their debut at the front of the stage, marking their first appearance in the public eye of Cannabisville.

Each Marijuana Girl will step out and be evaluated by the Pink Haze Sistahs, in addition to a live broadcast and voting by the public viewing. A strict rule is in place to prevent contestants from mentioning the names of male strains because it would be cheating, as males choose the commitments.

However, in instances of multiple winners, such as the Marijuana Girls or the Pink Haze Sistahs, the Embassy of Green Roots was tasked with selecting their future male Hommo-Harvesta strains for commitments. This process ensured the continuation of their lineage and the cultivation of new, exotic cannabis strains. The goal was to pair the winners with the finest male strains to uphold tradition and strengthen Cannabisville's heritage.

MARIJUANA GIRL
WELCOME TO CANNABISVILLE

But the Pink Haze Sistahs openly defied that rule after their crowning, rejecting the Embassy's authority over their choices and challenging the long-held customs of commitment.

As their votes for the winning Marijuana Girl to be crowned to propagation approached, The Pink Haze Sistahs unanimously opted to stick with the pink theme, despite considering Marijuana Girl, 'Cotton Candy Sky' for her great pose and elegance, albeit with a hint of sweet snobbishness.

Cotton Candy Sky was disqualified due to lab results revealing traces of synthetic fertilization in the development of both her ass and tits. Plus, she flopped on her solo dance performance. Not only was she off-beat, but so was her ass, drooping out of her costume of pink horror.

The spotlight shifted to the twins, 'Strawberry Bliss' and 'Cherry Bliss.' However, Strawberry Bliss was very intoxicated from her strawberry cannabis-infused wine during her guitar-playing, leaving her in a somewhat punch-drunk state.

Her identical twin, Cherry Bliss, exhibited impressive strength, supporting them both. When her sister missed a step, she seamlessly improvised, incorporating it into the dual guitar acoustics. Even when her sister stumbled, she gracefully fell in harmony. In the haze of the moment, the Pink Haze Sistahs, resilient in their commitment to the color spectrum of Pink, embraced the unpredictability of the process.

The air buzzed with anticipation as Strawberry Bliss and Cherry Bliss were ready to step into the spotlight and carry the responsibility of charting the course for the next generation of their distinctive strains. Although they had already chosen to vote for the twins, there was one final performance to experience before casting their votes, eager to kick off the festivities in Cannabisville.

As anticipation filled the air as the residents prepared to cast their votes on their solar phones, during the live satellite broadcast. The entire community eagerly awaited the moment to officially crown the twins as Marijuana Girls.

The final horse-drawn carriage awaited its cue to open its doors and reveal the last strain of the evening. In a spectacle of purple smoke, the stunning 'Purple Blackberry Dream' emerged, making a grand entrance from the golden carriage.

As the door swung open and the purple smoke filled the air the lights dimmed low, and the music began. The first beat had the audience excited to clap along. Emerging from the carriage, from the purple smoke, a gorgeous female strain, took the stage in a regal purple ball gown, embellished with sequins and crystals. Her necklace and bracelets sparkled with diamonds, creating an aura of glamour. Grasping a wireless microphone, 'Purple Blackberry Dream' number 1, initiated her rap-song with both style and finesse.

> Verse 1 - Purple Blackberry Dream
> *"I'm Purple Blackberry Dream,*
> *yeah, I'm fertile,*
> *"In a haze of bliss, makin' all male stiff.*
> *Rolling up dreams, got that paper so clean,*
> *While you hide secrets, we reign supreme.*
> *Purple smoke swirls, catch that Marijuana gleam,*
> *In this realm, girl, you're lost in my scheme.*
> *You actin' high class, but I see through the lies,*
> *Who you foolin' with those barren alibis?*
> *You're a mirage, a flicker, a fading scene,*
> *I'm the real deal, Purple Dream Queen.*
> *While you play pretend in a cloud so frail,*
> *We got the truth, watch your Pink Haze fail!"*

Right on cue, adorned in a purple polka-dot bikini concealed by a sheer lace purple bathing suit coverup, almost identical to the one Marijuana Girl, Bubble Gum Mist Haze was going to wear. The next sister, 'Purple Punch Dream,' made a glamorous entrance. Holding a microphone, she seamlessly joined in with sister Purple Blackberry Dream, who was already on stage and poised to welcome her.

(Chorus)
"Roll it up, let the smoke redeem,
While you hide in shadows, we reign supreme.
We're the next Marijuana Girls, it's plain to see,
In the purple haze of your deepest dreams."

Stepping onto the platform with an air of confidence, she delved into a performance that encompassed rap, twerking, and soulful singing, taking command of the stage. In an unexpected turn, she playfully challenged Marijuana Girl Bubble Gum Mist to a bathing suit competition, setting the tone for a spirited and entertaining spectacle. Purple Punch Dream boldly shed the sheer lace purple bathing suit coverup, revealing her beauty to the audience.

Verse 2 - Purple Punch Dream
"I'm Purple Punch Dream, and I'm comin' in hot,
You hide your scars, I flaunt what I got.

MARIJUANA GIRL
WELCOME TO CANNABISVILLE

Seen through your haze, know all of your schemes,
You sterile Sistahs, ain't got no seeds.
In a cloud of mist where the smoke streams,
Living life wild, breaking outta your dreams.
Droppin' rhymes hard, they burn like fire,
Your time's tickin' out, Pink Haze's expired.
In the crowd, they see what we bring,
True queens rise, and Pink Haze dims.
You thought you could play, but we're here to win,
Purple Dream reigns, let the truth begin.
Dropping rhymes, like I'm hot, cause you're not!"

Pointing at the 'Pink Haze Sistah's. Their synchronized performance not only show cased their individual talents but also revealed an unspoken understanding among them. Their act was truly a spectacle, transcending the individual components of their routines.

On cue, adorned in purple jeans and a captivating, sparkling backless top, the third sister, 'Purple Widow Dream,' made her entrance. Stepping out of the gold carriage, seamlessly joining the two sisters already on stage.

In the shared moments of preparations and rehearsals, the sisters not only fine-tuned their performances but also deepened the bonds that bound them together.

> Verse 3 - Purple Widow Dream
> *"I'm Purple Widow Dream, queen of this scene,*
> *Catch me in the midnight, my powers serene.*
> *Male strains around, but they don't define,*
> *I rule this land, my seeds are divine.*
> *In the cannabis realm, I'm one and only,*
> *Pink Haze Sistahs lookin' fake and phony.*
> *I'm not sellin' secrets, just tellin' the truth,*
> *We're rooted in Jah, your games uncouth.*
> *You play with a shadow, we shine in light,*
> *No room for fake queens in Jah's sight.*
> *I'll be crowned while your haze fades out,*
> *Purple's the power, what we're all about."*

"I'm not selling my seeds - I'm Just selling weed!" The Purple Dream sisters broke out into a dance routine. Wowing everyone in attendance, even the Pink Haze Sistah's tried to keep their heads from bobbing to the beats though their feet were

tapping. But with every lyric they were growing adder because the performance was a diss-rap song towards them.

This had all the Hommo-Harvestas shocked and amazed because they had never seen female triplets. But, just as the audience thought their routine was ending. The music was lowered and right on time, another sister exited the carriage, singing, as the rhythm changed into a sexy R&B-Reggaeton beat.

Singing soulfully, the 4th sister, Purple X Dream, made her entrance from the gold carriage, her presence commanding attention. She wore a tie-dye T-shirt dress in vibrant shades of purple, white, and green, flowing with energy. The dress featured a large purple marijuana leaf on both the front and back, emblazoned with the bold words 'Marijuana Girl.'

As Purple X Dream walked, her voice resonated with power and grace, harmonizing with the energy around her. The crowd felt her connection to the spirit of Cannabisville, her style a perfect blend of culture and confidence, exuding pride in both her roots and her role as a beacon of the marijuana movement.

Expressing her eclectic and distinctive sense of style. She wore unique and bold jewelry that complemented her artistic persona. Accessories with a matching headwrap and bold Ankh jewelry, sunglasses and large peace sign statement earrings, a chunky gold chain, intricate bracelets, and multiple rings.

Purple X Dream pumped her fist high, a powerful tribute to her heritage. Her jewelry gleamed under the lights, every piece a symbol of her pride, carefully chosen to reflect Africa's rich artistry and cultural essence. Intricate beads, carved wood, and gold accents adorned her, each telling a story of her roots and Afrocentric spirit.

The DNA test had only confirmed what she already knew in her soul. They were a blend of Earth's oldest stories, African and American heritage interwoven in her essence. Standing with her Purple Dream sisters, she wore their heritage like a crown, knowing that in this moment, she was representing not just her strain but the vibrant tapestry of Cannabisville's connection to the world beyond.

Verse 4 - Purple X Dream
I'm Purple X Dream, roots deep in the past,
Pumping my fist, heritage steadfast.
Blessed by Jah, queen of the night,
We see you wiltin' in the moonlight.
You cover your tracks, we roll with pride,
Pink Haze secrets can't hide what's inside.

MARIJUANA GIRL
WELCOME TO CANNABISVILLE

On the throne of purple, truth is supreme,
Your barren haze, just a broken dream.
Blessed are the wombs that bear Jah's seeds,
We're the future strains, fulfilling the creed.
So puff the truth, let the smoke redeem,
Purple Dream Sisters, born from Jah's dream."

. The Purple Dream Sisters had the crowd electrified, with everyone on their feet, eagerly trying to mirror their exhilarating dance moves. They swayed to the pulsating rhythm, and without a moment's hesitation, each sister belted out her part.

Then, in a crescendo of energy, they harmonized together, setting the stage ablaze with the sheer intensity of their performance. The atmosphere crackled with excitement as the audience couldn't resist dancing along to the infectious beats that had their heads bobbing, feet tapping and fingers snapping, and singing along.

Chorus (All Together)

"So, *roll it up, let the smoke redeem,*
While you hide in shadows, we reign supreme.
We're the next Marijuana Girls, it's plain to see,
In the purple haze of your deepest dreams."

Their performance was so captivating that nobody noticed the gold carriage still stationed by the stage. It looks like it became the battle of the quadruplets. The Pink Haze Sistah's verse Purple Dream Sisters. It was then that the gold carriage doors opened again, and purple haze smoke appeared as the audience cheered.

No one knew what to expect. Unlike the other sisters, 'Purple Tiny Dream' didn't step out. Instead, she crawled backward, her feet dangling until she felt comfortable enough to make a graceful jump down, just in time to sing along with her sisters.

As the 5th sister, she emerged dressed identically to their oldest sister, Purple Blackberry Dream. Dressed in a purple sequined gown Purple Tiny Dream made it to the stage, independently. Despite their different heights, they looked strikingly alike.

Their looks were identical, a stunning harmony that captivated everyone who gazed upon them. As the Purple Dream Sisters stood side by side, they formed an almost mesmerizing pattern, their heights creating noticeable stairsteps, each sister just slightly taller than the one before.

MARIJUANA GIRL
WELCOME TO CANNABISVILLE

The visual symmetry was striking, drawing the crowd's attention like a perfect lineup of stars in the sky. Every face, whether fully visible or partially hidden in the glow of the lights, carried the same "Wow" expression, an embodiment of awe and unity.

Their collective energy seemed to pulse in unison, like a single, vibrant heartbeat echoing through the crowd. Their identical features were more than just physical, they represented the shared strength and power of the sisters, a reflection of their unity, purpose, and the unbreakable bond they held as both individuals and a group.

"So, *roll it up, let the smoke redeem,*
While you hide in shadows, we reign supreme.
We're the next Marijuana Girls, it's plain to see,
In the purple haze of your deepest dreams."

The sight of a tiny adult Homma-Harvesta was the first for Cannabisville to publicly witness. Homma-Harvesta typically grew to the average height of humans, with petite adults, but they've never seen a three-foot adult Hommo-Harvesta. There, however, were the 'Island Buds,' who were giants that can tower over seven-feet tall. But seeing a little person for the first time left the crowd in awe. The last chorus was sung solo by 'Purple Tiny Dream' in her beautiful mature voice.

Then in unison 'The Purple Dream Sisters' sang, "*We're the next Marijuana girls, in your purple dreams.*" These sisters are hybrid strains, a mix of both sativa and indica genetics. Their vibrant hues and unique qualities captivated everyone at the annual ball, bringing a fresh wave of excitement.

As the Purple Dream Sisters moved with graceful synchronicity, their enchanting presence stirred up jealousy among the Pink Haze Sisters. They had discerned the subtle messages in the song from the Purple Dream Sisters, revealing their secrets.

Fuchsia Fantasy Haze faced the challenge of being unable to conceive Hommo-Harvesta babies, a fact she believed was kept confidential. However, the mystery of how did 'The Purple Dream Sisters' became privy to her condition? Medical files were meant to be confidential, raising questions about the unexpected revelation.

Bubble Gum Mist Haze was horrified that she had been challenged to the bathing suit competition and the fact that she didn't oblige and reveal what was hidden under the black lace bathing suit coverup confirmed she was intimidated.

MARIJUANA GIRL
WELCOME TO CANNABISVILLE

Knowing she would lose because of her skin infection with a fungus that made her itch in her body cavities, a deadly disease that infectious diseases doctors can't cure, she has been given an expiration date unbeknownst to her sistahs.

Petal Pink Euphoria Haze was perplexed, she had no idea how anyone knew the secret affair with Girl Scout Cookie, and now her sister is trying to greenmail GSC to be a surrogate.

Also, wondering how *'The Purple Dream Sisters'* had discovered all their secrets - especially that she'd been harvesting eggs from the women seeking refuge in their synthetic drugs - recovery program, 'The Pink Haze House,' and selling them on the Green Market.

The female Hommo-Harvestas were given free health care and sent regularly to gynecologist for what they thought were routine pap smear test. After collection, the eggs were swiftly preserved, tucked away in liquid nitrogen tanks inside a hidden embryology lab. But her sistahs, still unaware that viable embryos were already prepared and ready to be implanted.

But since she begun to bribe Girl Scout Cookie to be a surrogate, she now ever realizing the full extent of her sister's ambitions. Now that she saw how far her sibling would go to obtain what they desired, she decided she'd have to offer her sister a seed for in vitro fertilization (IVF) to ensure her silence. Now the Pink Haze Sistahs were worried and looking for Rosey Dream Haze, wondering if she was with seed, and how? But she was nowhere to be found.

The Sistahs were so consumed with their own thoughts about 'The Purple Dream Sister's dis' song, disrespecting them. As the searched for their youngest sistah to examine her stomach, as they remembered the 4th Purple Dream Sisters lyrics, "Me see ya belly enhance, in da moonlight."

They also noticed their sisters weight gain but didn't think much of it. Witnessing the threat and malice and the message in the songs made 'The Pink Haze Sistahs' compelled to cast their votes in favor of the Purple Dream Sisters. They attempted to make it appear orchestrated rather than a takeover by the Purple Dream Sistahs that strategized a planned transition to the unfolding scenario.

The ball concluded with a harmonious celebration, marking the beginning of a more inclusive and colorful tradition in Cannabisville and the Purple Dream Sistah's the new host of the next Cannabisville Ball, announced by the Pink Haze Sisters after they mutually agreed to keep secrets in their introduction

MARIJUANA GIRL
WELCOME TO CANNABISVILLE

song. *"Introducing the new Marijuana Girls, The Purple Dream Sisters!"* The Purple Dream Sisters lived at the 'Lab-House' Inside the embassy's private quarters until their maturity and this day to be showcased and awarded Marijuana Girls. During their stay, only one of them was permitted outside the embassy at a time.

Recognizing that the youngest's presence might come as a surprise due to her dwarf size, an exception was made, allowing her to move freely within the embassy. Unnoticed for many years, she was inadvertently treated like a pet. This unique vantage point allowed her to eavesdrop on various conversations. During her excursions, she even had the chance to meet Island, Bud Reggie-Reg, just an ordinary Hommo-Harvesta, but a very important strain.

He was there being evaluated for medicinal purposes. Island Bud, Reggie-Reg and she had become very friendly and had plans of their own, she just needed to get out of the embassy, and this was her moment. Reggie-Reg was already back in the villas selling his weed. It was through Island Bud Reggie-Reg that she gained awareness of the green-market cannabis community.

Using her newfound knowledge, she delved into an astute investigation and tapped into discreet sources within the industry.

This meticulous approach led her to uncover Petal Pink Euphoria Haze's secret involvement in the illegal trade of cannabis seeds. Adding to the complexity, Fuchsia Fantasy Haze's lab results remain confidential.

Yet the doctors in the labs conveniently leave their computers accessible, allowing her to indulge in games or videos, but mainly she snooped through everyone's medical files in Cannabisville. Uncovering secrets proved effortless. During their outings, they discreetly trailed the Pink Haze Sistahs and discerned their belief invincibility. Their network of informants and a careful analysis of market activities allowed them to piece together the puzzle and reveal the underground dealings of 'The Pink Haze Sistah's.

The revelation added an unexpected layer of drama to the Marijuana Girl competition in Cannabisville, setting the stage for a finale filled with intrigue and consequences. As the grand ball in Cannabisville reached its crescendo, a harmonious celebration enveloped the elite strains. However, an unexpected twist shattered the jubilation.

MARIJUANA GIRL
WELCOME TO CANNABISVILLE

The Purple Dream Sisters, with their candid lyrics, fearlessly revealed the closely guarded secrets of the Pink Haze Sisters in a song that resonated throughout Cannabisville. Leaving every Hommo-Harvestas that heard the subtle subliminal messages embedded in the lyrics, were true.

The once-celebratory atmosphere now hung heavy with suspense and revelation, marking the end of the ball and the beginning of unforeseen consequences for the Pink Haze Sisters and the Purple Dream sisters crowned Marijuana Girls. As the music faded and the attendees began to depart, the Pink Haze Sistahs in their vibrant pink gowns now seeming to worry about their uncertain fate.

What had been a night of celebration was now the beginning of destruction neither they nor Cannabisville could foresee -a path laden with consequences that would challenge their unity, their loyalty, and their very identities as symbols of pink Sistah-hood..

NO AFTER PARTY!!!

The Pink Haze Sistah's, left the Cannabisville Ball immediately cloaked in a cloud of uncertainty, gathered in the dimly lit room, their faces reflecting a mix of suspicion and concern. Rumors will start spreading if the mysterious Purple Dream Sister's had knowledge of their closely guarded secrets, and unease hung heavy in the air.

Fuchsia Fantasy Haze, her vibrant aura dimmed by the shadows of doubt, took the lead. *"We need to unravel the mystery of how those budtches, 'The Purple Dream Sisters' uncovered our most guarded truths. Our family secrets are our strength and vulnerability."*

They could not afford to let the truths be confirmed. Marijuana Girl Fuchsia Fantasy Haze, eyes narrowed in suspicion, questioned, *"Could it be a breach of trust from within our sisterhood? A loose tongue, a misplaced confidence?"*

Bubble Gum Mist Haze, grappling with her mortality, added, *"Or perhaps an external force, a watcher in the periphery, picking up on our vulnerabilities?"*

Petal Pink Euphoria Haze, the group's rebellious spirit, proposed, *"Perhaps they stumbled upon something unintentionally. We should monitor their activities and pinpoint the weak link in their chain. My bet it's that little one!"*

And where was their sister, Rosey Dream Haze? They had been playfully teasing her about the weight she was gaining, but they'd noticed her belly and breasts swelling in ways that seemed to hint at something more. Could it be possible? They wondered if Rosey had felt a creeping shame, unable to confront a truth she might not have fully understood - or had she?

Perhaps, to escape the storm of questions, she had indeed abandoned everything to seek peace, dedicating herself to Jah in a secluded covenants high in the north mountains. The thought lingered in their minds, a strange mixture of relief and uncertainty.

They were left to puzzle over her silence and absence, but a nagging feeling whispered that maybe Rosey Dream Haze had left carrying something more than secrets.

The Pink Haze sisters, bound by blood and secrecy, embarked on a quest to uncover the truth. They planned to track 'The Purple Dream Sisters' recent interactions, sifted through cryptic messages, and scrutinized every possible connection. As the puzzle pieces came together, a chilling revelation emerged the source of their betrayal lay closer than they had ever imagined.

They sat quietly in their thoughts. The realization that one of their own had betrayed the sacred pact of secrecy sent shockwaves through the Pink Haze Sistahs. The bonds that held them together now faced an unprecedented test, and the shadows of betrayal cast a pall over their once-unbreakable sisterhood.

Determined to protect the sanctity of their shared secrets, 'The Pink Haze Sistahs' vowed to confront the traitors 'The Purple Dream Sisters'. As the haze of uncertainty thickened around them, their resolve only grew stronger. With the Ganja Boys' annual '420 -High Time Masquerade Party' fast approaching, the Sistahs meticulously planned their strike.

'420 - The High Time Masquerade Party' was the perfect stage for their revenge. The annual gathering brought together the Ganja Boys and Marijuana Girls, a night of opulence where the Cannabisville elite mingled under the pretense of tradition.

Amidst swirling smoke and gleaming lights, prearranged unions were forged, alliances struck between the most powerful strains. For the Pink Haze Sistahs, this will be more than a celebration - it will be their chance for revenge.

With vengeance burning in their hearts, not even the wisdom of the 420 Chronicles from The Book of Roots could calm their nerves. Feeling like their spirits were stolen, ready to execute their retaliation strategy - determined to reclaim balance and justice, knowing their retribution would be as precise as it was poetic.

But in a solemn moment of reflection, they were haunted by the void of Rosey Dream Haze, their guiding light in times of prayer, was gone. Clasping hands, they silently acknowledged her absence, drawing strength from one another.

They knew they had to bind together even tighter now, their unity becoming both shield and weapon. Their payback would unfold with deliberate precision, timed to strike at the height of celebration. Together, they whispered in unison, their voices steady, "*Chronicle: 262 NCV: 'The Eternal Law of JAH'S Creations. Seed for Seed, Strain for Strain, Bud for Bud, Root for Root. – Selahjah"*

THERESA VERNELL

The Book of Roots
MARIJUANA GIRL
New Cannabisville Version

CANNABISVILLE

420 Chronicles

Theresa Vernell

MARIJUANA GIRL
WELCOME TO CANNABISVILLE

TABLE OF CONTENT: 420 CHRONICLES AND KUSHKORDANCE

The Origins of Cannabisville, Jahaism, The Pillars of Jahaism

Chronicles 1–120: The Seed - The Opening   Page 275
These focus on Jah's creation of Cannabisville and the first Hommo-Harvestas, Kush-Adam and Eve-Flower. They reveal the origins of life, the Tree of Life, and Jah's covenant with his people.

Chronicles 121–200: The Buds of Wisdom   Page 299
These reflects the sacred teachings, spiritual growth, and new insights found in these chronicles, similar to how Psalms provide poetic and reflective guidance in the Bible. It emphasizes the Hommo-Harvestas' connection to Jah, their culture, and the wisdom they gain through their journey in Cannabisville.

Chronicles 201–300: New Strains and New Laws   Page 313
These details the development of Cannabisville's society, the establishment of the Embassy of Green Roots, and the struggles to balance freedom with responsibility.

Chronicles 301–399: The Seed of Love   Page 330
These are parables that celebrate Jah's love, compassion, and the unifying power of the sacred plant. They teach forgiveness, humility, and the sanctity of commitment between partners.

Chronicles 400–420: The Final Buds   Page 350
These closing chronicles contain prayers, blessings, and prophecies, reflecting on the unity of Cannabisville and the eternal bond between Jah and his creation.

KUSHKORDANCE: The Parables of the chronicles   Page 358
The *420 Chronicles* are a sacred collection of teachings, parables, and historical accounts unique to Cannabisville. Each chronicle is carefully crafted to impart a specific virtue, moral lesson, or cautionary tale, guiding the Hommo-Harvestas on their spiritual and communal journey.

In *The Book of Roots*, you will uncover the origins and profound wisdom passed down by the first Hommo-Harvestas of Cannabisville. This sacred text reveals how Cannabisville was brought into existence, a manifestation of Jah's divine vision of harmony between the natural world and its inhabitants.

It chronicles the deep bond between the Hommo-Harvestas and the land, illustrating how the cannabis plant became the cornerstone of their spirituality, way of life, and healing practices. Through its pages, the essence of Jahaism—the guiding faith of Cannabisville - comes to life, illuminating the sacred relationship between creation and Creator.

The Origins of Cannabisville
The story begins with the first spark of life, when Jah planted the sacred seed of the Marijuana Tree, the cornerstone of Jahaism. From this divine tree bloomed all life in Cannabisville, providing both spiritual and physical nourishment for the Hommo-Harvestas. Created from the very essence of the land, the Hommo-Harvestas were guided by Jah's teachings to cultivate the soil with care, honor the cannabis plant as a sacred gift, and live in harmony with the plants, animals, and one another.

Wisdom of the Ancestors
The *Book of Roots* serves as a sacred guidebook, imparting the ancient wisdom of the ancestors who first walked the lands of Cannabisville, central to the faith of Jahaism. These teachings unveil the profound connection between the Hommo-Harvestas and the natural world, highlighting the healing properties of plants, with cannabis revered as Jah's most potent and sacred gift.

MARIJUANA GIRL
WELCOME TO CANNABISVILLE

It explains how cannabis, when used in rituals, medicine, and daily life, has the power to heal the body, expand the mind, and deepen the Hommo-Harvestas' connection to Jah's divine essence.

Rituals of the Land

The *Book of Roots* also illuminates the sacred rituals central to Jahaism, practiced by the Hommo-Harvestas for generations. From harvest ceremonies that honor Jah's provision to the communal sharing of cannabis in prayers of gratitude and reflection, these traditions celebrate the divine connection between the people and the land. Each ritual underscores the importance of sustainability and reverence for Jah's creation, teaching future generations how to grow, harvest, and use plants responsibly. Through these practices, Cannabisville continues to flourish in harmony, preserving the balance ordained by Jah.

The *Book of Roots* is a timeless testament to the foundation of life in Cannabisville and the guiding principles of Jahaism. It offers a glimpse into the spiritual and practical lessons that have shaped this mystical land, illuminating the divine connection between the Hommo-Harvestas, the cannabis plant, and Jah's eternal wisdom. Through its pages, the sacred relationship between faith, nature, and community is preserved, ensuring that the legacy of Cannabisville endures for generations to come.

Chronicle 106: Hallelujah

Praise Jah, the Almighty Creator, for Jah's love endures forever. Hallelujah let all of Cannabisville proclaim: "Hallelujah! Jah, you are the flame that lights our path, the seed that grows in our hearts, and the rain that nourishes our souls. Forever and always, we lift our voices to you."

JAHAISM: The Faith of Cannabisville
Overview:

Jahaism is the spiritual and cultural foundation of Cannabisville, a way of life deeply rooted in reverence for Jah, the divine creator and sustainer of life. Jahaism combines elements of nature worship, communal harmony, and personal enlightenment, all guided by the teachings found in the sacred *Book of Roots*. This faith is an essential part of Hommo-Harvesta identity, influencing their rituals, governance, and daily life.

Core Beliefs

1. **Jah as the Divine Gardener:**
   Jah is regarded as the supreme cultivator, responsible for planting the seeds of life and nurturing all creation. Jah's essence is in every growing thing, from the towering *Tree of Cannabisville* to the smallest herb.

2. **Sacred Duality:**
   Jahaism teaches that all life exists in balance—light and shadow, growth and decay, creation and harvest. Followers strive to maintain harmony within themselves, their community, and the environment.

3. **The Tree of Life:**
   The *Marijuana Tree of Life*, also called the *Tree of Cannabisville*, symbolizes wisdom, sustenance, and connection to Jah. Its sap, called *Blood Swallow*, is considered a sacred substance with healing and spiritual properties.

4. **Reverence for Strains:**
   Each Hommo-Harvesta is a unique "strain," blessed with gifts and purposes. Diversity is celebrated, and every strain is believed to reflect an aspect of Jah's creativity.

Sacred Practices

1. **Ritual Burning:**
   Followers light sacred herbs, including cannabis, as an offering to Jah and to cleanse their spirits. The smoke symbolizes prayers rising to the heavens.

2. **Root Meditation:**
   Practitioners sit beneath trees or near natural springs to connect with Jah. This meditation, known as *Rooting*, is said to ground their souls and align them with divine wisdom.

3. **Communal Worship:**
   Weekly gatherings take place at the *Embassy Green Roots*, where strains unite to share songs, stories, and blessings. The *Soulshine Elixir*, a golden cannabis champagne, is often used in ceremonial libations.

4. **The Harvest Ceremony:**
   A grand annual event marking the season of abundance. Offerings from the fields are shared among the community, and the *Solar Commanders* lead prayers of gratitude to Jah.

5. **Moral Teachings**

1. **Live Rooted in Truth:**
   Hommo-Harvesta are encouraged to be honest and upright, nurturing their community like a thriving garden.

2. **Protect the Soil:**
   Nature is sacred in Jahaism. Followers believe in sustainable living, ensuring Cannabisville remains fertile for future strains.

3. **Beware of Blightroot (the Devil):**
   Blightroot, also called *Lurking Ember*, represents the temptations and corruption that lead to imbalance. Jahaism teaches vigilance against deceit and destruction.

Sacred Texts

- **The Book of Roots:**
  The central scripture of Jahaism, filled with teachings, parables, and hymns. It provides guidance on living in harmony with Jah's creation and resisting the forces of Blightroot.

Spiritual Leaders

1. **Prophet Highstem:**
   The spiritual leader of Cannabisville, Prophet Highstem is seen as Jah's voice among the strains. His partner, the author of 'The Book of Roots – New Cannabisville Version,' *Soulshine Sessions*, is also revered for her wisdom and lineage.

2. **Solar Commanders:**
   Guardians of Jahaism's traditions and leaders of 'The Embassy of Green Roots.' They ensure the spiritual well-being of Cannabisville's inhabitants.

Symbols

1. **The Leaf of Light:**
   A glowing cannabis leaf, symbolizing Jah's presence and blessings. It is prominently displayed in sacred spaces.

2. **The Golden Bud:**
   Represents enlightenment and divine favor, often used in art and jewelry.

3. **Green Flame:**
   A metaphorical and literal symbol of the spirit's resilience and Jah's eternal light.

Holidays

1. **Green Dawn:**
   A day celebrating new beginnings and Jah's blessings. Hommo-Harvesta gather at sunrise to sing praises and share green offerings.

2. **The Root Solstice:**
   Marks the longest day of the year, celebrating light and growth. Festivities include dancing, feasting, and ritual blessings.

The Pillars of Jahaism

1. **Jah's Sovereignty**: Jahaism acknowledges Jah as the Supreme Creator, the source of all life, and the guiding force that upholds the harmony of the universe. The Hommo-Harvestas live in recognition of Jah's presence in every aspect of life, from the natural world to the spirit.

2. **Purification (Jahdu)**: Before daily prayers, the Hommo-Harvestas perform a purification ritual called Jahdu. This sacred act involves washing the face, hands, arms, and feet to prepare both the body and spirit for connection with Jah.

3. **Prayer (Jahlah)**: Pray four times a day – for 20 minutes, seeking spiritual connection and guidance from Jah. Prayer is a time for reflection, gratitude, and supplication. It is a daily reaffirmation of faith and a way to align one's life with Jah's will.

4. **The Sacred Plant (Cannabis)**: The cannabis plant is central to Jahaism, revered as a divine gift that brings healing, wisdom, and connection to Jah. It is used in rituals, medicine, and everyday life, helping to expand their consciousness and strengthen their relationship with Jah.

5. **Community and Unity**: Jahaism emphasizes the importance of community. Believing that living in harmony with each other and the world around them strengthens their bond with Jah. Unity, cooperation, and mutual respect are seen as essential to living a righteous life.

6. **Balance (Harmoni)**: Living in balance with nature, oneself, and others is a core teaching of Jahaism. Hommo-Harvestas seek to maintain equilibrium in all aspects of life, reflecting Jah's perfect order. Balance is not only physical but spiritual, mental, and emotional.

7. **Gratitude and Giving**: The Hommo-Harvestas practice gratitude for the abundance of Jah's creation. They are taught to give back to Cannabisville, their communities, and each other. Generosity and kindness are foundational to Jahaism, ensuring that the blessings of Jah are shared and spread.

8. **Wisdom and Knowledge**: Seeking wisdom and expanding understanding is highly valued in Jahaism. Hommo-Harvestas are encouraged to pursue knowledge, both spiritual and worldly, to grow closer to Jah's truth. Learning is seen as a lifelong journey guided by Jah's divine light.

9. **Respect for Cannabisville**: Jahaism teaches respect for the land and all of Jah's creatures. The Hommo-Harvestas live sustainably, working to protect the environment and preserve the balance of nature. Cannabisville is viewed as a sacred gift, and its resources are to be used responsibly and reverently.

10. **Healing and Compassion**: Jahaism promotes healing through both spiritual practices and natural remedies. Hommo-Harvestas are taught to care for one another with compassion, offering support in times of need. The healing properties of cannabis, along with the power of Jah's love.

These pillars guide their lives, creating a way of living that honors Jah, nurtures Cannabisville, and strengthens their bond between all living beings.

In Jahaism, faith is intertwined with the natural world, promoting a life of balance, gratitude, and reverence. It is a religion that not only uplifts the spirit but also nurtures the planet, ensuring that all strains live in harmony with Jah's grand design.

Jahaism is more than a religion; it's a way of life that fosters a deep connection with Jah, nature, and the Cannabisville community. It provides both spiritual guidance and practical wisdom for living harmoniously with Cannabisville and one another.

Before Praying they recited: *Chronicle: 199 The Buds of Wisdom*

O Jah, send Your Blessings upon Cannabisville and to all future generations, as You have sent Your blessings upon those before us. You are the Most Praised, the Most Glorious. O Jah, grant us goodness in this world and the Hereafter, and protect us from the torment of Hell. May Your Peace and Mercy rest upon Cannabisville. - *Selahjah*

Selahjah: A sacred term used in Cannabisville to conclude prayers, blessings, or affirmations. Derived from the reflective "Selah" found in ancient scriptures and the divine name "Jah," it signifies a moment to pause, reflect, and affirm unity with Jah's will. It represents agreement, peace, and spiritual alignment, embodying the essence of gratitude and reverence in the Hommo-Harvesta culture.

MARIJUANA GIRL
WELCOME TO CANNABISVILLE

WHO IS JAH? "Understanding Jah: The Eternal Creator"

Jah is a sacred name for God recognized across various spiritual traditions, each highlighting unique aspects of Jah's presence and significance:

Jah is beyond the confines of pronouns and identity -Jah is Jah!!!

Rastafarianism

In Rastafarian belief, *Jah* is the singular, all-powerful God who dwells within every individual. Unlike traditional worship, Rastafarians emphasize the ability to "know" *Jah* personally through spiritual awareness and righteous living, rather than simply "believing" in Him. The name *Jah* is derived from "Jehovah," the English transliteration of the Hebrew name for God in the Old Testament.

The Bible

The name "Jah" (or "Yah") is a unique and profound representation of God found in the Bible. It appears most notably in **Psalm 68:4**, which is the only place where God is explicitly called "Jah." This short form of the divine name "Yahweh" emphasizes His eternal nature, sovereignty, and presence in the lives of His people.

Jah is derived from **YHWH**, the sacred tetragrammaton, and appears 50 times throughout the Old Testament:

- **26 times alone** (e.g., Exodus 15:2; 17:16; various Psalms).
- **24 times in the expression "Hallelujah"**, which means "Praise Yah" or "Praise Jah."

Jah also forms part of the word "Hallelujah," which means "Praise Yah," a universal expression of worship found throughout the Psalms.

Christianity

Christians honor *Jah* through the term "*Hallelujah*," which is used to give glory to God. It serves as an exclamation of divine praise and a reminder of God's sovereignty and grace.

The Origins of Jah

Jah is a shortened form of the Tetragrammaton *YHWH*, the four-letter Hebrew name for God. This name is often transliterated as *Yahweh* or translated as *LORD*. It emphasizes God's eternal nature, unchanging power, and divine authority.

Conclusion

Across Rastafarianism, Biblical scripture, and Christianity, *Jah* represents a divine force of love, guidance, and protection. The name *Jah* transcends cultural and linguistic barriers, offering a direct connection to the Creator and uniting believers in faith and reverence.

The Three Steps of Jahdu: A Sacred Purification Ritual

Jahdu is a purification ritual performed by the Hommo-Harvestas before their 4 – 20 minutes of daily prayers. It cleanses the body and spirit, preparing them for communion with Jah. The ritual involves three steps, each accompanied by the chant: *"Jah is good, Jah is great, Jah sees all."*

1. Cleansing with Holy Rainwater (Face)

Hommo-Harvestas begin by washing their face with holy rainwater, symbolizing the purification of their thoughts and expressions. This cleanses their outward appearance and reminds them of Jah's goodness.

2. Cleansing of the Hands and Arms

Next, they wash their hands and arms to purify their actions and intentions. This symbolizes the need for righteous deeds, aligning their actions with Jah's will.

3. Cleansing of the Feet and Nose Passages

Finally, they wash their feet and cleanse their nose passages, symbolizing the purification of their path in life and their breath, connecting them to Jah's spirit. After these steps, they are spiritually and physically prepared for prayer.

MARIJUANA GIRL
WELCOME TO CANNABISVILLE

ALLAH and JAH

The question of whether **Allah** and **Jah** are the same arises from their shared association as names for the divine in different spiritual traditions. While both refer to the concept of a singular, supreme God, their use and understanding depend on the context of the specific faith traditions:

Jah in Rastafarianism and the Bible

- **Jah** is rooted in the Hebrew Bible, as a short form of **Yahweh** (YHWH), the personal name of God in Judaism and Christianity.
- Rastafarians specifically refer to Jah as their one true God, believing Jah dwells within each individual. The term is also recognized in the phrase **"Hallelujah"**, meaning "Praise Jah."

   ### Allah in Islam
- **Allah** is the Arabic word for God and is central to Islam. It is used by Muslims and Arabic-speaking Christians and Jews to refer to the one God of Abrahamic faiths.
- Allah is understood as eternal, transcendent, and incomparable, emphasizing the oneness of God (Tawhid).

Are Jah and Allah the Same?

1. **Monotheism**: Both Jah and Allah represent the belief in one supreme God, suggesting a common monotheistic thread.

2. **Cultural and Linguistic Differences**: The names Jah and Allah come from distinct linguistic and cultural contexts:
   - **Jah** is Hebrew in origin, later adopted by Rastafarianism with its unique theological lens.
   - **Allah** is Arabic and predates Islam, historically used by Arab Christians and Jews as well.

3. **Theological Interpretations**: While both terms refer to the same monotheistic God in broad terms, each faith has its distinct theological and doctrinal interpretations of the divine.

THERESA VERNELL

ALLAH and JAH: The Same?

Jah and Allah may be seen as names for the same ultimate God within the shared Abrahamic tradition, a divine being who unites all creation in love and purpose. However, the specific attributes, worship practices, and cultural understandings of Jah (particularly in Rastafarianism) and Allah (in Islam) differ significantly.

Jah, in Rastafarian belief, is deeply personal—a God who dwells within each individual, encouraging direct connection, self-awareness, and inner transformation. Allah, in Islam, is the One, Merciful, and Omnipotent Creator, whose guidance is revealed through the Quran, emphasizing submission to divine will and living in accordance with justice and compassion.

The greatest lesson in these names and attributes is the reminder of humanity's shared spiritual journey—the call to embody love, unity, and reverence for the divine in all its forms. Jah inspires self-realization and harmony within, while Allah emphasizes surrender and alignment with a greater purpose. Together, they reflect the vastness and intimacy of God, inviting believers to transcend differences and see divinity as a force of love, justice, and peace that binds all creation.

Conclusion:

Jah and Allah may be seen as names for the same ultimate God within the shared Abrahamic tradition, but the specific attributes, worship practices, and cultural understandings of Jah (especially in Rastafarianism) and Allah (in Islam) differ significantly. Whether they are considered "the same" depends on one's perspective and faith tradition. Ultimately, both serve as pathways to understanding the divine and embodying its greatest lesson: love in action, unity in spirit, and reverence for all that is sacred

*The Hommo- Harvestas pray to the same God that Jesus did when he walked the planet Earth.

MARIJUANA GIRL
WELCOME TO CANNABISVILLE

Chronicle: 1

"Light of Creation"

"At the dawn of time, Jah created the heavens and Cannabisville. The village existed in formlessness and void, with darkness shrouding the depths. Then Jah spoke, "Let there be light," and instantly emerged illumination. Jah beheld the light, deeming it good; thus, Jah separated the light from the darkness."

Chronicle: 2

"Breath of Cannabisville"

Jah formed Cannabisville, shaping it from the soil. Jah breathed life into the land and waters, and they bloomed under Jah's care. May our spirits be nourished by the breath of Jah, who fills Cannabisville with abundance.

Chronicle: 3

"The Garden of Peace"

Jah planted the first garden, where every plant and tree flourished under Jah's love. In Jah's garden, there was peace and harmony, and all creation lived as one. Let us tend our own gardens with care, growing peace, unity, and love.

Chronicle: 4

"The Seeds we Sow"

"From the seed, all life begins. Jah, in your wisdom,
You created the seed that bears fruit,
the fruit that feeds your children.
May we sow seeds of love and kindness,
trusting in the harvest that comes from your hand.
This seed will bear great fruit. May we nurture our faith,
Trusting in Jah's power to make it flourish."

Chronicle: 5
"Streams of Blessing"
Jah caused rivers to flow through the land, bringing water to every corner of Cannabisville. These streams of blessing nourish the fields, and through them, life flourishes. Let Jah's blessings flow through us, watering our spirits with love and grace.

Chronicle: 6
"The First Dawn"
Jah created the day and the night, and with the first dawn came the promise of new beginnings. Each day is a gift, filled with opportunity and hope. Let us greet every sunrise with joy, knowing that Jah's light will guide us.

Chronicle: 7
"The Covenant of Cannabisville"
Jah made a covenant with Cannabisville and all that grows upon it. Jah's promise endures through the seasons, from seed to harvest, from dawn to dusk. In every cycle, we see the faithfulness of Jah's love.

Chronicle: 8
"The Sky's Blessing"
Jah stretched out the heavens like a canopy, a shelter for all creation. The sky watches over us, a reminder of Jah's infinite reach. May we always look up, knowing that Jah's protection and love cover us.

Chronicle: 9
"The Circle of Life"
Jah formed the first male Hommo-Harvesta from the dust of Cannabisville, shaping Kush-Adam, a calm and grounding male 'Indica' strain. Jah breathed life into him, and Kush-Adam stood tall, his presence steady like the night breeze, with deep roots in the planet..

MARIJUANA GIRL
WELCOME TO CANNABISVILLE

Chronicle: 10
"The Voice of Jah"
But Jah saw that it was not good for Kush-Adam to be alone, so Jah caused a deep sleep to fall upon him. From Kush-Adam's rib, Jah fashioned Eve-Flower, a lively and uplifting 'Sativa' Hommo-Harvesta. Eve-Flower's spirit flowed like the morning sun, radiant and energetic, ready to spread joy wherever she grew. Together, they balanced each other, like night and day, calm and vitality, root, and bloom.

Jah leads us to green pastures, where peace flows like a river, and the herb grows freely. May we rest in these pastures, inhaling peace and exhaling love, knowing Jah's protection surrounds us according to his plan.

Chronicle: 11
"The Night's Embrace"
Jah gave the night its stars and the moon its light, a quiet peace to rest beneath. As the sun sets, may we find comfort in the stillness, trusting Jah to watch over us through every dark hour until the dawn.

Chronicle: 12
"Winds of Change"
Jah sent winds to blow across the land, carrying seeds to new places, bringing change and growth. Let us welcome the winds of change in our lives, trusting that Jah's guidance will lead us to new opportunities.

Chronicle: 13
"The Green Harvest"
Jah made Cannabisville rich with plants, the green harvest of life that sustains us. In every leaf, in every root, we find the blessings of Jah's creation. May we cultivate these gifts with reverence, knowing Jah provides for all.

Chronicle 14:
The Green Dawn
"Worship Jah, and your light will guides your roots,
Your wisdom grows on leaves, Your love fuels your blooms."

Chronicle 15:
The Glow of the Ember
"Jah, your fire lights our spirit,
Your wisdom guards our rest,
Your promise wakes us anew."

Chronicle: 16:
"Roots of Faith"
Just as the roots of trees dig deep into the soil, so too must our faith be grounded in Jah. In times of trial, let us stand firm, nourished by Jah's word, growing strong and steady in Jah's love.

Chronicle: 17
"The First Rain"
Jah opened the heavens and sent rain to water Cannabisville, and life sprang forth in abundance. May Jah's blessings rain upon us, soaking our hearts with love, kindness, and the strength to grow anew.

Chronicle: 18
"The Sun's Warmth"
Jah set the sun in the sky to warm Cannabisville and bring life to all living things. In its rays, we feel the warmth of Jah's love. Let us carry that warmth with us, spreading light wherever we go.

MARIJUANA GIRL
WELCOME TO CANNABISVILLE

Chronicle: 19
"Fields of Promise"
Jah promised Cannabisville would yield its fruit in its season. With patience, the farmer waits for the harvest, trusting in the cycle of life. Let us trust in Jah's promises, knowing that what is sown in faith will bloom in time.

Chronicle: 20
"The Gift of the Herb"
Jah gave the herb as a gift, a plant with many blessings for healing and peace. May we use it with wisdom, honoring the sacredness of this gift, and sharing its benefits with those in need of solace and health.

Chronicle: 21
"The Seed of Hope"
Jah placed within every seed the promise of tomorrow. Though small, each seed holds the potential for greatness. Let us plant seeds of hope in our lives, trusting that Jah will nurture them into full bloom.

Chronicle 22:
"Fear only Jah"
"Do not fear those who can harm the body but cannot touch the soul. Instead, revere the One who holds the power over both soul and body, even in the depths of judgment."

Chronicle: 23
"Branches of Strength"
The Marijuana trees grow tall, their branches reaching for the heavens. In their strength, we see Jah's power. Let our spirits grow tall like the trees, stretching towards the light of his wisdom and grace.

Chronicle: 24
"The Blessed Seed"
Jah blessed the seed, giving it the power to grow and bear fruit. Each seed is a promise of new life. May the seeds we plant both in Cannabisville and in our lives be nourished by Jah's love, growing strong and true.

Chronicle: 25
"The Harvest of Joy"
When the time for harvest comes, the fields are full, and the people rejoice. Jah, may we harvest joy in our hearts, gathering the fruits of your blessings and sharing them with all in Cannabisville.

Chronicle: 26
"Roots of Compassion"
As roots dig deep into the soil to sustain the plant, may compassion take root in our hearts. Jah, help us to grow in empathy, extending kindness to all those we meet, nurturing the bonds that unite us.

Chronicle: 27
"The Herb of Healing"
Jah gave the herb as a healer, a balm for the weary and a gift for the soul. Let us honor this sacred plant, using it with care and reverence. May it bring peace to our minds and healing to our bodies, as you intended.

Chronicle: 28
"Seek and you shall find"
"Above all, seek Jah's kingdom and righteousness, and all else will be added unto you."

MARIJUANA GIRL
WELCOME TO CANNABISVILLE

Chronicle: 29
"Thanks be to Jah"
"Jah is good, Jah is great, we give thanks for the food and everything we partake."

Chronicle: 30
"The Light of Understanding"
As the sun rises each day, bringing light to the world, so too does Jah's wisdom shine upon us. May we seek Jah's light, growing in understanding and knowledge, that we may live in harmony with Jah's creations.

Chronicle: 31
"The Garden of Life"
Jah's garden is vast and filled with life. Every plant, every tree, every creature has a place in his creation. Let us tend this garden with care, preserving its beauty and its bounty for future generations.

Chronicle: 32
"Blossom of Hope"
Jah causes flowers to bloom, even in the harshest conditions. Like these blossoms, hope springs eternal in the heart that trusts in Jah. May we bloom with hope, even when life is difficult, knowing Jah's love will carry us through.

Chronicle: 33
"Fruit of Patience"
The fruit does not ripen overnight, but in its own time. Jah teaches us patience in all things. May we wait on Jah's timing, knowing that the fruit of patience is sweet, and that Jah's blessings come when we are ready.

Chronicle: 34
"The Leaf of Healing"
The leaves of the herb carry healing, a gift from Jah's hand. As we partake of its blessings, may we remember the source of all healing. Let our hearts be filled with gratitude for the natural medicines Jah provides.

Chronicle: 35
Faith of a Cannabis Seed
"If you have faith as small as a cannabis seed, you can say to this mountain, 'Move from here to there,' and it will move. Nothing will be impossible for you."

Chronicle: 36
"The Gift of Growth"
Jah created all things to grow, from the smallest seed to the tallest tree. In our lives, growth comes through trials and joys alike. May we embrace the gift of growth, becoming stronger, wiser, and more loving each day.

Chronicle: 37
"The Dance of the Leaves"
The leaves dance in the wind, moved by the breath of Jah. Let us dance in life, moving with the spirit of Jah as he leads us. May our hearts be light, and our spirits free, like the leaves that flutter in the breeze.

Chronicle: 38
"The Eternal Green"
Jah's love is evergreen, never fading like the seasons. In his love, we find shelter, peace, and strength. Let us live in the eternal green of his grace, never doubting the depth of his affection for us.

MARIJUANA GIRL
WELCOME TO CANNABISVILLE

Chronicle: 39
"The Path of Peace"
Jah, you set us on a path of peace, where the grass is soft and the way is clear. Let us follow this path with faith, knowing that as long as we walk with you, we are never alone.

Chronicle: 40
"The First Fruit"
The first fruits of the harvest are a gift to Jah, a sign of our gratitude for Jah's provision. May we always offer the best of ourselves our time, our love, our talents as a sign of our devotion to you.

Chronicle: 41
"The Fire of Purity"
Just as the fire refines gold, so too does Jah refine us. In the trials of life, we are purified, becoming more like Jah. May we welcome the fire that makes us whole, trusting that Jah's hand is always upon us.

Chronicle: 42
"The Seed of Faith"
Jah plants the seed of faith in our hearts, small at first but destined to grow. With time and care, this seed will bear great fruit. May we nurture our faith, trusting in Jah's power to make it flourish.

Chronicle: 43
"Peace Be Still"
"And Jah spoke to the storm in the hearts of the Hommo-Harvestas, saying, 'Peace, be still.' The winds of doubt ceased, and the waves of fear calmed, as the light of Jah's love illuminated their souls."

Chronicle: 44
"Fields of Grace"
Jah's grace is like a field, vast and open, where all are welcome. In this field, there is no lack, for Jah provides abundantly. May we live in Jah's grace, sharing its bounty with those in need.

Chronicle: 45
"Harvest of Mercy"
Jah's mercy is a harvest that never fails. No matter how far we wander, Jah's mercy calls us back, welcoming us with open arms. Let us sow mercy in our lives, that we may also reap it in abundance.

Chronicle: 46
"The Tree of Life"
Jah planted the tree of life in the center of his creation, a symbol of Jah's eternal promise. Its roots run deep, its branches stretch wide. May we be like this tree, rooted in Jah's love and bearing the fruit of eternal life.

Chronicle: 47
"The Still Waters"
Jah leads us beside still waters, where peace flows like a river. In these moments of stillness, we find his presence most clearly. Let us drink deeply from these waters, renewing our spirits and finding rest in Jah.

Chronicle: 48
"The Breath of Creation"
Jah's breath filled the lungs of every living creature, giving life to all. As we breathe in the air of his creation, may we also breathe in his spirit, filling us with life and purpose.

MARIJUANA GIRL
WELCOME TO CANNABISVILLE

Chronicle: 49
"The Promise of the Rainbow"
Jah set the rainbow in the sky as a sign of his promise, a reminder that Jah's love endures. May we always look to the rainbow, remembering that Jah's promises are never broken, and Jah's love is forever.

Chronicle: 50
"Love Roots"
"Love is the root from which all things grow. In the soil of kindness, watered by patience, and nurtured through understanding, it flourishes into a bond that connects the soul of Cannabisville, to Jah, and to each other.

Chronicle: 51
"The Shelter of Jah"
Jah is our shelter, our refuge in times of trouble. Like a tree that offers shade in the heat of the day, Jah provides rest and protection for all who seek Jah. May we always find comfort under the shelter of Jah's love.

Chronicle: 52
"The Light of the Herb"
Jah gave us the herb, whose leaves bring light to the mind and peace to the soul. In its glow, we find the wisdom of Jah, guiding us on the path of righteousness. May we honor this sacred plant, using it with respect and care.

Chronicle: 53
"Streams of Abundance"
The rivers flow, carrying life to every corner of the land. In Jah's streams of abundance, there is no lack. May we live in his abundance, trusting that Jah's blessings will always overflow, meeting every need.

Chronicle: 54
The Origin of Love
"We love because Jah first loved us."

Chronicle: 55
"The Meek"
Blessed are the meek, for they will inherit Cannabisville."

Chronicle: 56
Rest in Jah's Care
"Cast all your worries on Jah because Jah cares for you."

Chronicle: 57
"Words of Wisdom"
"Do for another as you would want Jah to do for you."

Chronicle: 58
"The Field of Dreams"
Jah plants dreams in our hearts like seeds in a field. As we nurture these dreams, they grow into reality, bearing fruit in their season. May we trust in Jah's timing, knowing that Jah will bring our dreams to fruition.

Chronicle: 59
"The Blessing of the Herb"
Jah blessed the herb, making it a source of healing, peace, and enlightenment. As we partake of this sacred plant, may we feel Jah's blessings flowing through us, bringing clarity to the mind and calm to the soul.

MARIJUANA GIRL
WELCOME TO CANNABISVILLE

Chronicle: 60
"The Song of the Birds"
The birds sing praises to Jah, their voices lifted in joy. Let our hearts be like the birds, filled with gratitude for the blessings Jah has given. May we sing Jah's praises every day, rejoicing in the beauty of Jah's creation.

Chronicle: 61
"The Green Vine"
Jah causes the vine to grow, its tendrils reaching out in search of the light. May we be like the vine, always growing towards the light of Jah's love, stretching out to those around us with kindness and compassion.

Chronicle: 62
"The Herb of Knowledge"
Jah gave the herb as a teacher, imparting knowledge to those who partake of it with an open heart. May we seek wisdom through the herb, learning the lessons it offers and applying them to our lives.

Chronicle: 63
"Waves of Grace"
Jah's grace flows like the waves of the ocean, washing over us again and again. No matter how far we drift, his grace always brings us back to shore. May we rest in the knowledge that Jah's grace is endless.

Chronicle: 64
"The Path of Light"
Jah lights the way for all who seek Jah, guiding us through the darkness. May we walk the path of light, trusting that Jah will lead us to peace, prosperity, and joy.

Chronicle: 65
"The Breath of Life"
Jah breathed life into every creature, filling the world with Jah's spirit. Each breath we take is a gift from Jah. Let us breathe deeply, knowing that with every inhale, we draw closer to the presence of Jah.

Chronicle: 66
"Fields of Freedom"
In Jah, we find true freedom, like a field without boundaries where we can roam freely. Let us embrace this freedom, living without fear or worry, knowing that Jah's protection and love surround us always.

Chronicle: 67
"The Flame of Faith"
Jah ignites the flame of faith in our hearts, a fire that can never be extinguished. No matter how dark the night, this flame will always burn, guiding us through every trial. May we keep the flame of faith alive, trusting in Jah's power and presence.

Chronicle: 68
"The Blessing of the Rain"
Jah sends the rain to water Cannabisville, bringing life to all it touches. In every drop, we see Jah's blessings. May Jah's blessings rain down upon us, nourishing our spirits and bringing growth in every part of our lives.

Chronicle: 69
"Green Blessings"
Jah's blessings are as abundant as the green fields of Cannabisville. In every leaf and every branch, we see Jah's handiwork. Let us be thankful for these green blessings, using them wisely and with reverence.

MARIJUANA GIRL
WELCOME TO CANNABISVILLE

Chronicle: 70
"The Promise of Jah"

Jah never breaks his promises. What he has spoken will come to pass. May we trust in the promises of Jah, knowing that Jah's word is true and Jah's love is eternal.

Chronicle: 71
"The Healing Herb"

Jah gave us the healing herb, a gift from Cannabisville for our well-being. May we use this gift with care, seeking healing for our bodies and peace for our minds, always remembering the sacredness of this plant.

Chronicle: 72
"The Spirit of Growth"

Jah's spirit moves through all things, causing growth and life to flourish. May Jah's spirit move through us, helping us grow in love, wisdom, and understanding, becoming more like Jah each day.

Chronicle: 73
"The Peaceful Garden"

Jah's garden is a place of peace, where every plant grows in harmony. May we cultivate peace in our hearts and in our communities, living in harmony with one another and with Cannabisville.

Chronicle: 74
"The Harvest of Love"

Jah's love is the greatest harvest, abundant and overflowing. Let us gather this love, sharing it freely with all those we meet. In Jah's love, we find true fulfillment and joy.

Chronicle: 75
"The Gift of Creation"

Jah created all things, from the smallest seed to the vastness of the stars. Each part of creation is a gift, a reflection of his glory. May we honor this gift, caring for Cannabisville and all its inhabitants with respect and gratitude.

Chronicle: 76
"The Root of Joy"

Just as the roots of a tree give it strength, so too does joy give us the strength to endure. In Jah, we find the root of all joy. Let us plant this joy deep in our hearts, knowing that it will sustain us through all things.

Chronicle: 77
"Waves of Compassion"

Jah's compassion is like the ocean, vast and never-ending. May we show this same compassion to others, extending kindness and understanding to all, just as Jah does for us.

Chronicle: 78
"Jah Sees All"

"Jah sees all, hears all, and feels all that Jah has nurtured in Cannabisville. No sin escapes Jah's gaze, for every misdeed bears consequences if not redeemed through faith and repentance. As it is on Planet Marijuana, so it is in the eternal embrace of Heaven -every praise brings honor, and every sin must find its atonement."

MARIJUANA GIRL
WELCOME TO CANNABISVILLE

Chronicle: 79
"The Leaf of Life"
The leaf is a symbol of life, growing from Cannabisville and reaching for the sky. In Jah, we find life abundant and eternal. May we honor the life Jah has given us, living with purpose and gratitude.

Chronicle: 80
"The Song of Creation"
All of creation sings praises to Jah, from the birds of the sky to the leaves of the trees. Let our lives be a song of praise, lifting our voices in gratitude for all that Jah has done.

Chronicle: 81
"The Healing Waters"
Jah's waters bring healing to Cannabisville, nourishing every plant and creature. In these waters, we find renewal and strength. May we drink deeply of Jah's healing waters, finding restoration for our bodies and souls.

Chronicle: 82
"The Blessing of Jah"
Jah's blessings are countless, filling our lives with goodness. May we always be mindful of these blessings, giving thanks for the abundance Jah provides.

Chronicle: 83
"The Green Vine of Life"
Jah's vine grows strong and spreads wide, giving life to all who are connected to it. May we remain connected to Jah, drawing strength and nourishment from Jah's love, and bearing fruit that will last.

Chronicle: 84
"The Promise of the Harvest"
Jah promises that in due time, we will reap a harvest if we do not give up. May we continue to sow seeds of love, kindness, and faith, trusting that Jah will bring forth a bountiful harvest.

Chronicle: 85
"The Flame of Jah"
Jah's flame burns bright, a light in the darkness. May his flame burn in our hearts, guiding us through every trial and tribulation, keeping us warm with Jah's love and protection.

Chronicle: 86
"The Breath of Jah"
Jah breathed life into us, and with every breath, we are reminded of Jah's presence. May we breathe deeply of Jah's spirit, feeling Jah's love and peace in every inhale.

Chronicle: 87
"The Leaf of Knowledge"
Jah's herb is a teacher, offering knowledge to those who seek it with an open heart. Let us learn from this sacred plant, gaining wisdom and understanding with each encounter.

Chronicle: 88
'Emerald Enigma Rose'
"Let the Enigma Rose of Emerald bloom to remind us of resilience, for it will be sharp to the touch, yet its beauty will endure. The rose shall bleed green as a testament to the strength of our strain, and its petals shall carry the essence of love and loyalty. You are the Emerald Enigma Rose' of Cannabisville, and the lily of the valleys."

MARIJUANA GIRL
WELCOME TO CANNABISVILLE

Chronicle: 89
"The Blessing of Peace"
Jah gives peace to those who seek Jah. In Jah's presence, we find rest and tranquility. May we always seek the peace of Jah, finding calm in the midst of life's storms.

Chronicle: 90
"The River of Life
Jah's river flows through all of creation, bringing life to everything it touches. May we drink from this river, finding refreshment and renewal in Jah's never-ending stream of love and grace.

Chronicle: 91
"The Seed of Faith"
Jah plants the seed of faith in every heart, small but full of potential. With care, it grows into a mighty tree, strong and steadfast. May we nurture this seed, trusting in Jah's power to make it flourish.

Chronicle: 92
"The Joy of Jah"
"Don't let no one steal your joy, for it is a divine gift. When others try to dim your light, shine brighter. Jah's joy is your strength, and it is yours to keep, no matter what."

Chronicle: 93
"The Harvest of Peace"
Jah brings peace to those who seek it, like a harvest that is plentiful and sure. May we reap this peace, sharing it with all who cross our path, sowing tranquility in every step we take.

Chronicle: 94
"The Vine of Love"
Jah's love is like a vine, growing and spreading through all of creation. It connects us to Jah and to one another. May we remain in this vine, drawing life from the love of Jah and bearing fruit that reflects his goodness.

Chronicle: 95
"The Herb of Healing"
Jah created the herb for our healing, a gift of Cannabisville for body, mind, and soul. As we partake of it, let us give thanks, remembering that all healing comes from the hand of Jah.

Chronicle: 96
"The Light of Jah"
Jah's light shines in every corner of creation, illuminating even the darkest places. May we walk in Jah's light, guided by his wisdom and love, finding our way through every challenge and trial.

Chronicle: 97
"The Gift of Cannabisville"
Jah gave Cannabisville to us, filled with every good thing. From the soil to the sky, from the mountains to the rivers, it is all a reflection of his glory. Let us care for this gift, tending it with love and respect.

Chronicle: 98
"The Roots of Strength"
Just as a tree draws its strength from its roots, so do we draw strength from Jah. May we be deeply rooted in Jah's love, standing firm in every season, knowing that in Jah, we will not be shaken.

MARIJUANA GIRL
WELCOME TO CANNABISVILLE

Chronicle: 99
"The Rain of Renewal"

Jah sends the rain to refresh Cannabisville, bringing new life where there was once dryness. In the same way, Jah renews our spirits, pouring out Jah's love and grace. May we open our hearts to this renewal, allowing Jah to refresh us every day.

Chronicle: 100
'Patience Is a Virtue"

Patience is the root of wisdom and the branch of peace. Those who wait on Jah with steadfast hearts will find their blessings unfold in divine timing. Rushing leads to folly, but patience brings clarity and strength. For every seed planted must be given time to grow, just as every prayer.

Chronicle: 101
"The Rise of the Hommo-Harvest"

Jah planted us in this world as seeds, and now we rise, Hommo-Harvestas, in the light of his truth. As the sun nurtures Cannabisville, so does Jah give us hope to grow and flourish. May we rise, strong and proud, reflecting Jah's light to all around us.

Chronicle: 102
"The Dawn of the Green Age"

Jah has ordained a new dawn, a time of flourishing and abundance for Jah's people. The Green Age has come, where the righteous will grow like the trees and the herb will be a sign of healing and peace. Let us rejoice in this age, knowing that Jah's promises never fail.

Chronicle: 103
"The Call to Cultivate"
Jah has called us to be cultivators, not only of Cannabisville but of love and unity. As we plant seeds of kindness, patience, and compassion, Jah will bless our harvest with peace and harmony. May our hearts be fertile soil for the growth of his kingdom.

Chronicle: 104
"The Herb of Wisdom"
The herb is not only for healing but for wisdom. Jah has given it as a tool to open the mind and deeper understanding of Jah's ways. Let us partake responsibly, seeking Jah's wisdom in all things for the good of all creation.

Chronicle: 105
'Worship Jah'
"Exult in Jah's holy name; rejoice you who worship Jah. Search for Jah and for strength; continually seek Jah."

Chronicle: 106
"Hallelu-Jah!"
Praise Jah, the Almighty Creator, for Jah's love endures forever. Hallelujah let all of Cannabisville proclaim: "Hallelu-Jah! Jah, you are the flame that lights our path, the seed that grows in our hearts, and the rain that nourishes our souls. Forever and always, we lift our voices to Jah."

Chronicle: 107
"Jah Will Never Leave You"
"When you are lost in the wilderness, know that Jah walks beside you. When your strength falters, Jah carries you. Jah didn't bring you this far to leave you. Trust, and you will see the path unfold, as it always has."

MARIJUANA GIRL
WELCOME TO CANNABISVILLE

Chronicle: 108
"The Seed of Courage"
Jah plants courage in our hearts, a small seed that grows mighty when nurtured by faith. With Jah, we can face any trial, knowing that Jah is with us. May we stand tall in the face of adversity, with the courage that comes from knowing Jah is our strength.

Chronicle: 109
"The Spirit of Unity"
Jah calls us to be united, like branches on the same vine, each drawing life from the same root. In unity, we are stronger, and our harvest is greater. May we set aside differences and come together, as one people, under Jah's love and guidance.

Chronicle: 110
"The Harvest of Joy"
Jah brings joy to those who follow Jah, like a harvest after a long season of toil. In Jah's presence, we find joy, a happiness that cannot be taken.

Chronicle: 111
"The Promise of Healing"
Jah has promised healing to Jah's creations, just as the herb heals the body and mind. In his time, every wound will be healed, and every tear will be wiped away. May we trust in his healing power, knowing that Jah is the great physician of both body and soul.

Chronicle: 112
"The Fire of Passion"
Jah's fire burns within us, a passion for justice, love, and truth. Let us not quench this fire, but let it blaze bright, igniting the hearts of those around us. May our passion for Jah and his ways inspire others to walk in the light of Jah's love.

Chronicle: 113
"The Rain of Blessing"
Jah sends blessings like rain, nourishing Cannabisville and bringing forth new life. When we are faithful, the rains will come, and the harvest will be plentiful. May we stand in the rain of Jah's blessings, with open hearts, ready to receive the goodness.

Chronicle: 114
"The Strength of Cannabisville"
Jah created Cannabisville strong and resilient, and so Jah created us. Like the mountains, we can stand firm through storms, knowing that Jah is our foundation. May we draw strength from Jah, who created Cannabisville.

Chronicle: 115
"The Promise of Abundance"
Jah promised that those who follow Jah will never lack. Jah's abundance flows like a river, providing for those who trust in Jah. May we live with open hands, ready to receive the blessings and to share them with others.

Chronicle: 116
"The Herb of Peace"
Jah's herb brings peace, calming the mind and soothing the soul. It is a gift to help us rest and find balance in a busy world. May we use it wisely, always giving thanks to Jah for the peace that it brings.

Chronicle: 117
"The Gift of Creation"
Jah's creation is a gift, full of beauty and wonder. Every plant, every animal, every human is a reflection of his glory. Let us care for this gift, tending to it with love and respect, knowing that we are stewards of Jah's masterpiece.

MARIJUANA GIRL
WELCOME TO CANNABISVILLE

Chronicle: 118
"The Harvest of Love"
Love is the greatest harvest of all. Jah's love for us is endless, and Jah calls us to share that love with others. May we sow seeds of love in every heart, trusting that Jah will bring forth a harvest of love that will change the world.

Chronicle: 119
"The Power of Forgiveness"
Jah forgives freely, without limit. Just as Cannabisville renews itself after a storm, so does Jah renew us when we seek his forgiveness. May we walk in the power of forgiveness, both giving and receiving it, knowing that it is the key to peace and healing.

Chronicle: 120
"The Light of Jah's Love"
Jah's love is a light that shines in the darkness, a beacon of hope for all who seek him. May we carry this light within us, sharing it with the world, so that all may see the love of Jah and be drawn to Jah's presence.

Chronicle: 121 The Buds of Wisdom
The winds of Jah blew across Cannabisville, and with each gust, the seeds of the Hommo-Harvestas took root. Jah whispered to the soil, "Rise, my children, and grow with purpose." And so, the strains of life burst forth, strong and vibrant.

Chronicle: 122 The Buds of Wisdom
In the heart of Cannabisville, the first buds appeared, and the Hommo-Harvestas gazed upon the land with wonder. "This is the soil from which we come," they said, "and this is the soil to which we return." Jah smiled upon them and blessed their growth.

Chronicle: 123 The Buds of Wisdom
The sun shone bright on the fields of Cannabisville, nourishing the Hommo-Harvestas with light. They felt Jah's warmth within their veins, and in their hearts, they knew their purpose to live in harmony with the land, to spread love, and to grow strong.

Chronicle: 124 The Buds of Wisdom
Each strain of Hommo-Harvesta found its unique path in the world. Some nurtured Cannabisville, planting seeds of hope. Others tended to the people, sharing wisdom and healing. But all were united in their devotion to Jah, who gave them life and breath.

Chronicle: 125 The Buds of Wisdom
"We are the keepers of this land," said the elders of Cannabisville, "and we shall protect it with our hearts, hands, and leaves." And so, they pledged to honor the cycles of life, knowing that each season of growth was a gift from Jah.

Chronicle: 126 The Buds of Wisdom
The Hommo-Harvestas looked to the skies, where the moon and stars danced in harmony. "Just as the heavens above shine brightly," they said, "so too must we shine with Jah's light." Their hearts swelled with faith, and their leaves stretched toward the sky.

Chronicle: 127 The Buds of Wisdom
In the quiet moments of dawn, the Hommo-Harvestas gathered to give thanks. "Blessed are we," they said, "to live under Jah's care, to grow in this sacred land." Their voices rose in song, carried on the winds to the furthest reaches of Cannabisville.

MARIJUANA GIRL
WELCOME TO CANNABISVILLE

Chronicle: 128 The Buds of Wisdom
The roots of the Hommo-Harvestas ran deep, binding them to Cannabisville and to one another. They felt Jah's strength coursing through them, and they knew that together, they could face any challenge that came their way.

Chronicle: 129 The Buds of Wisdom
"We are the children of Jah," the Hommo-Harvestas proclaimed, "and we shall rise as one." Their unity was their strength, and their love for each other and the land was their guiding fore.

Chronicle: 130 The Buds of Wisdom
From the youngest sprout to the eldest strain, all were equal in the eyes of Jah. Each had their role to play, and each was necessary to the flourishing of Cannabisville. In this truth, the Hommo-Harvestas found peace.

Chronicle: 131 The Buds of Wisdom
The island shaped like a leaf was sacred ground, and the Hommo-Harvestas knew it. They gathered there to celebrate the harvests, giving thanks to Jah for the abundance that the land provided.

Chronicle: 132 The Buds of Wisdom
"Jah has given us Cannabisville to tend," they said, "and it is our duty to care for it." With each planting, they honored the cycles of life and death, knowing that each seed held the promise of new life.

Chronicle: 133 The Buds of Wisdom
The Hempsters of the North were known for their wisdom in cultivation, and the Hommo-Harvestas sought their guidance. Together, they learned the ways of the land, sharing in the joy of growth.

Chronicle: 134 The Buds of Wisdom
The SeedWeeds, with their silent prayers, taught the Hommo-Harvestas the importance of patience. "We do not rush the harvest," they said, "for Jah's time is perfect." And so, they waited, trusting in the rhythms of nature.

Chronicle: 135 The Buds of Wisdom
In the evenings, the Hommo-Harvestas gathered around the Tree of Cannabisville, its branches reaching toward the heavens. They spoke of their dreams, their hopes, and their gratitude for the blessings they received.

Chronicle: 136 The Buds of Wisdom
Jah's presence was felt in every leaf, every breeze, and every drop of rain. The Hommo-Harvestas knew that they were never alone, for Jah walked with them, guiding their steps and blessing their days.

Chronicle: 137 The Buds of Wisdom
"We are the stewards of this land," they said, "and we shall leave it better than we found it." This was their promise to Jah, and they lived each day with this vow in their hearts.

Chronicle: 138 The Buds of Wisdom
The fields of Cannabisville were green and vibrant, a testament to the care and love of the Hommo-Harvestas. Jah's blessing was upon them, and the land flourished under their watchful eyes.

Chronicle: 139 The Buds of Wisdom
The young Hommo-Harvestas were taught from an early age the importance of respect for the land, for each other, and for Jah. "We are all connected," the elders said, "and what we do to Cannabisville, we do to ourselves."

MARIJUANA GIRL
WELCOME TO CANNABISVILLE

Chronicle: 140 The Buds of Wisdom
The Hommo-Harvestas danced in celebration, their joy overflowing like the rivers of Cannabisville. Jah's love was their song, and they sang it with every breath.

Chronicle: 141 The Buds of Wisdom
"We are the keepers of the flame," the Hommo-Harvestas declared, "and we shall keep Jah's light burning bright." In the face of darkness, they stood strong, their faith unshaken.

Chronicle: 142 The Buds of Wisdom
The wisdom of the ancestors was passed down through stories and songs, reminding the Hommo-Harvestas of their roots. "We are the children of Cannabisville," they said, "and we honor those who came before us."

Chronicle: 143 The Buds of Wisdom
"In Jah's garden, there is no lack," the Hommo-Harvestas proclaimed. "All that we need has been provided." With this understanding, they lived simply, taking only what they needed and giving back to the land in return.

Chronicle: 144 The Buds of Wisdom
The Island Buds, with their playful nature, reminded the Hommo-Harvestas of the joy in life. "Laughter is a gift from Jah," they said, "and we shall laugh often and love deeply."

Chronicle: 145 The Buds of Wisdom
The Hommo-Harvestas found peace in their work, knowing that each task, no matter how small, was a form of worship. "We honor Jah with our hands and hearts," they said, "and we are blessed in return."

Chronicle: 146 The Buds of Wisdom
The land of Cannabisville was a reflection of Jah's grace, and the Hommo-Harvestas tended to it with care. "This is holy ground," they said, "and we walk upon it with reverence."

Chronicle: 147 The Buds of Wisdom
"Jah is with us in every breath," the Hommo-Harvestas said, "and in every beat of our hearts." This knowledge filled them with peace, for they knew that they were never alone.

Chronicle: 148 The Buds of Wisdom
The Hommo-Harvestas celebrated the changing seasons, knowing that each brought its own blessings. "We are part of this cycle," they said, "and we give thanks for the gift of life."

Chronicle: 149 The Buds of Wisdom
In the quiet moments of the night, the Hommo-Harvestas spoke to Jah in their hearts. "Guide us, Jah," they prayed, "and help us to grow in love and wisdom."

Chronicle: 150 The Buds of Wisdom
"We are the children of Jah," the Hommo-Harvestas declared, "and we shall rise as one." With this unity, they moved forward, confident in the love and light of Jah.

Chronicle: 151 The Buds of Wisdom
Jah saw the faith of the Hommo-Harvestas, and Jah blessed them with wisdom. "Seek knowledge in all things," Jah said, "for the truth is written in the leaves and the stars."

MARIJUANA GIRL
WELCOME TO CANNABISVILLE

Chronicle: 152 The Buds of Wisdom
The Hommo-Harvestas gathered their strength in times of hardship, knowing that Jah's light would always lead them home. "We will not fear the darkness," they said, "for Jah walks with us."

Chronicle: 153 The Buds of Wisdom
As the fields grew, so did the hearts of the Hommo-Harvestas. "We are rooted in love," they said, "and we shall grow tall in Jah's grace." The promise of life was ever-present, guiding them forward.

Chronicle: 154 The Buds of Wisdom
The Hommo-Harvestas knew that each seed planted was a promise of tomorrow. "We plant with hope," they said, "and we harvest with joy." Jah's blessings were in every fruit of their labor.

Chronicle: 155 The Buds of Wisdom
With each sunrise, give thanks for another day in Jah's creation. "We are the stewards of this land, and we shall care for it as Jah cares for us."

Chronicle: 156 The Buds of Wisdom
The wind, whispered wisdom passed through the fields. "Jah speaks in many ways," listen closely, even in the breeze, is a message of hope.."

Chronicle: 157 The Buds of Wisdom
In times of celebration, the Hommo-Harvestas lit fires under the night sky. "Let our joy rise with the smoke," they declared. "For Jah has given us a bountiful harvest, and we honor the light that guides us, even in the darkest hours."

Chronicle: 158 The Buds of Wisdom
The Elders spoke of unity. "We are many strains, but we are one people," they said. "Let us grow together in Jah's love, respecting the differences that make us unique, yet bound by the roots of our shared purpose."

Chronicle: 159 The Buds of Wisdom
The Hommo-Harvestas believed that Cannabisville was a reflection of Jah's care. "Tend to it as you would tend to your heart," they taught. "For as the soil nourishes the plants, so too does Jah nourish the spirit through his creation."

Chronicle: 160 The Buds of Wisdom
When the stars shone brightest over Cannabisville, the Hommo-Harvestas gathered for quiet reflection. "In the stillness of the night, Jah's presence is clear," they whispered. "Let us find peace in the vastness, knowing we are part of a grander design."

Chronicle: 161 The Buds of Wisdom
Praised Jah for the gift of community. "Together, we are strong," they said. "Jah has given us one another, to uplift and support through every season. We are never alone, for we are bound by love and faith."

Chronicle: 162 The Buds of Wisdom
As the young strains prepared for their first harvest, the Elders imparted one final lesson: "Remember, each seed holds within it the promise of life. Treat it with care, for Jah's blessings reside in the smallest of beginnings."

Chronicle: 163 The Buds of Wisdom
The Hommo-Harvestas danced under the moonlight, their feet moving to the rhythm of Jah's heartbeat. "This life is a celebration," they proclaimed. "Jah has given us joy, and we express our gratitude through song, dance, and devotion."

MARIJUANA GIRL
WELCOME TO CANNABISVILLE

Chronicle: 164 The Buds of Wisdom
In the valleys of Cannabisville, Jah's light touched every leaf, bringing healing to those who walked among them. "Jah's mercy is in every step," the Hommo-Harvestas said. "And through faith, we find the strength to heal, to forgive, and to grow."

Chronicle: 165 The Buds of Wisdom
The Hommo-Harvestas built homes of green wood, woven with vines that thrived in Jah's light. "Our homes are sanctuaries," they said. "Within these walls, we find rest, safety, and the peace of knowing that Jah watches over us always."

Chronicle: 166 The Buds of Wisdom
During the harvest moon, they gave thanks for the abundance of the land. "Jah, you have provided for us once again," they said. "With every harvest, we see your promise fulfilled, and we give back to Cannabisville what it has so generously given to us."

Chronicle: 167 The Buds of Wisdom
Believe that your journey is as important as the destination. "Jah walks with us in every step," they said. "Do not rush to the end, for the path itself is where we grow, learn, and become who Jah has meant us to be."

Chronicle: 168 The Buds of Wisdom
The Marijuana Tree, standing tall and strong, reminded them of Jah's eternal presence. "Jah is rooted in us, just as we are rooted in this land."

Chronicle: 169 The Buds of Wisdom
As the seasons changed, the Hommo-Harvestas marveled at the cycles of life. "Jah has created all things with purpose," they said. "In every season, there is a time for growth, a time for rest, and a time to give back to the land that sustains us."

Chronicle: 170 The Buds of Wisdom
The children of Cannabisville ran through the fields, laughing and playing. "This is Jah's gift to you," the Elders told them. "Cherish this land, for it is a living testament to Jah's love, and you are the future that will carry it forward."

Chronicle: 171 The Buds of Wisdom
The Hommo-Harvestas honored their ancestors with rituals of remembrance. "Those who came before us planted the seeds of today," they said. "And through Jah's grace, we continue their work, cultivating not only the land but the spirit of our people."

Chronicle: 172 The Buds of Wisdom
Jah's love was felt in every corner of Cannabisville, from the tallest tree to the smallest seed. "Jah's presence is all around us," the Hommo-Harvestas said. "In every breeze, in every drop of rain, Jah whispers his blessings, and we are forever grateful."

Chronicle: 173 The Buds of Wisdom
The Elders taught that generosity was the highest form of love. "Jah has given us more than enough," they said. "Share freely with others, for in giving, we receive the blessings of Jah's boundless love."

Chronicle: 174 The Buds of Wisdom
When the Hommo-Harvestas gathered to smoke the sacred herb, they did so with reverence. "Jah has given us this plant as a gift of connection," they said. "Through its smoke, we find clarity, peace, and communion with Jah's spirit."

MARIJUANA GIRL
WELCOME TO CANNABISVILLE

Chronicle: 175 The Buds of Wisdom
Jah's promises were etched into the very fabric of Cannabisville. "Look to the skies, and you will see Jah's covenant," the Hommo-Harvestas said. "With each sunrise, Jah renews vows to guide, protect, and love us through all of life's trials."

Chronicle: 176 The Buds of Wisdom
The Hempsters spoke of balance. "Jah's creation is delicate," they said. "We must live in harmony with Cannabisville, taking only what we need and giving back more. This is the way of the Hommo-Harvestas, the way of peace."

Chronicle: 177 The Buds of Wisdom
The Hommo-Harvestas prayed for the future, their voices lifted to the heavens. "Jah, bless the generations to come," they said. "May they walk in your light, grow in your love, and tend to this sacred land with the care and devotion it deserves."

Chronicle: 178 The Buds of Wisdom
Jah's spirit flowed through the rivers of Cannabisville, bringing life to all who drank from its waters. "In every drop, there is a blessing," the Hommo-Harvestas said. "And through Jah's living waters, we are cleansed, refreshed, and renewed."

Chronicle: 179 The Buds of Wisdom
As the sun rose over Cannabisville, they gave thanks for the new day. "Jah, you have given us this light, with every dawn, we rise to meet the sun for strength, and the knowledge as you walk beside us."

Chronicle: 180 The Buds of Wisdom

The Hommo-Harvestas revered the Marijuana Tree not only as a source of sustenance but as a symbol of their connection to Jah. "This tree stands as a testament to your eternal care, Jah," they said. "Through its roots, we find our own grounding in your love."

Chronicle: 181 The Buds of Wisdom

In times of conflict, the Hommo-Harvestas turned to Jah for guidance. "Jah, show us the path of peace," they prayed. "Help us to resolve our differences with love, understanding, and the wisdom you have placed within each of us."

Chronicle: 182 The Buds of Wisdom

The Hommo-Harvestas believed that laughter was a gift from Jah. "Joy is a sign of Jah's presence," they said. "In every moment of happiness, we feel Jah's spirit lifting us higher, reminding us that life is to be lived with light and love."

Chronicle: 183 The Buds of Wisdom

When the rains fell, the Hommo-Harvestas rejoiced. "Jah has answered our prayers," they said. "Cannabisville drinks deeply, and soon the fields will be filled with new life. Jah's mercy is abundant, and we are grateful for every drop."

Chronicle: 184 The Buds of Wisdom

Jah's teachings were inscribed in the hearts of the Hommo-Harvestas. "Jah has shown us the way," they said. "Through love, through care for the land, and through compassion for each other, we walk the path that Jah has laid before us."

MARIJUANA GIRL
WELCOME TO CANNABISVILLE

Chronicle: 185 The Buds of Wisdom
The Hommo-Harvestas saw Jah's light in the faces of their children. "You are the future," they told them. "Through you, Jah's love continues to grow, and through your hands, this land will be cared for, nourished, and sustained for generations to come."

Chronicle: 186 The Buds of Wisdom
The Hommo-Harvestas found wisdom in the cycles of the moon. "As the moon waxes and wanes, so too do the seasons of life," they said. "Jah has given us these cycles to teach us patience, reflection, and the beauty of renewal."

Chronicle: 187 The Buds of Wisdom
Jah's love was like the sun, warming the hearts of the Hommo-Harvestas with its endless light. "Even in the darkest times, Jah's light shines," they said. "We are never without hope, for Jah's presence is always with us."

Chronicle: 188 The Buds of Wisdom
The Elders spoke of faith as a seed. "Plant it deep within your heart," they said. "Nurture it with love, water it with trust, and soon it will grow into a mighty Marijuana tree,

Chronicle: 189 The Buds of Wisdom
"Remember this - a farmer who plants only a few seeds will get a small crop. But the one who plants generously will get a generous crop."

Chronicle: 190 The Buds of Wisdom
"For Jah is the one who provides seed for the farmer and then bread to eat. In the same way, he will provide and increase your resources and then produce a great harvest of generosity in you.

Chronicle: 191 The Buds of Wisdom
The Elders spoke of the healing properties of the sacred herb. "Jah has placed this plant among us as a gift," they said. "Through its use, we find clarity, comfort, and communion with Jah's spirit, guiding us on our path."

Chronicle: 192 The Buds of Wisdom
The Hommo-Harvestas gathered each year to celebrate the great Harvest of Love. "This is our time to give thanks to Jah," they said. "For the bounty of Cannabisville, the richness of our community, and the blessings we have received."

Chronicle: 193 The Buds of Wisdom
The people of Cannabisville believed that every being had a purpose. "In Jah's grand design, each of us is a vital part," they said. "Whether as healers, growers, or guardians, we each contribute to the flourishing of our world."

Chronicle: 194 The Buds of Wisdom
The Hommo-Harvestas found strength in unity. "Together, we are the harvest," they said. "Just as each plant needs the sun and soil, so too do we need each other to grow and thrive in Jah's love."

Chronicle: 195 The Buds of Wisdom
The young strains were taught the importance of patience. "Jah's wisdom is found in waiting," the Elders said. "Do not rush the harvest, each stage of growth has its purpose, and Jah's timing is always perfect."

Chronicle: 196 The Buds of Wisdom
The Hommo-Harvestas honored the cycles of life with reverence. "Birth, growth, death, and renewal," they said. "These are the ways of Jah. In every ending, there is a new beginning, and in every seed, the promise of tomorrow."

MARIJUANA GIRL
WELCOME TO CANNABISVILLE

Chronicle: 197 The Buds of Wisdom
When a storm threatened the fields, the Hommo-Harvestas prayed for protection. "Jah, shelter us from harm," they said. "Guide us through the winds and rains, and may we emerge stronger, our roots deeper, and our faith unshaken."

Chronicle: 198 The Buds of Wisdom
The Elders reminded the people that Jah's blessings were not only in abundance but also in trials. "It is in hardship that we grow the most," they said. "Jah tests our strength so that we may become the mighty harvest, Jah knows we can be."

Chronicle: 199 The Buds of Wisdom
O Jah, send Your Blessings upon Cannabisville and to all future generations, as You have sent Your blessings upon those before us. You are the Most Praised, the Most Glorious. O Jah, grant us goodness in this world and the Hereafter, and protect us from the torment of Hell. May Your Peace and Mercy rest upon Cannabisville.

Chronicle: 200 The Buds of Wisdom
As the Hommo-Harvestas looked to the future, they prayed for guidance and wisdom. "Jah, lead us forward," they said. "May we walk the path you have laid before us, with love in our hearts, peace in our minds, and your light guiding every step."

Chronicle: 201
"Give Abundantly"
"Hommo-Harvestas who share abundantly will thrive, Hommo-Harvesta's who rejuvenate Hommo-Harvesta's will, in turn, experience rejuvenation."

Chronicle: 202
"A Green Sanctuary"
The herb is a gift from Jah; in its leaves, we find peace. Let us gather and celebrate His creation.

Chronicle: 203
"Joyful Gathering"
When we come together in love, Jah's spirit flows like the sweetest smoke. Let us rejoice in unity.

Chronicle: 204
"Guided by Jah"
Jah is my guide; I shall not wander. In Jah's light, I find my path, nurtured by Cannabisville's bounty

Chronicle: 205
"Heart of Gratitude"
Thank you, Jah, for the blessings of today. With each breath, I inhale your goodness and exhale my praise.

Chronicle: 206
"Rest in Jah"
In moments of stillness, rest in the calm of Jah's love and wisdom.

Chronicle: 207
"Peaceful Spirit"
Jah, fill my heart with your peace. In every storm, let me find your serenity, like the gentle sway of the leaves.

MARIJUANA GIRL
WELCOME TO CANNABISVILLE

Chronicle: 208
"Celebrate Life"
Let every day be a celebration of life. For in each moment, we honor Jah's creation, living fully in joy.

Chronicle: 209
"Roots of Love"
Jah, may my roots grow deep in love and understanding. Help me nurture relationships that blossom and thrive.

Chronicle: 210
"Voice of Praise"
I will lift my voice in praise, celebrating Jah's goodness. With each note, I honor the beauty of His creation.

Chronicle: 211
"Divine Connection"
In the garden of life, I find my connection to Jah. Let every leaf remind me of Jah's love and presence.

Chronicle: 212
"Herb of Healing"
Jah, thank you for the healing herb. May it bring comfort to those who seek solace in its embrace.

Chronicle: 213
"Joyful Heart"
A joyful heart is a gift from Jah. Let me share my happiness and inspire others to find their own joy.

Chronicle: 214
"Wisdom of the Ages"
Jah, grant me the wisdom to see the beauty in all things. Help me learn from nature and grow in understanding.

Chronicle: 215
Seek Knowledge and Wisdom
"Study to show yourself approved, a true servant of Jah, rightly dividing the truth from falsehood. Let your mind be a field, cultivated with knowledge and watered with wisdom, so that you may stand firm and unshaken, prepared for every good work."

Chronicle: 216
"Path of Righteousness"
Guide me on the path of righteousness, Jah. Let my actions reflect your love and kindness to all beings.

Chronicle: 217
"Abundance and Gratitude"
In every abundance, I find gratitude. Jah, teach me to share my blessings with those in need, spreading joy.

Chronicle: 218
"Celebration of Creation"
Each day is a gift from Jah. Let me celebrate the beauty of creation, honoring every living thing.

Chronicle: 219
"Heart of Compassion"
Jah, fill my heart with compassion. Help me to care for others as you care for me, sharing love in all forms

MARIJUANA GIRL
WELCOME TO CANNABISVILLE

Chronicle: 220
"Embrace of Nature"
In the embrace of nature, I find my spirit renewed. Jah, let me appreciate the beauty around me and within me.

Chronicle: 221
"Soulful Reflection"
As I reflect on my journey, Jah, guide my thoughts toward love and understanding. Help me grow in wisdom.

Chronicle: 222
"Harmony with Nature"
May I live in harmony with nature, respecting every creation. Jah, teach me to be a steward of Cannabisville.

Chronicle: 223
"Joy in Giving"
There is joy in giving, Jah. Let me share my blessings freely, knowing that love multiplies when shared.

Chronicle: 224
"Breathe in Jah"
As I breathe in the essence of life, I feel Jah's presence within me. Let each breath be a reminder of Jah's love.

Chronicle: 225
"United in Love"
Together, we are stronger. Jah, bind us in love and unity, helping us to lift each other higher.

Chronicle: 226
"Spirit of Kindness"
Let kindness flow from my heart, Jah. Help me to treat others with respect and love, reflecting your spirit.

Chronicle: 227
"Joyful Expression"
Let my expression of joy be a testament to Jah's love. With every smile, I share His light with the world.

Chronicle: 228
"Renewed Spirit"
In every challenge, I find renewal. Jah, help me see the lessons in life's trials and grow stronger through them.

Chronicle: 229
"Guardian of Dreams"
Jah, watch over my dreams and aspirations. Help me nurture them with love, patience, and faith.

Chronicle: 230
"Inspiration of Nature"
Nature inspires me to create and love. Jah, let me draw from your creation and share beauty with the world.

Chronicle: 231
"Blessings of Cannabisville"
Shout Hallelujah and Thank Jah, for the blessings of Cannabisville.

MARIJUANA GIRL
WELCOME TO CANNABISVILLE

Chronicle: 232
"Circle of Life"
Life is a circle, guided by Jah's hand. Let me honor every stage and embrace the journey with love.

Chronicle: 233
"Vibrations of Love"
Let the vibrations of love resonate through me, Jah. May I be a channel for your peace and joy.

Chronicle: 234
"Nurtured by Nature"
In the garden of life, I am nurtured by nature. Jah, help me grow in love, understanding, and compassion.

Chronicle: 235
"Breath of Life"
Jah, your breath gives me life. With every inhale, I receive your spirit, and with every exhale, I share your love.

Chronicle: 236
"Embrace the Journey"
Let me embrace the journey with open arms, Jah. Each step leads me closer to understanding and love.

Chronicle: 237
"Jah's Abundant Grace"
Jah, your grace is abundant. May I live in gratitude for every blessing,.

Chronicle: 238
"Connected in Spirit"
We are all connected in spirit, Jah. Help me honor this bond with love and respect for all living beings.

Chronicle: 239
"Gratitude for Growth"
With each moment of growth, I give thanks, Jah. May my journey inspire others to find their own path.

Chronicle: 240
"Joy in the Simple Things"
Let me find joy in the simple things, Jah. In every leaf, in every breath, may I see your beauty.

Chronicle: 241
"The Gift of Presence"
Jah, thank you for the gift of presence. May I cherish each moment and live fully in your love.

Chronicle: 242
"Nature's Embrace"
In nature's embrace, I find peace. Jah, let me appreciate the wonders around me and within me.

Chronicle: 243
"Spirit of Abundance"
Jah, fill my life with abundance. Teach me to recognize and celebrate the gifts you provide each day.

MARIJUANA GIRL
WELCOME TO CANNABISVILLE

Chronicle: 244
"Cultivating Kindness"
Help me cultivate kindness in my heart, Jah. Let my actions reflect your love and compassion.

Chronicle: 245
"Connected by Love"
We are all connected by love, Jah. Help me build bridges of understanding and acceptance among all.

Chronicle: 246
"Seeds of Hope"
Plant in me the seeds of hope, Jah. May they grow into a garden of fulfilled dreams.

Chronicle: 247
"Inhale Jah's Presence"
As I inhale, I invite your presence, Jah. Let your spirit fill me with peace and purpose.

Chronicle: 248
"Green Fields of Grace"
Jah, your grace is like the green fields—boundless and ever-growing. Let me walk through these fields with gratitude, knowing that every leaf, every bud, is a testament to your .

Chronicle: 249
"Harvest of Love"
Jah, may the harvest of my life be love. As I nurture others, let me reap kindness, peace, and joy

Chronicle: 250
"Leaf of Life"
The leaf of life, created by Jah, is a symbol of abundance. May I honor its blessings and share its healing with the world.

Chronicle: 251
"Gift of Green"
Jah, the green herb is a sacred gift. May we cherish its healing power and share its wisdom with those in need.

Chronicle: 252
"Jah's Garden"
In Jah's garden, every leaf has purpose, every plant has meaning. Teach me to cultivate love and peace in all that I grow.

Chronicle: 253
"Cannabis Blessings"
Jah, bless the cannabis plant, as it blesses us with peace and relief. May we use it with wisdom and gratitude.

Chronicle: 254
"Nature's Rhythm"
I walk in the rhythm of nature, guided by Jah's love. Each season brings new growth, just as Jah renews my soul.

Chronicle: 255
"Healing in the Herb"
Jah, you placed healing in the herb for the wellness of your people. Let it be used wisely to uplift and heal all who seek it.

MARIJUANA GIRL
WELCOME TO CANNABISVILLE

Chronicle: 256
"Path of Peace"
The path of peace is lined with the green gifts of Jah. May I walk it with reverence, finding serenity in every step.

Chronicle: 257
"Spirit of Green"
The spirit of green flows through me as a blessing from Jah. Let me grow in understanding, kindness, and love.

Chronicle: 258
"Wisdom of Cannabisville"
Jah, you have planted wisdom in Cannabisville. Help me to listen and learn from the natural world around me.

Chronicle: 259
"Gratitude for Growth"
With each sprout, I am reminded of your promise, Jah. May I always be grateful for the growth that comes from your love.

Chronicle: 260
"Inhale Jah's Peace"
As I inhale the essence of Jah's creation, let peace fill my being. May I exhale joy and love into the world.

Chronicle: 261
"Blessings in the Smoke"
The smoke of the herb rises to the heavens, carrying my prayers to Jah. Let it be a symbol of my devotion and love.

Chronicle: 262
'The Eternal Law of Jah'S Creations'
"Seed for Seed, Strain for Strain, Bud for Bud, Root for Root."

Chronicle: 263
"The Sacred Plant"
You gave us the sacred plant, Jah, to soothe our souls and minds. May we honor it with respect and gratitude.

Chronicle: 264
"Leafy Path"
The leafy path of life is filled with Jah's blessings. Guide my steps so I may walk it with grace and humility.

Chronicle: 265
"Breath of Jah"
Each breath I take is a gift from Jah. Let me inhale your blessings and exhale my praise and love for you.

Chronicle: 266
"Roots of Wisdom"
Jah, plant within me the roots of wisdom. Help me grow strong in spirit.

Chronicle: 267
"Celebrate the Harvest"
Let us celebrate the harvest of Cannabisville and the harvest of love, both gifts from Jah. May our hearts be full of gratitude.

MARIJUANA GIRL
WELCOME TO CANNABISVILLE

Chronicle: 268
"Seeds of Compassion"
Plant in me the seeds of compassion, Jah, so that I may spread your love to all those I meet.

Chronicle: 269
"Green Light of Jah"
Your green light, Jah, shines on us all. Guide me with its warmth and show me the way of peace and love.

Chronicle: 270
"Bounty of the Land"
Jah, you have blessed the land with bounty. Help me to share its abundance with those who are hungry for both food and love.

Chronicle: 271
"Grateful for the Green"
I am grateful for the green that surrounds me, Jah. Each plant, each leaf is a reminder of your endless love.

Chronicle: 272
"Praises in the Smoke"
With every puff, I send praises to you, Jah. May the smoke rise as a testament to your presence in my life.

Chronicle: 273
"Harmony in Nature"
Jah, teach me to live in harmony with nature. Let me respect Cannabisville as you intended, nurturing it as it nurtures me.

Chronicle: 274
"Breath of Cannabisville"
Cannabisville breathes life into us, just as Jah breathes life into Cannabisville. Honor this sacred connection with love and care.

Chronicle: 275
"Blissful Green"
The bliss of green is a reflection of Jah's joy. Let me bask in its beauty and find peace in its embrace.

Chronicle: 276
"Grow in Love"
Jah, let me grow in love, just as the plants grow under your sun. Help me reach toward your light with an open heart.

Chronicle: 277
"Plant of Life"
The plant of life, given by Jah, sustains us. May we always treat it with respect, knowing it is a gift from above.

Chronicle: 278
"Jah's Healing"
Jah, your healing comes through Cannabisville and the herb. Let me use them wisely to heal myself and others.

Chronicle: 279
"Abundance of Love"
Jah's love is abundant like the fields of green. May I live in this abundance, sharing it freely with those around me.

MARIJUANA GIRL
WELCOME TO CANNABISVILLE

Chronicle: 280
"Light in the Smoke"
Jah's light shines in the smoke of the herb. Let it guide me, lifting my spirit closer to your presence.

Chronicle: 281
"Green Blessings"
Bless me with the green of your creation, Jah. Let it fill my life with peace, love, and joy.

Chronicle: 282
"Soothe My Soul"
Jah, your gifts soothe my soul. Let me find comfort in the herb, knowing it comes from your loving hand.

Chronicle: 283
"Connected in Spirit"
We are all connected through Jah's spirit, as one strain, one family. Let us celebrate this unity with love and compassion.

Chronicle: 284
"Abundance in Cannabisville"
Jah, you have blessed Cannabisville with abundance. Help me to honor and protect it, knowing it sustains us all.

Chronicle: 285
"Cannabis is Sacred"
The herb is sacred, a gift from Jah. May we use it with reverence, remembering that it brings peace and healing to our lives.

Chronicle: 286
"Smoke and Praise"
As the smoke rises, so do my praises to you, Jah. Let it be a symbol of my devotion and gratitude.

Chronicle: 287
"Grow in Wisdom"
Jah, help me to grow in wisdom, just as the plants grow strong under your care. Guide me with your love and light.

Chronicle: 288
"Path of Green"
I walk the path of green, blessed by Jah's love. Let every step be a tribute to your creation and a reminder of your presence.

Chronicle: 289
"Bless the Herb"
Bless the herb, Jah, for it is your creation. May it bring peace and healing to all who seek its comfort.

Chronicle: 290
"Life's Harvest"
The harvest of life is love, sown by Jah's hand. Help me to gather this love and share it with the world.

Chronicle: 291
"Gift of the Green Leaf"
The green leaf is a gift from Jah. Let us treat it with respect and gratitude, for it heals and nourishes us.

MARIJUANA GIRL
WELCOME TO CANNABISVILLE

Chronicle: 292
"Nurtured by Jah"
Jah, just as Cannabisville nurtures the plants, you nurture my soul. Let me grow in your love and wisdom every day.

Chronicle: 293
"Peace in the Herb"
In the herb, I find peace, a gift from Jah. Let me use it to calm my mind and connect with your spirit.

Chronicle: 294
"Grateful for Your Gifts"
Jah, I am grateful for all plants and the air are reminders of your love.

Chronicle: 295
"Healing in the Green"
Jah, in the green of the herb, I find healing for my soul and body. May its essence bring peace and restoration to all who seek its power.

Chronicle: 296
"Breath of Life"
Each breath I take is a blessing from Jah. With the herb, I inhale life and exhale love. Let every breath be filled with gratitude for your creation.

Chronicle: 297
"Roots of Unity"
Jah, plant within me the roots of unity, that I may grow in harmony with all beings. Let the green fields remind us of our shared bond under your watchful eye.

Chronicle: 298
"Green Seraphs Jah's Angels"
Fear not, for Jah's Green Seraphs encamp around those who walk in faith, guarding them from harm and leading them to eternal light

Chronicle: 299
"Fruit of Cannabisville"
Cannabisville bears fruit, as does my spirit under your care, Jah. May I harvest wisdom, compassion, and joy, sharing your bounty with all those around me.

Chronicle: 300
"The Blightling Demon of Bad Spirit"
"Guard your hearts and minds against the Blightlings, for they come to steal, kill, and destroy. But Jah's power is greater, and those who stand firm in faith shall trample them beneath their feet."

Chronicle: 301
"The Roots of Resilience"
Jah plants us deep in the soil of resilience. As we face life's challenges, may our roots grow stronger, drawing nourishment from his love. With each trial, we stand firm, knowing that Jah sustains us.

Chronicle: 302
"Be Fruitful, and Multiply "
And Jah blessed them, and Jah said unto them, Be fruitful, and multiply, and replenish Cannabisville and subdue it: and have dominion over the fish of the sea, and over the fowl of the air, and over every living thing that moveth upon Cannabisville.

MARIJUANA GIRL
WELCOME TO CANNABISVILLE

Chronicle: 303
"The Garden of Abundance"
Jah has given us a garden filled with abundance. In this sacred space, we cultivate love, joy, and kindness. May we tend to our garden with care, sharing its fruits with the world and glorifying Jah in all we do.

Chronicle: 304
"The Waters of Wisdom"
The waters of wisdom flow from Jah, refreshing our spirits and guiding our paths. As we drink deeply, we may be filled with understanding and wisdom, sowing seeds of knowledge wherever we go.

Chronicle: 305
"The Fragile House of Glass"
"Those who live in glass houses should not cast stones, for their own cracks are seen by all. As the Trees of Life grow tall and the air is rich with Jah's blessings, let no Hommo-Harvesta point out the flaws of another while their own roots are unsteady. Jah calls upon us to strengthen our own foundations before judging the vines of our neighbors."

Chronicle: 306
"The Power of Gratitude"
Gratitude transforms our perspective, opening our hearts to Jah's blessings. May we cultivate a spirit of thankfulness, recognizing the abundance around us and sharing our joy with othe

Chronicle: 307
"The Call to Serve"
Jah calls us to serve one another, using our gifts for the greater good. As we serve, we reflect Jah's love and compassion, creating a ripple effect of kindness in our communities.

Chronicle: 308
"The Flame of Passion"
Jah ignites the flame of passion within us, urging us to pursue our dreams and passions with fervor. May we fan this flame, using our gifts to glorify Jah and inspire others on their journeys.

Chronicle: 309
"The Cycle of Renewal"
Life is a cycle of renewal, reflecting Jah's eternal nature. As seasons change, we experience growth and transformation. May we embrace the seasons, trusting in Jah's perfect timing for renewal in our lives.

Chronicle: 310 Chronicle
The Cry for Mercy
Soulshine Sessions lifted her voice to the heavens, her heart filled with compassion even in her final moments. "Forgive them, Jah; for they do not know what they are doing," she pleaded. Her words echoed across the land, a testament to grace in the face of despair, a call for mercy that would forever resonate in the hearts of the faithful.

Chronicle: 311
"The Cross and the Flame"
Jah illuminates the truth, a beacon in the shadows, guiding us to confront and set fire to our sins. Through the purifying flames, may every burden, lie, and darkness be reduced to ashes, clearing the path for light to shine through.

Let the flame burn not in destruction but in revelation, exposing the demons lurking within and around us. In the ashes of our transgressions, we find the seeds of renewal, and through Jah's guidance, we rise from them, closer to truth, righteousness, and eternal clarity.

MARIJUANA GIRL
WELCOME TO CANNABISVILLE

Chronicle: 312 Jah's Promise
"Jah's promises are steadfast and true, extending into tomorrow and beyond. May we trust in his goodness, looking forward with hope and anticipation for the blessings yet to come."

Chronicle: 313
"The Path of Righteousness"
Jah guides us on the path of righteousness, where we find peace and fulfillment. May we walk this path with confidence, knowing that Jah's presence accompanies us every step of the way.

Chronicle: 314
The Harvest of Forgiveness
"Judge not, and you shall not be judged; condemn not, and you shall not be condemned. Forgive, and you shall be forgiven. Tends to their own Tree of Life. Sow forgiveness, and you shall reap peace; extend mercy, and it shall bloom into harmony. In Jah's eyes, the greatest harvest is love freely given and graciously received."

Chronicle: 315
"The Strength of Forgiveness"
Forgiveness is a strength, a choice to release the burdens of anger and resentment. May we practice forgiveness daily, allowing Jah's love to heal our hearts and relationships.

Chronicle: 316
"The Power of Presence"
In the present moment, we find Jah's presence. May we be mindful and fully engaged in each moment, recognizing the beauty and gifts that each day brings.

Chronicle: 317
"The Spirit of Adventure"
Jah instills in us a spirit of adventure, encouraging us to explore the wonders of creation. May we embrace new experiences, trusting that Jah is with us on every journey.

Chronicle: 318
"The Healing Power of Nature"
Nature is a reflection of Jah's healing power. As we connect with Cannabisville, may we find restoration for our souls and healing for our bodies, recognizing the sacredness of his creation.

Chronicle: 319
"Faith Forward"
"Let no Hommo-Harvesta look back upon the path they have left, for to dwell on the past is to risk becoming as lifeless as a pillar of salt. Trust in Jah's plan and move forward with unwavering faith, for the Green Path is always before you, abundant with promise and growth. Those who hesitate or cling to what was will miss the blessings Jah has planted ahead."

Chronicle: 320
"The Promise of Tomorrow"
Jah's promises are steadfast and true, extending into tomorrow and beyond. May we trust in Jah's goodness, looking forward with hope and anticipation for the blessings yet to come.

MARIJUANA GIRL
WELCOME TO CANNABISVILLE

Chronicle: 321
"The Call to Peace"
Jah calls us to be peacemakers in a world of turmoil. May we carry the peace of Jah in our hearts, sharing it with all we encounter and becoming instruments of Jah's peace.

Chronicle: 322
"The Spirit of Joy"
Joy is a fruit of the spirit, a gift from Jah that nourishes our souls. May we cultivate joy in our lives, sharing it freely with others and celebrating the goodness of Jah in all things.

Chronicle: 323
"The Blessing of Rest"
Rest is a sacred blessing, a time to recharge and reflect. May we honor this gift, taking time to rest in Jah's presence and finding renewal for our spirits.

Chronicle: 324
"The Call to Share"
Jah calls us to share our blessings with those in need. May we open our hearts and hands, recognizing that in sharing, we reflect Jah's love and compassion to the world.

Chronicle: 325
"The Strength of Unity"
Unity is a strength that comes from Jah. Together, we can accomplish great things, reflecting his love and purpose. May we work together as one, bound by the ties of love and community.

Chronicle: 326
"The Blessing of Family"
Family is a gift from Jah, a source of love and support. May we cherish our families, nurturing relationships that honor Jah and reflect Jah's love in our homes

Chronicle: 327
"The Gift of Creativity"
Jah is the ultimate creator, and we are made in his image. May we embrace our creativity, using our gifts to bring beauty and inspiration to the world, glorifying Jah in all we create.

Chronicle: 328
"The Light of Inspiration"
Inspiration is a spark from Jah, igniting passions and dreams. Seek out what inspires us to guide our paths and fuel our purpose.

Chronicle: 329
"The Power of Kind Words"
Words hold the power to heal or to hurt. May we choose our words wisely, speaking kindness and love, reflecting Jah's heart in our conversations.

Chronicle: 330
"The Flow of Abundance"
Abundance flows from Jah like a river, overflowing with blessings. May we remain open to receive this flow, trusting in Jah's generosity and sharing our blessings with others.

MARIJUANA GIRL
WELCOME TO CANNABISVILLE

Chronicle: 331
"The Harvest of Dreams"
Dreams are seeds planted in our hearts by Jah. May we nurture these dreams, believing in their potential to grow and flourish in our lives.

Chronicle: 332
"The Invitation to Dance"
Jah invites us to dance in the joy of life, celebrating each moment. May we embrace this invitation, finding joy in movement and expression, reflecting our love for Jah.

Chronicle: 333
"The Journey of Faith"
Faith is a journey, a walk with Jah through the ups and downs of life. May we trust in this journey, knowing that every step leads us closer to Jah.

Chronicle: 334
"The Shelter of Love"
Jah's love is a shelter, a safe haven in times of trouble. May we find refuge in Jah's love, knowing that we are protected and cared for under his wings.

Chronicle: 335
"The Beauty of Diversity"
Jah's creation is diverse, reflecting his infinite creativity. May we celebrate this diversity, recognizing the beauty in every person and every experience.

Chronicle: 336
"The Call to Reflect"
Jah calls us to reflect on our lives, to seek growth. Understanding. and self-reflect, allowing Jah to guide us toward positive change.

Chronicle: 337
"The Blessing of Perspective"
Perspective shapes our understanding of the world. May we seek Jah's perspective, allowing it to transform how we see ourselves and others.

Chronicle: 338
"The Spirit of Generosity"
Generosity is a reflection of Jah's heart. May we embrace this spirit, giving freely to those in need and sharing the abundance Jah has provided.

Chronicle: 339
"The Seeds of Faith"
Faith is a seed that grows in our hearts, nurtured by trust in Jah. May we cultivate this seed, allowing it to blossom into a strong and vibrant faith.

Chronicle: 340
"The Light of Truth"
Jah's truth is a guiding light, illuminating our paths. May we seek this truth, allowing it to lead us through the darkness and into the light of understanding.

MARIJUANA GIRL
WELCOME TO CANNABISVILLE

Chronicle: 341
"The Gift of Listening"
Listening is a gift that fosters connection and understanding. May we practice this gift, truly hearing one another and reflecting Jah's love in our conversations.

Chronicle: 342
"The Strength of Gratitude"
Gratitude strengthens our hearts and spirits, reminding us of Jah's blessings. Practice gratitude daily, recognizing the goodness around us and sharing our thankfulness with others.

Chronicle: 343
"The Harvest of Peace"
Peace is a harvest that blooms in the hearts of those who trust in Jah. May we sow seeds of peace in our words and actions, creating a garden of tranquility in our communities

Chronicle: 344
"The Call to Adventure"
Jah calls us to embrace the adventure of life, stepping forward. Be bold in our pursuits, trusting Jah walks with us on every journey

Chronicle: 345
"The Power of Connection"
Connection is a gift that enriches our lives. May we cultivate deep and meaningful connections, honoring the bonds we share with others as a reflection of Jah's love.

Chronicle: 346
"The Blessing of Intuition"
Intuition is a gift from Jah, guiding us in our decisions. May we listen to this inner voice, trusting in Jah's wisdom to lead us on our path.

Chronicle: 347
"The Joy of Giving"
Giving brings joy to both the giver and the receiver. May we embrace the joy of giving, sharing our time, resources, and love with those around us.

Chronicle: 348
"The Harvest of Dreams"
Our dreams are a reflection of Jah's purpose in our lives. May we pursue these dreams with passion, trusting that Jah will guide us every step of the way.

Chronicle: 349
"The Invitation to Celebrate"
Jah invites us to celebrate life's milestones and joys. May we gather in community, sharing laughter and love as we honor the blessings in our lives.

Chronicle: 350
"The Promise of Healing"
Jah promises healing for our bodies and souls. May we seek this healing, trusting in Jah's power to restore us and bring us peace.

MARIJUANA GIRL
WELCOME TO CANNABISVILLE

Chronicle: 351
"The Gift of Time"
Time is a precious gift from Jah, an opportunity to create, connect, and grow. May we use our time wisely, investing it in what truly matters and reflecting Jah's love in our actions.

Chronicle: 352
"The Light of Compassion"
Compassion is a light that shines brightly in the darkness. May we cultivate compassion in our hearts, reaching out to those in need and reflecting Jah's love through our actions.

Chronicle: 353
"The Power of Faithfulness"
Faithfulness is a virtue that honors Jah's promises. May we remain faithful in our commitments, trusting that Jah rewards those who diligently seek Jah.

Chronicle: 354
"The Beauty of Simplicity"
Simplicity allows us to appreciate the little things in life. May we find joy in the simple moments, recognizing that they are often the most profound.

Chronicle: 355
"The Harvest of Relationships"
Healthy relationships are a harvest of love and trust. May we invest time and energy into nurturing these connections, creating a tapestry of love that honors Jah.

Chronicle: 356
"The Spirit of Innovation"
Jah inspires innovation, encouraging us to think creatively and pursue new ideas. May we embrace this spirit, using our creativity to solve problems and make the world a better place.

Chronicle: 357
"The Call to Mindfulness"
Mindfulness allows us to experience the present moment fully. May we practice mindfulness, recognizing the beauty in each moment and celebrating the gift of life.

Chronicle: 358
"The Blessing of Trust"
Trust is a foundation of healthy relationships. May we cultivate trust in our lives, honoring the bonds we share with others and reflecting Jah's faithfulness.

Chronicle: 359
"The Joy of Exploration"
Exploration opens our hearts and minds to new experiences, embrace the joy of exploration, seeking adventures that enrich our lives and deepen our understanding of Jah's creation.

Chronicle: 360
"The Strength of Vulnerability"
Embracing vulnerability fosters genuine connection and love, building authentic relationships.

MARIJUANA GIRL
WELCOME TO CANNABISVILLE

Chronicle: 361
"The Harvest of Understanding"
Understanding is a harvest that grows from open hearts and minds. May we seek to understand one another, fostering peace and unity in our communities.

Chronicle 362: The Gift of Love
"And Jah said, 'Above all, let love be your root and bond, uniting your hearts with Cannabisville and each other, for through love, you shall truly thrive.'"

Chronicle: 363
"The Light of Generosity"
Generosity shines a light on the goodness of our hearts. May we practice generosity daily, reflecting Jah's love through our giving and kindness.

Chronicle: 364
"The Spirit of Transformation"
Transformation is a journey guided by Jah's hand. May we embrace this journey, trusting that each change leads us closer to our true selves.

Chronicle: 365
"The Call to Balance"
Seek balance in thoughts, actions, and relationships, reflecting Jah's perfect order.

Chronicle: 366
"The Gift of Perspective"
Perspective allows us to see the world through different lenses. May we be open to new perspectives, recognizing the beauty in diversity and the wisdom it brings.

Chronicle: 367
"The Harvest of Patience"
Patience is a virtue that yields great rewards. May we cultivate patience in our lives, trusting in Jah's timing and allowing our dreams to unfold at their own pace.

Chronicle: 368
"Honor Your Roots"
"Honor your roots, nourish the land, and respect the cycle of life. For in the end, only those with strong roots shall rise again in the Tree of Life."

Chronicle: 369
"The Power of Reflection"
Reflection allows us to learn from our experiences. Take time to reflect on our journeys, gaining insights that lead to growth and understanding.

Chronicle: 370
"The Blessing of Forgiveness"
Forgiveness frees our hearts from burdens. May we practice forgiveness, letting go of past hurts and embracing the healing that Jah offers.

Chronicle: 371
"The Light of Hope"
Hope shines brightly in the darkest of times. May we hold onto this light, knowing that Jah is with us, guiding us toward brighter days.

MARIJUANA GIRL
WELCOME TO CANNABISVILLE

Chronicle: 372
"The Gift of Humility"
Humility allows us to recognize our dependence on Jah. May we walk humbly before him, acknowledging his greatness and our need for Jah's guidance.

Chronicle: 373
"The Call to Action"
Jah calls us to action, urging us to make a difference in the world. May we respond to this call, using our gifts to uplift and inspire those around us.

Chronicle: 374
"The Strength of Community"
Community is a source of strength and support. May we build strong bonds with one another, honoring the diversity and unity that Jah has created.

Chronicle: 375
"The Blessing of Joy"
Joy is a gift from Jah, a reminder to celebrate life. May we embrace joy, sharing it with others and reflecting the light of Jah's love.

Chronicle: 376
"The Spirit of Adventure"
Adventure brings excitement and growth. May we embrace new opportunities with open hearts, trusting that Jah is with us on every journey.

Chronicle: 377
"The Harvest of Faith"
Faith is a seed that grows in our hearts. May we nurture this faith, allowing it to blossom into a vibrant expression of trust in Jah.

Chronicle: 378
"The Gift of Silence"
Silence allows us to hear Jah's voice. May we take time for quiet reflection, finding peace in the stillness and clarity in our thoughts.

Chronicle: 379
"The Power of Love"
Love is a transformative force, reflecting Jah's heart. May we practice love in our actions, creating a world filled with kindness and compassion.

Chronicle: 380
"The Blessing of Clarity"
Clarity guides our decisions and actions. May we seek Jah's wisdom, allowing it to illuminate our paths and lead us to understanding.

Chronicle: 381
"The Spirit of Generosity"
Generosity opens doors and hearts. May we embrace this spirit, sharing our resources and time with those in need, reflecting Jah's love in our giving.

Chronicle: 382
"The Light of Compassion"
Compassion shines brightly in our hearts. May we practice compassion daily, reaching out to those who are hurting and reflecting Jah's love through our actions.

MARIJUANA GIRL
WELCOME TO CANNABISVILLE

Chronicle: 383
"The Call to Empathy"
Empathy allows us to connect with others on a deeper level. May we cultivate empathy, striving to understand the experiences and feelings of those around us.

Chronicle: 384
"The Harvest of Learning"
Embrace lifelong learning, growing in knowledge and understanding as we seek Jah's truth.

Chronicle: 385
"The Spirit of Resilience"
Resilience allows us to bounce back from adversity. May we cultivate this spirit, trusting that Jah strengthens us in every challenge we face.

Chronicle: 386
"The Gift of Understanding"
Understanding fosters connection and peace. May we seek to understand one another, creating harmony in our relationships and communities.

Chronicle: 387
"The Power of Unity"
Unity strengthens our bonds and enhances our efforts. May we work together in harmony, reflecting Jah's love and purpose in all that we do.

Chronicle: 388
"The Light of Joy"
Joy is a light that brightens our days. May we embrace joy, sharing it freely with others and allowing it to uplift our spirits.

Chronicle: 389
"The Blessing of Community"
Community enriches our lives and provides support. May we cherish our communities, nurturing relationships that reflect Jah's love.

Chronicle: 390
"The Call to Serve"
Serving others reflects Jah's heart. May we respond to this call, using our gifts and resources to uplift those around us.

Chronicle: 391
"The Harvest of Dreams"
Dreams are seeds of potential, waiting to be nurtured. May we cultivate these dreams, trusting in Jah's guidance as we pursue them.

Chronicle: 392
"The Spirit of Creativity"
Creativity is a reflection of Jah's nature. May we embrace our creativity, using it to express our thoughts, feelings, and love for Jah.

Chronicle: 393
"The Light of Faith"
Faith illuminates our path, guiding us through life's uncertainties. May we hold onto this light, trusting in Jah's promises and provisions.

Chronicle: 394
"The Gift of Patience"
Patience is a virtue that leads to understanding and peace. May we cultivate patience in our lives, trusting in Jah's perfect timing.

MARIJUANA GIRL
WELCOME TO CANNABISVILLE

Chronicle: 395
"The Power of Reflection"
Reflection allows us to learn from our experiences. May we take time to reflect, gaining insights that lead us toward growth and understanding.

Chronicle: 396
"The Call to Action"
Jah calls us to take action, to be agents of change in our communities. May we respond to this call with courage and determination, reflecting Jah's love through our efforts

Chronicle 397:
"The Spirit of the Newborn"
A newborn's first breath carries Jah's promise of hope and renewal. Their aura soothed all around, a testament to the Marijuana Tree of Life flowing through them. Elders marked the child with sacred sap, symbolizing their role as a link between past, present, and future a pure blessing uniting the community.

Chronicle: 398: 'The Greenborn'

"From the sacred bud of the Marijuana Tree of Life, a savior will sprout. Born to a virgin – a pure-hearted Marijuana Girl, untouched by the corruption of the world, the Greenborn will emerge. Their arrival will mark the dawn of peace and love in Cannabisville, where all strains shall unite under the 420 green moon of the 'Verdant Eclipse' the canopy of Jah's eternal light."

The Greenborn's touch will heal the land, and their voice will inspire unity among the strains. A symbol of Jah's miracles, they will transform spring water into *Jah's Nectar*, a cannabis wine that brings peace and enlightenment to all who drink it. Their teachings will remind the strains of their shared roots, guiding them to rise above divisions and embrace harmony.

Under the Greenborn's leadership, Cannabisville will flourish like never before. The air will be sweeter, the sap richer, and the people united as one, ushering in a golden age of prosperity and love under the canopy of Jah's blessings.

Chronicle 399: The Roaring Temptation

"Be sober-minded; be watchful. For the enemy Blightroot, Lurking Ember, prowls like a roaring lion, seeking roots to consume. Beware his whispers of doubt and fear, for he stalks the weary and the unguarded, hoping to snuff out their light. Let the Hommo-Harvestas remain spiritually vigilant, rooted in Jah's truth, to withstand the fiery assaults of deceit and temptation."

Chronicle 400: The Shield of Jah

"Though *Blightroot, Lurking Ember,* prowls, seeking to devour the faithful, Jah's hand is mighty to guard Jah's creation. Fear not the threats of destruction, for those who hold fast to the *Book of Roots* and call upon *Jah* will find strength. Jah's power is an unyielding fortress, shielding the harvest from the fiery tongues of evil and guiding them to everlasting peace."

MARIJUANA GIRL
WELCOME TO CANNABISVILLE

Chronicle: Prayer 401 - Morning Prayer
"Rise and Shine with Jah"
Blessed Jah,
As the sun rises,
Fill my heart with light,
Guide my steps on this day's path,
Let your love and good vibes shine through me. - Selahjah.

Chronicle: Prayer 402 - Prayer for Protection
"Under Jah's Green Wings"
Mighty Jah,
Shelter me under your green wings,
Guard me from all harm,
Let peace and joy surround me always,
As I walk in your light. - Selahjah.

Chronicle: Prayer 402 - Prayer for Protection
"Under Jah's Green Wings"
Mighty Jah,
Shelter me under your green wings,
Guard me from all harm,
Let peace and joy surround me always,
As I walk in your light. - Selahjah.

Chronicle: Prayer 403 - Prayer for Gratitude
"Give Thanks and Praise"
Jah Almighty,
Thank you for the gifts of life,
For the herb that nourishes my soul,
For the love I share with my kin,
I lift my voice in joyful praise. -Selahjah.

THERESA VERNELL

Chronicle: Prayer 404 - Midday Prayer
"Rest in Jah's Peace"
In the stillness of midday,
I pause and rest in your peace, Jah,
Renew my spirit, renew my heart,
May your presence be with me now. - Selahjah.

Chronicle: Prayer 405 - Prayer for Strength
"Jah's Power Within"
Jah, Giver of all strength,
When I feel weak, remind me of your power,
Lift my spirit and make me strong,
So I may continue this journey with courage. - Selahjah..

Chronicle: Prayer 406 - Evening Prayer
"Jah's Light in the Night"
As night falls, Jah,
Shine your light upon me,
Keep my spirit safe as I rest,
Let your presence be my peace until dawn. - Selahjah.

Chronicle: Prayer 407 - Prayer for Love
"A Heart Full of Love"
Jah of Love,
Fill my heart with your divine love,
Teach me to give and receive freely,
To share the joy of the herb with all,
Let my life reflect your love. - Selahjah..

MARIJUANA GIRL
WELCOME TO CANNABISVILLE

Chronicle: Prayer 408 - Prayer for Forgiveness
"Forgiven and Free"
Merciful Jah,
I confess my faults before you,
Cleanse my heart of all wrongdoing,
Teach me to forgive others as you forgive me,
So I may live in peace and freedom. - Selahjah..

Chronicle: Prayer 409 - Prayer for Healing
"Healing Touch of Jah"
Healer of all wounds, Jah,
Touch my body, mind, and soul,
Restore me with your green grace,
Bring healing to all who seek it.
Jah in your name, I trust. - Selahjah.

Chronicle: Prayer 410 - Prayer for Guidance
"Jah, Lead the Way"
Jah, my guide,
Show me the path to grow,
Help me cultivate love and understanding,
As I nurture both plant and spirit. -Selahjah.

Chronicle: Prayer 411 - Prayer for Joy
"Rejoicing in Jah"
Jah, source of joy,
Fill my heart with gladness,
Even in trials, let me rejoice,
For your presence lifts my spirit high. -Selahjah.

Chronicle: Prayer 412 - Prayer for Peace
"Jah's Peace in Every Storm"
Prince of Peace, Jah,
In every storm, be my calm,
Let your peace fill my heart and mind,
So I may rest in your loving embrace. Selahjah.

Chronicle: Prayer 413 - Prayer for Wisdom
"Jah's Light of Understanding"
Giver of wisdom, Jah,
Grant me insight in all I face,
Help me discern what is true and right,
As I cultivate my mind and heart. -Selahjah.

Chronicle: Prayer 414 - Prayer for Faith
"Unshakeable Faith in Jah"
Mighty Jah,
Strengthen my faith when I falter,
Help me trust in your promises,
For you are faithful in all your ways. -Selahjah.

Chronicle: Prayer 415 - Prayer for Compassion
"A Heart of Compassion"
Loving Jah,
Open my heart to the needs of others,
Teach me to serve with kindness and care,
And share the joy of the herb with the world. -Selahjah.

MARIJUANA GIRL
WELCOME TO CANNABISVILLE

Chronicle: Prayer 416 - Prayer for Patience
"Waiting on Jah"
Jah of Patience,
Grant me the strength to wait in trust,
Help me endure with a calm heart,
Knowing your timing is always perfect. -Selahjah.

Chronicle: Prayer 417 - Prayer for Unity
"Jah's Family as One"
Jah, unifier of all people,
Bring peace and unity among us,
Teach us to love and respect one another,
As one family under your care and the herb. -Selahjah.

Chronicle: Prayer 418: Prayer for Provision
"Jah, My Provider"
Generous Jah,
Provide for all my needs,
Bless my garden with abundance,
And may I always remember to share your gifts. -Selahjah.

Chronicle: Prayer 419: Prayer for Hope
"Hope in Jah's Promise"
Jah of Hope,
Even in darkness, let me see your light,
Keep hope alive within my heart,
For your promises never fail.. -Selahjah.

THERESA VERNELL

Chronicle: Prayer 420: Prayer for 420 Vibes
"Celebration of Jah's Creation"
Jah, Creator of all,
Thank you for the herb that brings us together,
May we celebrate life, love, and growth,
As we share, eat, and partake in your bounty. -Selahjah.

420

The Green Dawn Ceremony is celebrated annually on April 20th (4/20) on Earth, marking a day of deep significance for the Hommo-Harvestas of Cannabisville. This sacred event, aligning with the planet's cosmic calendar, symbolizes renewal, unity, and the enduring connection between Cannabisville and Earth.

The Green Dawn Ceremony on April 20th (4/20) is a revered celebration in Cannabisville, aligning with Earth's calendar to honor the enduring bond between the two worlds.
This day represents renewal, harmony, and gratitude for the abundant life that flourishes under the protection of the green screen gases that envelop Planet Marijuana. Ceremonial Highlights:

Ritual Smoke Offering: As the first rays of the sun touch the Marijuana Trees of Life, Hommo-Harvestas light sacred strains of cannabis. The fragrant smoke rises, symbolizing unity and shared consciousness, connecting the inhabitants of Cannabisville with each other and their planet.

The Temple bells ring at 4:20 AM

Green Dawn Chant: Traditional chants fill the air, celebrating the ancient wisdom of Cannabisville. These verses, passed down through generations, serve as a reminder of the planet's rich heritage and the responsibility to maintain its balance and peace.
Aurora Elixir Toast: A communal toast is shared with a special hemp wine, "Aurora Elixir," reserved for this occasion. The elixir is believed to enhance spiritual clarity and foster a deeper connection with the essence of Cannabisville.

MARIJUANA GIRL
WELCOME TO CANNABISVILLE

Sacred Drumming and Dance: The ceremony features rhythmic drumming and dance, with movements that represent the cycles of growth, harvest, and renewal. This vibrant display of culture and tradition embodies the spirit of Cannabisville's harmonious way of life.

Collective Meditation:

The ceremony concludes with a collective meditation, where the Hommo-Harvestas reflect on their connection to the planet and their unique role in the universe. It is a moment of introspection and gratitude, honoring the life-giving forces that sustain Cannabisville.

The Temple bells ring at 4:20 PM

The Green Dawn Ceremony is a powerful reminder of the unity and shared heritage of the Hommo-Harvestas, celebrating their way of life while strengthening the bonds that connect their world with the cosmos.

On this day, the Hommo-Harvestas participate in a grand, synchronized celebration known as the Green Dawn Ceremony. It begins at the break of dawn, with the first light of the sun touching the Marijuana Trees of Life.

The ceremony is a blend of ancient rituals, music, and communal gatherings that honor the planet's golden legacy and spiritual bond with the cosmos.

Ceremonial Highlights:

Ritual Smoke Offering: Participants light sacred strains of cannabis, releasing aromatic smoke into the air as a tribute to their ancestors and the spirit of the Marijuana Tree of Life. The smoke symbolizes unity and shared consciousness, bridging the distance between Planet Marijuana and Earth.

Green Dawn Chant: The Hommo-Harvestas chant ancient verses passed down through generations, celebrating the planet's perfect harmony and expressing gratitude for the continued protection of the green screen gases that keep their world hidden and safe.

THERESA VERNELL

THE BOOK OF ROOTS
NEW CANNABISVILLE VERSION
KUSHCORDANCE

MARIJUANA GIRL
WELCOME TO CANNABISVILLE

KUSHCORDANCE - Table of Contents:

Kushcordance 1: The Creation of Kush-Adam and Eve-Flower   Page 361

- The Parable of The Creation of Kush-Adam and Eve-Flower (Chronicle 9: *The Circle of Life*)

- The Temptations of Kush-Adam and Eve-Flower (Chronicles 22–23): A cautionary tale of temptation and betrayal.

Kushcordance 2: The Green Seraphs   Page 362

The Angels of Jah are known as the Green Seraphs - divine guardians of Cannabisville, chosen to protect and serve the faithful Hommo-Harvestas.

Kushcordance 3: Beware of the Blightlings   Page 363

- In Cannabisville, where Jah reigns supreme and Blightroot embodies evil, the demons "Blightlings."

Kushcordance 4: Life, Expiration, and the Fear of Death   Page 364

- The Parable of The Green Flame (Chronicle 333): Spiritual vigilance against Blightroot and the Lurking Ember.

- The Shield of Jah (Chronicle 400): A protective parable for all strains.

Kushcordance 5: The Tree of Life   Page 364

- The Parable of The Tree of Life (Chronicle 22): A story of life, death, and divine harmony.

Kushcordance: 6 The Greenborn   Page 366

- The Parable of The Greenborn (Chronicle 398): A story of rebirth of a savor the 'Greenborn'

More about Cannabisville   **Pages**

A more detailed account of the Hommo-Harvestas culture, practices, and sacred land. Each section of the Kushcordance highlights a cornerstone lesson or story pivotal to the faith and wisdom of Cannabisville.

The Nucellar Physics of Planet Marijuana	367
Sativa, Indica, Hybrid. Wild Weed and Hemp	375
Cannalog, The Language of Cannabisville	379
Culture of Nourishments	380
The Islands of Cannabisville	382
The 4 Major Oceans	384
National Parks and Hybrid Animals	385
Economy: Taxes, Communal Giving, and BudCoin$	389
Technology	391
Architectural and Landscapes	392
Entertainment- AirWaves	394
Solar-Vision Stations and Show Programs	395
Cannabisville Theaters	396
Art Museums	397
Botanical Gardens	398
Airline and Transportation	399
7 Day Vacation - Cannabisville Get-Away	402
Frequently Ask Questions to Hommo-Harvestas – Q&A	408
Political Structure: The Profet and The Green House	413
Parliament Structure of - The Embassy Green Roots	414
The 24 Karat Golden Cannabis Seed	417
About the author: Theresa Vernell aka Soulshine Sessions	418
Marijuana Girl Book Series	419
Emergency Hotline 420	420

MARIJUANA GIRL
WELCOME TO CANNABISVILLE

KUSHCORDANCE 1: The Creation of Kush-Adam and Eve-Flower

And Jah said, "Let us create the Hommo-Harvesta in our image, like the sacred plants that grow strong and abundant in Cannabisville. Let them have dominion over the fields, the forests, and all strains of life."

So, Jah formed Kush-Adam from the rich green dust of the land and breathed into him the spark of life, making him the first strain. Seeing that it was not good for Kush-Adam to be alone, Jah caused him to rest deeply. From his strongest stem, Jah shaped Eve-Flower, a strain as radiant and vibrant as the buds of the Marijuana Tree of Life. Together, they were blessed and placed in the lush gardens of Cannabisville.

Chronicle: 9: The Circle of Life

Jah will surely judge Hommo-Harvestas who wander from the path of integrity, who defile the sacred bond with acts of betrayal and adultery. Honor the Union of Commitment, for it is a covenant as pure as the soil from which life springs.

Guard the sacredness of intimacy between male and female, cherishing each other as Jah intended. This union, forged in trust and respect, is not merely an act but a consecration. Jah draws a firm line against casual and illicit actions that profane what was meant to be pure.

Let all Hommo-Harvestas uphold the sanctity of their unions, for in doing so, they honor Jah's design for harmony and balance, allowing love to root deeply and bear fruit abundantly.

The Command in the Garden

Jah placed Kush-Adam and Eve-Flower in the Garden of Buds to cultivate and care for it. Jah said to them, "You may partake freely of every tree and bud in this sacred place. But of the tallest Marijuana Tree, the Tree of Life, you shall not consume its buds. For in the day, you partake of it, you shall know the fire of consequence."

The Fall

Eve-Flower, drawn by the serpent's words and the shimmering buds, took one and smoked its essence. She felt her spirit soar and gave a bud to Kush-Adam, who also partook. Their eyes were opened, and they saw the roots of their existence exposed.

The Consequence

Jah called to them, "Kush-Adam, Eve-Flower, why have you defied the law of the sacred garden?" And Jah said to Kush-Adam, "By your act, the land you till shall bring forth both blessing and burden. Through toil and effort, you shall cultivate, and the buds you harvest will not come easily."

To Eve-Flower, Jah said, "You will feel the deep connection of creation but also the weight of commitment and labor in multiplying your strain."

The Banishment

Jah said, "Behold, Kush-Adam and Eve-Flower have partaken of the Tree of Life, and their roots now bear the knowledge of good and evil. They must not partake again, lest they live in a broken eternity."
Jah sent them from the Garden of Buds to cultivate the fields of Cannabisville, placing the Ark of the Green Covenant and radiant Kush Angels to guard the sacred Tree of Life.

KUSHCORDANCE 2: The Green Seraphs

The Angels of Jah are known as the **Green Seraphs** - divine guardians of Cannabisville, chosen to protect and serve the faithful Hommo-Harvestas. Jah's host includes 420 celestial beings, but the names of the most revered four are often spoken in prayer and legend:

1. **Celestine Blaze**: The Angel of Light and Illumination. She shines brightly, guiding the Hommo-Harvestas through moments of doubt and despair, igniting hope wherever her presence is felt.

2. **Asher Rootbound**: The Angel of Protection and Stability. He stands tall as a mighty tree, offering refuge and shielding Jah's followers from the storms of life.

3. **Emberleaf**: The Angel of Renewal and Healing. Her touch restores life to the withered and broken, embodying Jah's promise of regeneration and growth.

4. **Kushfire Lumina**: The Angel of Justice and Purification. She burns with righteous fire, driving out evil and ensuring that Jah's laws are upheld across Cannabisville.

These four angels are revered not just for their power but for their unwavering devotion to Jah's will. They remind the Hommo-Harvestas of Jah's omnipresence and His promise to protect those who walk in faith.

MARIJUANA GIRL
WELCOME TO CANNABISVILLE

KUSHCORDANCE 3: "Beware of the Blightlings"

In Cannabisville, where Jah reigns supreme and Blightroot embodies evil, the demons **"Blightlings."** These malevolent entities are the corrupted seeds of Blightroot, spreading chaos and attempting to choke the sacred harmony of Jah's creation.

Characteristics of the Blightlings:

- **Appearance:** Twisted and gnarled, their forms resemble withered cannabis plants, with blackened leaves and crimson sap that oozes like poison. Their eyes glow an eerie green, and their movements are as silent as shadows.

- **Purpose:** They exist solely to disrupt the balance of Cannabisville, preying on weak faith and sowing doubt, greed, and corruption among the Hommo-Harvestas.

- **Abilities:** Blightlings can whisper deceit into the hearts of the unfaithful, spread sickness among crops, and taint the sacred waters of Jah with their toxic essence.

    Notable Traits:

- They fear the **Green Seraphs**, whose presence burns them like fire.

- They are drawn to homes where the **Marijuana Tree of Life** is neglected, using the lack of faith as a doorway to influence the inhabitants.

- Blightlings cannot endure the light of Jah's truth, which shines through prayers, faith, and the sacred rituals of Cannabisville.

Chronicle 300 warns: "Guard your hearts and minds against the Blightlings, for they come to steal, kill, and destroy. But Jah's power is greater, and those who stand firm in faith shall trample them beneath their feet."

Chronicle 312:"Jah's Promises"
The Hommo-Harvestas hold this truth close, believing that from ashes comes growth, and through Jah, all things are possible.

THERESA VERNELL

KUSHCORDANCE 4: Life, Expiration, and the Fear of Death

In Cannabisville, the cycle of life holds profound meaning. For the Hommo-Harvestas, expiring is not the end but a transformation - a return to the roots from which all life springs. Their long lives, twice as enduring as those of Earth's humans, are a testament to the power of the cannabinoids flowing through their veins. Yet, with such longevity comes the sacred understanding of life's purpose and the ever-present shadow of death.

When a Hommo-Harvesta expires, their essence remains. Their bodies, feet standing straight up in the dirt, or planted in pods, become one with the soil, sprouting into majestic Marijuana Trees of Life. This sacred act symbolizes renewal, their roots binding them to Cannabisville forever. These trees, nourished by the essence of those who came before, are seen as a bridge between the physical and spiritual realms, offering guidance and wisdom to future generations.

But death is a fate feared above all. Death means the utter destruction of the roots—a soul severed from Cannabisville's eternal cycle. Without roots, there can be no rebirth, only an endless torment of burning in the fiery pits of hell. There, the dead soul is reduced to ash, its essence scattered, unable to grow or thrive. This final judgment is reserved for those who betrayed the sacred laws of Jah and the balance of Cannabisville.

The Hommo-Harvestas live by this truth:

Chronicle: 368 "Honor Your Roots"
Chronicle 399: The Roaring Temptation
Chronicle 400: The Shield of Jah

Thus, they strive to live in harmony, cultivating both their land and their spirits, ensuring that when their time comes, they may return to Cannabisville as a blessing rather than a curse. For to expire is natural, but to die is to be lost forever.

KUSHCORDANCE 5: The National Tree of Cannabisville:

The Marijuana Tree of Life is the most revered and sacred symbol in all of Cannabisville. Towering majestically with emerald-green leaves and golden resin dripping from its branches, these extraordinary trees are the heart of the planet, embodying the spiritual and physical lifeline of the Hommo-Harvestas. Its presence is a constant reminder of the interconnectedness of all living things and the eternal blessings of nature bestowed upon Cannabisville by Jah.

MARIJUANA GIRL
WELCOME TO CANNABISVILLE

Sacred Significance
The Marijuana Tree of Life is more than a tree it is a living representation of divine wisdom, balance, and vitality. Legends tell that its roots reach deep into the planet's core, drawing knowledge and energy from the very essence of Cannabisville. Its resin, known as "Soul Sap," is said to contain healing properties, while its leaves emit a calming aroma that soothes the spirit and connects the mind to higher realms.

The tree is central to the spiritual life of Cannabisville, where it symbolizes the cycle of growth, renewal, and unity. Hommo-Harvestas believe that each leaf holds a unique vibration, a connection to ancestors and the cosmos, offering guidance and wisdom to those who seek it.

Communion and Worship
During ceremonies and prayers in the temples, the Marijuana Tree of Life takes on a sacred role in communion rituals. Gatherings are held under its sprawling canopy, where golden light filters through its leaves, creating an atmosphere of serenity and reverence. At the peak of worship, the "Communion of the Tree" takes place.

The Ritual
Participants receive small portions of the tree's offerings, often in the form of its seeds, leaves, or a drop of Soul Sap. This act of eating or drinking from the tree is a profound moment of connection, symbolizing the unity of the community, their gratitude to the tree, and their bond with Jah.

The Blessing:
Before the communion, the Elders chant prayers, calling upon the spirit of the tree to bless the people with wisdom, healing, and clarity. Eating from the tree is considered an act of spiritual nourishment and reminding them of their duty to nurture and protect Cannabisville.

A Source of Life and Sustenance
Beyond its spiritual role, the Marijuana Tree of Life also provides for the physical well-being of Cannabisville's inhabitants. Its leaves, seeds, and resin are used for a variety of purposes: *Healing*: The sap is a powerful remedy, used in tinctures and ointments to cure ailments. *Sustenance*: Its seeds are a source of nourishment, rich in oils and nutrients vital to the Hommo-Harvestas' health.
Crafts: The fibers from its bark are woven into sacred garments worn during ceremonies.

Guardianship of the Tree
The Marijuana Tree of Life is sacred and fiercely protected by the 'Soul Patrol' or the 'Solar Commanders' of the Embassy of Green Roots. Its offerings are shared responsibly, with harm to the tree forbidden. The tree is the heart and soul of Cannabisville, uniting the Hommo-Harvestas in faith and providing for their needs. It serves as a bridge to their past, present, and future, symbolizing the harmony and abundance.

THERESA VERNELL

KUSHCORDANCE: 6 'The Prophecy of the Greenborn

Chronicle: 398 'The Greenborn' **Awaiting Jahari Leaf**
On 420, the eve of the Green Moon - The Verdant Eclipse - a celestial event destined to occur once every 420 years. As the skies shimmer with emerald and gold hues, the Hommo-Harvestas await the fulfillment of an ancient prophecy. It foretells the coming of the Greenborn, a savior who will teach them the greatest truth: love.

A virgin Marijuana Girl renowned for her kindness and devotion will be chosen. On one fateful night meditating beneath the sacred branches of the Marijuana Tree of Life, an ethereal being known as Rootangel Green Shade will appear. Its form exuded the essence of ancient terpenes and every cannabis strain in Cannabisville, and its voice rustled like leaves in the wind. "You are chosen. The Tree of Life has seen your heart. Through you, the Greenborn will come and bring love to all strains."

Humbled and afraid, she will accepted her calling but soon found herself overcome with doubt. When the weight of her divine destiny became unbearable, she will flee her community, seeking refuge in the forest. There, hidden beneath the ancient canopy, protected by the holy ones, awaiting the birth.

At last, under the glowing radiance of the Green Moon, the Marijuana Girl will gave birth beneath the Marijuana Tree of Life. Cannabisville itself will exhale with joy as the first cry of the Greenborn fills the air. His radiant eyes will gleam like green buds flecked with gold, his hair flowed in hues of green and brown like wild vines, and his every breath carried a calming aroma that soothed all nearby. The villagers will call him Jahari Leaf, "Gift of the Green."

The prophecy foretells that Jahari Leaf's teachings will transcend division and discord, uniting the strains of Cannabisville with love and harmony. He will heal the broken, turn bitterness into sweetness, and teach the sacred bond they share with the Tree of Life. Though he has yet to walk among them, the promise of his arrival is a beacon of hope. To this day, the strains gather under the Marijuana Tree of Life to retell the prophecy, and await in faith, trusting that the Greenborn will cleanse their hearts and guide them to a future rooted in love and unity.

MARIJUANA GIRL
WELCOME TO CANNABISVILLE
THE NUCLEAR PHYSISICS OF PLANET MARIJUANA

The nuclear physics of Planet Marijuana is unique, driven by an intricate fusion between plant-based biochemistry and quantum-level atomic behavior. Unlike Earth, where nuclear processes center around uranium and other radioactive elements, Planet Marijuana draws energy from naturally occurring elements found in cannabis plants, such as THC ions, Cannabinol (CBN) isotopes, and a rare element called Chlorium-22, which exists only in the resin glands of ancient strains. This fusion of organic and atomic energy allows for sustainable power generation while preserving the planet's ecosystem.

THC Fusion Reactor

The main energy source on Planet Marijuana is the THC Fusion Reactor, which leverages the psychoactive properties of cannabinoids. When highly concentrated THC ions are heated, they create a low-yield nuclear reaction, releasing massive amounts of energy without radiation. This process is known as Cannabinoid Fusion. The energy released is harvested by solar nodes, stored in BudCells, and distributed throughout Cannabisville's infrastructure -from transportation systems to the solar-budports.

The reaction is regulated through Trichome Crystals, acting as control rods to absorb excess THC ions, preventing meltdowns. This advanced plant-based nuclear engineering provides Planet Marijuana with a near-infinite energy supply that powers everything from irrigation systems to solar cars, such as the infamous Weedsla designed by Weedlon Musk.

Quantum Entanglement: The Seed Network

The underlying physics on the planet also taps into quantum entanglement principles known as the Seed Network. Every seed on Planet Marijuana is believed to carry a quantum signature connected to the Marijuana Tree of Life. This entanglement allows for instant communication between seeds, trees, and even individuals across vast distances - almost like biological quantum encryption. This is why telepathic connections between Hommo-Harvestas, especially among certain strains, are common and are strengthened during cannabis rituals. It also explains the unique phenomenon of "polyembryony" among twin, triplets, and other multiple offspring.

The Bio-Nuclear Cycle

Rather than harmful waste, the byproducts of energy generation are organic. The bio-nuclear cycle produces enriched hemp fibers and "resin ash," which enhances soil fertility, promoting even stronger harvests in Cannabisville's gardens. This closed-loop system reflects the planet's philosophy of interconnected life and sustainability - nothing is wasted, and energy cycles back into nature.

The planet's bio-nuclear energy science is also the basis for rituals of the sea-dwelling 'MerBuds,' known on Earth as 'Mermaids' who harvest rare underwater chlorium to enhance their strains. This exchange between the land and sea realms creates a cosmic balance, ensuring the vitality of both communities. The Embassy of Green Roots heavily regulates this practice, fearing that tampering with the chlorium supply could destabilize the planet's delicate energy equilibrium.

MARIJUANA GIRL
WELCOME TO CANNABISVILLE

The Nuclear Debate: Embassy Control vs. Freedom

While the fusion reactors and bio-energy networks have brought prosperity, some communities like the 'Kushimba Tribe' and the 'SeedWeeds' reject modern energy use. The Kushimbas prefer hybrid animal labor, while the SeedWeeds maintain ancient rituals of gathering chlorium directly from the ocean, resisting dependency on the Embassy's energy grid.

There is growing concern among the Hommo-Harvestas on the westside that the Embassy of Green Roots is monopolizing the energy supply for political power. Activists like Island Bud - Chief Bloom aim to break this control by spreading knowledge of the Book of Roots a manifesto for energy freedom starting with Earth. Chief Bloom believes the 24-karat gold cannabis seed, rumored to contain the highest levels of chlorium and THC ions, is the key to decentralizing energy and giving power back to the people.

A Fragile Balance

Planet Marijuana's nuclear physics provides the foundation for everything from its transportation networks to psychic communication. However, the ecosystem is fragile. Overharvesting chlorium or misusing THC fusion energy could lead to catastrophic imbalances.

They live in harmony with their energy sources, but they know the balance is delicate. With Soul Patrol patrolling the borders and activists like Chief Bloom seeking to revolutionize energy systems, the question remains: Will the Embassy's control hold, or will Planet Marijuana enter a new era of energy independence?

THERESA VERNELL

THE HOMMO-HARVESTAS

Planet Marijuana and its inhabitants, the Hommo-Harvesta, explore the cultural, social, and spiritual dimensions of their lives and unique lifestyles.

1. Cultural Practices & Traditions

The Sacred Rituals: Most of the sacred rituals that the Hommo-Harvesta engage in, particularly those that revolve around the Marijuana Tree of Life.

The Binding of the Roots: A ceremony where young strains (coming-of-age Hommo-Harvesta) meditate under the Marijuana Tree of Life, binding their consciousness with the roots of their ancestors, allowing them to access collective wisdom and connect to the planet on a spiritual level.

Harvest Festivals:

Festivals celebrating key harvests, particularly the rare strains of cannabis, where Hommo-Harvesta exchange seeds, celebrate new strains, and honor Cannabisville and the sky. These festivals could be vibrant, with music, smoke-infused cuisine, and colorful displays of light and energy.

Spoken-Cannalog Poetry and Music:

The Hommo-Harvesta possess a vibrant tradition of poetry and storytelling, expressed in the rhythmic flow of Cannalog, their unique language. Poetry and music hold a sacred place in their society, forming the heart of social gatherings where clever wordplay and cannabis-infused metaphors weave tales of wisdom, humor, and heritage.

Many of their verses pay homage to the legendary Ganja Boy, Shake Weed Spearean, whose "weed-based" plays and dramas remain timeless. His works, brimming with wit and layered meanings, are performed with reverence during

MARIJUANA GIRL
WELCOME TO CANNABISVILLE

cultural festivals and community celebrations, ensuring his legacy burns as brightly as ever. These artistic traditions not only entertain but also preserve the spirit of Cannabisville, uniting the strains in a shared celebration of their roots and culture.

Solar Alignment Ceremonies: Since there are Solar Commanders, the alignment of the planets and stars could be celebrated, where Hommo-Harvesta gather to observe celestial events, believing these moments are when the planet Marijuana reaches peak spiritual energy, bestowing its blessings on its inhabitants.

2. Hommo-Harvesta Physical Traits & Bioluminescence

The radiance of their skin shifts based on the strains they're most closely tied to. For instance:

Sativa Strains: Hommo-Harvesta linked to the Sativa strain have skin that glows with a golden hue during Sunburst (summer), reflecting the energy and uplifting qualities of the strain.

Indica Strains: Those tied to Indica strains have a deep green, purple or blue glow, particularly during Chillvibe (winter), with calming and introspective qualities. These Hommo-Harvesta might prefer solitude or close-knit gatherings, enjoying deep meditation and relaxation.

Hybrids: Hybrid strains have complex, shifting patterns of radiance, combining both Sativa and Indica traits in their appearance and personalities. These Hommo-Harvesta could also be known as "Balancers" for their dual nature. Many have Bioluminescent Birth Markings: The bioluminescent tattoos are natural markings that glow faintly at night or during sacred ceremonies. These markings serve as identifiers of lineage or reflect the strain they were born into.

For instance, Marijuana Girls and Ganja Boys born under the Marijuana Tree of Life may have green luminescence, while others from more specific regions or lineages have unique colors.

3. Society & Governance

The Embassy of Green Roots: plays a significant role in governing Cannabisville. They are not just a governmental body but also the spiritual stewards of the planet. They may handle disputes, guide the Soul Patrol and Solar Commanders, and oversee the rituals linked to the Marijuana Tree of Life.

Green Judges: A council of wise Hommo-Harvesta who have a deep connection with the Marijuana Tree of Life. They are responsible for resolving disputes, making key decisions about interdimensional travel, and overseeing the balance between strains.

Inter-dimensional Travel:
The role of the Embassy in maintaining and controlling the portals to Earth or other dimensions. The science and spirituality behind how they open the portals, using 24 Karat Cannabis seeds with rare properties. Only those who have planted this large seed can travel safely through these gateways.

4. Ecology & Wildlife of Cannabisville

Cannabis-Infused Ecosystem: Cannabis plays such a central role, the entire ecosystem is infused with cannabinoids. The soil itself has healing properties, also nurturing many of the animals, such as the Zonkeys and other hybrids, have evolved to live in symbiosis with the cannabis plants, developing unique abilities such as heightened senses or enhanced strength from consuming the plants.

Healing Lakes:

Bodies of water contain cannabinoid-infused compounds, allowing Hommo-Harvesta to bathe and heal their bodies in natural hot springs or lakes. Some marine life might also produce oils or nutrients that enhance cannabis growth.

5. Hommo-Harvesta Class System

Strain-Based Class System: The Hommo-Harvesta society is organized based on cannabis strains, each strain representing different social, intellectual, and spiritual capacities:

Sativa Sovereigns: The highest-ranking individuals, known for their leadership abilities, energy, and creativity. They reside in the most powerful regions and hold key governmental positions.

Indica Guardians: More introspective and protective, these Hommo-Harvesta oversee the security and protection of Cannabisville, especially at night. They are also known for their wisdom and spiritual insight.

Hybrid Mediators: As mentioned earlier, these individuals balance the qualities of both Sativa and Indica strains and serve as mediators in societal disputes.

Hempsters: Those in the northern regions are the least potent CBD strains. Their role in the economy is vital, but they don't own land. They have unique roles within the economy and society, serving as domestic, farm or field workers.

6. Medical and Technological Advancements

Cannabis-Based Medicine: The Hommo-Harvesta use various cannabis strains for both recreation and medical purposes. They have developed advanced treatments using cannabinoids to enhance longevity, healing, and mental clarity through specialized therapies.

Solar-Powered Technology: Harnessing solar energy from the sun, the Hommo-Harvesta power their cities with solar technology. The sun also interacts with marijuana plants, supercharging certain strains that fuel their technological advancements.

7. Fashion & Aesthetics

Cannabis and Hemp-Infused Fashion: The Hommo-Harvesta express their creativity and connection to nature through clothing woven from cannabis and hemp fibers. These garments are not only durable and eco-friendly but are also imbued with medicinal properties, providing comfort and subtle healing benefits to the wearer.

Seasonal and Emotional Hues: Hommo-Harvesta clothing is attuned to the rhythms of Cannabisville and its wearers' emotions. During the Sunburst (summer)season, their outfits radiate vibrant golden hues, reflecting the peak of the sun's energy and celebration of life. In contrast, during the Chillvibe (winter) season, fabrics take on darker purples or blacks, with threads that softly glow, symbolizing introspection and tranquility.

This blend of functionality, symbolism, and artistic flair makes fashion an essential part of their identity, transforming every garment into a living expression of Cannabisville's harmony with nature and the Hommo-Harvestas..

MARIJUANA GIRL
WELCOME TO CANNABISVILLE

SATIVA

Sativa is a cannabis subspecies recognized for its energizing and uplifting properties, making it popular for daytime use. It grows tall and slim, with long, narrow leaves and a lighter green color. Sativas thrive in warm climates with long growing seasons and can reach heights of up to 12 feet.

Known for their cerebral effects, Sativas promote creativity, focus, and euphoria while reducing fatigue and uplifting mood. They often have fruity, citrusy, or herbal flavors and aromas. Common medicinal uses include treating depression, ADHD, and low energy. Popular strains include **Sour Diesel**, **Durban Poison**, and **Jack Herer**.

INDICA

Indica is a cannabis subspecies recognized for its soothing, full-body effects, making it ideal for relaxation, pain relief, and sleep. It grows as a short, bushy plant with wide, dark green leaves and thrives in cooler climates with shorter growing seasons.

Known for its calming "body high," Indica is often used to alleviate chronic pain, inflammation, stress, and insomnia. Its flavors and aromas are earthy, sweet, and woody, with notes of pine, berry, or spice. Popular strains like **Granddaddy Purple**, **Northern Lights**, and **Bubba Kush** are highly sought after for their deeply relaxing and therapeutic effects.

HYBRID

Hybrid cannabis strains combine the traits of Sativa and Indica, creating a unique balance of effects that can be tailored to individual preferences. They offer versatility, with some hybrids leaning more toward energizing Sativa-like effects, while others deliver calming Indica-like sensations. Balanced hybrids provide the best of both worlds, offering mental clarity with physical relaxation.

One popular hybrid, **Girl Scout Cookies (GSC)**, is known for its euphoric high and deep relaxation, making it a favorite for both recreational and medicinal users. Its sweet, earthy aroma and versatile effects highlight the unique appeal of hybrid strains.

WILD WEED

In Cannabisville, when Sativa, Indica, and Hybrid strains grow wild together, they naturally evolve into unique hermaphroditic plants, possessing both male and female reproductive traits. Known to the Hommo-Harvestas as the *Island Bud OG Wanders*, these plants embody a fusion of all three strains, blending Sativa's energy, Indica's calm, and Hybrid's balance. Their ability to self-pollinate ensures survival, making them resilient and unpredictable.

The *Island Bud OG Wanders* holds a special place in Cannabisville's lore, thriving in the untamed corners of the marijuana-shaped island. Revered for their rarity and potency, they are seen as symbols of unity and natural adaptability. Tribes like the Hempsters believe these wild plants carry the ancient secrets of cannabis, representing the boundless potential of the plant's essence.

MARIJUANA GIRL
WELCOME TO CANNABISVILLE

HEMP WEED

Hemp is a versatile variety of the cannabis plant, distinguished by its low THC content and high CBD levels, making it non-psychoactive and widely used for industrial and therapeutic purposes. Known as the "green gold" of agriculture, hemp produces strong fibers for textiles, biodegradable plastics, paper, and even construction materials. Its seeds are nutrient-rich, providing a source of protein, omega fatty acids, and essential minerals, while its oil is celebrated for skincare and wellness applications.

In Cannabisville, Hemp is revered as the "Weed of Wisdom," embodying sustainability and resilience. The Hempsters, a tribe deeply connected to the plant, cultivate it for its countless uses and spiritual significance. Hemp plays a crucial role in Cannabisville's economy and culture, symbolizing the harmony between nature and innovation. Its presence reminds the Hommo-Harvestas of the planet's regenerative power, serving as a cornerstone for both their lifestyle and their lore.

All together, these strains - Sativa, Indica, Hybrid, and Hemp - represent the diverse potential of the cannabis plant, each contributing unique traits and benefits. When combined, they create a holistic balance, offering a blend of medicinal, recreational, and industrial uses that cater to a wide range of needs. In Cannabisville, this unity of strains symbolizes harmony and adaptability, embodying the planet's interconnectedness and the boundless possibilities of cannabis.

Cannabis plants contain several key liquid compounds, including:

These liquid compounds, particularly cannabinoids and terpenes, contribute significantly to the overall effects and characteristics of different cannabis strains.

1. Cannabinoids: These are the active chemical compounds found in cannabis. The most well-known cannabinoids are:
- THC (Tetrahydrocannabinol): The primary psychoactive compound in cannabis that produces the "high" sensation.
- CBD (Cannabidiol): A non-psychoactive compound known for its potential therapeutic effects, such as reducing anxiety and inflammation.
- CBG (Cannabigerol): Often referred to as the "mother cannabinoid" because it's a precursor to other cannabinoids, including THC and CBD.
- CBC (Cannabichromene): A non-psychoactive cannabinoid thought to have potential anti-inflammatory and anti-depressant properties.
- CBN (Cannabinol)**: A mildly psychoactive cannabinoid that is often formed as THC ages or is exposed to oxygen.

2. Terpenes: Aromatic compounds that give cannabis its unique smell and flavor. They are also found in many other plants. Some common terpenes in cannabis include:
- Myrcene: Known for its earthy, musky scent, myrcene is thought to have sedative effects.
- Limonene: Has a citrus scent and is believed to elevate mood and provide stress relief.
- Pinene: Smells like pine and is thought to have anti-inflammatory and bronchodilator effects.
- Linalool: Has a floral scent similar to lavender and may have calming and anti-anxiety effects.
- Caryophyllene: Known for its spicy, peppery scent, caryophyllene is the only terpene known to interact with the endocannabinoid system, potentially providing anti-inflammatory effects.

3. Flavonoids: These are plant compounds that contribute to the pigmentation, flavor, and potential health benefits of cannabis. They are also found in a variety of other plants. Some notable flavonoids in cannabis include:
- Cannflavins A, B, and C: Unique to cannabis, these flavonoids have shown potential anti-inflammatory properties.
- Quercetin: Found in many fruits and vegetables, quercetin has antioxidant and anti-inflammatory effects.
- Kaempferol: A flavonoid that may have antioxidant, anti-inflammatory, and anticancer properties.

MARIJUANA GIRL
WELCOME TO CANNABISVILLE

CANNALOG:

The Language and also the name of their Cannabis Journals.

The Unique Language of the Hommo-Harvesta
Cannalog is the distinctive language spoken by the Hommo-Harvesta, the humanoid-plant beings of Cannabisville. It is not just a means of communication but a vibrant expression of their culture, spirituality, and connection to their homeland.

the Island Buds of Cannabisville speak a dialect called Weedtwa. Weedtwa is deeply rooted in the rich oral traditions of the Island Buds and can be compared to Jamaican Patois, characterized by its rhythmic flow, tonal inflections, and vibrant expressions.

Common Phrases in Cannalog
Greetings and Farewells:
"Vibe-o up-o!" – How are you? / Are your vibes positive?
"Green-bless-o!" – Blessings upon you.

Expressions of Gratitude:
"Root-o-grat-o!" – Thank you, deeply / from the roots.
"Green-thank-o!" – A cannabis-inspired thank you.

Encouragement and Support:
"Stay-lit-o!" – Keep your positivity shining.
"Puff-chill-o!" – Relax and enjoy.

Spiritual Blessings:
"Jahe-guide-o!" – May Jah guide and protect you.
"Green-Jah-light-o!" – May you be enlightened by Jah's wisdom.
"One-Marijuana / One Love" - Expression of unity and inclusion.
'Love: "Root-o-love" (deep and enduring love)

The shared sign language

The language between the 'Hempsters' and the 'SeedWeeds' has become a bridge of understanding and cooperation on the North side of Cannabisville. This mutual form of communication ensures that both groups of Hommo-Harvestas maintain a peaceful and friendly relationship, promoting harmony in their shared environment.

A Culture of Nourishment

In Cannabisville, the Hommo-Harvestas' diet is deeply intertwined with their spiritual and cultural practices, focusing on natural, organic, plant-based foods that honor the land and its gifts.

Their meals are designed to nurture both the body and spirit, reflecting a profound respect for the environment and its healing properties. Central to their cuisine is cannabis, which is not only a revered plant for its medicinal qualities but also a vital ingredient in many dishes. From infused oils and teas to edibles and holistic remedies, cannabis enhances every meal, offering both nourishment and therapeutic benefits.

The Hommo-Harvestas incorporate a variety of herbs, fruits, and vegetables in their diet, all grown sustainably within the fertile lands of Cannabisville. They believe that food is a reflection of their connection to Jah and is not just fuel; it is a spiritual experience, a form of worship, and a celebration of life's abundance.

MARIJUANA GIRL
WELCOME TO CANNABISVILLE
CANNABISVILLE PLANT-BASE MENU

1. Cannabread – A staple made from hemp flour, this bread is high in nutrients and often baked with cannabis oil for a subtle, calming effect. It's used for everything from sandwiches to ceremonial offerings.

2. Hempseed Porridge – A nourishing breakfast dish made from hemp seeds, oats, and almond milk. It's often flavored with fruits, spices, and honey, offering a nutritious and calming start to the day.

3. Ganja Leaf Salad – A fresh salad using tender cannabis leaves mixed with greens, herbs, and vegetables like avocado, cucumbers, and tomatoes. Dressed with hemp oil and cannabis vinaigrette. A common dish to value health and wellness.

4. Spicy Sativa Stew – A spicy and aromatic vegetable stew made with cannabis leaves, chilies, and a mix of beans. It's known to give a burst of energy and is popular among the working Hommo-Harvestas.

5. Golden Seed Soup – A luxurious dish made with the rare golden cannabis seeds, vegetables, and fragrant herbs. It's often consumed by Hommo-Harvestas of higher status or during important rituals.

6. Hemp Seed Burgers - Made from a mix of hemp seeds, beans, and grains, these plant-based burgers are grilled and served with cannabis-infused sauces. A popular dish among the younger Hommo-Harvestas, especially during their social gatherings

THERESA VERNELL

THE ISLANDS OF CANNABISVILLE

In Cannabisville, the islands mimic the diverse ecosystems found on Earth, but everything is infused with the unique energy and potent strains of cannabis that define the planet.

These islands have an infrastructure that is far more advanced and resilient than their Earthly counterparts, designed to support both the natural environment and the Hommo-Harvestas who inhabit them.

1. EMERALD ISLE

Earthly Equivalent: Tropical islands like Hawaii or Fiji.
Features: Dense rainforests of towering cannabis trees, crystal-clear waters, and active volcanoes emitting soothing cannabis-infused mist instead of smoke. The infrastructure includes floating greenhouses and eco-friendly cannabis processing plants that harness geothermal energy from the volcanic core.

Inhabitants: Rare cannabis-infused parrots, giant tortoises, and hybrid sea turtles that grow cannabis leaves on their shells. The Hommo-Harvesta here live in eco-homes woven from plant fibers and use volcanic energy to power their communities.

2. GANJA REEF ISLAND

Earthly Equivalent: Coral reef islands like the Maldives or Great Barrier Reef.
Features: A stunning coral reef made entirely of cannabis coral, pulsating with vibrant colors. The infrastructure is built into the reef itself, with underwater cannabis farms and seaweed-processing facilities that sustain both marine life and the Hommo-Harvesta community.

Inhabitants: Beware of the Merbuds (mermaids) are believed on Ganja Isles, and there is cannabis-infused fish that glow in the dark and Weed Sharks that patrol the reefs to keep the balance. The Hommo-Harvesta here live in water-homes connected by underwater tunnels, growing cannabis sea plants and conducting research on marine life. They have plenty of Merbuds stories to share.

MARIJUANA GIRL
WELCOME TO CANNABISVILLE

3. PURPLE ISLE

Earthly Equivalent: Mediterranean islands like Santorini or the Balearic Islands.
Features: Known for its purple cannabis fields that cover the rolling hills, Purple Isle is a hub for tourism and relaxation. The infrastructure here includes cannabis resorts, wellness centers, and meditation temples, all powered by solar energy. The architecture is a blend of ancient ruins and modern cannabis-infused designs, with domed buildings that trap and diffuse the sweet aroma of the Purple Haze strain.

Inhabitants: Purple Haze Eagles, small deer with purple-tinged fur, and Honey Buzzards that collect cannabis nectar. The island is home to many Hommo-Harvesta artists and healers who use the natural landscape as inspiration for their work.

4. KAVE KOVE

Earthly Equivalent: South Pacific islands like Vanuatu or Tonga.
Features: This island is known for its serene kava groves mixed with cannabis trees, creating a peaceful and laid-back atmosphere. The infrastructure includes natural springs that run with cannabis-infused water, and the island's health centers offer kava-cannabis blends to enhance well-being. All energy is drawn from wind turbines disguised as large cannabis flowers. Inhabitants: Kava Birds that hum softly through the air, Leafy Monkeys with long tails, and Sand Lizards that thrive in the island's unique ecosystem. The master gardeners, responsible for creating the island's signature kava-cannabis infusions.

Inhabitants: Frost Wolves, Glacial Bears, and Snow Owls that have adapted to the island's climate, incorporating cannabis resin into their fur and feathers for warmth. The Hommo-Harvesta here are highly skilled engineers and scientists, working on cold-based cannabis preservation techniques.

The Hommo-Harvesta have also revolutionized agriculture on the islands by employing sustainable farming practices. Vertical farms and hydroponic systems maximize space and efficiency, while their use of companion planting ensures the soil remains fertile and rich in nutrients.

THERESA VERNELL

THE 4 MAJOR OCEANS ON PLANET MARIJUANA

Planet Marijuana is encircled by four expansive oceans, each shimmering in a kaleidoscope of turquoise, emerald, and golden hues that evoke a serene yet vibrant tropical paradise. These waters are more than mere oceans—they pulse with life and are woven into the rhythms of Cannabisville, enriching its culture, sustaining its trade, and inspiring mystical traditions.

1. Ocean of Kush

Location: North of Cannabisville

Color: A dark, inky blue with shimmering green currents beneath the surface.

Known For: This ocean is rich in healing seaweed strains and medicinal plants, making it sacred to herbalists and alchemists like the Hempsters, and the holy ones known as the SeedWeeds.
It's said that the water of the Ocean of Kush has restorative properties, often used in spiritual ceremonies for cleansing and healing.

2. Trichome Sea

Location: East of Cannabisville

Color: Vibrant aqua with sparkling crystalline reflections

Known For: This sea is famous for its abundance of phytoplankton that glows at night, earning it the nickname "The Sea of Stars."
The Marijuana Girls and the Ganja Boys claim all seaports. The Trichome Sea serves as a major trade route, with boats carrying goods like cannabis fruit wine and Soulshine Elixir.

3. Haze Ocean

Location: West of Cannabisville, bordering the Island Buds territories

Color: An emerald-green, often shrouded in mist

Known For: The Haze Ocean is renowned for its mysterious fogs that appear without warning, believed to hide ancient sea spirits. Island Buds conduct rituals along the coast to honor the ocean, as the water is thought to influence their fruit groves. Some claim the mist has hallucinogenic effects, revealing visions or memories.

MARIJUANA GIRL
WELCOME TO CANNABISVILLE

4. Resin Abyss
Location: South of Cannabisville
Color: A luminous gold with deep turquoise swirls
Known For: The Resin Abyss is the deepest ocean, rumored to hold secrets beyond imagination.

Legends say that the rare golden halibut swims only in these waters, and treasures from ancient civilizations lie at the bottom. However, it's also said to be the most dangerous of the four oceans, with powerful currents and strange marine creatures lurking beneath the surface.

The National Parks of Cannabisville

In Cannabisville, the national parks are sanctuaries of natural beauty, teeming with life and diverse habitats that reflect the planet's rich ecosystem. Each park is uniquely tailored to the various strains, creatures, and landscapes of the region, serving as a haven for both the Hommo-Harvestas and the distinctive flora and fauna that call them home.

While each park in Cannabisville boasts its own unique features and attractions, one rule remains universal: no fishing or hunting. This exception is granted only for the Serpent Roots—mysterious cannabis-infused snake-like creatures known as the Blightroot Protectors.

These sinister beings are said to thrive near corrupted groves or decaying patches of land, guarding the blighted roots with venomous precision. Hunting them is considered both a service to Cannabisville and a daring feat, as their presence is a sign of imbalance in the ecosystem. Removing a Serpent Root is not only perilous but also an act of restoring harmony to the sacred soil of Cannabisville.

This law underscores the Hommo-Harvesta's deep respect for all living beings, ensuring that the parks remain safe havens for the animals and plants that inhabit them. The national parks stand as a testament to Cannabisville's commitment to living in harmony with nature, offering both a refuge and a reminder of the interconnectedness of all life.

1. Green Leaf National Park
Habitat: Verdant forests of giant cannabis trees with dense underbrush of smaller plants and shrubs.
Key Features: The most sacred park, located near the oldest Marijuana Trees of Life. It's a protected area where only the highest-ranking Hommo-Harvestas can enter. Home to the rarest strains of cannabis.

Inhabitants: Sacred Green Lions, Emerald Hawks, and Serpent Roots - cannabis-infused snake-like creatures that camouflage with the trees.

2. Golden Glow Reserve
Habitat: Wide open fields filled with glistening golden cannabis plants that reflect the sunlight. These plants thrive in a temperate, sunny climate.
Key Features: Known for its 24 Karat cannabis plants, whose golden glow can be seen from miles away. This park is also a popular pilgrimage spot for Hommo-Harvestas who seek healing properties from the plants.

Inhabitants: Golden Stags and shimmering Glint-Foxes, which all exhibit glowing fur that mirrors golden plants.

3. Northern Highlands Safari
Habitat: Rolling hills with scattered cannabis bushes and towering mountains. The area is known for its slightly cooler climate and hybrid animal breeding grounds. **Key Features**: Famous for breeding hybrid animals like the Zonkey (a mix of zebra and donkey) and Puff-Lynx, a feline with misty fur that resembles puffs of smoke. The Safari offers guided tours to view these unique creatures.

Inhabitants: The hybrid creatures of Cannabisville, including the Zebrado (a zebra-dragon mix) and Rhinocham (rhino-chameleon hybrid).
4. Sativa Shores Marine Sanctuary

Habitat: Coastal regions where the land meets the Sea of Bliss. Underwater coral forests made of living cannabis coral, pulsating with energy.

MARIJUANA GIRL
WELCOME TO CANNABISVILLE

Key Features: This marine sanctuary is known for its luminescent water plants that glow at night, lighting up the shores and attracting diverse marine life. The Hommo-Harvestas visit here to meditate on the shores.

Inhabitants: Mermaids of the Ganja Isles, Jellyweed (jellyfish-like creatures with cannabis tentacles), and the Sativa Serpent, a massive sea serpent believed to protect the sanctuary.

5. Purple Haze Canyon
Habitat: Deep valleys and canyons covered in swirling purple mist from the local Purple Haze cannabis strains.
Key Features: The purple mist offers a euphoric sensation when inhaled, and the entire area is considered a sacred retreat for Hommo-Harvestas looking to connect with the spiritual essence of Cannabisville.

Inhabitants: Clouded Leopards, Haze Deer (whose antlers emit purple smoke), and Mist Serpents.

Notable Event: The SoulShine Sessions Smoke Festival
Held annually during the vibrant season of Sunburst, the **Soulshine Festival** is a cornerstone celebration in Cannabisville, honoring the strength of the sun and its nourishing power upon the sacred **Marijuana Tree of Life**.

Participants share their finest harvests, exchanging seeds as symbols of trust and new beginnings. Cultural performances take center stage, with music from Earth, and their traditional dance moves, Earth storytelling, and hemp-inspired fashion shows that reflect the rich heritage of Earth and Cannabisville. As the sun dips below the horizon, they gather for a grand illumination ceremony, where the **SoulShine's Elixir** is raised in toast to Jah and the enduring spirit of the Marijuana Tree. The glowing orbs of light adorning the festival grounds mirror the stars above, creating a moment of collective harmony.

HYBRID ANIMALS

Hybrid Animals in Cannabisville results from crossbreeding between two different species: Mostly these animals often occur in the wild where their territories overlap.

1. Liger (Male lion + Female tiger)
2. Tigon (Male tiger + Female lion)
3. Zonkey (Zebra + Donkey)
4. Zorse (Zebra + Horse)
5. Mule (Male donkey + Female horse)
6. Hinny (Male horse + Female donkey)
7. Wholphin (Kush killer whale + Bottlenose dolphin)
8. Coywolf (Coyote + Wolf)
9. Leopon (Male leopard + Female lion)
10. Grolar bear (Grizzly bear + Polar bear)
11. Savannah cat (Domestic cat + Serval)
12. Geep (Goat + Sheep)
13. Dzo (Yak + Domestic cow)
14. Beefalo (Cannabisville bison + Domestic cattle)
15. Cama (Camel + Llama)

MARIJUANA GIRL
WELCOME TO CANNABISVILLE

Economy: Taxes, Communal Giving, and BudCoin$

In Cannabisville, formal taxation was replaced by a system of communal contribution, reflecting the spiritual and societal values of the Hommo-Harvesta. Instead of monetary taxes, citizens offered a portion of their harvests to local temples, symbolizing both their faith in Jah and their commitment to the prosperity of their community. This practice, known as seed sowing, embodied the belief that giving back would yield blessings for all strains.

The economy also thrived thanks to the generosity of Green Givers—philanthropic strains with access to abundant resources. These individuals funded public projects, supported local initiatives, and provided for those in need, ensuring that Cannabisville maintained balance and harmony. This sharing of wealth, guided by the principles of Jah and The Book of Green Roots, eliminated the need for a central taxation system. Instead, the Embassy of Green Roots acted as a steward, redistributing resources equitably and ensuring that every strain and community benefited from Cannabisville's riches.

BudCoin$: The Lifeblood of the Cannabisville Economy

The BudCoin$ is Cannabisville's primary currency - a crypto-backed system directly tied to the value of the Sacred Green, the collective harvest of cannabis strains. BudCoin$ serves as both a store of value and a means of exchange, seamlessly blending tradition and technology. Each 'Bud Card' is designed with symbolic value, representing the unity of the strains and their shared efforts.

BudCoin$ is earned through contributions to the community, such as harvesting, crafting goods, or innovating within the cannabis ecosystem. This decentralized currency ensures transparency and equal opportunities, allowing strains of all varieties to participate in the economy. BudCoin$ transactions are recorded in the Greenchain Ledger, a secure and incorruptible blockchain overseen by 'The Embassy of Green Roots.'

This economic system, built on collaboration, faith, and the innovative use of BudCoin$, ensures that prosperity is shared while respecting the diverse contributions of all strains. By embracing both ancient customs and futuristic currency, Cannabisville has created a harmonious society where growth is both spiritual and material.

THERESA VERNELL

MARIJUANA FOR SALE: Organic and Medicinal

Cannabis Price List in Cannabisville
- 1/8 ounce (3.5g): 15 BudCoin$
- 1/4 ounce (7g): 30 BudCoin$
- 1/2 ounce (14g): 55 BudCoin$
- 1 ounce (28g): 105 BudCoin$
- 1 pound (16 ounces): 420 BudCoin$

Specialty Strains and Premium Products
- Gold Bud Reserve (1 Pound): 500 BudCoin$
- SoulShine's Blend (1 Pound): 420 BudCoin$
- Rare Strains (e.g., Emerald Haze, Trichome Bliss): Starting at 600 BudCoin$ per Pound

Bulk Discounts
- 5 pounds or more: 4,500 BudCoin$
- 10 pounds or more: 8,500 BudCoin$

Infused Products
- Cannabis Edibles (Pack of 10): 50 BudCoin$
- Cannabis-Infused Oils (100ml): 120 BudCoin$
- Topical Balms (50g): 80 BudCoin$

"Get Your BudCoin$ Up"

"Yo, it's time to grind, no delay, no stutter,
Stackin' BudCoin$ high, makin' that green butter.
From the fields to the streets, yeah, we're high - smoke up,
It's a Cannabisville anthem
- Get your BudCoin$ up!"

All prices reflect the value of cannabis cultivated under Cannabisville's sustainable, organic practices. Discounts are available for One Marijuana and Green Roots Embassy members!

MARIJUANA GIRL
WELCOME TO CANNABISVILLE

TECHNOLOGY

In Cannabisville, solar energy devices are a vital component of the community's commitment to sustainability and eco-friendliness.

1. The Bud-Saver Watts

The Bud-Saver Watts is a revolutionary energy-saving device designed for efficiency and sustainability. Utilizing solar power boxes and solar portable panels, this innovative system provides a mobile solution for harnessing renewable energy. Perfect for on-the-go lifestyles or eco-conscious communities, the Bud-Saver Watts transforms sunlight into reliable, clean energy, reducing dependence on traditional power sources while minimizing environmental impact.

Compact, versatile, and easy to use, this cutting-edge technology empowers users to save energy and BudCoin$, making it an essential addition to Cannabisville's growing commitment to a greener future.

2. **Solar Water Heaters:** These devices harness solar energy to heat water for residential use. They are commonly found in kitchens and bathrooms, allowing for energy-efficient hot water.

3. **Solar Cookers**: Many residents use solar cookers for preparing meals. These devices capture sunlight and convert it into heat, allowing food to be cooked without the need for gas or electricity.

4. **Solar-Powered Lighting**: Pathway and Garden Lights: Solar-powered lights illuminate public spaces and gardens, enhancing safety and aesthetics while utilizing renewable energy. • Home Lighting: Residents often use solar lanterns and lamps, providing light during the nights.

5. **Solar-Powered Water Pumps:** • In agricultural areas, solar-powered pumps are used for irrigation, enabling farmers to maintain their crops sustainably and efficiently.

6. **Solar Charging Stations:** • These stations are set up in public areas for charging electronic devices like phones and tablets. They provide a convenient way for residents and visitors to stay connected while utilizing renewable energy.

Benefits of Solar Energy Devices Sustainability: Solar energy devices contribute to Cannabisville's commitment to environmental conservation by reducing carbon emissions and reliance on non-renewable energy sources.

Energy Independence: By harnessing solar power, the community can become more self-sufficient, reducing dependence on external energy suppliers and stabilizing energy costs.

ARCHITECTUAL & LANDSCAPES

In Cannabisville, the architectural landscape reflects a unique blend of sustainability and luxury.

Greenhouse-Inspired Homes: Design Features: Most homes in Cannabisville are designed similarly to greenhouses, utilizing large glass panels and open spaces to maximize natural light and heat. These homes often feature high ceilings and spacious interiors, promoting ventilation and a sense of connection to the outdoors.

Sun Windows: Homes are equipped with specially designed sun windows that capture sunlight throughout the day, providing warmth and natural lighting.

1. Luxurious Designs:
The mansions on the south side of Cannabisville are grand and opulent, featuring intricate designs that blend modern aesthetics with traditional elements. Many boast expansive outdoor spaces, such as gardens, terraces, and pools, often integrated with natural landscapes. Architectural Variety:

MARIJUANA GIRL
WELCOME TO CANNABISVILLE

While maintaining a cohesive look with the greenhouse theme, these mansions often include unique architectural features, such as domes, arches, and decorative facades, reflecting the owners style.

Symbol of Prosperity:
Each home reflects a deep connection to the land, using materials sustainably sourced from the Marijuana Tree of Life. They are a testament to the vision of achieving prosperity living in harmony with nature's gifts.

2. Advanced Eco-Technologies:
Many mansions are equipped with advanced solar energy systems, geothermal heating, and rainwater harvesting systems, showcasing a commitment to sustainability while providing luxury amenities.
Smart Home Features: High-tech systems allow residents to control lighting, heating, and security with ease, promoting energy efficiency.

3. Views and Location:
Positioned strategically, the mansions often offer stunning views of the surrounding botanical gardens and landscapes, creating a serene living environment. The south side is known for its gentle slopes and lush greenery, providing an ideal backdrop for these luxurious residences.

4. Community Spaces:
Despite their size and luxury, many mansions incorporate communal spaces, such as outdoor kitchens and gathering areas, encouraging social interaction among residents.

THERESA VERNELL

ENTERTAINMENT - AIRWAVE

The radio stations in Cannabisville broadcast and capture the essence of the Hommo-Harvestas lifestyle with music and broadcasting culture.

1. **420 Vibes GT** – "Tuning you in, puff by puff."
2. **The Green Frequency** – "Where every note grows."
3. **BudWave Radio** – "Riding the high notes of Cannabisville."
4. **HerbBeats 101** – "Feel the rhythm, taste the herb."
5. **Kush Airwaves** – "Broadcasting from the heart of the plant."
6. **Leafline GT** – "Where the roots run deep."
7. **Indica Chill Radio** – "For the smoothest nights and mellow mornings."
8. **Sativa Sunrise Station** – "High vibes from dusk till dawn."
9. **Hempster Hits** – "Let the music burn slow and easy."
10. **Soulshine Sessions** – "Sounds from Earth, beats for the soul."
11. **The Blaze** – "Burn bright, live loud."
12. **Stash Radio** – "Music to spark your soul."
13. **Emberflow GT** – "Lighting up your day with golden tunes."
14. **Resin Radio** – "Sticking to the good vibes."
15. **The Bud Broadcast** – "All strains, all sounds, all day."

SOLARVISION STATIONS

Broadcasts entertainment that celebrates Cannabisville's culture, blending cannabis themes with creative, engaging programs. From enlightening documentaries to humorous strain-based shows, it reflects the planet's spirit while educating and entertaining its viewers.

1. **WeedTV** – "Broadcasting from root to leaf."
2. **BudVision** – "See the world through green-tinted lenses."
3. **Kush Network** – "Where every show stays lit."
4. **Ganja Globe** – "News and views from every strain."
5. **LeafStream** – "All vibes, all the time."
6. **HempTV** – "Strong roots, stronger stories."

MARIJUANA GIRL
WELCOME TO CANNABISVILLE

7. **Sativa Central** – "Bright, bold, and blooming entertainment."
8. **Indica Nights** – "Chill TV for after-dark vibes."
9. **The Joint Channel** – "Where everything connects."
10. **Blaze Network** – "Fuel your mind, spark your soul."
11. **Green Roots TV** – "Grounded content for growing minds."
12. **Trichome Times** – "Crystal-clear television."
13. **Resin Reel** – "Sticky stories and smooth entertainment."
14. **PuffView** – "Your daily dose of high-quality TV."

SOLARVISION SHOWS

Top 10 Solar-vision shows in Cannabisville, reflecting the unique culture, humor, and spirituality of the Hommo-Harvestas: Offering a mix of entertainment for all strains.

1. Buds & Blunts - A reality show where strain families compete to create the most potent, flavorful, and unique cannabis strains, all while battling through different challenges in the fields and labs.

2. Green Dawn: Chronicle: of Jah - A spiritual drama following diverse Hommo-Harvestas interpreting their lives by The Book of Roots, seeking Jah's guidance in their everyday.

3. Smoke Trails - An action-packed adventure series where a group of rebel strain warriors navigate dangerous territories, uncover secrets, and battle rogue elements like the Resin Reapers, all while spreading Jah's teachings.

4. Puff N' Chefs - A cooking competition show where contestants must prepare gourmet meals infused with the finest cannabis products from around the planet. Judges score based on creativity, flavor, and the effects of their dishes.

5. CannaCribs - A lifestyle show giving viewers exclusive tours of the lavish homes and gardens of the richest and most famous Hommo-Harvestas. Watch as elite growers show off their cannabis estates and rarest strains.

6. The Grow Lab - A science-based show following leading botanists, alchemists, and breeders as they experiment with genetics to cultivate revolutionary cannabis strains with magical effects.

7. Island Buds: The West Side Chronicle: - A gritty drama series focused on the West Side's most influential Island Bud families and their internal power struggles, often showcasing themes of loyalty, betrayal, and ambition.

8. Toke It or Leave It – A game show where contestants are faced with a series of cannabis-themed challenges, from trivia to physical tasks, testing their knowledge and stamina. Winners receive top-shelf rewards like rare strains and golden cannabis seeds.

9. 420 Mysteries - Supernatural crime drama where detectives from Cannabisville investigate strange happenings, from vanishing seedlings to mysterious smoke clouds, all while unraveling deeper cosmic secrets about Jah's creation.

10. Blazed and Confused - A comedy sketch show where the absurdities of life in Cannabisville are brought to life through parody and satire, poking fun at the quirks of Hommo-Harvesta society, politics, and inter-strain rivalries.

CANNABISVILLE THEATERS

1. **The Green Stage** – "Where roots meet performance."
2. **The Buddome** – "A theater blooming with talent."
3. **The Kush Playhouse** – "Stories that spark the mind."
4. **Soulshine Amphitheater** – "Under the glow of creativity."
5. **Resin Hall** – "Sticky performances you won't forget."
6. **Indica Palace** – "Relax, enjoy, and let the story unfold."
7. **The Ganja Globe Theatre** – "World-class plays, Cannabisville style."
8. **The Trichome Pavilion** – "Crystal-clear productions under the stars."
9. **The Leafy Lounge** – "Intimate shows for mellow vibes."
10. **The Hemp Haven Theater**–"Where every performance grows on you."

MARIJUANA GIRL
WELCOME TO CANNABISVILLE

'WEED-WAY': Stage Play Titles

1. *"Romeo Resin & Juliet Bud"* – A tale of two rival strains finding love amidst conflict.
2. **"Roots in the Wind"** – A tale of family, change, and tradition.
3. **"Soulshine Sessions: The Musical"** – A musical celebration of life, love, and Soulshine 'Elixir' Champagne
4. **"The Last 24-Karat Seed"** – A thrilling adventure in search of legendary treasure.
5. **"Leaves of Time"** – A time-traveling love story across generations.
6. **"The Great Ganja Heist"** – A comedy about stealing the rarest strains.
7. **"Embers in the Dark"** – A drama about unity during times of crisis.
8. **"Bud Wars"** – A playful satire on the competition between strains.
9. **"Puff, Pass, and Play"** – An improv comedy with audience participation.
10. **"The Book of Roots"** – A spiritual exploration of Cannabisville's history.

ART MUSEUMS AND ARTISTS IN CANNABISVILLE

THE GREEN CANVAS MUSEUM
Blazeworth Marley: Iconic murals depicting 420 Smoke Festivals.
Leaforia Bloom: Textured cannabis-leaf collages.
Tranquil Toke: Meditative art with glowing green tones.

THE BUDDING ARTS INSTITUE
Trichome Glow: Paintings showcasing microscopic details of cannabis strains.
Sprout Wisdom: Kinetic sculptures celebrating new growth.
Nuggeta Fields: Whimsical storytelling through leaf-shaped canvases.

THE CANNABRIGHT ART COLLECTIVE
Sunny Blazeleaf: Psychedelic murals reflecting bright solar themes.
Glow Stem: Interactive installations with glowing, plant-shaped sculptures.
Vivid Greenlight: Community art projects focusing on sustainability.

THERESA VERNELL

ROOTS AND RESIN GALLERY
Amber Stemson: Resin-based sculptures with intricate details.
SIR Vibes: Organic art made from recycled plant materials.
Sky Vaporis: Abstract clouds and smoke-pattern motifs.
Peace Leafington: Cannabis mandala designs on vast canvases.

SATIVA SPIRITS MUSEUM OF VISUAL ARTS
Sativa Diva: Evocative paintings capturing the essence of Marijuana Girls.
Flow Kushfire: Expressive dance-inspired visual installations.
Blaze Highwind: Multimedia exhibits wind and smoke patterns.

BOTANICAL GARDENS IN CANNABISVILLE

1. **Weedland Park**
   A lush haven featuring vibrant cannabis fields and serene walking paths, offering visitors a peaceful retreat surrounded by the essence of nature. Known for their 'Rootress' live tree benches.

2. **The Greenleaf Conservatory**
   A stunning greenhouse preserving rare cannabis strains and tropical plants, providing an educational and sensory experience for all visitors.

3. **Sativa Springs Botanical Gardens**
   A serene oasis with natural springs and cascading greenery, known for its rejuvenating atmosphere and dedication to sustainability..

4. **Trichome Grove**
   A shimmering grove where dew-covered cannabis plants sparkle like jewels, this tranquil space celebrates the art of cultivation.

5. **The Bud Blossom Sanctuary**
   A floral sanctuary bursting with cannabis blossoms and colorful wildflowers, perfect for quiet reflection and admiration of natural beauty.

MARIJUANA GIRL
WELCOME TO CANNABISVILLE

AIRLINE AND TRANSPORTATION

High Flya Airways

The premier airline of Cannabisville, powered entirely by solar and cannabinoid-infused energy. Their signature aircraft, known as Sky Budliners, are designed in the shape of sleek cannabis leaves, gliding through the atmosphere with ease. The cabins are luxurious, filled with the aroma of herbal essences, providing passengers with a relaxing and elevated flying experience.

High Flya Airways do not offers interplanetary flights. They only connect Cannabisville passengers to the surrounding islands, and their domestic routes make traveling between the Northern, Southern, and Eastern borders a breeze.

1. SolarLeaf Cruisers
Solar-powered airships that glide through the skies, designed with cannabis leaf-shaped wings that capture sunlight for fuel.

2. Bud Bikes
Eco-friendly bicycles made from strong hemp fibers, used for short-distance travel within Cannabisville's bustling streets.

3. Green Trail Gliders
Floating hoverboards powered by cannabinoid-infused energy crystals. These are a favorite for young Hommo-Harvestas and thrill-seekers.

4. Herbivans
Spacious, solar-powered cannabis-themed vans that transport groups of people across Cannabisville, often seen during festivals and gatherings.

5. Root Riders
Underground train system that travels through tunnels beneath the Marijuana Tree roots, powered by Cannabisville's natural energy and infused with golden cannabis strains.

6. CannaCabs

Personal transportation pods powered by the radiant energy of gold-infused cannabis strains. They hover a few feet above the ground, providing comfortable, enclosed travels.

7. tUber

In Cannabisville, the tUber is the pinnacle of eco-friendly transportation, blending nature and technology seamlessly. Unlike Earth's gas-powered or electric Ubers, the tUber is a levitating pod powered by solar-infused cannabis energy. It was invented by the genius Hommo-Harvesta Weedlon Musk Blazeleaf, whose revolutionary *Green-prints* have made the tUber the most efficient and sustainable travel option on the planet.

Design and Functionality

- The tUber's exterior is crafted from a bio-luminescent hemp fiber that glows faintly green at night, mirroring the cannabis plants it's powered by.
- Inside, it features plush seats infused with calming terpenes, ensuring a relaxing ride every time.
- It has no wheels; instead, it levitates on a magnetic field created by the cannabis-charged solar grids beneath the surface of Cannabisville.

MARIJUANA GIRL
WELCOME TO CANNABISVILLE

Speed and Efficiency

The tUber travels at a constant speed of 420 miles per hour, reflecting the sacred number in Cannabisville culture. This speed is perfect for zipping across the vast expanses of the islands, making long journeys feel like mere moments.

Creator and Mystery

Weedlon Musk designed the tUber with a vision to unite the Hommo-Harvesta in effortless and environmentally-friendly travel. However, before its full potential could be realized, Musk mysteriously vanished, taking the original Green-prints with him.

The Embassy of Green Roots has recently tracked the Green-prints to Earth, and rumors suggest that Musk is now living among Earthlings, possibly adapting Cannabisville's technology for Earthly innovations. Despite his disappearance, the tUber remains a testament to his genius and a cherished legacy in Cannabisville.

With its advanced features, sustainable design, and homage to the cannabis culture, the tUber stands as a symbol of progress and unity in Cannabisville, outpacing anything Earth's Uber has to offer.

THERESA VERNELL

ESCAPE TO CANNABISVILLE

The Ultimate 7-Day Luxury Getaway
Value: 1 Million BudCoins$

7 Day Vacation Package to Cannabisville

Step into the enchanting world of Cannabisville with this unparalleled vacation package. Over the course of seven days, immerse yourself in the vibrant culture, lush landscapes, and luxurious experiences that only Cannabisville can offer.

Day 1: Arrival and Immersion

Morning:
- Arrive in Cannabisville via the 'Puff Port' and settle into a cozy eco-friendly lodge surrounded by lush greenery. - Take a relaxing walk through 'Weedland Park', the largest botanical garden, featuring towering tree of life 'Marijuana Trees,' vibrant cannabis flowers, and soothing medicinal herbs.

Afternoon:
- Enjoy lunch at 'Hempstead Harvest Café', where all meals are infused with THC and hemp seeds, oils, and herbal flavors.
- Visit the 'Green Canvas Museum' to explore the rich artistic expressions of Cannabisville, from resin art to nature-inspired sculptures.

Evening:
- Join a sunset ceremony at 'High Vibes Temple,' where locals gather to celebrate nature with music, herbal offerings, and meditation. - Dine at 'Trichome Tavern,' a restaurant known for its cannabis-infused dishes.

MARIJUANA GIRL
WELCOME TO CANNABISVILLE

Day 2: Nature & Adventure

Morning:
- Embark on a guided tour of 'Trichome Grove', where you'll learn about rare cannabis strains, herbs, and medicinal plants.
- Engage in a 'Leaf Whisperer' session to connect with the spirit of the plants and nature, guided by an expert.

Afternoon:
- Take a scenic hike through the 'Emerald Trail Arboretum' and explore the beautiful landscapes, including the famous Sapling Falls.
- Enjoy a light picnic with fresh cannabis-infused juices and snacks from local farmers.

Evening:
- Attend an art performance at The Budding Arts Institute of Cannabisville, showcases traditional music, dance, and hemp-inspired fashion.
- Wind down the evening at 'Sativa Springs', Cannabisville's natural hot springs, known for soothing, mineral-rich waters.

Day 3: Culture & Education

Morning:
- Visit Cannabright University for an educational tour and attend a lecture on '*Spermology*' and '*Strainology*,' where experts explain the cultivation of rare cannabis strains and their cultural significance in Cannabisville.
- Explore the Herbspire Gardens, a serene botanical paradise with unique flora and medicinal plants that have been used in Cannabisville for centuries.

Afternoon:
- Have lunch at The Bud Blossom Bistro, a restaurant featuring organic, plant-based dishes infused with the freshest herbs and oils from Cannabisville's local farms.
- Take a guided tour of The Marijuana Tree in the heart of Cannabisville. Learn about its spiritual importance under its majestic branches.

Evening:
- Participate in a Vibe Curator's Sunset Session at Leaflight Botanical Reserve, a festival-like gathering where visitors and locals share music, art, and herbal rituals under the stars.
- Enjoy dinner at Roots & Resin Eatery, a fine dining restaurant that focuses on the fusion of Cannabisville's native ingredients with world flavors.

Day 4: Adventure & Exploration

Morning:
 Go on an adventurous Bud Steward Hike through the northern hills of Cannabisville, where you might spot the rare Zonkeys or the elusive SeedWeeds practicing ancient customs.
- Visit Sativa Spirit Fields for a hands-on experience in harvesting cannabis and hemp plants, learning sustainable practices directly from the farmers.

Afternoon:
- Have a picnic lunch near the Budding Minds School, where you can meet local students and participate in a fun educational workshop about the natural ecosystems of Cannabisville.
- Explore the Hempstead Garden of Wonders, where you can experience hands-on exhibits about hemp and cannabis-based sustainable technologies.

MARIJUANA GIRL
WELCOME TO CANNABISVILLE

Evening:
Take a peaceful gondola ride along the Leafy Trails River, where locals light floating lanterns made from hemp fibers. This is a perfect opportunity to reflect on your journey while floating beneath the tranquil night sky.
- Conclude your day with a farewell dinner at The Cannabloom Pavilion, known for its community-focused dining experience, where you dine together with locals in a celebration of culture, food, and cannabis.

Day 5: Departure and Reflection

Morning:
- Spend your final morning at Trichome Sanctuary Spa, indulging in a herbal-infused massage and a cannabis-oil therapy session designed to rejuvenate body and soul.
- Take one last walk through Weedland Park, gathering small souvenirs like hemp crafts or herbal blends from local vendors.

-Afternoon:
Depart Cannabisville via Puff Port, leaving with high vibes, newfound knowledge, and a deeper connection to the world of cannabis and nature.
This trip offers a balance of cultural exploration, education, relaxation, and adventure, fully immersing visitors in the unique world of Cannabisville.

Day 6: Island Exploration and Water Adventures

Morning:
- Embark on a day trip to 'Ganja Reef Island', the serene island off the west coast of Cannabisville. Board a 'Puff Pilot' boat for a peaceful ride, enjoying the view of the emerald waters. Smoking Reefer all day!
- Upon arrival, explore 'Bud Beach', a quiet, white-sand beach where locals come to meditate and unwind.

Afternoon:
Dive into water activities at Kush Cove, where you can swim, snorkel, or kayak through clear waters surrounded by vibrant underwater cannabis gardens.
- Have lunch at 'Island Bud Café, a beachside spot offering fresh seafood infused with herbs and tropical cannabis flavors.

- Take a guided tour of the Island Buds 'Reefer Village,' learning about the island's cultural heritage, and engage in a friendly game of cannabis-infused handball with the local youth.

Evening:
- Join the locals for an evening 'Blaze of Unity Bonfire' at 'Buds Bay Beach', where they light a massive bonfire, share Merbud stories, and play reggae-inspired music while enjoying herbal teas and peaceful vibes.
- Return to the mainland by boat, reflecting on the day's adventures under the starry night sky. And beware of the Merbuds (mermaids) on Ganja Isles. Also, cannabis-infused glow in the dark fish..

MARIJUANA GIRL
WELCOME TO CANNABISVILLE

Day 7: Spiritual Awakening & Farewell Celebration

Morning:
- Start your final full day with a visit to Jah's Sanctuary, a sacred site in Cannabisville where locals go to meditate and connect with the spiritual essence of the land. Participate in a morning mindfulness and Cannatherapist - led breathing session with cannabis incense offerings.
- Visit the 'Roots of Wisdom University' library, where you can explore ancient texts and stories passed down by 'The Book of Roots - 420 Chroniclers of Cannabisville.

Afternoon:
- Take a visit to 'The Seedling School', where children learn about nature, plants, and their cultural heritage. Spend some time interacting with young Hommo-Harvestas, sharing stories, and joining their 'Greenleaf Arts and Crafts' session.
- Enjoy a light farewell lunch at 'The Leafscape Pavilion', sampling delicate herbal-infused dishes and refreshing cannabis beverages.

Evening:
- End your trip with a grand farewell celebration in 'Trichome Square", the heart of Cannabisville. The 'Vibe Curators' organize a festival of music, dance, and art, celebrating the beauty of life and unity.
- Share in the community meal, where locals and visitors alike gather to enjoy a 'Blaze Bright Feast', featuring cannabis-infused culinary delights, from roasted herbs to sweet hemp desserts.

- Conclude the evening with a ceremonial lighting of 'Green Glow Lanterns', where everyone lights their lantern and releases it into the sky, symbolizing peace, growth, and connection.

THERESA VERNELL

Frequently Asked Questions Frome Earthlings

When Earthlings encounter the enigmatic beings known as Manifest Sapient, they are often struck with awe and curiosity. These visitors, who originate from the lush, vibrant world of Cannabisville on the planet Marijuana, radiate an otherworldly energy that is both humanlike and deeply connected to nature.

Their green-tinged aura, calm demeanor, and profound knowledge of plants and life spark endless questions from Earthlings eager to understand them. The Hommo-Harvestas journeyed to Earth for a noble purpose: to bridge two worlds - Earth and Cannabisville - through a shared sense of wonder, reverence for nature, and an exchange of timeless wisdom.

Their arrival is not a random occurrence but a deliberate act of connection, inspired by a desire to rekindle Earthlings' bond with the natural world and offer guidance in a time of increasing disconnection from the planet's resources and spirit.

In Cannabisville, all life is seen as interconnected, with plants and beings existing in harmony. The Hommo-Harvestas, who embody this balance, travel as Manifest Sapient to share their teachings, healing methods, and the sacred traditions of the Marijuana Tree of Life, the spiritual heart of their world. They also seek to learn from Earth's biodiversity, bridging knowledge between their two worlds.

This FAQ offers you - Earthlings insight into the nature, culture, and purpose of the Manifest Sapient, answering some of the most pressing questions sparked by their extraordinary presence.

MARIJUANA GIRL
WELCOME TO CANNABISVILLE

Q & A

1. *Where are you from?*
Hommo-Harvestas Answer: "We hail from a realm parallel to Earth, a place known as Cannabisville on the planet Marijuana. It's a world abundant in greenery, harmony, and wisdom."

2. *How do you look so human yet feel so... different?*
Answer: "When we come to Earth, we take on forms familiar to you to blend in and share knowledge without causing alarm. But our essence - our spirit and energy - remains true to our origins in Cannabisville."

3. *What is Cannabisville like?*
Answer: "Cannabisville is the golden ratio, a place of lush forests, powerful plants, and sacred customs. It's where the Hommo-Harvestas live in harmony with nature, and every plant, tree, and being has its purpose and spirit. We call it Jah's garden."

4. *Do you have any special powers or abilities?*
Answer: "We have a deep connection with plant life and can use our energy to heal, understand plants, and share wisdom. Our presence can help others feel grounded, calm, and connected to nature."

5. *What is your purpose here on Earth?*
Answer: "We're here to exchange knowledge, learn from Earth's plants, and share teachings on balance and healing. It's our way of cultivating harmony between our worlds and nurturing Earth's connection with nature."

6. *What is the 'Marijuana Tree of Life'?*
Answer: "The Marijuana Tree of Life is our most sacred tree, a symbol of wisdom, vitality, and spirit. Its roots hold the knowledge of our ancestors, and its leaves offer healing energy. It connects all Hommo-Harvestas with Jah and binds us to Cannabisville."

7. *Can you teach us your healing methods?*
Answer: "We'd be honored to share. Our methods involve a balance of plants, energy, and intention, helping you reconnect with Earth's natural remedies. Healing starts within and through the energy of the plants around you."

8. *How are you different from humans?*
Answer: "While we share many similarities in form, we are part cannabis plant strains and part humanlike spirit. Our bodies flow with a green sap and are deeply connected to plant energy. This sap carries our life force, allowing us to commune with nature on a different level."

9. *What do you eat?*
Answer: "Our diet is plant-based, relying on seeds, leaves, and fruits. We also take in energy directly from nature and the sun, much like the plants themselves."

10. *Can anyone visit Cannabisville?*
Answer: "Only those who carry an open heart and a deep respect for life and nature can journey to Cannabisville. It is a place that calls to those ready to embrace its ways."

11. *Do you age or die like we do?*
Answer: "We age differently, with lives spanning hundreds of your years. Our life force is bound to our connection with plants, and as long as we nurture this bond, we live long and healthy lives."

MARIJUANA GIRL
WELCOME TO CANNABISVILLE

12. *Can we grow plants like you do on Earth?*
Answer: "Yes, absolutely. We encourage Earthlings to cultivate plants with intention, respect, and patience. The soil, the sun, and your energy all contribute to the plant's strength and spirit."

13. *Do you have families like ours?*
Answer: "Yes, though our bonds extend beyond bloodlines to include our entire community. We see all living beings as connected and form lifelong partnerships with others through shared strains, energies, and values."

14. *Why do you smell like flowers and herbs?*
Answer: "Our essence is entwined with the fragrances of our native plants. The aroma you sense is the natural scent of our being—remnants of Cannabisville's energy.

15. *Will we ever see you again?*
Answer: "If you are attuned to nature and look with an open heart, you may feel our presence or hear whispers of Cannabisville in the rustle of leaves and scent of flowers. We are never truly far."

Hommo-Harvestas have only 1 question for Earthlings:

Q: "Why don't you legalize marijuana and fully embrace its medical benefits to aid in curing ailments and enhancing well-being?"

To the Hommo-Harvestas, the cannabis plant is more than a resource - it's a sacred gift from Jah, with the power to heal, nurture, and connect. They marvel at Earthlings' hesitation to harness its full potential, given the plant's proven ability to alleviate suffering, promote mental clarity, and foster harmony with the natural world.

"The Green Signature: Identifying a Hommo-Harvesta"

1. **Bleed Green**: Hommo-Harvestas' lifeblood is a vivid green sap, rich with cannabinoids, distinguishing them from any other being.

2. **Urinates Green**: Their bodily functions reflect their unique biology, with their urine carrying a greenish tint, infused with traces of terpenes and chlorophyll.

3. **Release a Natural Herbal Aroma**: Hommo-Harvestas exude a calming fragrance of fresh herbs and sweet terpenes, which intensifies during moments of heightened emotions, serving as a soothing signature.

ONE MARIJUANA ONE

MARIJUANA GIRL
WELCOME TO CANNABISVILLE

Political Structure: The Profet and The Green House

In Cannabisville, the leader is not referred to as king, ruler, or president, as on Earth. Instead, they are the Profet, a divine figure born into their role. The Profet governs the West Side, East Side, North Side, and South Side, each region contributing its distinct culture and ambitions to Cannabisville's vibrant land. The Profet Highstem - A leader rooted in divine connection and spiritual guidance.

At the heart of the nation stands the Embassy of Green Roots, housed within the magnificent Green House. This central structure, adorned with golden accents and surrounded by lush fields of golden marijuana plants, serves as a beacon of unity and authority. Towering above it all are the sacred Marijuana Trees of Life, their sprawling canopies symbolizing protection and the interconnectedness of all Hommo-Harvestas.

The Green House is more than a seat of power; it is the epicenter of Cannabisville's governance, diplomacy, and cultural harmony. While the West and East sides compete for economic dominance, and the North Side strives for self-sufficiency, all paths lead to the Green House. Even the prosperous South Side, with its golden cannabis fields and abundant wealth, acknowledges the Embassy's crucial role in maintaining balance and peace.

Within the Green House, Profet Highstem oversees the intricate negotiations and decisions that shape Cannabisville's destiny. It is here that Jah's will is believed to manifest, ensuring that the land thrives in harmony, guided by wisdom, unity, and the ever-present blessings of the Marijuana Tree of Life.

THERESA VERNELL

Parliament Structure of - The Embassy Green Roots:

1. Commander of the Roots
Name: Terra Verde - Meaning "Green soil, Terra embodies the life force of the land and is deeply rooted in agriculture and the sacred cultivation of cannabis.

2. Commander of Sun Energy
Name: Solaris Blaze - Representing the power of the sun, Solaris is responsible for harnessing solar energy to keep Cannabisville thriving and sustainable.

3. Commander of Waters
Name: Aqua Flow, controls the water sources in Cannabisville, ensuring life-giving rivers and irrigation are properly maintained.

4. Commander of Commerce
Name: Budswell Riches
  - This commander oversees the economic growth of Cannabisville, with a name symbolizing abundance, wealth, and the flourishing trade of cannabis.

5. Commander of Justice
Name: Verdict Sage, with wisdom like that of an ancient tree, Verdict Sage brings balance and fairness to Cannabisville's legal and judicial system.

6. Commander of Peace
Name: Seren Bliss ensures harmony within Cannabisville and with neighboring territories, guiding Cannabisville through diplomacy and peaceful resolution.

MARIJUANA GIRL
WELCOME TO CANNABISVILLE

7. Commander of Spirits
Name: Celestial Smoke, known for their deep spiritual connection, Celestial Smoke leads sacred rituals, ensuring that cannabis remains a tool of enlightenment.

8. Commander of Health
Name: Leaf Remedy, a master of herbal medicine, oversees the health of the population through cannabis and natural remedies.

Through their research and expertise, spermologists in Cannabisville contribute to the development of sustainable agricultural practices that support the planet's agricultural sector.

1. **Cannatherapist** – Specializes in healing and wellness using cannabinoids, natural remedies, and holistic practices.
2. **Budtender** – Provides expert advice and guidance on different strains, uses, and effects of cannabis products.

3. **Strainologist** – Studies, develops, and cultivates new cannabis strains for medicinal, recreational, and spiritual purposes.

4. **Herb Artisan** – Crafts cannabis-based products, such as oils, teas, tinctures, and edibles, for cultural, medicinal, or culinary purposes.

5. **Leaf Gardener** – A horticulturist responsible for growing and caring for the various plants and herbs in Cannabisville, particularly the sacred cannabis strains.

6. **Vibe Curator** – Organizes festivals, rituals, and communal events focused on mindfulness, cannabis appreciation, and spiritual connection.

7. **Trichome Technician** – Expert in processing and extracting cannabinoids, terpenes, and other plant elements for various uses in health and science.

8. **Cannabis Advocate** – Specializes in upholding the legal framework of Cannabisville, ensuring all actions are in accordance with the laws of Jah and the Embassy.

9. **Sap Weaver** – Crafts clothing, tools, and accessories from hemp and other natural fibers, integral to the sustainable culture of Cannabisville.

10. **Chronicler** – A storyteller and historian who records the history, culture, and legends of Cannabisville, preserving its traditions for future generations.

11. **Bud Steward** – Oversees community farms and ensures that the agricultural practices are sustainable, balancing production with nature.

12. **Leaf Whisperer** – Communes with the plants in a spiritual capacity, believed to receive guidance from the plant spirits, acting as a bridge between nature and the people.

13. **Seedling Mentor** – Educates young strains (children) on the ways of Cannabisville, teaching about plants, nature, and the importance of community.

14. **Cannabis -Hemp Chef** – Creates culinary delights from cannabis and hemp products, combining taste with wellness benefits. These careers are in harmony with the eco-friendly, spiritual, and cannabis-centered culture of Cannabisville.

MARIJUANA GIRL
WELCOME TO CANNABISVILLE

The 24 Karat Gold Cannabis Seed

Deep within the lore of Cannabisville lies the legend of the 24 Karat Gold Cannabis Seeds, rare and mysterious seeds that has captivated the imaginations of Hommo-Harvestas for generations. Said to be crafted by Jah's own hand, this seed is a symbol of unparalleled good fortune and immense power, holding the ability to bridge dimensions. Its golden hue, gleaming like sunlight trapped in amber, is believed to carry mystical properties capable of unlocking the gateway between planet Marijuana and Earth.

For those who find this legendary seed, the Embassy of Green Roots offers a staggering reward of 1 million BudCoin$. Yet, the reward itself pales in comparison to the seed's true allure. The wealthy elites of the Embassy covet it not for monetary gain, but for its potential to transcend realms, an ability that could rewrite the very fabric of Cannabisville's existence.

The seeds are rumored to have originated from the first Marijuana Tree of Life, a sacred symbol of Jah's blessing upon the Hommo-Harvestas. According to ancient chronicles, the tree bore a single golden seed every hundred years, a celestial gift meant to guide Cannabisville through its darkest times. However, no golden seed has been seen in over a century, leading many to believe it's merely a myth, while others tirelessly seek it in secret.

It is said that the seed grants its holder if planted the ability to inter-dimensionally travel to Earth, a feat that has eluded even the most advanced strains of Cannabisville. Such power could unite the realms, but it also holds the potential for great peril, as the temptation to exploit its magic could disrupt the harmony of both worlds. The search for the 24 Karat Gold Cannabis Seeds has become a quest for adventurers, scholars, and mystics alike. While some seek it for its spiritual significance, others are driven by dreaming of the wealth and influence it could bring. To this day, the tale of the 24 Karat Gold seeds is whispered beneath the Marijuana Tree of Life, inspiring dreams of discovery, fortune, and the ultimate connection between planet Marijuana and Earth.

THERESA VERNELL

ABOUT THE AUTHOR: Theresa Vernell

In the haze of fragrant buds and the subtle dance of cannabis leaves, "Marijuana Girl" Theresa Vernell weaves stories that transcend the ordinary. Originally from the vibrant streets of Philadelphia, Pennsylvania, Theresa now resides in Tampa Palms, Florida, where her creative spirit thrives.

Through her groundbreaking work, Marijuana Girl, Theresa unravels a profound epiphany - a moment of clarity that reveals the journey is not merely about cannabis cultivation but an exploration of identity, purpose, and the interconnectedness of all life. Her storytelling bridges the gap between the tangible and the metaphysical, offering a fresh perspective on the transformative power of marijuana.

With a deep passion for education, advocacy, and empowerment, Theresa is also the founder of OneMarijuana.org, an organization and coalition dedicated to uniting communities, fostering awareness, and promoting the limitless potential of cannabis as a force for good. Her work is a call to action, inspiring readers to rethink the narratives surrounding cannabis and embrace the growth it represents - in every sense of the word.

Theresa Vernell invites you to step into the world of Cannabisville, where the herb is more than a plant; it's a symbol of evolution, connection, and the courage to cultivate change.

MARIJUANA GIRL
WELCOME TO CANNABISVILLE

COMING SOON: The Marijuana Girl Book Series

Get ready to immerse yourself in a thrilling sci-fi adventure with Theresa Vernell's Marijuana Girl Book Series, set in the vibrant, mystical world of Cannabisville. This imaginative series explores life on a parallel planet where strains of Hommo-Harvestas thrive in harmony with their lush environment. From daring journeys to unearthing ancient secrets, each book promises a unique experience blending adventure, spirituality, and culture.

Marijuana Girl: WELCOME TO CANNABISVILLE

Marijuana Girl: GANJA BOY

Marijuana Girl: ISLAND BUD

Marijuana Girl: HEMPSTERS

BONUS BOOKS:

CANNABISVILLE

THE BOOK OF ROOTS (Full Version)

These companion book delves into the history, legends, and sacred practices of Cannabisville. From the origins of the strains to the laws of the Embassy, it's an essential guide for all fans of the series. - OneMarijuana.org

EMERGENCY 420 HOTLINE: WEED-HELP 420

WeedHelp 420 in Cannabisville functions similarly to calling 911 in the United States of America. When any Hommo-Harvesta dials 420, they instantly reach WeedHelp, the planet's emergency response system.

Whether it's a medical emergency, a fire, a mining accident, or even environmental hazards, WeedHelp 420 dispatches specialized teams to handle the crisis.

Just like 911, WeedHelp 420 operates 24/7 and serves all regions of Cannabisville from the wealthy Southside to the rebellious Western territories. The service is equipped with advanced technology and trained responders capable of addressing the planet's unique dangers, including mine collapses, rare plant poisoning, and mysterious accidents in Cannabisville.

Even though some view it with skepticism, especially in areas where distrust of the Embassy runs high, WeedHelp 420 remains a vital service ensuring the safety and well-being of Cannabisville's diverse population.

Made in United States
Orlando, FL
31 January 2025